TWO BOYS

TWO BOYS

LAUREL ADAMS

Thanks, read &
enjoy
Laurel Adams

Willoheart Enterprises
PO Box 111, McMinnville, OR 97128-0111

First Edition 2010
ISBN-13: 978-0-9845642-0-0
Library of Congress Control Number (LCCN): 2010927018

Printed and bound in the United States of America by
Print Northwest, McMinnville, Oregon

2 4 6 8 10 9 7 5 3 1

Two Boys is a work of fiction. The author uses individuals from history to set the context of era and place; otherwise, names, characters, places and incidents are the product of the author's imagination. Any resemblance to actual persons, living or dead, businesses, companies, events or locales is entirely coincidental.

Book and Cover Design by Katherine Huit
Published by
Willoheart Enterprises
PO Box 111, McMinnville, OR 97128-0111

ACKNOWLEDGEMENTS

I would like to thank my wife, Janet Adams, for the time she spent reading and correcting my mistakes and my editor, Katherine Huit. Then there is the crew at the Evergreen Aviation Museum and particularly former B-17 crewmen Russ Barney and Chris Lindsley, who provided valuable input. And, of course the 3:00 o'clock coffee group known as "The Goats" provided input, asked good questions and gave me encouragement over many cups of coffee.

PROLOGUE

Lowell Andersen was born in a small town in Northern Nebraska in January 1924. His father owned a small automotive shop where he repaired cars and tractors. At the height of the depression in 1931, his father lost the shop and was encouraged to move out to Oregon where Lowell's uncle, Norwood Andersen, was a Lutheran minister in Willamette. Gathering all the funds possible, the Andersens (mother, father and seven-year-old Lowell) moved to Oregon in the summer of 1931.

Ethan Andersen, by arrangements of his brother and his skills as a mechanic, had a job at a local gas station and repair shop in the town of Drayville, (about ten miles from Willamette), owned by Milo Adams. They found a house in a nice neighborhood that they could rent and were able to purchase after a few years. It was next door to the Rothsteins, the only Jewish family in town. They had one boy, Myron who became Lowell's best friend. Lowell started school at the local grade school that fall in the second grade.

Times were hard for the Andersens, but with their faith and Ethan's hard work, they managed to survive the awful early 1930s. In the summer of 1935, Milo Adams passed away suddenly and his widow asked Ethan to take over the management of the station and shop. By 1938, the depression was beginning to wane and business was improving. Mrs. Adams wanted to move back to North Dakota to be near family and offered Ethan a chance to buy the station. Because of his reputation and a guaranteed starter loan from Mr. Speer, owner of the local lumber yard, the local bank approved a mortgage and Ethan became the owner of a gas station and repair shop once again.

SUMMER 1941

Lowell opened his eyes and realized it was very warm for Oregon in July when from down stairs his mother called to him, "Lowell, it's time to get up. Your father is expecting you at the station by ten this morning. Remember this is bank day."

The door to his room suddenly flew open and Diane, his nine-year-old sister flew into the room and jumped on his bed followed by David, her twin brother.

"Lowell, make David stop chasing me!"

"All right you guys, get out of my room and quiet down!"

Lowell sounded gruffer than he intended. He thought a lot of his brother and sister, but at times they could be a real trial to a teenager.

Lowell slowly dragged himself out of bed and sat on the edge. He thought of Helen as he did most of his waking hours. Most of the boys at Drayville High considered Helen Speer, a dark haired girl with very striking dark eyes, as the cutest girl in school. She was a year behind him and he had first 'really' noticed her two years ago when as a mighty high school sophomore, he and the rest of his friends stood in the hall on registration day and observed the incoming crop. He knew the family because her father owned the local lumber yard and his father serviced their trucks at his service station. He did not, however, remember she was so good looking. Of course, being a mighty sophomore and her only a freshman, he did not lower himself to speak to her, but notice her he did.

It was not until the next school year when he found her in his forensics class that he finally got around to talking to her as an equal. They both participated in After Dinner Speaking at The Emmons College Speech Tournament. Emmons was the local college across town and Lowell found himself sitting beside Helen in the hall while waiting his turn to deliver his speech.

"Are you scared?" he asked.

"No, not scared but very nervous. I don't suppose you are because this isn't your first tournament is it?"

"Well, yes it is. I didn't take speech last year because I chose shop as my elective."

"Oh."

Lowell could feel his pulse rate skyrocket as he began to formulate his next words.

"Are ... aw ... are you going to go back to school after you're done?"

"Yes I am, why?"

"Well, aw, well I have my father's car and I wondered if you wanted a ride."

"Hum, I really don't want to walk all across town, so I guess that would be swell."

Lowell was on cloud nine and he breezed through his speech and was thoroughly convinced that he had probably won a blue ribbon though he didn't remember much about the presentation.

He thought about Helen and what Jew would say when he told him he had given her a ride back to school. Jew, or Myron Rothstein, was his best friend and they always shared their thoughts about everything including the girls they would like to take out on a date. Jew had a somewhat steady girl friend in Betty Miles.

Lowell remembered that afternoon and had relished it in his memory many times. As Helen came out of the room after delivering her speech, she looked very scared, red faced and seemed to have been perspiring. He felt sorry for her as she seemed to be on the verge of tears and when he asked how it went, she said, "Okay I guess."

On the way back to school he suggested that they stop by Smith's Ice Cream Store and have a pop or something, but Helen said she had to get back, her father expected her to come to the lumber yard and help this afternoon. Mr. Speer was one of the richest men in town and had helped his father purchase the service station.

When they arrived at the high school, Helen said something that he would never forget, "Lowell, you know all the girls think you are one of the nicest boys in school."

He still had nightmares about his response, which was nothing as she looked at him and then jumped out of the car and ran into the school.

*****

His mother called him again, "Come on Lowell, your father is expecting you in forty minutes."

He got up from the bed and walked across the hall to the bathroom, wet a washcloth and scrubbed his face. He was almost past that age when pimples burst out everywhere, but he was still very careful to wash every morning. He was one of the lucky adolescents in that respect. He had very little acne, unlike his best friend Myron Rothstein who since eighth grade had fought the pimple battle and had still not achieved victory. His father owned the local furniture store and Lowell heard about a family connection to a large Jewish chain of stores, but he didn't care because Myron was his best friend.

They were not only best friends and neighbors, but rivals as well. Myron played end on the football team and Lowell halfback and they constantly competed for top scorer. On the baseball team, Myron played third base and Lowell was the catcher, but for basketball, they put the rivalry aside for the good of the team; Lowell played guard and Myron forward. Lowell always looked for Myron when he brought the ball down the floor because he was the best shot on the team. Their junior year they just missed going to state by three points as their traditional rivals, the Johnson City Beavers beat them in the last few minutes of the District Tournament to determine which school would go to State. This coming year, everyone expected Drayville to make it to the State Tournament. Lowell and Myron had pledged they would do everything possible to see that that happened their senior year, even if it meant feeding the ball to

Vernon Dickerson, the other forward and Lowell's chief rival for Helen's affections.

Vernon was a tall nice looking boy who had a very high opinion of himself. His family owned the local bank in town and he had his own car, a very important status symbol to high school boys. He probably wasn't all that bad, but Lowell and Myron had, since grade school, tried to surpass him in everything they did. All three were in the top four or five of the class academically and tapped for Honor Society at the same time. Nevertheless, the State Tournament was so important that they put aside their personal rivalries.

Lowell was not totally aware of what being a Jew was all about. He did know that on Friday nights, when there wasn't a game, Myron and his family went in to Portland to Synagogue. One day in the summer of 1939, he went over to see Myron and his mother answered the door. She was very red eyed and it was obvious she had been crying.

Lowell was somewhat embarrassed but asked, "Is Myron home?"

"Yes, of course; come in Lowell."

Entering the house, Lowell knew something was terribly wrong. Myron's father was sitting in the living room looking very sad. Lowell thought it odd that Myron's father was home in the middle of the day.

Mrs. Rothstein called Myron and he looked at her in a very strange way when she said, "It's okay Myron, you can go out with Lowell."

When they got outside, Lowell turned to Myron and said, "What's going on?"

"My mom got a letter from her uncle's wife in Poland and her uncle has been arrested by the Nazis."

"What did he do?"

"Nothing, he's just a Jew."

"I don't get it, what do you mean."

"The Nazis are arresting all the Jews and stealing their property."

"They can't do that, can they?"

"Well, they are,"

"That's awful!"

"Yea, well let's go downtown and see what's happening."

As they walked towards town, Lowell thought about what happened to Myron's uncle. He still did not understand how any government could just walk in and take your property and arrest you for nothing at all.

As Lowell dressed in his green station uniform, he thought of what he was going to do that night after work. He had to work until eight P.M. when the station closed and if business were slow he would call Myron and arrange to do something after work.

Business was slow that night so about seven o'clock, Lowell went to the phone and gave the operator Myron's number.

"Hello." it was Myron's father answering.

"This is Lowell, is Je– Myron there?"

"Yes, just a minute."

After a short pause, there was, "Hello."

"Jew, this is Low. I close in forty-five minutes. Want to meet me at Smith's for a sundae?"

"Sure, that sounds swell."

All of Myron's close friends called him Jew. It didn't bother him because he had always lived in Drayville and had never experienced the prejudice of larger cities. Lowell hoped the operator had not been listening to the conversation. His dad did not like him to use the station phone for personal reasons but what he didn't know wouldn't hurt him, although the local phone operators some times mentioned to his father that the station line was busy for quite a while especially if he happened to call Helen. His dad was pretty understanding, however, and would usually just say, "Talked on the phone for a bit last night did you?"

The summer passed with Lowell working five nights a week at the station and if Helen wasn't out with Vernon on the weekends, he'd take her to the movies or for a walk or if he could get the car, out to the river where all the teens with cars would park. Helen was always game for a little kissing and petting, but would draw the line when it led to touching in the wrong places. It would frustrate him when she would say no and stop him, but he always was glad and respected her all the more for it. Most of his friends would brag about how far they got with girls, but in those quiet times with close friends like Myron, they would admit that they didn't get anywhere and their innermost feelings were usually of relief.

Fall & Winter 1941-42

Football summer workouts started in the middle of August when it was very hot in Oregon, but it was very important that anyone who wanted to play make those practices. When school started they had been practicing for three weeks and were well on the way to becoming a team. Myron was again playing left end and Lowell left half. There was a new boy, Gerald Olson, who had just moved to town and had won the quarter back position. He was a good passer who could throw the ball over fifty yards with great accuracy. With Gerald, the coach decided to run the new "T" formation that meant a lot of passing. Lowell was somewhat concerned because he knew that would mean Myron would probably be receiving a lot of passes and just might surpass him in scoring.

By mid-season, Drayville's plans to win the championship were not to be, they had lost two games and were in third place but if they could win their last game, they could move in to a tie for second. Their opponent was Mitchell High School. Mitchell was a quite a bit bigger school than Drayville and had a better record at six and one. Lowell was also determined to beat Myron this year in scoring. Tied with eight touchdowns each, it had been raining all day and he didn't think they would pass that much in this game.

After getting dressed and listening to the coach's inspirational speech, they all yelled and ran out of the dressing room.

In the tunnel to the field, Jew came up to Low and said, "Well, Low, I hope you finish second again this year!"

"You bastard, I'm going to score two touchdowns to your none tonight." Low, realizing what he had said looked around to see if Coach Roberts had heard him because coach was very tough on swearing.

"Yea, well just don't get in my way as I catch three or four TD passes tonight."

That night as they took the field, the fans cheered and the rally girls (Helen was junior team captain) jumped up and down in the mud in front of the stands. It was a typical November night in Oregon, forty-eight degrees and raining.

After warm up Coach Roberts called them together and said, "Look boys, this is the last game for many of you so let's make it a good one. You all know that Mitchell is a tough team but so are we, so let's go get 'em."

They all touched hands in the center and yelled, "Go" and went back onto the field.

Drayville won the toss and elected to receive. Lowell took the kick and returned it to their forty-one yard line.

In the huddle Olson instructed, "Pass left on three."

The play so surprised Mitchell because of the weather that Myron was able to catch the ball on the forty-fifth and run it all the way for a touch down.

Though he was very happy for the score, Lowell thought, *Damn, now I'm going to have to score two times to beat him.*

As the first half drew to a close the game had see-sawed back and forth and ended at half time with the score Mitchell fourteen, Drayville seven.

Walking into the dressing room, Lowell went over to Myron and said, "Look out buddy; I'm going to beat you."

"The devil you are!"

They patted each other on the rear and sat down to wait for another of Coach Robert's famous half time speeches. They always laughed about him trying to copy Knute Rockne's half time speech at Notre Dame.

Short gains and slipping running backs dominated the third quarter preventing both teams from gaining an advantage. Near the end of the quarter, Mitchell was driving for what could be their third touchdown putting the game out of reach for Drayville. Their big full back was tearing holes in the Drayville line and it looked like nothing could stop them. With third down and two yards to go for a first down, Mitchell ran an end sweep to Lowell's side of the field. The big 195-pound full back came around the end with a look on his face that dared anyone to try and stop him. Lowell moved out to meet the steamroller, and just as they were about to make contact, the wet muddy football slipped out of the big fullback's hands and right into Lowell's.

After a quick recovery from the surprise, Lowell took off for the end zone some seventy-five yards away. The good fake around the right end pulled most of the Mitchell's backs and most of Drayville's players in that direction. Trying to recover the ball in mid-air, the big full back fell into the mud. With no one in his path Lowell went all the way for the score, tying him with Myron's at nine touchdowns each and tying the game, fourteen to fourteen.

The fourth quarter was again a see-saw battle back and fourth until with just three minutes to go, Drayville got the ball after Mitchell punted on fourth down. The ball was on Mitchell's forty-seven yard line and the rain had increased. Gerald looked over at the bench and seemed uncertain what play to call.

After a moment of indecision, he bent into the huddle and said, "Okay, Andersen, do you think you can make it to the end zone?"

"Sure, if they will open a hole for me."

"Okay, twenty-three dive on three."

They broke the huddle and Gerald called signals, "Hut one, hut two, hut three."

The center snapped the ball and Olson handed off to Lowell. There was a small hole and Lowell was able to slip through, but when he looked up, there was Mitchell's 195-pound fullback/line backer standing directly in his path. He lowered his head and waited for the impact, but none came. When he raised his head, he saw nothing but open field in front of him all the way to the goal line, giving Drayville a twenty to fourteen lead and leading Myron for the team scoring record at ten to nine.

In the huddle for the extra point, everyone was congratulating Myron on a great block and it was only then that Lowell remembered that it was the end's assignment to block the linebacker and block him he did. As he looked at Jew, he noticed his nose was bleeding; however, he was smiling.

The conversion was not good and Drayville's lead was only six points. Before the kickoff, Lowell went over to Myron and said, "I owe you one buddy."

"Yea, well I'll get you back some day."

The game ended in a twenty to fourteen victory for Drayville, a tie for second in the league, and Lowell beating Myron for the team-scoring record with ten touchdowns to nine for Myron.

That night at the after game dance, the student body greeted the team as heroes. A resounding round of applause greeted Lowell, Myron and Gerald when they entered the gymnasium. Lowell was somewhat taken aback but Myron reveled in the recognition. Betty, his steady girl friend came up to him and gave him a little peck on the check. Lowell noticed Helen Speer was standing back a little ways smiling. He did not have the courage to approach her, but she came up to him and said, "Nice game Lowell."

They had several dances that night, but Lowell could not muster up the nerve to ask her if he could take her home and as the dance ended, he did not know who did, probably Vernon Dickerson. Jew made quite a fuss about it the next day as they talked on the phone. Lowell was working at the station and Myron was at his father's store.

"You idiot, can't you see that Helen wants to go out with you. Come on buddy, wake up."

Lowell lay in bed that night thinking about why he was so bashful around Helen. She seemed to like him and pay attention to him, but he could just not get up enough nerve to ask her out or to go steady.

*****

With football season behind them, the boys had only a few days off before the start of basketball practice. Those boys who played both sports, and most of them did, had very little rest between seasons. However, being winter Lowell and Myron looked forward to their other passion, duck hunting. They were both avid hunters and duck season was their favorite. They could just sit in a duck blind for hours talking with only an occasional interruption to shoot at a stray duck or two.

It was on such a day during Thanksgiving vacation that the subject of the war in Europe came up.

"Hey Jew, do you think we will have to go to the army if the country gets in to this war?"

"Well I'm not going in to no army. I'll enlist in the air corps if we get in the war."

"What? You want to fly an airplane?"

"You bet. That's better than sitting in some cold mud hole."

"You mean like we are now!"

They both laughed and then fell silent each to their own thoughts until Lowell asked, "Has your mother heard anymore from your uncle and his family?"

"No, some agency told my dad that they were probably in a camp over there."

"What kind of camp?"

"Oh I don't know, I guess it's like a prison or something."

"That's awful!"

"Yea."

Suddenly a distant quacking interrupted their thoughts and they both gripped their shotguns and peered up through the slit in the blind looking for the flight. There was no flight, only a single duck came in to look over the decoys and both boys raised up and fired, bringing the duck down.

"I got him!"

"The heck you did Low, I got him!"

"Oh BS, it was my shot that brought him down!"

The argument went on while they waded out in the pond but just as they reached the fallen duck, they heard another loud quack. They both froze and then slowly looked up. There was a flight of at least twelve ducks circling calling loudly for permission to land. Lowell slowly turned his head and shouted "NOW!"

The loud report of both shotguns ripped through the afternoon air and when it was over, three ducks fell into the water.

"Boy did you see that flight?"

"Yea and did you see me shoot two ducks?"

"Oh that's bull, I got all three; you missed 'em all!"

These little friendly arguments never went on very long. They were only bantering between two very good friends.

"Well, we each have two ducks to take home today, no matter who shot them."

Myron answered "Yea," giving Lowell that little smirked smile of his which always meant everything is okay.

After gathering up all their gear, Lowell and Myron mounted their bikes and started for home. The pond where they hunted was just outside the city limits and was only about two miles from their houses. It belonged to a very good friend of Lowell's father who had to give up hunting because of health problems and he allowed the boys to hunt anytime they wanted.

They rode in silence the rest of the way and upon reaching Myron's house said their good byes with a "See ya later."

As Lowell entered the house his mother hollered, "Is that you dear?"

"Yea!"

"Did you get anything?"

"Yea we got two apiece."

"Well bring them in here so I can clean them."

Lowell entered the kitchen where his mother was as she was most of her waking hours. She was a fairly tall woman, slightly over weight in her mind, but a beautiful woman never the less.

"Here, put them in the sink. Did you have a good time?"

"Yea."

"Well you better go clean up. Dinner will be ready in a few minutes."

Sunday dinner at the Andersen's house was a tradition even though it was only three days after Thanksgiving, and it was mandatory for the entire family. To get permission to miss church during hunting season was stretching it enough without missing dinner as well.

Dinner went as usual with a lot of family talk punctuated by Diane and David's fighting over the last drumstick until father stepped in and said, "No! Neither of you can have it. You've both had two already and for a two legged chicken, that's pretty good!"

To which David said, "Aw Dad!"

After dinner, Lowell went to his room and did a little math homework but couldn't get Helen out of his mind. He went downstairs and asked his father if he could make a phone call to Helen.

"Yes," his father replied. "Go ahead, but don't stay on too long."

The Andersens were on a party line with four other families and Mr. Andersen always tried to be considerate of them.

Picking up the phone, Lowell gave the operator Helen's number. Mr. Speer answered and he asked, "Is Helen there Mr. Speer? This is Lowell."

"No, she's out."

"Okay, well I'll call back later."

"Do you want me to tell her you called?"

"Yes, please. Goodbye."

"Oh Lowell, are you working next Saturday at the station?"

"Yes till noon."

"Would you come by the yard and pick up the truck for service? We don't have any deliveries Saturday."

"Okay, I'll be there a little after nine o'clock."

"Fine, I think Helen will be working."

"Oh! Thanks Mr. Speer!"

As Lowell hung up the phone, he thought to himself, *What am I going to do to get old Vernon out of the picture?*

When he walked back into the room, his mother and father were listening intently to a news program on the radio and Diane and David were doing a puzzle on the dining room table.

His mom said, "Helen not home?"

"No I think she's out with Vernon."

"Well dear, a young girl as pretty as Helen probably has many dates," said his mom as she looked over at her husband and they smiled at each other.

Lowell had heard all the stories about his parent's courtship he wanted to, so he said, "I think I'll go up and play some records."

*****

The next week after basketball practice on Thursday, which was a little lighter being the day before full court scrimmage, Lowell said, "Hey Jew, why don't we get Betty and Helen and find something to do Saturday afternoon. I only have to work half a day."

Betty was Betty Miles, Myron's somewhat steady girl friend. She was a tall red head and had been in the boys' class since third grade. Her father worked in the next town in a lumber mill and she was not only on the rally team, but she also served as the senior captain.

"Nah I can't, Dad wants me to work at the store all day; we're getting in a large shipment for Christmas."

"I thought you Jews didn't work on Saturdays or celebrate Christmas?"

"We're not that Orthodox."

"Well, are we going hunting on Sunday?"

"I thought you Swedes didn't do anything on Sundays?"

"Were not that Orthodox, and besides, I'm Norwegian, I've told you that a hundred times!"

"Same difference!"

Lowell reached over and slugged Myron on the shoulder; Myron retaliated with a slug on Lowell's shoulder. They looked at each other for a minute, agreed to go hunting on Sunday and turned and walked away with a "See ya later."

Sunday morning just before dawn, Lowell's alarm clock woke him. As he did every morning when he and Myron were going hunting, he dressed, went down stairs, and had a piece of toast and glass of milk. He was always careful not to wake the rest of the family, but he knew his mom was probably already awake. After eating his meager breakfast, he went out to the garage, got his bike, tied the bag of duck decoys on the back luggage rack, strapped his shotgun to the handlebars and shoved off to Myron's house. When he reached the Rothstein's house, the lights were on in the back room and he knew that Myron would be out soon.

With his bike similarly loaded, Myron came around the house and said, "Ready to go?"

"Been ready for some time, where have you been?"

"Oh Yea! I looked out a few minutes ago and you weren't here."

They rode in silence the two miles to the pond, placed the decoys and settled down on the straw they had placed on the floor of the blind. It looked like it was going to be a clear day, which didn't bode well for shooting ducks. Contrary to popular belief, ducks, did not like to fly in the rain and wind so they would look for places to land making rainy, windy days best for hunting.

After a very fruitless hunting morning, Lowell and Myron loaded their equipment and rode back to town. At Myron's house, they said their goodbyes and Lowell rode home.

When he entered the house, he got the usual greeting from his mom, and he reported, "We got skunked today."

"Well, go on up and get ready, dinner will be on the table in about fifteen minutes."

As they sat down to dinner, Lowell noticed Diane wasn't at the table. "Where's Diane?"

"Oh she had a little cold so I told her to stay in bed and I would bring dinner up to her." This provoked a response from David.

"Yea, I'll bet she is faking it just to get to eat in bed."

"Now David, didn't you get to eat in bed that time you had a cold?" Mother said.

"Yea, but I was really sick!"

Lowell looked at his little brother and smiled both inwardly and outwardly.

Following dinner, Lowell set about on the usual Sunday afternoon activities, homework, listening to some records and thoughts of Helen. He decided to go down and call her. After the usual admonishment, Lowell obtained permission to use the phone.

"Hello."

It was a women's voice and for a moment, Lowell thought it has Helen, but soon realized it was her older sister.

"Is Helen there?"

"No, she isn't home right now."

"Oh. Well, will you tell her Lowell called?"

"Oh hi Lowell! I thought it was you. This is Linda."

Helen's sister, Linda, was six years older than Lowell. He remembered how all of the junior high boys thought she was one of the most beautiful girls in town. She was now married to a lawyer and lived in Portland.

As he went back into the living room, his mother asked, "No luck honey?"

"No I guess she is out with Vernon again."

"Well, maybe you will see her at school tomorrow."

"Yea, well I think I'll walk over to Jew's house and see what he's doing."

"Lowell!" His father said, "Don't call him that, in some areas that is a very derogatory term!"

"Yea, okay Dad."

Walking down the sidewalk to Myron's house, he thought of how much he liked Helen and how jealous he was of Vernon. Being from the richest families in Drayville and having his own car made him pretty tough competition indeed. Well, he would talk it over with Myron. Maybe he'd have an idea.

He walked up on the porch and knocked on the door. Mr. Rothstein opened the door and Lowell was so preoccupied with his thoughts he said, "Is Je—I mean is Myron here?"

Mr. Rothstein looked at him with a slight but warm smile saying, "It's okay Lowell, we know what you boys call each other and we know it is a term of endearment and not a derogatory slur."

Lowell could feel his face flushing as Mr. Rothstein opened the door for him and said, "He's up in his room."

Glancing into the living room, Lowell noticed that Mrs. Rothstein had a handkerchief to her face and he wondered what was going on.

Climbing the stairs Lowell banged on Myron's door and walked in. He was lying on his bed reading a hunting magazine. He looked up and greeted him by throwing the magazine at him.

"How ya doing Low?"

"Well, not so good, I tried to call Helen again and she was out, probably with old Vernon in his almost new 1935 V8 Ford Coupe!"

"Yea, that's a swell car isn't it?"

They both sat in silence for a minute when Lowell finally said, "Ya want to walk down to Smith's for a coke or some ice cream?"

"Yea, that sounds great. Let me get my shoes and I'll be right with you."

As they went downstairs, Lowell noticed that Mr. and Mrs. Rothstein were both sitting on the couch and he had his arm around her. Myron went over and gave his mother a peck on the forehead and told them that they were going down to Smith's.

As they walked down the sidewalk, Lowell asked. "Jew, was your mother crying again?"

"Yea."

"What happened?"

"We got word that her uncle and all his family had been killed by the Nazis."

"That's awful, how can they get away with something like that?"

"I guess they just do. I would like to join the British army and go kill every one of those bastards!"

After a short pause he said, "God, I hate to see my mother cry. Those dirty bastards!"

After a short while, Lowell asked. "Jew wasn't your mother born here in the United States."

"That's right."

"How come your uncle was still in Europe?"

"It isn't my uncle. It's my great uncle, my mom's uncle."

"Oh. Did you know them?"

"No, only from pictures and what Mom said about them."

"Did your mom know them?"

"Yea, remember in the third grade when Mom was gone for a month and Aunt Sara came to stay with us?"

"Yea."

"Well Mom, my grandparents, and my uncle from Chicago traveled to Poland and visited them."

"I thought your uncle and aunt lived in Portland?"

"That's my dad's sister and her husband, Uncle Jules and Aunt Sara."

"Oh."

"Uncle Simon is my mother's brother. He owns a bank in Chicago."

"So it must be true that all Jews are very rich."

"Well, I know a few rich Swedes too."

"I told you, I'm Norwegian!"

"Same difference!"

Lowell reached out and gave Myron a slug on the shoulder and Myron returned the act. They both laughed and their eyes met for a minute and then embarrassed they both looked down.

"Jew."

"Yea?"

"There is something I want to talk to you about."

"Yea?"

"You and Betty are sort of going steady aren't you?"

"Well, sort of."

"Did you ask her to or did it just happen?"

"Well, it kind of just happened. One night out at the river, I said, 'Are we going steady?' and she said, 'Yea, I guess so.' And that's how it happened."

"Boy that sounds romantic."

"What are you leading up to?"

"Well, I am tired of Vernon chasing Helen and I'm thinking of asking her to go steady. Has Betty ever told you anything about how Helen feels about me?"

"Listen dork, if you don't know how Helen feels about you, you're dumber than I thought."

"Whada'ya mean?"

"Haven't you noticed how she lights up and squirms when see sees you in the hall?"

"Well, yea!"

"Look dummy, that means she likes you!"

By this time, they had reached the front door of Smith's. Lowell opened it to allow Myron to enter first. Immediately upon stepping inside the door, Myron turned running into Lowell and said, "Hey, let's go down to the Cozy Corner today!"

"What, are you nuts, that place would be full of families with kids."

"That's okay, let's just walk then." Myron began to push Lowell out the door.

"What's the matter with you? Are you crazy?" Lowell looked over

Myron's shoulder and saw what was causing such crazy behavior. Helen and Vernon were sitting in a booth and he was holding her hand.

Lowell's heart jumped into his throat and he could hardly get his breath. He stood frozen for what seemed like several minutes until Myron gave him a shove backward almost making him fall to the sidewalk. The disturbance caused everyone in the place to look at the door and when Helen saw who it was, her face fell and she jerked her hand from Vernon's.

As they walked down the street, Myron felt sorry for his friend as he kept repeating. "Darn it, darn it, darn it. I hate that guy!"

"Hey, did you see the look on her face? It reminded me of someone who had just suffered terrible pain."

"Whada'ya mean?"

"You didn't notice when she saw you. She jerked her hand away from him and her expression looked like a wounded fawn."

"Whada'ya mean?"

"I think she had nothing to do with holding his hand. I think she was embarrassed to death."

"You think so?"

"Sure!"

"Okay, okay that settles it, when I see her at school next week, I'm going to ask her to the after game dance and then, I'm going to ask her to go steady."

"Well good; I'm glad that's settled!"

The next week at school Lowell had no opportunity to see Helen alone until Tuesday after fourth period when he spotted her walking down the hall towards the home economics room. He quickened his pace and caught up to her.

"Hi Helen!"

"Hi."

Lowell got that old feeling when he saw her face light up with the smile that only Helen could display. That must have been what Jew was talking about.

She asked, "What are you doing down at this end of the hall?"

"Well, I just wondered what you were doing after the game Friday and if you have no plans, would you like to go to the dance with me?"

"Oh sure!"

"Okay swell. Well, I'll see ya around. I had better get to class."

As Helen turned into the home economics room she looked over her shoulder and gave him one of those heart stopping smiles making Lowell giggle all over as he skipped down the hall toward his math class.

"Hey Low, what's your big hurry and what's the big smile for?"

"Oh, hi Jew! I just made a date with Helen for after the game on Friday."

"Yea, well finally, but you better not spend too much time thinking about your dame. Coach will want to be really ready and try to knock off Grant."

"Yea. How big is Grant anyway?"

"I don't know Low, I guess it's around 1,000 kids."

"Wow, that's nearly a third of the population of Drayville!"

"Yea, well here we are, old Miss 'Large Bottom's' Social Econ."

"Yea."

GAME DAY, GRANT

The big day dawned dark and wet as most winter days in Oregon. Friday, December 5, 1941, the day of the big non-league game with Oregon's largest school, and the day Lowell would start going steady with Helen, he hoped.

He crawled out of bed, started across the hall to the bathroom only to find the door locked and he could hear his brother and sister arguing over something.

Banging on the door, he said, "Hey you guys, open the door, you've been in there long enough."

As the door was unlocked and flew open, Diane came out and yelled, "Lowell, make him give me my toothbrush!"

"It's not hers, it's mine!"

"It is not! Lowell, he left his downstairs and he wants to use mine. Uck!"

"Okay David, go downstairs and get your own toothbrush and let me use the bath room for a minute."

"That's not fair. We were in here first!"

"Yes, but you don't have a toothbrush and besides, you shouldn't brush your teeth before you eat breakfast anyway."

He finished in the bathroom and began to dress. He was so nervous he could hardly button his pants. He didn't know if it was from thinking about Helen or about the game.

When he came downstairs his father looked up and said "Hey, a big day today huh?"

For a terrible moment, Lowell thought he was referring to Helen, but then realized he meant the game.

"You, you bet. "Dad, do you know how big a school Grant is?"

"Well, I think it must have nearly 1,000 kids doesn't it?"

"Je—Myron said over a 1,000."

"Well, good luck tonight. We'll be there to cheer you on."

That day at school, Lowell could hardly keep his mind on classes. Though it was important to him, he wasn't thinking about the game at all but rather about asking Helen to be his steady girl. He saw her in the hall for a moment and she seemed to sense that tonight was an important night as well. When he walked up to her locker, she turned and put her hand on his chest and wished him good luck; he wanted to kiss her so bad it hurt.

The rest of the day was a blur even when Myron and Betty came up to him between fourth and fifth period and wished him well with both his endeavors. Obviously, Jew had told her about what he planned to do after the dance.

At dinner that night, his father told him he could be a little late to work the next day after such a big night. Lowell again had the feeling that his father knew more than he was letting on. After dinner, he went to his room and for the 100th time, rehearsed what he was going to say to Helen and was still dissatisfied with it. Oh well, it will have to do.

As the team took the floor that night for the big game with Grant, the band was playing the fight song, which was a version of On Wisconsin, and the cheerleaders were jumping up and down, and the fans were yelling and clapping. Grant was already on the floor and they looked very big. However, Drayville had one of the tallest centers in the state in Bill Vickers, just a junior, at six feet-four inches. When Coach Roberts called them to the sideline for the last minute pep talk, Lowell caught a glimpse of Helen looking straight at the bench and he hoped she was looking at him and not Vernon.

"Okay boys, this is a non-league game so it doesn't count toward any statistics," said Coach Roberts. "They are the big school from the big city, so let's show them what us hicks from the sticks can do with a basketball."

*****

The starters for Drayville were Bill Vickers at center, Myron and Vernon as forwards and Lowell and Roger Wilson as guards. The referee threw up the ball and blew his whistle to start the game. Bill won the tip and he tipped it to Roger. Lowell broke for the basket and Roger threw the ball; it slipped right through Lowell's hands out of bounds and Grant got the ball. Lowell was mortified. He knew then he must concentrate on the game and not the dance or what might happen after the dance.

Grant scored on their first possession and Lowell took the in bounds pass and started to dribble down the floor. Vernon broke out in front of his man and Lowell passed him the ball and broke across the key. Vernon passed back to him and he set and shot from the top of the key, the ball swished through the net, score tied.

The first thirty seconds set the tone for the entire game. It was a back and forth struggle with Grant pulling ahead by two then by four and then Drayville closing the gap to tie and pull ahead by a basket. The game see-sawed back and forth until late in the second quarter when, Coach Roberts, sensing some fatigue from his starters, substituted for Roger, Vernon and Bill, leaving Lowell and Myron in the game. Gerald Olson, the football quarterback who was over six feet played back-up center to Bill and replaced him. Bob Porter and Larry Majors came in for Roger and Vernon. That lineup finished the half and they went to the dressing room behind by four points, Grant leading twenty-two to eighteen. Coach Roberts delivered another of his inspiring half time speeches and the team went out for the last two quarters.

Lowell redeemed himself on the second half tip off by breaking for the basket and Myron passed him the ball for a lay up. Grant failed to score on their possession and Drayville tied the score. A Grant player ran into Vernon sending him to the line and the referee called a foul against Grant.

Lowell went over to Vern and said, "Just relax, you can make it."

The ball swished through net giving Drayville the twenty-three to twenty-two lead with five minutes to go in the third quarter. The quarter ended with Drayville still leading thirty-one to twenty nine. In the fourth quarter, the fans went crazy. The entire gym seemed to rock back and forth emulating the flow of the game. With only forty-five seconds left and down by one point, the Grant coach called a time out. As the boys went to the bench, Coach Roberts didn't say a word he just had them sit down and rest.

When the whistle blew calling the teams back on to the floor, Coach just said, "I can't help you now boys. It's up to you."

Grant in-bounded the ball and each player on the team ran to a different spot on the floor. It confused the Drayville boys to the point where they just stood for a minute giving Grant's guard time to break for the basket with the ball for a lay up, taking the lead, forty-one to forty. Drayville in-bounded the ball and Lowell started down the floor when the little Grant guard suddenly swept the ball away from him and dribbled towards the basket. Lowell followed but was unable to check him so his next choice was to foul.

In the act of shooting, the foul gave the Grant guard two free throws. The first swished right through the basket giving Grant a two-point lead, but the second bounced off the rim and was rebounded by Roger. Myron, Bill and Vernon broke for the other end of the floor as Roger began to dribble down floor. The little Grant Guard again tried to steal the ball, but Roger was too quick and passed it to Lowell. He dribbled a few times and seeing Myron break out, he passed it to him who in turn passed it to Bill Vickers, the six-foot four-inch center. Bill spun, faked a shot and Grant's center fouled him.

He went to the foul line with two shots. Bill was, like so many big men, not a very good foul shooter. Lowell went over to him and gave him the admonishment to relax. The first shot hit the rim, bounced twice and fell through. As Bill readied himself for the game-tying basket, Lowell could see him shaking from nerves.

He walked over and said, "I told you to relax and it worked, now do it again!"

Bill's shot hit the rim so hard that the ball bounded almost to the centerline. Lowell quickly recovered it and dribbled around the key a few times looking for an opportunity to shoot, but the Grant guard was sticking close to him. Suddenly Lowell saw Vernon fake his man and break for the basket, he rifled the ball to him and he made the lay up giving Drayville a one-point lead with just under fifteen seconds to play. As the Grant guards hurriedly brought the ball into their end of the court, every fan and every player not in the game yelled, "Check 'em, Check 'em!"

The Grant players were breaking this way and that trying to get free of their guards. At five seconds left, the little Grant guard worked the ball to the top of the key where he put up a set shot that hit the side of the rim and caromed into Bill Vicker's arms just as the horn sounded ending the game with a one-point victory for Drayville.

From the turmoil in the Drayville dressing room, one would have thought they had just won the State Championship instead of the first non-league game.

Lowell went over to Vernon to congratulate him on the shot but before he could say a thing, Vernon said, "Lowell, thanks a lot for that pass, it was all your doing."

They shook hands and as Lowell walked back to his locker, he thought, "Maybe Vern isn't such a bad guy after all."

As the team came up from the basement dressing room to the main gym, the dance was in progress; everything stopped and there was a great round of applause. Lowell spotted Betty and Helen standing together with large smiles on their faces and he walked over.

Helen reached up and gave him a peck on the cheek saying, "Great game Lowell. You were the star."

Lowell was somewhat embarrassed but he took her hand and asked if she would like to dance. On the way to the dance floor, he spotted his father coming towards him with a big smile on his face. He extended his hand and said great game son. Lowell noticed Mr. Rothstein standing beside his father with an equally large grin on his face.

His father reached into his pocket and handed him the keys to the car saying, "Here son, you and Myron can have the car tonight. The Rothsteins have offered us a ride home. It's parked over on Second Street."

Lowell danced every dance with Helen until he was so tired he couldn't stand any more. She suggested they sit down or go get a cup of lemonade, which he readily did. Myron and Betty joined them and talked about leaving before eleven o'clock and going to Smith's for some ice cream. About 10:45, the four teenagers left in Lowell's family car. There was a tradition for those few who had cars, called dragging the gut. That meant driving up and down the main street back and forth any number of times. That night Lowell, Helen, Myron and Betty dragged the gut for awhile and then decided to drive out to the river and park.

After thirty minutes or so of some kissing and listening to music on the radio, Betty said she had to get home. This provided the opportunity Lowell was hoping for, to be alone with Helen. They took Betty home, dropped Myron at his house and then drove up to Helen's.

After shutting down the engine and turning off the radio to save the battery, Lowell took Helen in his arms kissed her longingly and told her he had something to ask her, but could not get the words out.

Helen said, "What were you going to ask me?"

"Well, you know I really like you don't you?"

"And I really like you Lowell."

After a long silence, Helen said, "What was it Lowell?"

"Well, I ah, I really like you Helen and I was wondering if ah, well if you – – ."

Before he could get it out, Helen finished it for him with, "Do you want to go steady?"

"Why yes, YES I do!"

"Oh Lowell, I like you, no I love you so much and I thought you would never ask me to be your steady girl."

The evening ended with more heavy kissing, but nothing beyond that except ecstasy. Lowell was in seventh heaven; he had a steady girl for the first time in his life. As he put the car in the driveway, it finally occurred to him that she had been the one doing the asking, but what the heck. It worked anyway.

*****

That night he slept the sleep of angels and when his mother called him to get up and get ready for work he looked at the clock and discovered it was almost noon. He crawled out of bed went across the hall to the bathroom and could hear Diane and David arguing over something down in the living room. He shook his head and thought; those two will never get along.

When he arrived at the station, his father had several jobs lined out for him. First, he had to clean the rest rooms, scrub the lubrication room (known as the "lube" room floor), and wash Mrs. Booker's 1932 Hudson, which was one of the prize cars envied by all the teenage boys. It was a beautiful green with only 8,000 miles on it and probably never saw a speed over twenty miles an hour. He would have loved to own that car but had to settle for driving it around the station lot when she brought it in for a wash or a lube.

Lowell was very busy most of the day but every once in awhile got that warm feeling from the events of the night before. He decided he would use the station phone and call Helen when his dad left for home. Lowell was just finishing with the lube room floor when the bell signaling someone pulled into the gas pumps.

His dad yelled from the back office, "Lowell, can you get that? I'm working on the books."

"Sure Dad!"

When he went out to the pumps, there was Myron in his dad's delivery truck.

Lowell smiled and said in an over professional tone, "Filler up sir?"

"No, just give me a couple of dollars worth, but check the tires and oil as well, boy!"

"How you doing Jew?"

"Okay. Well, come on, how did it go?"

"Great, we are now going steady."

"When did you ask her?"

"Well, I didn't exactly ask her. I kind of suggested it and she agreed."

"What? What did you say?"

"Well, I sort of stammered around a bit and she asked if I wanted to go steady."

"What? You mean she asked you?"

"No, not exactly and if you say anything around school, I'll kill you!"

"O ho! That's really swell, she asked you!"

"Now just keep your dang mouth shut, okay?"

"Yea, okay. Well how about that gas or does Helen have to come over here and tell you to pump it?"

"Oh, really funny."

As Lowell was pumping the gas, he yelled up to Myron, "Hey, you want to go hunting in the morning?"

"Sure, same time?"

"Yea, I guess. That will be two dollars please."

"Hey, what about the tires and oil?"

"Check 'em yourself!"

"Boy, I'm telling you; wait till I tell the manager what kind of service I'm getting here."

At six o'clock, Lowell's mother came by in the car with a hot meal for him and picked up his dad to take him home. Before he left, Mr. Andersen reminded him to be sure and turnoff all the lights. Last time he closed, he left the back room light on all weekend.

"I will dad, see ya about 8:30."

"Bye son."

As soon as his parents were off the lot, Lowell ran to phone in the back room that served as an office and asked the operator to connect him with 964, the Speer's number. Mrs. Speer answered, after three rings.

"Hello."

"Mrs. Speer, this is Lowell Andersen. Is Helen there?"

"Yes Lowell, I'll get her. She has just about driven us all nuts today asking if she has had any calls."

"Hello Lowell."

"Hi Helen, sorry to wait so long to call but after you kept me out so late last night I slept until it was time to go to work."

"Now, who kept who out?"

"Never mind. What have you been doing today?"

"Oh, I helped Dad at the yard this morning and then came home and did my homework and cleaned my room."

After ten minutes of small talk, the pump bell rang again and Lowell quickly made arrangements to call her tomorrow after he got home from hunting. Lowell had several late customers that night mostly purchasing only two or three dollars worth of gas. At eight o'clock, he turned off the front light and began to gather the money from the cash register, put it in a money sack and hid it in the back room under some oil cans. After making sure he had turned off all the lights and the gas pumps, he started to walk home. Rain was beginning to fall and it was quite cold, but temperature was not a problem to any teenage boy who was now going steady!

Sunday morning, the alarm went off at 5:00 and Lowell reached over, shut it off and then rolled over on his back thinking, *What am I doing getting up this early?* Rolling out of bed, getting dressed in warm dry clothes he went downstairs to the kitchen where his mother had placed a sack lunch for him. He smiled and thought, *What a great mother I have. I'll bet Helen will be that kind of mother too.*

Hunting

After putting the decoys out and settling in on the straw at the bottom of the duck blind, Lowell and Myron began to talk about the rest of their senior year in school.

"Do you think you will go to college Jew?"

"I don't know. Maybe, but I think my dad wants me to take over the store some day so I think I'll need to know something about business. I'll probably go to some college."

"You think you'll go to Emmons?"

"I don't know – maybe, or the University of Oregon."

"You want to be a Duck?"

"I don't know. I hear they have a good business school there."

Suddenly they heard that tell tale *quack* and both froze and looked up. One of the biggest flights they had seen in some time was circling the decoys. Myron brought the duck call to his mouth and began to *quack* back. Among the high school boys who hunted, Myron was the best duck caller.

The flight set wings and began to float down to the water a mere twenty yards from the blind. Lowell yelled, "Now!" and they both rose up and emptied their guns into the flock of ducks. Several ducks fell to the water as the smoke from their guns cleared.

"Great shooting Jew!" Lowell yelled.

"You too Low!"

"We must have gotten several."

As they wadded out in the water, they saw four ducks lying still among the decoys.

"Well I think you got one Low!"

"BS, I got all four!"

"Oh yea. Will you settle for two each?"

"Okay!"

As the boys gathered up their kill and checked the time, they decided it was time to go.

Lowell said, "Well, if I'm to get home for dinner today, I guess we'd better take off."

"Yea, I guess so."

"They picked up the decoys, loaded them in the sacks, strapped them on the bikes and set off for town.

Entering town, they had to ride down Main Street to get to their homes. As they peddled along, they began to notice that there were people standing in small groups on corners and in front of stores talking in very serious tones.

At Fifth and Main, the boys noticed Mr. Teague, the owner and editor of the weekly paper, the Drayville Advertiser standing with Mr. and Mrs. Johnson and two people they didn't know. They rode over to the curb and Lowell said to Mr. Teague, "What's going on?"

Mr. Teague said, "What do you mean?"

"I mean, why are all the people here on Main Street today?"

"You mean you haven't heard?"

Myron said, "Heard what?"

"About the attack?"

"What attack," Lowell Asked.

"The Japs have bombed Pearl Harbor. Where have you boys been?"

"We've been duck hunting."

"Where's Pearl Harbor?" Myron asked

"In Hawaii!"

"Why would they do that?" replied Lowell

"They want us in the war and by golly we're going to beat those little yellow bastards!"

Lowell and Myron looked at each other and smiled in disbelief not understanding quite what that meant but they did realize that something momentous had taken place.

When Lowell got home, he heard the radio and saw his mother and father listening to it as he entered the house. He could smell dinner on the stove and noticed that his mother had been crying.

She immediately jumped up and ran to him throwing her arms around his neck and saying, "Oh Lowell, this is terrible!"

"Mom, what is the matter? Pearl Harbor is way out in the Pacific. It won't affect us that much."

Mr. Andersen rose and said, "Well, Son I'm afraid you're mistaken. This means war and I'm sure Germany will jump right in and we'll have another world war."

"Dad, didn't Uncle Norwood get wounded during World War I?" Lowell asked.

"Yes, at Bella Woods in Europe," his father replied.

Just then, David and Diane came running down the stairs arguing about something and were both yelling for justice from their mother.

Mrs. Andersen said, "Kids, will you be quiet? We have something important to discuss."

Lowell asked, "What's going to happen, Dad?"

"I don't know Son, but I am sure that young men your age will be involved!"

"Oh Ethan, let's don't think about that; he is only seventeen-years-old and hasn't finished high school yet!"

*****

The next day at school, the major subject discussed both in the halls and in the classrooms was the event in the far off Hawaiian Islands. Mr. Black, the history teacher, had maps on the wall showing the locations of Pearl Harbor and Japan. He explained that the Japanese had carefully planned the attack, otherwise they could not have gotten close enough to bomb the harbor.

At lunch that day, Lowell and Myron sat very silent for some time and then Myron said, "I'm going to enlist as soon as I graduate."

"Why Jew. Dad said they probably would not take any one under nineteen years old."

"Hey, you forget, I will be nineteen in July."

"Oh yea, that scarlet fever thing."

Myron was a year older than Lowell though in the same grade. He had been six and ready to start school when he contracted scarlet fever in August and his folks decided to keep him out of school that year.

The bell rang for the start of fifth period and Myron looked at Lowell and said, "Let's skip!"

After a pause, Lowell, said, "Okay, where will we go?"

"I don't know. Let's just walk around, maybe go by the store and get dad's car and just drive and talk."

"Great, let's go!"

When they walked in to Rothstein's Furniture store, the clerk, Mr. Fowler greeted them with, "Hi boys. Aren't you supposed to be in school?"

"Is Dad here?"

"Yes, he's back in the office."

"Thanks Mr. Fowler."

When they entered the office, Mr. Rothstein looked up with the same greeting as Mr. Fowler. "Aren't you boys supposed to be in school?"

"Yea Dad, but we didn't feel like it. We just wanted to get away and talk."

Drafted into World War I at nineteen-years-old, Mr. Rothstein fully understood.

"Boys, I was in exactly your situation when we entered the Great War."

"Dad, can we have the car this afternoon? We want to just drive around and talk."

Mr. Rothstein looked at them for a minute and then reached in his pocket and threw Myron the keys to their 1940 Pontiac four-door sedan.

"Be careful boys, we might need you soon."

They got in the car just as it started to rain. They had no idea where they were going but they knew they didn't want to hear anything about economics or how to diagram a sentence. They just wanted to be alone with each other and talk.

As they drove out of town, Myron asked, "Where do you want to go?"

"I don't care; why don't we just drive out in the country."

After a few miles, Myron hit the steering wheel and exclaimed, "Dang it. Dang it any way, those dang Japs have sure messed up our plans haven't they?"

"What do you mean?"

"Well, I was going to ask Betty to marry me after graduation."

"No kidding?"

"Well you knew we were serious didn't you?"

"I don't know. I guess I did. After all you have been dating for over a year."

"I love her Low; I love her a lot!"

"Yea, I guess I love Helen like that to."

"Aren't we something, here we are talking about being in love, getting married and all, and we aren't even out of high school yet. We haven't even finished basketball or baseball season yet."

They both laughed and gave each other that look which meant *I love you too* but for two teenage boys, that must always remain unsaid.

They drove around for nearly an hour and finally found themselves in Masonberg, the neighboring town and fierce rival. There was a small soda shop on the main street so they pulled up in front, parked and walked in.

Both had their Drayville letterman sweaters on and the lady behind the counter looked up and said, "What brings two Drayville boys to town in the middle of the day? You're not skipping school are you?"

"Yea, well kind of; we just felt like going for a drive."

"Yea, I understand. What can I get for you?"

"Oh, I don't know. What do you want Lowell?"

"Oh, I don't know, maybe a coke."

"Okay, two cokes."

As the waitress opened the bottles and placed them before the boys, she said, "That was a great game you played against Grant Friday night."

"Yea, thanks. It seems like a hundred years ago now."

"Yea, it sure does!"

As they took the first sip of their cokes, the door opened and two boys wearing the black and orange letterman sweaters with the big M on them entered. Low and Jew recognized them as two of the most outstanding athletes from Masonberg High School. They nodded to each other as the Masonberg boys took a seat in the window booth.

The waitress walked over and asked what they wanted and they gave her their order.

Before she served them, the taller of the two Masonberg boys raised his voice and said, "What are you guys doing over here on a school day?"

Low turned on the stool and said, "Oh, I don't know, we just didn't want to go to class this afternoon so we skipped."

"Yea, that's the way we felt too. You guys want to join us?"

Low looked at Jew who nodded and they moved over to the booth.

"I'm Lowell Andersen and this is Myron Rothstein."

The smaller of the two Masonberg boys said, "I'm Bill Brooks and this is Dick Toguard."

Low and Jew nodded and Low said, "Glad to meet you. We know who you are Toguard. You just killed us in football this year."

"Yea, I had a pretty good season."

His friend said, "Yea, all league and second team all state."

They were silent for awhile and then Brooks said, "What do you guys think about this war we're going to have?"

"I don't know, I don't think it will last too long. Maybe it will be over before we graduate."

"Oh bull Low; it's going to go on for a long time." Jew said.

Brooks said, "I think I am going to join the Marines the day I graduate."

Toguard, said, "Why?"

"Because they are the toughest and best outfit in the whole country!"

Myron said, "I'm going to join the Army Air Corps so I can bomb the crap out of those damn Nazis bastards!"

"You mean you want to fly?"

"You're damn right!"

The waitress came around from behind the counter and approached their booth, "Look boys, you've got to watch your language. I would throw you out for the way you've been talking except for the present situation, I fully understand."

"We're sorry; I guess we just got carried away," said the Brooks boy.

Low and Jew finished their cokes, got up from the booth and did something they would never have consider any other time. They extended their hands to the two Masonberg boys and said, "Good luck in basketball this year."

The two boys in orange and black sweater somewhat taken aback by the gesture, responded with their hands and repeated the well wishing.

*****

Christmas of 1941 was not celebrated anywhere in the United States as other Christmases had been. The events some three and a half weeks prior had detracted from the usual merry celebrating of the season. However, Lowell's happiness at having Helen as a steady girl made the season memorable for him. He talked to his mother about what he might get her on their first Christmas as boy friend and girl friend. She suggested jewelry and he thought that was a good idea. He managed, with his mother's help, to find a nice necklace that she sincerely loved. He received a very nice hunting jacket from her making this sad Christmas season one of the most memorable of his life.

With the holidays over, the league basketball season began. The first game was against Rickered, a school about the same size as Drayville whom they beat forty-nine to forty-three. The next night they beat Amsville fifty-one to forty-one. After the game and the dance Lowell, Helen, Myron and Betty did their usual thing: Smiths, followed by a short park at the river. Because both boys and Helen worked at their father's stores the next day, they ended the night early.

The '33

The next morning as Lowell came around the corner of the garage on the way to work, he noticed a gray 1933 Ford, four-door sedan with suicide front doors in the repair bay. His father and George, the other station employee, were both leaning in under the hood looking at the motor.

Lowell said, "Hi Dad, got a new job?"

Lowell thought it very odd that both men jumped and hit their heads on the hood of the 1933 Ford.

His father seemed ill at ease as he answered, "Yea, it has a blown engine and George and I are trying to figure out just what it would take to fix it."

"I haven't seen that around town. Whose is it?"

Lowell's father looked at George and somewhat sheepishly said, "No, it's from over in Hill Dale. Say, Lowell, today I think we should wash down the lot, some of the fall leaves are still in the back."

"Okay Dad, but can I wait until it warms up a bit?"

"Sure."

Lowell put the 1933 Ford out of his mind in favor of more important things even though it sat in the repair bay for some time until one Saturday he came to work and it was gone.

He asked George, "What happened to the '33?"

"Oh, ah, your dad delivered it."

With basketball and seeing Helen whenever he could, he forgot all about the '33. He even forgot about his upcoming birthday, which fell on a Saturday. That morning his mom woke him with, "Happy birthday, old man!"

David and Diane came running into his room and jumped on his bed with a package between them, and as usual, they were fighting.

David said. "I get to give it to him!"

"Mom, you said we could both give it to him!"

"Well Diane I did but I thought we would do it down at breakfast, you haven't even given your brother time to get his eyes open."

Lowell smiled at both his brother and sister as they insisted that he open package right there in bed.

He raised it to his ear and shook it several times and said, "Doesn't rattle; must not be anything very important."

"Open it. Open it!"

"Okay."

Lowell tore off the ribbon and the paper to expose a plain cardboard box with the words Shock Absorbers (Front).

Faking excitement he said, "Oh boy, I got new shocks!"

"No! Dad gave us the box. It's from the station; open it!" Diane said with some disgust.

As he opened the box, the twins could hardly contain themselves and both started to help until mom restrained them. When the flaps of the box opened, Lowell saw a beautiful red sweater carefully wrapped in tissue inside. Lowell lifted it out and admired it with much delight and some awe.

"Try it on. Try it on!" Both twins yelled in unison, so Lowell got out of bed and put it on; it was a perfect fit.

Diane said, "I picked it out!"

David retorted, "I wrapped it!"

Lowell reached over and gathered both twins in his arms and said, "It's great kids, I love it. I'll wear it tonight when I go out with Helen."

"Well Lowell, you had better come on down and have some breakfast, your Dad will be expecting you at the station at ten."

"Okay."

Lowell decided he would wear the sweater down to breakfast to please the twins, it was a great looking sweater and he wanted to wear it anyway. During breakfast while Diane and David kept reaching out feeling the sweater, Lowell heard a car pull into the garage, which meant his father was home. *How strange*, he thought.

The back door opened and his father came in smiling, looked as his mother and put his arm around her and asked, "What's going on?"

"I was about to ask you the same question, Dad."

Diane and David said in unison, "Look at Lowell's sweater we gave him Dad!"

"Yea, it is a beauty; that will look good on him when he is greasing a car at the station." Mr. Andersen said with a twinkle in his eye.

Diane exclaimed, "Oh Dad, it's not for working at the station!"

"Dad, you haven't said why you're home in the middle of the morning," said Lowell.

"Well, I'll show you. If you've finished breakfast, come in the garage a minute."

Lowell got up from the table somewhat hesitantly and followed his father out to the garage. They entered by the side door followed by Mrs. Andersen and the twins. Mr. Andersen switched on the lights. There sat the 1933 gray Ford with suicide front doors and a ribbon on it that said, HAPPY 18TH BIRTHDAY SON FROM MOM AND DAD.

Spring 1942

The basketball season ended in March with Drayville finishing second in the league behind Clarkston, but that didn't indicate who went to state. The State Tournament participants were from local tournaments held in districts around the state. Drayville's district consisted of Masonberg, Amsville, Shelton, Rickered, and Compton. Held at the Emmons College gym, the tournament schedule called for three nights of play with the final on Saturday, March 10. The Drayville boys thought they had a good chance to win the district and enter state; however, they didn't figure on the hot shooting of the Rickered team who beat them forty-three to thirty-nine in the final game on Saturday night.

After the game Jew and Low collected their respective girl friends and went to Smith's for some ice cream and cokes. The mood was not very good but the jukebox and the food cheered them up a bit and the evening went okay from then on. Of course, Lowell drove the '33 with Jew and Betty in the back seat and when Jew suggested they go to the river, Helen thought they should just go home. The group evaluated her suggestion and thought it wise.

At Helen's front door, Lowell said, "Are you okay tonight?"

"No, not really."

"I thought something was wrong. Are you mad at me?"

"Oh heavens no! Linda called today and said that John was called up for his physical."

"Oh, it was that. Just so there is nothing wrong between us."

"Oh Lowell. When are you going to learn? There will never be anything wrong between us!"

Lowell hugged her even harder and then leaned back and planted a kiss on her forehead.

She said, "You can do better than that," and proceeded to kiss him directly on the lips.

They parted and Lowell said, "I'll call you tomorrow."

"Good night honey," Helen said and turned to enter the house when Lowell reached out and took her by the shoulder, turning her back in to his arm.

"Oh Helen I love you so much!"

"And I love you too Lowell!"

Driving home, Lowell wondered if asking Helen to marry him was out of the question at their age. After all, he was only eighteen and she was not yet seventeen.

Sunday mornings after duck season meant driving over to Willamette to attend his uncle Norwood's church. Lowell didn't mind because uncle Norwood's wife usually invited them to stay for dinner, which was most always fried chicken, mashed potatoes and some very good homemade pies. This Sunday was no exception.

As they sat around the living room, Lowell's father said, "Well, Norwood. That was one hell of a sermon today."

"Obviously it didn't have a great effect on you – you still use that pool room language."

Lowell chuckled at the exchange between his father and his older brother. It was an ongoing banter that he thought must have been going on most of their lives. Norwood, Lowell's uncle, was three years older than Lowell's father and he knew that he'd had a very diverse life. He was once a farmer, then a railroad worker, then a barber, and finally after serving in World War I, found Jesus in his life and became a preacher. Lowell liked uncle Norwood because he had enough life experience to be able to speak with some authority.

One time after he and Myron had gone hunting with uncle Norwood, Myron said, "If I ever decide to become a Gentile I think I would like to join your uncle's church."

That meant a lot to Lowell to find out that his best friend thought as much of his uncle as he did, though he doubted it would ever come to pass.

Lowell rode in the back seat with Diane and David on the way home. The family discussed how the war might affect them. His Father thought it would hurt his business because of probable gas rationing. Though he knew the meaning of the word ration, he didn't understand why it would apply to gasoline. His father explained that the country would need all the gasoline for the planes, tanks and trucks needed for the war. As they drove through the countryside towards Drayville, Lowell wondered if it would mean he couldn't get gas for the '33.

*****

The disappointment of not getting into the State Tournament in basketball eased with the start of baseball season. Though Lowell was the starting catcher on the team and the pitchers and catchers who were not on the basketball team had been working out for several weeks, he was nevertheless welcomed to the work out on Monday following the District Tourney on Saturday night. Lowell looked forward to the season because everyone thought Drayville had a chance of winning the league championship. They had two very good pitchers in Vernon Dickerson and Gerald Olson, the new boy who quarter-backed the football team. Everyone said he had a chance for a pro career. He had a very quick fastball and a curve that fooled every one, even the second string catcher who had been working out with him. Lowell knew that Vernon had a wicked fastball from last year but had some control trouble.

Coach Roberts called Lowell to his office one day, asked him to close the door and sit down.

"Lowell, as my starting catcher this year, you have a tough job ahead of you. You're aware that Vernon has been our back up and relief pitcher for two years, but Gerald is somewhat better. He throws a better fastball, better curve and has much better control. He'll be our starter this year."

"Yea, I understand that coach."

"Well, with Larry's graduation, we need both of them this year and it is your job to make sure they both feel they are important to the team."

Larry was Larry Worden, the starting pitcher who was now a freshman at Oregon State College.

"Okay coach."

"I don't think you understand what I am asking of you. I need you to encourage both, help them both, and make sure there's no rivalry between them that could hurt the team!"

"Okay coach, I'll do my best."

"I know you will Low, and between you, Jew and Bill, I expect a great deal of leadership."

The coach's use of their nicknames surprised Lowell. He didn't realize any of the teachers knew what the kids called each other.

By mid-season, with Gerald Olson and Vernon Dickerson on the mound, Drayville was having one of the best seasons in many years. Myron was at third, Lowell behind the plate and Bill Vickers at first. They had one of the best defensive infields in the league as well. As for hitting, Lowell led the team at mid-season with a 427 average and four home runs. Bill was just behind him at 417 and Myron at 394. With only four games left on a fourteen game schedule, they led the league with a nine and one record having lost only to Masonberg who was in second place with an eight and two record.

*****

Baseball was far from Lowell's mind as he was dressing for one of the most important nights of his life, the junior-senior prom. Of course, he was taking Helen and double dating with Jew and Betty. He had offered to drive, but Myron was able to get the family Pontiac with a near full tank of gas.

The dance was somewhat subdued compared to other school dances due to the world situation. There were two boys there in uniform with their dates. One of them was Robert Smith who lived just down the street from Myron and Lowell and who had quit school in January to join the navy; the other was Frank Mayham, a boy who had graduated a year ago but was dating a senior girl. They were the center of attention for the boys. They all crowded around asking questions about boot camp and where each was going to serve.

After the dance, Lowell and Myron took their dates to Smith's for ice cream and cokes and then the girls said they would like to go home and change their clothes to be more comfortable. Betty had brought her change over to Helen's that night so it meant only one stop. The boys merely took off their ties and jackets and waited in the car for the girls. They discussed the dance and who was dating whom.

"Boy old Bob and Frank really looked good in their uniforms."

Myron agreed but said, "I would never wear those tight pants with no pockets."

The girls finally finished changing and came out. They drove around town for awhile and then over to Masonberg to an all night diner for something to eat. Afterwards they drove to the river; that was part of the plan. The boys, in anticipation of this, had been sure they had two Indian blankets in the trunk.

When they arrived at the river, they got out, got the blankets from the trunk, and along with their dates, went their separate ways. Lowell walked down the beach past several couples wrapped up in blankets. They found a secluded spot behind some willows and spread the blanket on the sand.

After rolling up in the blanket, they began to kiss and hug. Lowell had so much respect for Helen that he never would do something she wouldn't want him to do, but that night there was much touching and petting. They lay rolled up in the blanket hugging and kissing and expressing their love for each other until the cold night finally got to them and Helen suggested that they get up and find Myron and Betty. Just then, they heard Myron and Betty calling out softly to them.

"Low, Helen."

"Over here Jew," Lowell said in a soft voice as he unwrapped himself from both the blanket and Helen's arms. "Are you ready to go?"

"Yea, Dad said not to stay out all night and in a couple of hours, night will be over. Besides, don't you think it is getting a little cold?"

"Yea."

Lowell and Helen folded up the blanket and followed Myron and Betty up the beach to where they had parked the car. They put the blankets in the trunk, got in and Myron turned the car around and started back to town.

In the back seat, Lowell and Helen snuggled together and pecked away at each other's lips. Lowell said, "Hey, why don't you come to church with me tomorrow?"

"Tomorrow?"

"I mean today," Lowell replied with a slight laugh.

"I don't know – I would have to write mom a note because I'm sure she will be asleep."

"Well if you can why don't you call, say around eight, I'm sure either my mom or the twins will be up."

They dropped Helen off first, which was an unwritten rule for double dating. You always dropped the back seat girl first and then her date. This gave the driver a few minutes alone with his date.

Lowell walked Helen to her door, gave her a loving hug and kiss, and said, "Try to make it today, will you."

"Yes I will."

At the un-Godly hour of 8:15 the twins barged into Lowell's room yelling in unison, "Helen's on the phone."

Lowell stretched and with as much speed as he could muster with only four hours of sleep ran down stairs to the phone.

"Hello."

"Hi, this is Helen."

"Well I sure hope it is."

With a slight laugh, she said, "Mom said it would be okay if I went with you this morning, if there's room."

"Sure there's room. That's swell! We'll pick you up around ten."

"Okay. See ya then."

*****

On the way over to Willamette, David sat in front with his folks and Lowell, Helen and Diane sat in back. Diane was always delighted when she got to be with Helen and thought of her as the sister she never had. Diane would snuggle up to her and when Helen put her arm around the little girl, it made a very cute scene. Some how church seemed so much better when Helen was with him. Lowell listened to the sermon, greeted the little old ladies more pleasantly, introduced Helen to those who had not met her, and always liked the way Uncle Norwood greeted her and made her feel welcome.

Lowell's aunt had invited some new people in the congregation for dinner, so the Andersens drove straight back to Drayville. On the way, Mrs. Andersen suggested that maybe Helen would like to come home with them and have a light lunch.

Diane sat up and said, "Oh yes Helen, please do."

Lowell said, "Yea I don't know – that would be okay I guess."

Helen punched him in the ribs and Diane said, "Oh shut up Lowell you know you want her to."

"I would love to, but I need to let my folks know." Helen responded.

The "light lunch" consisted of meat loaf, mashed potatoes, salad and left over cake. The subject of discussion during lunch was the major topic of almost every table discussion in the United States for the past five months. The War!

Lowell's dad talked about World War One when he was just an early teenager and how he wanted to get in the service and serve his country. Mrs. Andersen kept admonishing him to quit glorifying war and killing, making it sound like something noble and true. Lowell mostly listened to his parents discuss something that he knew nothing about, but was very concerned.

"Do you think you will have to go to the army?" asked Helen.

"I don't know, I will do my duty, but it won't be in the army."

Mrs. Andersen said, "Oh Lowell don't even talk about it; you know they are not taking anyone under nineteen."

"But that will undoubtedly change as the need for more and more troops are necessary," Mr. Andersen said.

Mrs. Andersen replied, "Oh Ethan, don't be so pessimistic; the war might be over before Lowell reaches nineteen."

Throughout this discussion, Lowell sat quietly and listened to his folks with thoughts of conversations he and Jew had in the last few months. Jew was determined to join the air corps and bomb the crap out of the Nazis.

After dinner, Lowell suggested a call to Myron to see if he and Betty would like to catch the matinee at the Broadway, the local theater downtown. An Abbot and Costello film was showing.

Mother said, "Lowell, you shouldn't go to a movie on Sunday."

To which he replied, "Oh Mom, that's such old thinking!"

Jew and Betty joined them and after the movie. Myron suggested that they drive over to Willamette to that great hamburger drive in and have something to eat.

Lowell said, "Good idea Jew, but I don't have enough gas and Dad won't give me more for another two weeks."

"Okay, let's just go to Smith's then for a coke."

As they sat in the booth at Smith's, Helen, who had been quiet said, "Do you think you boys will have to go in the army?"

"Yea, I think that is a very good possibility," replied Myron.

"What, are you now resigned to the army?" said Lowell.

"Well, the Army Air Corps."

Betty spoke up with, "You guys sound like it is something you want to do. My dad was in World War One and he said it was terrible!"

"Oh yea, but they didn't have airplanes that could fly at 30,000 feet in World War One," replied Myron.

"This kind of talk scares me to death," said Helen.

Lowell replied, "Yea, let's change the subject."

The evening gave way to night and the boys dropped the girls off and went for a little ride by themselves. "Are you really considering signing up for the air corps?" asked Lowell.

"Well, I told you that I wanted to bomb the crap out of those Nazis and I don't think the army has many bombers."

"When do you think you will sign up?"

"I don't know. When we graduate, I'll be nineteen and a half, just the right age for the draft. I will probably try to sign up in June or so."

Lowell, thought for several minutes as they drove by the lumber yard and then said, "God I would like to go in with you. But, Mom and Dad are working on me to go to college for at least a year."

"Well, in your case, I think that would be a good idea."

"Why am I so different than you? If you can go in, why can't I?"

"You can, but you have a year to wait, take it!"

As Lowell dropped Myron off and drove home he was very confused and needed advice that he couldn't get from his friends. When he came in the house, his mom and dad were in the living room. His dad was reading the paper with his unlit pipe hanging from the corner of his mouth; his mom was working on the constant knitting project and David and Diane were lying on the floor coloring.

He came in and without taking off his coat, he sat on the sofa and said, "Do you think it would be dumb for me to join the air corps right after graduation?"

His mom nearly dropped her knitting and his dad put the paper down with some force. They looked at each other showing great concern in the expression.

His dad finally said, "Lowell, I thought we had worked this all out. You are going to register at Emmons next fall."

"Yea I know, that's what we talked about, but Je—Myron is going to enlist right after graduation and I would really like to go with him."

"Lowell, Myron is a year older and he would be drafted before he finished his first year, you wouldn't!"

His mother added, "And Myron hasn't really got any college plans; you do!"

"What do you mean? I have no idea what I want to do or what I want to take in college."

The twins, sensing a different tone to their parent's voices, looked up and began to listen to the exchange.

Both parents looked at Lowell for some time and finally his dad said, "Son, can we discuss this at some other time; it's getting late and I think you kids should go to bed!"

Lowell knew that his father did not mean he had to go to bed at nine. It was for the benefit of the twins to settle a long-standing come back from them of "Why doesn't Lowell have to go to bed too?"

Nevertheless Lowell sighed and got up, looked at his parents and said, "Okay. See ya in the morning."

As he climbed the stairs to his room, he thought about his future. He would like to have more time with Helen and a year at Emmons would give him that. On the other hand, he and Myron had been doing things together for more than twelve years and it would be difficult to break away from that.

Lying on his bed, he picked up a hunting magazine and began to thumb through it when the door to his room quietly opened and Diane and David came in very uncharacteristically quiet for them.

Diane said, "Lowell?"

"Yes."

"Are you going to war?"

Lowell patted the bed beside him and both twins jumped up on his bed. "Well kids, I probably will have to some day."

David got a glint in his eyes and said, "Will you get a uniform and everything?"

"Yea, I suppose I will."

Diane said, "Mrs. Fletcher said that some times solders get killed in wars."

"Yea, that's right."

She snuggled closer to her older brother and said, "I don't want you to get killed Lowell!"

He leaned back and looked at her and she had big tears in her eyes.

He smiled and said, "Okay, I promise I will not get killed."

"Promise!"

"Yes!"

David was taking this all in with a look of non-understanding, but joined his sister in giving Lowell a big hug.

Lowell said, "Besides, we don't have to worry about this for a long time, I'm going to college next year. Okay guys? I think you should go back to your room and go to sleep now.

"Good night Lowell," they both said in unison as they raced out.

Lowell stared at the door for a minute thinking how much he loved those two little warts. They could be pains in the neck, but they were his brother and sister.

*****

Even with the war, Helen and his best friend Myron monopolized most of Lowell's thoughts and baseball was still important to him. They finished the last four games with victories, ending the season with a record of thirteen and one. Although Coach Roberts tried his best, the State Athletic Association did not choose them for the State Championship.

He called the team together after receiving the final ruling and said, "Well boys, I have bad news, the State Association has not chosen us to compete for the championship. It seems that there are eight teams with undefeated records and I guess they deserve the spot."

The room was silent until the left fielder, David Clark spoke up with, "That's okay coach. I feel bad for the seniors, but maybe we'll make it next year."

Refusing to be outdone, Jew broke the solemn mood.

"Yea, maybe some of us will flunk and we can come back and help you children."

ALL-STAR

On Thursday, the week before graduation, an announcement came on the public address system calling Lowell and Gerald Olson to the office. When Lowell entered, Gerald was sitting in the outer office looking very perplexed.

Lowell walked over to Gerald and said, "What's this all about Ole?"

"I don't know. I thought you might know."

The door to the principal's office opened and Coach Roberts stepped out and summoned the boys. When they entered, both the coach and Mr. Vernon, the Principal, were smiling. This relieved the tension somewhat, but did not explain the summons.

The coach said, "Boys, we've got some very good news for you. You have both been selected to the Down State All Star Baseball Team!"

Both Gerald and Lowell sat spellbound. They looked at each other in wonder and then they smiled and said to the coach, "Thank you coach!"

"Well I had very little to do with it. Maybe it was your season record. You were eight and zero on the mound with one no-hitter and three shut outs and a batting average of 437 with five home runs. You are two of the best ball players I have ever coached and you deserve this."

Mr. Vernon then entered the conversation.

"There is only one problem with your selection. The night of the all-star game against Metro is also our graduation night. You will have to decide, along with your folks, which is most important to you. Of course you will still graduate, but will not go through the exercises. I suggest that you both go home tonight and discuss it with your parents and let coach know in a day or so."

Lowell left the principal's office and went directly to the junior English class to wait for Helen. He wanted her to be the first to know. When the bell rang, the students began to spill out into the hall. Lowell spotted Helen in the room talking to another girl. He entered the room and took her by the arm saying, "Come on, I've something to tell you."

With a puzzled look on her face, Helen followed saying, "What is it?"

When they got out in the hall in a semi private corner, he said, "Guess what!"

"I don't know. What?"

"I've been picked for the All State Team to play against Metro in Municipal Stadium in Portland."

"Really, how swell; I am so proud of you!"

She reached up and gave him a little peck on the cheek, which he thoroughly enjoyed but caused him to look around. There was a strict rule against necking in the halls that included kissing. Lowell next had to tell Jew, whom he would see in fifth period trigonometry, but his surprise was taken away from him when at the beginning of fourth period, Mr. Vernon came on the public address system, calling for everyone's attention for a very important announcement.

After waiting a few seconds for their attention, the metallic voice said, "We have just been notified by phone that two of our boys have been selected to play on the Down State All Star Team against the Metro All Stars. They are Gerald Olson and Lowell Andersen. Congratulations boys! That is all."

The announcement caused somewhat of a shock in Miss Large Bottom's class when all the kids looked at Lowell and began to congratulate him. Miss Large Bottom gave the kids a few minutes and then said, "Congratulations Lowell, now we must get back to work."

That night the topic around the Andersen's dinner table was the all-star selections and the pros and cons of missing his high school graduation.

There was no doubt in Lowell's mind or apparently in his father's. His mother was the holdout when she said, "But dear, you only graduate once in your life and to miss it – –."

His dad said, "That's not quite right son, there's always college, and besides this is the only time he will have a chance to play in an all-star game."

That seemed to settle it, but Lowell could tell that his mother was not completely convinced.

The Game

Lowell sat next to Gerald on the bench in the dressing room of Municipal Stadium in Portland, Oregon listening to the state coach's final instructions.

"Okay boys I've done all I can. The rest is up to you."

By virtue of having two of his boys selected to the team, Coach Roberts became one of the assistant coaches. As they got up to go to the field, he walked by the boys and winked, not wanting to show any preferential treatment to them. Gerald looked at Lowell and they both smiled; there was that Knute Rockne thing again.

As Lowell put on his catcher's equipment, he looked around the stands to see if he could see his folks and Helen. There must have been several thousand people there but he suddenly spotted David waving at him from the tenth row just off the first base side. Next to David he saw his father and mother, Helen, and to his surprise, Helen's folks. As his eyes moved back towards his folks, he saw another person sitting between Helen and his mom. There was a fan sitting directly in front of the person and it took him awhile to see him clearly. *My God, there's Jew!*

Lowell had an outstanding game and earned most valuable player status by going two for three with a line drive double off the left field fence that drove in two runs giving State their first victory over Metro in three years. State won five to four and though he didn't start, Gerald got credit for the win in relief.

As Lowell left the dressing room, Helen ran up to him and gave him a big hug and kiss. Myron walked up to him with that smirk on his face, took his hand and said, "A little more left hand and that would have been a homer."

"Bull Sh-- I mean crap. I hit it good; it was just too much of a liner."

Jew gave him a punch on the shoulder and said, "Great game buddy!"

Lowell said, "By the way fella, what are you doing here or did you find out you didn't graduate anyway?"

"Nah, I wanted to come and after several hours of arguing with my dad he said okay, but I'm not sure that my mom will ever speak to me again."

Mrs. Andersen said, "Oh Myron your mom will too, she just didn't want you to miss your commencement."

Mr. Andersen invited everyone out for dinner to celebrate Lowell's MVP and the team's victory. Lowell asked if they could invite Gerald and his mother along as well and of course, his father said yes. After Gerald's father died in a logging accident down in southern Oregon, they moved to Drayville, his mother's hometown.

Post Graduation

After graduation and the all-star game, Myron and Lowell spent as much time together as possible. Their summer activities consisted of working at their father's businesses and going to movies and to the river with their girl friends. Dragging the gut was no longer possible because of gas rationing, which took effect in May of that year. They talked a lot about going into the army, but nothing serious. Lowell was going to honor his mother's wishes and start college anyway; he didn't know if he would even finish his first year. Myron said he definitely was going to join the air corps.

One day in late June, Myron called and said he had something he wanted to talk about and could he come by the station. Of course, Lowell said yes, and then spent the next forty minutes trying to figure out what it was. Did it have something to do with him and Betty? God he hoped Jew hadn't done something stupid like getting her in the family way. Maybe he just wanted to talk. Lowell went in the back office and told his dad about the call and asked if he could have a few minutes off. His dad said, okay but don't stay away all afternoon.

When Myron walked in he had that little smirk on his face and Lowell knew something important was up.

"What's up Jew?"

"I've done it, joined the air corps!"

Lowell stood perfectly still for a few minutes until he recovered his senses and then said, "When do you go?"

"The recruiting sergeant thought probably within a few weeks."

"Come on Jew, let's walk and talk about this!"

"Nothing to talk about Low; I've enlisted and now I'm going. You knew I had always planned to!"

"Yea, but I thought you would come and tell me before you did it."

"Yea, well I'm sorry but I didn't want you to try and talk me out of it."

Fall & Winter 1942-43

That day in June when Myron announced his enlistment was about as close to an argument as Low and Jew had ever had. As the recruiting sergeant said, Myron left for Sheppard Field in Texas in early July to start basic training. Shortly after Myron left for the air corps, Lowell received a phone call from Coach Palmer, the football coach at Emmons, asking him if he would consider going out for football this fall. He considered it and decided to try it. Emmons was in a small college league called the North Pacific Conference and like the other colleges, was having a difficult time getting enough boys to turn out. Most boys, who would have normally gone out for sports, had instead gone into military service.

Lowell received a letter nearly every week from Myron telling him how hot it was in Texas in the summer and how much weight he had lost. He couldn't or wouldn't say much about the training except that it made football practice look like a Sunday school outing. Lowell wondered how Jew knew anything about Sunday school.

As winter approached, the letters suddenly stopped. Lowell was worried that something had happened to him so he went by the Rothstein's house to see his parents. They were surprised that Myron hadn't written Lowell. He had washed out of flight school and had transferred to Maxwell Training center for navigator and bombardier training. Mr. Rothstein said that he was sure Myron would write to him soon.

True to the prediction, the next week Lowell received a letter from Jew.

Dear Low,

Sorry I haven't written for several weeks but I have been very busy and somewhat embarrassed. I washed out of flight school and I've transferred to Navigator and Bombardier school at Maxwell Field in Montgomery Alabama. It's OK, but it isn't flying. I guess if I navigate the guys to the target, I'm still bombing the crap out of those Nazi bastards.

Myron went on to tell a little about Maxwell Training Center and then asked about Lowell and Helen. He was especially interested in news about Betty.

Have you seen Betty? I receive at least three letters a week from her . I can hardly wait to see her. I'll probably get my first leave in about six weeks as soon as the commissioning is over.

Lowell wasn't sure what *the commissioning* was, but it was good to know that he would soon see his friend.

The fall went by fast with working, football and classes, which he found to be much harder than high school. He also found football a lot harder. Emmons had a fairly good season finishing with four wins and two losses. Two of the colleges in their league had to cancel their season due to lack of players. Emmons was discussing doing the same as they only had twenty players out. Lowell again starred as halfback and scored seven touch downs. He wrote once to Jew and asked him how many he had scored. Although he knew Myron wasn't playing he wanted to keep the rivalry alive.

Lowell accompanied Helen to several high school functions as well. She invited him to the Christmas dance on December 22, and asked if he cared if Betty went with them. She didn't want to miss it but was not going to accept any other invitation while Myron was away.

During the first dance Helen said, "Low, please ask Betty to dance."

"Well I was going to if you will ever let go of my hand."

"Oh you, why don't you do it right after this dance."

"Okay."

The dance finished and Lowell and Helen started back toward the table where they had left Betty. Suddenly Helen caught her breath and put her hand to her mouth.

"What's the matter?"

"Look!"

Lowell turned and looked in the direction Helen was pointing and saw Betty in the arms of a soldier. It took a minute, but Lowell recognized his friend and without thinking he began running toward the pair shouting, "JEW!"

Colliding in a bear hug with Myron and Betty, he realized he'd attracted the attention of everyone in the high school gym as many of the kids migrated toward the couple. Embracing Betty with one arm, he reached out with the other to shake hands with as many as possible. Betty's happiness and pleasure was uncontrollable as she cried, hugged and kissed Myron, as well as hitting him on the arm and scolded him for not letting her know.

"Well, I wasn't sure I could get home; I only had a nine day pass and transportation was a mess."

Lowell asked, "How did you finally get home."

"I ran into a captain who was flying a C-47 up to Portland with a load of parts and I asked him if I could hop."

"What's hop mean," asked Helen.

"That's kind of like hitch-hiking. Anyway, we had to land twice for fuel, but made it this afternoon and I called Dad and he came right up. I had called from Maxwell and told them I thought I had a hop and that if so, they would hear from me in Portland."

Betty hit him on the chest again and said, "I will never forgive you for not letting me know!"

"Well, I've got to report back on the twenty-seventh but I think the hop might leave before Christmas."

"You mean you won't be able to be home for Christmas?"

"Well I made the dance didn't I? You can't have everything. Ya know, there's a war on and you know I don't celebrate Christmas!"

Betty hit him again on the chest and then reached up and kissed him on the lips.

The rest of the evening was pure pleasure for most everyone in the gym especially Betty, Lowell, Helen and it goes without saying, Myron.

After the dance, Lowell said, "Well Soldier, shall we take these ladies out for a little after-dance dessert?"

"I believe that would be okay, Mr. Civilian."

Lowell had been saving his gas rationing stamps and so had a near full tank of gas, allowing them to drive around some that night talking. They went to Smith's and several other teenage hangouts, but Lowell could tell Myron was somewhat ill at ease with everyone coming up to the table and all the boys asking how it was in the army.

The next day, Lowell told his folks that he was not going to church but going hunting with Myron. His mother said, "Now Lowell, let him spend some time with his folks."

"I will Mom, but he wants to get in a little shooting in the morning."

Still having gas left over, Lowell picked up Myron in his car and he came out of the house smoking a cigarette.

"Oh, I see you've picked up some bad habits in the air corps."

"Yea I have; I even have learned to like a beer now and then."

They didn't talk much more the rest of the way but Lowell had a million questions to ask.

When they got their decoys spread and sat down in the blind, Lowell asked, "Well, how is it?"

"I'll tell you, I was so disappointed after I washed out of flight school that I did not know what to do. I actually went in the latrine and cried."

"What's the latrine?"

"The bathroom."

"Oh, go on."

"Well when I first got there we were treated like crap by the training cadre. They screamed and called us every dirty name in the book, made us do pushups until our hands bled, and then finally when the actual training began, we found them to be quite helpful though still pretty rough on us."

Myron went on to describe pre-flight and then primary where he failed the test that washed him out as a pilot.

"They said I didn't have enough peripheral vision. Can you imagine me, a receiving end, not having enough peripheral vision? Well that was okay because I found out I was going to either navigator's school or bomb training and not to the ground pounders. The training at Maxwell is tough, but with my interest in math, it isn't very hard. I guess Mr. Prichard did a good job with me in math. Anyway, I'm about halfway through training and they offer us a nine-day pass for Christmas."

"Yea and you don't even celebrate Christmas," replied Lowell.

"Well, don't tell 'em!"

"What's bomb training?"

"Bombardier training."

"Oh, well navigator's training sounds more interesting anyway, doesn't it?"

"Yea, I like it fine; we'll finish in about four months and get our commission and wings and then off to the war."

They only had a couple of flights of ducks come in that day and got two. The boys each took one and towards afternoon, Myron said, "Well, Mom said not to stay out all day so I guess we maybe should take off."

"Yea, my mom chastised me about taking you away from home."

They picked up the decoys and loaded them into the '33 and headed for home to be with their families.

The next day Lowell was working at the station when the phone rang and George yelled that it was for him. "Okay, be right there."

He wiped his hand and picked up the phone, "Hello."

"Low, this is Jew."

"Oh hi Jew, what's up?"

"Well I checked with that captain and he said we probably would leave Thursday."

"Thursday, but that's Christmas Eve."

"Yea I know, but when the army calls, we must answer."

"Well let's try to get together some night before you leave maybe take the girls to a movie or something."

"That sounds swell. Now I have to call Betty and give her the *good* news, Mom's still in the bedroom crying."

Thursday morning as Lowell was finishing a grease job on Mr. Smith's car, he heard a familiar "Hi!"

Lowell jumped and banged his head on the hood of the car. When he turned around, there stood Myron in civilian clothes.

"What the devil are you doing Jew, have you run away from the army?"

"No the captain called, he ran into a sergeant he knew at the Portland Airbase and he said the sergeant found "all kinds of stuff wrong" with the plane and it will take three days to fix it. I don't know if the pilot being from Longview had any effect on the condition of the plane or not," Myron said with a smirk in his face.

"Gee, what a shame! Now you'll have to spend Christmas here watching all us Gentiles celebrate. Are all you Army Air Corps guys dishonest?"

"Stay out of my way Swede. I'll show you some celebrating!"

"I've told you, I'm Norwegian!"

"Same difference!"

Christmas was one that Lowell would never forget. Though they were Jewish, the Rothsteins did celebrate the holiday with an open house the day after Christmas and invited the Andersens, the Speers, the Miles, and Gerald Olson and his mother. It was marvelous and everybody had a great time.

Later in the afternoon, Myron left the room and motioned for Lowell to follow him.

"I want to show you something."

He opened a sideboard drawer and took out a ring box, opened it and said, "I'm going to propose to Betty tonight and give her this ring."

"You mean, here, now?"

"Yes, don't you think that will be just swell?"

"Well, I think that will be a big shock to everyone."

"Everyone but Mr. and Mrs. Miles, I've already talked to them and they have given their approval."

"There is one other person who has to give her approval!"

"Yea, well we've talked in general terms and I think she will."

"Buddy, you never cease to amaze me. Congratulations Jew, of course I'm going to be your best man."

"Well maybe, I really was thinking more about Vernon Dickerson."

"You bastard!"

"Boys, what are you doing in there?" Mrs. Rothstein yelled.

"Oh nothing Mom, we'll be right in, and yes Low, you will be my best man."

As they came back in to the parlor, Myron could hardly keep a straight face nor could Lowell. He looked over at Mr. and Mrs. Miles, smiled and Mr. Miles, who looked accepting but not entirely approving, nodded. Mrs. Miles had her handkerchief out and ready but was all smiles.

After clearing his throat several times, Myron asked Betty to come to him, which she did with a frown and some hesitancy.

"Folks I have a question to ask someone in this room."

Lowell spoke up and said, "Sure, we can go hunting tomorrow."

"Oh shut up, Low."

"Anyway, as you know I'm an only child. When my folks had me, how could they improve?"

Everyone laughed and he continued, "So, this is a very important day in my life and my folk's life. I would like to start the ball rolling to bring Mom that daughter she has always wanted."

The room had fallen totally silent by this time and Mr. and Mrs. Rothstein looked as though they were about to pass out.

Myron continued, "I say start the ball rolling because it is just the first step in my long range plan to, as I said, bring my mom a daughter."

Betty caught on to what he planned to do and began to cry.

"Betty Miles, will you be my wife?"

Mrs. Rothstein's mouth fell open and Mr. Rothstein looked like he had been struck by lightning. Helen screamed, Mr. and Mrs. Andersen looked stricken, Gerald Olson and his mother stared in disbelief and David and Diane came running in from the back room where they had been listening to the radio yelling, "What happened?"

There was no doubt what Betty's answer was, she jumped into Myron's arms and started kissing him furiously. Everyone else in the room gathered around the couple offering their congratulations. Mrs. Rothstein and Mrs. Miles hugged each other and the fathers shook hands.

Gerald came up to Myron smiling and said to Betty, "Do you know how much better you could have done with me?"

Betty reached over and gave him a peck on the cheek and Myron shook his hand.

Mr. Rothstein said, "Well folks, I think this calls for something a little stronger than coffee and tea, I just happen to have a few bottles of champagne I was going to use at New Years, but how can we have a better reason to celebrate than this?"

David and Diane, looked to their mother and said in unison, "Can we have some too Mom?"

"No you can't."

But their father said, "Well maybe just a sip," which brought a scowl from his wife.

Winter & Spring 1942-43

The winter of 1942-43 went along as planned. The news from the war was not good; the Philippines fell to the Japanese, the Germans seemingly were running wild across Africa and rationing was hurting the Andersen's business. Even the news from Myron was not good. He had finished first in his navigation and bombardier school and as a result, his instructors encouraged him to stay on and teach. Lowell knew that this would be a problem. Myron wanted to go bomb those damn Nazis.

As spring came, life for Lowell Andersen improved. Baseball season at Emmons was a highlight for him. The team did very well, winning the conference; Lowell became a member of the all-star team and he and Helen had begun to talk about something beyond going steady. With every date, Lowell fell further in love and convinced that he wanted to spend the rest of his life with her. After much prompting by both Lowell and her parents, Helen decided she would go to college. The only logical choice was Emmons, with Lowell.

However, Lowell had other plans. One Sunday afternoon in late April he was in his room studying for Monday's exam in western civics. He could not concentrate because of the decision he had made last week. He had gone down to the local draft board and asked Mr. Tupper, the director, if he could find out how he stood in the draft.

Mr. Tupper looked at him for several minutes and then said, "Lowell, I'm not really supposed to do this, but I think I can trust you not to tell anyone. You will probably get your notice some time in either June or July. It depends on how many men are needed at that particular time"

"Thank you so much Mr. Tupper, I thought that would be the case."

Mr. Tupper went on, "You probably would have been called by now, but the board felt they wanted to give you a chance to finish the term."

"Thanks."

As he closed his textbook, he decided it was time to tell his parents. He went down stairs and found them in the living room. His father was smoking his pipe and reading a magazine, his mother was working on the constant knitting project. He came in to the room and sat on the edge of the sofa.

His mother said, "Finished studying son?"

"No, there is something I want to talk to you about."

Mr. Andersen put the magazine down, looked over at his wife and said, "Son, I've been dreading this for a long time, but I guess I know how you feel and that it had to come sometime."

His mother put down her knitting and came over to sit beside him on the sofa.

She put her arm around him and said, "Lowell, you and the twins are the most important things in our lives. You were first and so I guess that gives you a special place. We know that you will probably not be able to start the second year at Emmons."

She looked over at her husband and went on, "If there was any way to keep you out of this war we would do it, but there doesn't seem to be."

His father stepped in with, "Your mother and I have spent many nights talking about this and what I think she is trying to say is go. Go with our blessing and prayers!"

Lowell looked at his mother and saw tears well up in her eyes. He gave her a big hug and then reached over and shook his dad's hand.

"Thanks, folks, thanks for making it easier for me. I've been dreading talking with you about this for some time, but I have made up my mind."

"When are you going to enlist son?"

"I don't know. I've got to find out if I qualify first. Also, I want to talk to Helen."

His mom asked, "What about her? I mean, well you kids have been going steady for a long time now and in these times, well are you going to propose before you leave?"

Mr. Andersen interrupted, "Mary, that's none of our business!"

Lowell laughed and said, "Well we've talked about it and I think I might just give her a ring after graduation."

"That's fine son. We couldn't asked for a better daughter-in-law," his mother said as she rose from the couch and put her arms around him.

Lowell took this as her blessing as well. Soon after, Lowell received word that he could take the Army Air Corps qualifying test the next week at the Army Induction Center in Portland.

So began his entry into the World War II.

Enlistment

In April, two months before completing his freshman year in college, Lowell enlisted in the United States Army Air Corps. Though she hated the idea of losing him, Helen understood and supported him going.

When he told her about his acceptance, Helen said, "Oh Lowell, I don't want you to go!"

"I know honey, I don't want to go, but I have to. The draft board is breathing down my neck and Mr. Tupper says that I will probably get my notice in June or July."

"Oh Lowell, let's spend as much time together in the next few weeks as we can." Helen said as she threw her arms about his neck and kissed him longingly.

Of course, Lowell accompanied Helen to her junior-senior Prom in May, but really didn't enjoy it as much as he should. He passed the test for pilot training, which delayed his call to duty until after finishing his freshman year in college.

The talk of marriage dominated almost every conversation between the couple. He had never officially proposed to her, though it was an accepted understanding that they would some day get married. Lowell insisted that they wait to see what the next few years would bring and like so many men going off to war, he did not want to leave a widow at home. On May 3, he received a letter directing him to report to the Induction Center in Portland for induction into the army no later than June 5, 1943. That gave him only a few weeks to get his affairs in order, but the worst news was that he would miss Helen's graduation. The major affair to which he had to attend was purchasing an engagement ring for Helen.

The engagement was far less spectacular than Myron's to Betty. They were going to a movie one night and as Helen came down the stairs, she noticed a small box sitting on the coffee table in the living room and her folks sitting around with the cats-that-ate-the-canary smirks on their faces. Lowell was sitting on the davenport just looking at the ceiling.

When she came up to the table, she said, "What's this?"

Lowell said, "Oh just something I picked up today."

As she opened it, her eyes lit up with that beautiful glow Lowell loved so much and she said, "Oh Lowell, it's lovely. Yes! Yes, I will."

She slipped it on her finger and ran over to show it to her mom and dad who gave her kisses on the cheek and wished them both much happiness.

That night neither Lowell nor Helen could have told anyone what the movie was about. They hugged, kissed and just generally snuggled together in the back of the theater. After the show, they went to Smith's for an ice cream sundae and Helen had an opportunity to show off her ring to several of her friends. All the girls congratulated her, but the boys all made smart remarks to Lowell, who just grinned back at them.

The weeks until Lowell left for induction were a whirlwind of activity. He had put his '33 Ford up on blocks in the back of his father's garage, turned his room over to David who was elated because by now he had become tired of sharing a room with Diane. Lowell then said goodbye to all his friends still in town and of course spent as much time with Helen and his folks as possible.

"Do you think we will have to wait to get married until you get out of the army?"

"Well, I don't know, I sure don't want to, but you know how I feel about that."

They had discussed those young people who got married just before the man left for the army and the chances of his being killed and leaving her a widow. Lowell always said he would never want to do that.

"Oh Lowell, I know how you feel, but let's say we don't get married and something should happen to you, I would feel just as bad as if we were married and I would have never gotten to be your wife at all."

Lowell thought for a minute because he had never considered that and said, "Honey, let's just see what happens in my training and where I end up. I'm not saying we definitely should not get married, but we shouldn't rush into it before I leave."

"Oh Lowell, I love you so much if anything should happen to you, I don't know if I could go on."

"Don't be silly Helen; of course you would go on."

The conversation ended as it usually did with that topic of discussion, in a passionate embrace and a pledge of loving each other forever.

"Oh darling, I wish you could get an assignment like Myron and stay in the States!"

"Honey, I don't want to be an instructor, I want to fly airplanes and there is only one place to do that. Overseas."

Myron was now on the staff at navigators school in Alabama. He didn't like it, a fact he made clear in the letters he sent Lowell, but he accepted his assignment.

INDUCTION & TRAINING

On the morning of June 5, Lowell awoke with the heavy feeling of knowing that this was going to be the last morning he would awake in this room for a long time. He had packed his bag the night before and said a tearful good by to Helen. He'd asked her not to come to the bus station. When he went down to breakfast, his father was home from the garage and his brother and sister and mother were waiting for him in the kitchen. He did not feel much like breakfast so he just had a glass of milk and a piece of toast.

His father said, "All packed and ready?"

"Yea Dad, I am."

"Well, I guess it's time to leave then."

As he hugged his mother she sobbed uncontrollably, which was the hardest thing for him.

Diane was also in tears, but David said, "Don't forget Lowell, you promised to send me some army insignias!"

He and his father then left the house and drove to the bus station. The bus to Portland had not come yet so they sat in the car not saying much until it pulled into the station.

Lowell said, "Well Dad, I guess this is it."

Reaching out for his dad's hand, he looked him in the face and saw tears running down his cheeks. Instead of shaking hands, he gave him a hug and his father kissed him on the forehead. When he got out of the car, he realized this was the first time he had ever seen his father cry.

Induction consisted of a cursory physical, raising the right hand and swearing to protect and defend the United States of America, followed by directions to wait for a bus that would take them to the train and their first duty station at Santa Ana Army Air Base, known as SAAAB. They ate a fine meal of meatloaf, potatoes and some kind of vegetable that Lowell could not identify. The train ride to SAAAB was fairly uneventful. Most of the boys slept, read, smoked cigarettes or just talked. Lowell and another inductee decided to walk through the train. When they came to the end of their car, a sergeant asked where they were going and they told him for a walk. He said to get back to their seats and sit down. This was Lowell's first experience with army discipline.

Lowell's arrival at the SAAAB was quite a shock for him. A bus, driven by an army corporal, met them at the train station. After a short ride, they arrived at the base and received orders to get off the bus and fall in. He had a vague idea what "fall in" meant, as did most of the other cadets. A sergeant marched them to the barracks where they were told to leave their personal belongs and fall out to go draw bedding and what they would need for the night. The sergeant giving instructions was quite gruff when he addressed them. Going through the line at the supply room was another experience in humility as the men working behind the counters kept yelling at them to "Move on!" After drawing bedding, they returned to the barracks where they received rudimentary instruction on how to make a bunk, army-style.

The next few days were very busy indeed. They drew their uniforms, learned how to wear them and how to sew on the patches signifying them as air cadets. Lowell remembered David's request to send him some insignias, but had no idea how to get any extras. They were tested, examined, tested again, examined again, and tested once more, given a series of shots and then tested again. They learned that the tests would rate them in three areas on a scale of zero to nine and those scores would determine their suitability to become a pilot, navigator or bombardier. The whole time they were being marched, yelled at by the sergeants who were their training cadre, and told exactly when and where to do everything.

Lowell tried to write every night to Helen, but several times he was just too tired. Mail call was always a highlight for all the cadets. After the first week, he began to get letters from both Helen and his mother. He hated to admit it, but he was very homesick.

For the short time they were together in classification, he made some very good friends. Charles (Charlie) Smith was on one side of him in the barracks and Bill Porter on the other. When they could stay awake for awhile, they told each other about their hometowns, their girl friends, and what their parents did. Charlie was from Utah and his father owned a clothing store. He was a slight built young man with dark hair and gave an air of seriousness and intelligence. Bill was from Montana and his father owned a cattle ranch and was just the opposite from Charlie. He always seemed to find fun in everything and loved to tell stories of exploits he and his friends had in high school. Of course, they all wanted to be pilots.

One night after lights out, Bill said, "Ya know, I remember one night when I was a junior in high school, a bunch of us boys went out and got some beer. There was a tavern in the next town that was famous for selling beer to high school boys. Well, we guzzled it down and got so stinko that we slept in the car all night. It was a very cold night and I guess that if we hadn't had so much antifreeze in our blood, we probably would have frozen to death. You every get drunk Low?"

When they first introduced themselves, Lowell said that his nickname was Low.

He answered, "Well, I had a couple of beers with my friend Jew one night, but I can't say I was ever drunk. How about you Charlie?"

"Nah, I haven't; my folks are very strict about that sort of thing. My family is LDS."

It took Lowell a minute to figure out what that meant, but then remembered it was for the Church of Latter Day Saints, Mormon and he said, "Yea my folks were pretty strict too; my uncle is a preacher."

Bill added, "Boy, you two have really led sheltered lives. What do you do for fun in Oregon and Utah?"

Lowell answered, "Oh, we go the library a lot, walk down our paved streets; of course you Montana people don't know what paved streets are!"

Charlie said, "Yea, and we read our Bibles every day and are not allowed to date until we reach the age of twenty one."

"Oh BS you two, I'm going to sleep!"

Finally the test results and next assignments appeared on the bulletin board. Lowell walked over to the orderly room with much excitement and some trepidation. As he looked at the list, his name was third. He scanned across to his assignment. To his great relief his assignment was to SAAAB for pre-flight training.

Lowell exclaimed loudly, "Hurrah!" and turned around to leave.

Charlie was standing there quietly starring at the list. "What did you get Charlie?"

"I don't know – I'm afraid to look."

"You want me to look for you?"

Charlie shook his head, "No, I'll do it."

Lowell waited for him and when he turned around he looked very sad and his face was quite red. "What did you get?"

"Well, I'm going to pre-flight with you!" he said as he broke in to a grin.

"Did you see Bill's name?" Lowell asked.

"No, although I bet he made it to pre-flight as well."

When they saw Bill later in the barracks, he was lying on his bunk with his hands behind his head. Lowell asked, "Well, where are you going?"

"I guess I'm going to be a radio operator. I'm going to radio school."

There was not much Charlie or Lowell could say except to express their sympathy to him.

Bill responded with, "I asked the captain what this meant and he said I must not have scored high enough on the test, but that I could re-apply for pre-flight later. So I guess that's what I'll do."

"Yea, why don't you do that," said Charlie.

Pre-Flight – Santa Ana, California

The cadets who made it to pre-flight transferred to a different part of the base and received assignment to small rooms that housed ten men. Lowell was pleased to find Charlie assigned to the same room along with another cadet, Marvin Chapell, whom he had gotten to know during classification. Marvin, or Marv, was from Seattle, Washington and had been a sophomore at the University of Washington. He was a good looking blond boy who looked like he just stepped off a poster advertising the advantages of becoming a college boy. Both Lowell and Charlie had known him slightly during classification and decided he would be a good replacement for Bill.

That evening, a lot of talk about the future went on in the room. The subjects ranged from hopes to get pilot training in fighters to home, to girl friends and several other things young men talk about when they are together.

The mornings started very early, as Lowell had discovered was typical in the army. Reveille at 0530, breakfast at 0600, return to the barracks, make up the bunks, clean up the barracks. Then fall out for the day's activities, which usually meant more tests, physical exercise and running. The training cadre was men who had just recently washed out of pre-flight and were waiting for new assignments. They seemed to take great pleasure in yelling at the cadets and making them feel they had very little worth.

On Friday nights, cadets G.I.'d the barracks. "G.I.'ing" the barracks meant getting down on your hands and knees and scrubbing the floor with stiff bristled brushes to prepare for the Saturday morning inspection.

As they crawled around with their brushes, Lowell said, "I used to think my dad was particular about the floor of our garage, but this is ridiculous!"

"Yea, I thought the modern army was supposed to be mechanized," Marv replied.

Charlie said, "I bet your dad didn't wear white gloves when he inspected the floor though."

"I don't think my dad ever wore any gloves, white, brown or any other color."

This was a particularly important G.I. because if they passed, they got freedom of the post, which meant they could go to the service club or PX (Post Exchange) without being marched. The other important G.I. they looked forward to was when they would get a weekend pass to go in to town.

Pre-flight was where the men got their first taste of what being an air cadet was all about. Training covered alot of mathematics, physics, rudimentary map reading, aircraft recognition and several other topics relating to military flight training. The most important phase of training was the tests, both physical and mental. The cadets all knew if they didn't do well on such tests as eye-hand coordination and eye-exams including peripheral vision, they would have no chance of becoming pilots. The cadets found out that there was another hazard to them as underclassmen: upperclassmen. These cadets had made it through half of the ten week pre-flight and had the authority to treat the underclassmen with as little respect as possible. Nowhere was this more evident than in the mess hall during meals, where underclassmen were required to eat square meals. Square meals had nothing to do with nutrition, but rather how food moved from plate to mouth. There were several upperclassmen at each table to oversee this procedure. Underclassmen were required to sit at rigid attention, looking straightforward, and bring the spoon or fork straight up from the plate to the mouth. The men never really knew what they were eating.

One evening Lowell, Marv and Charlie walked down to the Day Room to have a little relaxation. On the way, they met several upperclassmen. As required, they hit a brace position of rigid attention while the upperclassman walked around them inspecting their uniforms.

One upperclassman came right up to Marv and shouted in his face, "Cadet, do you know you have a smudge on your left shoe?" As Marv started to look down, the upperclassman yelled even louder, "You are at attention cadet, why are you looking down?"

Of course, Marv gave the standard answer, "No excuse sir!"

The upperclassmen kept them in the brace position for several more minutes and then said, "Dismissed!" Then they walked on, laughing among themselves.

Marv said, "Bastards!"

"Well, let's remember how we felt when we get to be upperclassman," replied Charlie.

Marv said, "Yea, you always look on the bright side of things don't you Charlie?"

Charlie just poked him in the shoulder and then went on to the Day Room. As they entered, there were several upperclassmen and some underclassmen from their class. They were trying to play cards, but the upperclassmen had insisted they sit in the brace position and it didn't look like very much fun for the classmates.

When they saw the situation, Lowell said, "Let's get out of here, okay?"

Marv and Charlie agreed so they left and returned to the barracks.

When they entered their room, Lowell got out his writing kit and thought of what he could tell Helen tonight. She was probably tired of hearing about the training. Nevertheless, he wrote:

My Darling Helen,

Today was a very rough day. The cadre had us out running all afternoon in 95-degree heat. We had to run up Kill Hill twice because they said we didn't run fast enough; I could hardly walk after the first trip.

Then they gave us a ten- minute break and started calisthenics. It was really rough and we all thought the cadre were just being mean, but when you realize they are doing the same thing, you have to admire them somewhat.

Are you getting excited about college? You had better not meet any good-looking boys! Do you spend any time with Betty? I haven't heard from Jew for a couple of weeks now; I hope he is OK.

Lowell wrote two more pages with small talk and ended with the same words as he always did.

As always to you I give my love and life,
Lowell

As he sealed the envelope, he thought he should write to his folks as well, but he was so tired he decided he would write tomorrow.

The classes in pre-flight were not difficult for Lowell. He had always been a good student and he read very well. He had good oral learning skills and almost never forgot anything he heard. The instructors were pretty good; they made most of the classes interesting and fun. Some were able to put a lot of humor into them. One class on military courtesy was particularly funny. There were demonstrations on how a soldier should report to his commanding officer.

One instructor acted as the CO and another reported to him.

The private said, as he held his salute, "Private Jones reporting to the commanding officer as ordered sir."

The CO returning the salute, said, "At ease Private Jones. It has come to my attention that you have been eating out of the garbage cans, is this correct?"

"Yes sir!"

"Now see here, Jones, that must stop immediately, is that understood!"

"Yes sir!"

"So from now on you will eat in the mess hall like all the other cadets. You are no better than anyone else. Is that understood?"

"Yes sir!"

"That is all. You are dismissed!"

And the instructor playing Private Jones did a correct about face and left the office to much laughter from the cadets. As the cadets from class 43-L moved through pre-flight their lives became easier. The threat of meeting an upperclassman disappeared when they became upperclassmen. Lowell, Charlie, and Marv remembered their discussion about how to treat lowerclassmen. They did not harass them over petty little things, but when something major happened, they did perform their duties.

A situation occurred one Sunday as the three were walking to church. An underclassman came across the street with his shirttail hanging out of his pants.

Lowell said, "Look at that cadet!"

Marv said. "Yea, we can't let that go. Come on!"

They confronted the underclassman and he just looked at them when they called him and said, "What's the matter?"

Charlie said, "Cadet, stand at attention when you speak to an upperclassman!"

The underclassman said, "I didn't think we had to on Sunday."

"That's where you are wrong cadet, now do as you are told!" Charlie replied.

The underclassman hit the attention position and Marv said, "What is your name cadet?"

"Cadet Setnicker!"

"That's Cadet Setnicker, sir!"

"Cadet Setnicker, sir!" he replied.

Lowell jumped in and said, "Cadet, do you know why we stopped you?"

"No Sir!"

"Well," Lowell said, "Are you aware of the dress code on this post?"

"Yes sir!"

"Do you think you meet that code the way you're dressed?" asked Lowell.

The underclassman answered, "I don't know what you mean sir?"

"Does a shirttail hanging out of your pants meet the dress code?" Lowell asked.

The cadet looked down and then up in great horror and replied, "Oh my God, oh my God, I must have forgotten to tuck in my shirt. I'm on my way to church and – –."

Marv jumped in saying, "Cadet Setnicker, the answer to that is 'no excuse sir'!"

"No excuse sir!"

Lowell said, "Setnicker, tuck in your shirt and be on your way. Dismissed!"

The three went on their way smiling to each other.

"Well," said Charlie. "That was funny. He didn't even realize it wasn't tucked in."

Marv said, "Or he was a very good actor and put one over on us."

They all three laughed and went on their way.

The next day Lowell received a letter from Myron.

Dear Low,

Well how is everything with you? Watch that peripheral test; it's a killer. Things go along here just the same. We just started the fourth class. There has been some change; we no longer get cadets for both navigator's school and bombardier's school. They are now dividing them into the individual training.

Every month I go in to see the major and apply for a transfer and he accepts it but says he will not approve it, which generally means it will not be granted. (Army regulations permit a soldier to request a transfer once a month and the commanding officer has the option of approving it or not, but is required to forward it up the chain of command.) The major said I should stop this and accept the fact that I am where the air corps wants me to be, but I just can't. I've got to get into combat and relieve this frustration. The only thing that keeps me from being very mad at the major is that there is a rumor around that he also submits a request every month and is very frustrated as well. I do enjoy instructing the cadets and think when I get out I might look into becoming a teacher. Of course, my folks and Betty are perfectly happy having me stuck here in Texas.

What do you hear from Helen? I get a letter every other day from Betty and she says everything is going OK. We have talked about our wedding day and look forward possibly tying the knot if I can get home at Christmas. If we do, is there any chance you can make it?

Myron went on to describe a funny incident that occurred in one of his classes and then signed off.

Your Friend,
Jew

Lowell thought about getting home and had no idea if they would get any Christmas leaves. Getting home would not be a big problem since it was only a couple of days drive up to Drayville from Santa Ana but he had no idea where he would be by Christmas because pre-flight would be over in a few more weeks and hopefully he would go on to primary. He decided to ask the lieutenant the next time it was convenient. It should work out just fine because if he made it on schedule primary flight training should just about be finished by Christmas. Pre-flight ended on September 19 and as that date neared, the stress and excitement of the cadets grew. The barracks talk was of nothing else but whether they would become navigators, bombardiers or pilots. Lowell knew he had done well and was fairly sure of an assignment to a primary pilot training base. He hoped it would be in California so that getting home for Christmas would be a possibility.

Laying on their bunks studying for a test the next day, Marvin dropped his book on his chest and said, "Wouldn't it be great if we would all three make it through training and be assigned to the same base overseas and be flying the P-47?"

Lowell answered, "Yea, but only if we would be flying the P-38."

"Nah, I like the P-47 better," answered Charlie. "It's a very tough airplane."

"Oh well, dream on. We will probably all end up flying the C-47."

"Aw shut up Marv; don't even think that!" said Lowell.

One day in mid September, the training officer announced to the cadets that they would see their assignments posted the next day on the orderly room bulletin board.

Marv said, "What will we do if we don't make primary?"

"What do you mean? We're all three in the top ten percent of the class."

"Yea, but one of the cadre told Johnson that it depends more on what the air corps needs than on how we did in pre-flight," said Marv.

Lowell chimed in with, "Come on Marv, I told you not to even think that."

That night after training, the three friends walked down to the PX to get a beer. As they entered, the place was not it's usually loud boisterous self. Most of the cadets were thinking the same thing as Lowell, Marv, and Charlie. Marv and Lowell bought a beer and Charlie his usual soft drink. They looked around and found a table with three empty chairs. There were two cadets at the table and the boys asked if they could join them and received an affirmative. The conversation went right to their assignments.

Minor, one of the other cadets said, "Well guys, what do you think our chances of getting primary are?"

Marv responded, "Oh I don't know, I guess about fifty-fifty."

Lowell said, "God I hope they're better than that!"

Johnson said, "If I get any assignment that leads anywhere other than flying fighters, I think I will just ask to be dropped from the cadet program."

"And become a ground-pounder? Are you crazy?" Charlie said.

"Yea, becoming a bombardier or navigator is still flying, isn't it?" Minor said.

Lowell said, "My best friend from home is a navigator instructor down in Alabama. He says it's not bad, but he really wants to get a combat assignment."

"God, I never thought of that. What if they keep us here as instructors?" said Marvin.

"Oh they won't, we aren't even commissioned yet," replied Charlie.

The conversation went on through another round of drinks and then the three decided to return to their barracks. They all three flopped down on their bunks and then Lowell reached in his footlocker and took out his writing kit.

Marv said, "There he goes again. Another letter to Helen."

Lowell just grinned and began to write.

Dearest Helen,

Well, by the time you get this, I will be on my way to becoming a pilot, navigator or bombardier. They're going to post the assignments tomorrow after training. Everyone is pretty subdued tonight. Marv, Charlie and I went down to the PX and had a couple of beers and that was what everyone was talking about.

How is everything with you? I got a long letter from Jew yesterday describing how he is so frustrated and upset about being stuck in a training command. I suppose it could be worse. He says he likes the teaching and is thinking about maybe becoming a teacher after the war. Can you imagine that, him becoming a Mr. Phillips?

(Mr. Phillips was considered to be the worst teacher in Drayville High School.)

I don't think there is much chance of that happening, however, I mean him becoming a bad teacher.

He also dropped a slight bombshell on me when he said he and Betty might be getting married at Christmas and asked if I thought I could get home to be his best man. Has Betty said anything to you? If she hasn't mentioned it, please don't say anything to her.

Lowell went on for another page and then closed the same as always.

As always to you I give my love and life,
Lowell

*****

Not one cadet could have told you much of what that day's training was all about. Everyone was thinking about the assignments. As they were marched back to the area, the cadre tried to get a good marching song going, but even their favorite one, which was quite spicy, didn't glean much enthusiasm.

Upon dismissal from formation, some of the cadets ran to the orderly room bulletin board. There was mixed reaction at the results. Some yelped in a gleeful manner, some swore, several were seen with tears in their eyes and of course some did not give their feelings away. As Lowell approached, Marvin was looking over several of the cadet's heads. When he turned around Lowell saw a large smile on his face indicating much pleasure.

He slapped him on the shoulder and said, "Congratulation Marv!"

"Thanks, have you looked yet?"

"No, where are you going?" asked Lowell,

Marv responded, "Santa Maria, just up the coast."

As Lowell walked closer to the bulletin board, his anxiety increased. He kept his head down until he was sure he could see the list well enough to read it all. He looked up and there it was:

CADET ANDERSEN, LOWELL, ASSIGNED PRIMARY FLIGHT TRAINING, SANTA MARIA ARMY AIR CORPS BASE SANTA MARIA, CALIFORNIA.

A feeling of great elation swept over him as he looked around into the very smiling face of Charlie. He jerked his head around and scanned to the lower part of the list and there it was:

CADET SMITH, CHARLES, ASSIGNED PRIMARY FLIGHT TRAINING SANTA MARIA ARMY AIR CORPS BASE SANTA MARIA, CALIFORNIA.

Lowell grabbed him in a big bear hug and said, "Marv got the same assignment."

Someone slapped him on the back and Lowell turned around to see Bill Minor with a big smile spread across his face and he asked, "What did you get?"

Minor, replied, "Primary at Santa Maria, just like you guys."

"Congratulations! We're going to Santa Maria! What did Johnson get?"

"I haven't talked to him, but I looked on the list and he got bombardiers school some where in New Mexico."

Charlie said, "Yea, we had better be a little careful celebrating in front of those guys who didn't get primary."

They all agreed as they turned towards their barracks.

Primary Flight Training, Santa Maria California

It was a short 200-mile-trip from Santa Ana to Santa Maria so the transportation was a bus. Upon arriving at Santa Maria, they went through some of the same procedures. The training cadre yelled at them to get off the bus, line up, and march to the supply room to draw bedding. By this time, the cadets knew how to fall in, turn left face, march, column left and so on. The experience at the supply room was much the same as well.

"Move along! Move along!" shouted the supply orderlies.

There was one big difference from their first experience and that was they also had a forty-pound duffel bag to contend with. Lowell did not have a great deal of trouble because he was fairly strong, but some of the smaller men could barely carry their duffel bags and their bedding. The barracks at this base were slightly different. They were divided into small four man rooms so it did not seem to be as crowded as at Santa Ana. The men marched to their barracks and received their room assignments. Lowell was pleased to find he and Marvin were assigned to the same room but Charlie was across the hall. The other cadets sharing the room with Marv and Lowell were Bill Minor and Oscar Chadwick whom they had known in pre-flight. Ordered to go to their rooms, select a bunk and make it up, they prepared for a bunk inspection in fifteen minutes. Most of the cadets had been in the army long enough to know that fifteen minutes was usually closer to twenty or thirty minutes, but just in case, the men hurried in and followed instructions.

Lowell was somewhat sorry that he didn't get to room with Charlie, but Marv, Bill and Oscar were okay guys. Besides, Charlie was just across the hall. The cadre came through the barracks, gave each bunk a cursory inspection and told the cadets to fall out. Next, they marched past the other barracks to a classroom building where they fell out and entered.

They sat for several minutes before hearing someone yell "ATTENTION!"

The men jumped up as two officers entered from the rear of the classroom. They both climbed up the stairs to the stage in front and the lead officer said, "At ease men. Take your seats!"

"I'm Major Arnett, the commandant of the Cadet Training School here a Santa Maria. I would like to welcome class 43-L to Santa Maria and wish you all good luck. You are now in a very select group of air cadets. Some of you may not make it to final graduation but, if you follow orders, pay attention to your instructors and work hard, I am sure you will all end up being very good pilots. It is in primary flight training that you will all get your first taste of flying and believe me men it's a thrill. I am now going to turn you over to your training instructor, Captain Peterson."

Someone else yelled, "ATTENTION," and all the cadets jumped to attention as the major left the building. Captain Peterson was a short well-built man who had flown thirty-five missions in the famous P-47 *Thunderbolt*. All the cadets were very much impressed with Captain Peterson.

He said, "At ease; sit!"

They all sat and waited in much anticipation.

He began, "You have all made it this far and as Major Arnett said, if you work hard and pay attention to your instructors, you will have no trouble getting through primary."

"This is where you will get your first taste of flying. Your training plane will be the Fairchild PT-19. It's a good airplane but it doesn't suffer fools lightly. You will have 10 to 15 hours of instruction and if your instructor feels you are ready, you will then solo."

All the cadets stirred at that and looked at each other.

Captain Peterson waited a few minutes for that to sink in and then went on, "Don't think for one minute that soloing will make you an Army Air Corps pilot; it doesn't! Now, when we dismiss you, you will march back to the barracks, take the rest of the day to settle in and unpack your duffel bags. After chow, get to bed as early as possible because tomorrow will begin at 0500. It will be a very busy day."

When Captain Peterson started to leave the stage, someone shouted the expected "ATTENTION!" The cadets jumped to their feet as the drill instructor moved to the front of the room and told them to fall out in front.

That night in the barracks, Lowell and Marv lay in their bunks staring at the ceiling. The captain had told them to get a good night sleep, but not a man in the barracks was asleep.

"Low, are you asleep?" asked Marv.

"No, I can't help thinking about what will happen tomorrow."

"Neither can I; do you think we have a chance to make it through?"

Lowell thought of that for awhile and responded, "I don't know, but I'm going to give it a very good try."

"Yea, so am I."

With that, they both were quiet and finally fell asleep.

First Flight

The day began with the usual 0500 reveille, falling out for breakfast, returning to the barracks, cleaning their rooms, and standing a brief inspection. They were marched to the supply room and issued their flight- gear, which consisted of a pair of very baggy coveralls, gloves and a World War I leather helmet with a tube sticking out of each ear. As they came out of the supply room, they all laughed about the tubes until a cadre called for a fall-in and explained these appendages. He said they were for the "gosport" tube. Lowell looked at Marv with an inquiring expression on his face and Marv shrugged his shoulders; neither one had the foggiest idea about how the gosport tube was used.

Lowell said, "These coveralls are just like I used to wear in my dad's garage."

"Yea, but I'll bet they fit better." responded Marv.

"Not really."

After donning their new flight gear, they heard the order to fall out into formation. Double-timed to the flight field, they entered a building, received their issued parachutes and instructions how to put them on and doubled-timed it to the flight line. By this time, the temperature had climbed into the upper 70s and the cadets were sweating profusely, but the sight of a PT-19 on the apron excited everyone and made them forget about the temperature. They were told to stand easy by their training officer, Captain Peterson.

"Men, before you is the P-19. It will be your primary trainer during this phase of your training. It is a very good airplane for training cadets to be pilots."

Lowell could hardly contain his excitement. A real airplane. He had seen several airplanes at the landing strip in Drayville, but had never been close to one before. He also noticed several civilians standing beside the airplanes and wondered what they were doing. Captain Peterson soon cleared up the mystery.

"Gentleman, the men you see standing by the airplanes are your instructors. Yes, they are civilians because this is a contract base, but don't think they aren't up to the job. They have more hours of instructing cadets than you have in the air corps."

With that Captain Peterson called off the name of each instructor and his assigned cadets. Lowell drew Mr. Cochran along with Charlie, which made Lowell happy to think he and Charlie would be together once more. Marv drew Mr. Dalton. There was one woman, Miss Chandler, and the cadets who drew her were somewhat taken aback which proved to be a mistake in the future; more cadets who trained under Miss Chandler made it through primary than any other instructor.

Lowell walked up to Mr. Cochran, saluted and said, "Cadet Andersen reporting as ordered sir!"

To which Mr. Cochran responded with, "You don't have to salute me men, I'm a civilian and don't call me sir; that's my father."

Mr. Cochran went on to say, "Men, today some of you will get your first ride in an airplane; it will be only a ride because you will not be flying."

He looked down at his list and said, "Let's see, how about doing this alphabetically. Cadet Andersen, you're first."

Lowell went cold, his blood pressure must have gone up 100 points, but he responded with. "Yes sir!"

Mr. Cochran went through the procedure to introduce him to the airplane. He walked Lowell around to review the various parts; ailerons, rudder, elevator and landing gear which Lowell had learned in pre-flight.

"Well cadet, are you ready to go for a little airplane ride?"

Lowell answered, "Yes sir!"

"Well, get your helmet on and climb aboard!"

Lowell put his leather helmet on and climbed aboard as instructed. Mr. Cochran climbed up on the wing and told him how the flight was going to go. He showed him how to buckle in the harness, hook up the gosport tube to his helmet and pointed out various dials on the instrument panel. The cadets had been taught in pre-flight what the basic instruments in an airplane were and how they were used. Then he talked Lowell through the instrument checklist. He called out the instrument and Lowell pointed it out.

He called out, "Manifold pressure gauge, RPM, temperature, turn and bank, and air speed."

Lowell identified all correctly and Mr. Cochran was satisfied. Having worked in his father's garage, the gauges were not a problem for Lowell; he knew what they were and what they measured.

"Now Cadet Andersen, I will be flying the airplane, but I want you to put your right hand on the control stick and your feet on the rudder peddles, but under no circumstances are you to exert any pressure on the controls, that is unless I die or fall out of the airplane."

Mr. Cochran smiled and climbed into the rear cockpit. He talked into the gosport tube and told Lowell to shake his head either yes or no if he could hear him.

Lowell nodded his head and Mr. Cochran said, "Okay, Mr. Andersen, here we go."

He went through the start up procedures, yelled "CLEAR," and started the plane.

Lowell felt the shudder of the plane and then the gust of wind from the prop and the plane was running. He let the engine warm up for several minutes and Lowell noticed the gauges responding. Mr. Cochran, speaking through the gosport tube, told him to watch all the gauges. Lowell indicated that he had understood. Mr. Cochran then told him he was going to release the brakes and begin to taxi out to the runway.

At the end of the runway, he stopped the plane again and explained to Lowell what he was going to do and ended with, "Are you ready?"

Lowell nodded his head just as he felt the engine increase revolution the wind also increased. The plane began to move slowly at first and then as the throttle was increased, the speed increased as well. In a short time, the tail of the plane lifted and just as quickly, the whole plane left the runway and was airborne. He was flying.

Mr. Cochran reminded him to keep his hand on the controls and his feet on the rudder.

"Now, feel the controls move as we do a slight bank to the left."

Lowell felt left pressure on the control stick and the left rudder pedal moved ever so slightly. The left wing of the PT-19 dropped and the nose seemed to go down a bit as the airplane made a shallow turn to the left.

Mr. Cochran said, "Watch your instrument!"

Lowell motioned that he understood and saw that the RPM had increased slightly, the air speed had dropped a little and the turn and bank indicator had swung slightly, duplicating the movement of the plane.

Mr. Cochran did several more turns and banks then said, "Well I guess that's enough for the first flight," and began his return to the field.

He told Lowell he could look around a little but to keep his hands and feet on the controls. Lowell took a quick look at the altimeter and saw that they were at 1,200 feet and then looked over the edge of the cockpit and was taken by how small every thing on the ground appeared. Mr. Cochran spoke over the gosport tube to tell Lowell to pay particular attention to how the controls felt during landing.

After landing and taxiing up to the parking apron, Mr. Cochran climbed out of the rear cockpit on to the wing, indicating to Lowell to unplug the gosport tube and remove his helmet. Lowell did so and Mr. Cochran asked him how he liked his first ride.

Lowell could only respond with, "That was swell; that was really swell!"

As Lowell excitedly crawled out of the plane and started to walk across the apron to the flight center, Marv yelled for him to wait up.

As he caught up he said, "Wasn't that just the greatest feeling in the world?"

Lowell in equally exited terms said "Boy, it sure was; did you feel how smooth the instructors turned?"

"Yea, maybe some day we can fly like that!"

The next item on the schedule for this momentous day was double timing to the mess hall for noon chow. There was a lot of talking and excitement at chow. Everyone wanted to tell his individual story.

After chow, they were marched back to the field and told they were to fly again that afternoon. After donning their parachutes they walked to the flight line where Mr. Cochran was standing by the PT-19.

When the cadets came up he said, "Well men, are you ready for another ride this afternoon?"

Pausing for effect, he said, "We'll keep the same order as this morning so you're up Mr. Andersen."

Lowell stepped forward, climbed up on the wing and into the cockpit. The parachute made it very difficult to perform that simple task but adrenaline helped. Mr. Cochran climbed into the back seat and spoke to Lowell through the gosport asking him if he was ready, to which he nodded his head up and down. They went through the startup procedure, taxied out to the runway, and added power, lifting gently into the air. Lowell kept his hands and feet on the controls while watching the instruments.

Suddenly at about 2,800 feet, Mr. Cochran said, "You want to take it awhile?"

Although somewhat shocked Lowell managed to nod yes.

Mr. Cochran said, "Okay, you've got the airplane."

Lowell had never felt anything so exhilarating. He held the stick with such force that his knuckle turned white.

Mr. Cochran, through the gosport said, "Just relax son; watch your airspeed and keep it as you were taught in pre-flight."

Lowell, watching the turn and bank indicator swing would correct and it would swing the opposite way.

Mr. Cochran said, "Okay, now take your hand off the stick."

Somewhat confused he did as he was told and the airplane immediately straightened out and flew level.

Mr. Cochran said, "Now, that is your first lesson, the airplane will fly better without you than with you. I have trimmed it for level flight. Alright take the controls again and we'll try a few simple turns."

Lowell, as instructed from the rear seat pushed the stick to the left, put in slight left rudder and the plane made a gentle turn to the left. After several more gentle turns and some slight climbs, Mr. Cochran again took the controls and landed. Climbing out of the plane Lowell was even more elated than in the morning's simple ride. He could hardly wait to get back to the barracks and write Helen.

Lowell waited in the ready room for Marv or Charlie to come in and talk about the day's activities. When he saw Marv coming across the apron, he didn't look too happy.

As he entered the room, Lowell said, "Well, how did it go?"

"I don't know, I couldn't keep the wings level."

"Well, neither could I until my instructor told me to take my hand off the control stick and the plane leveled out and flew straight."

"How did that help?"

Lowell smiled and said, "Well, it showed me you had to let the plane fly itself and when I did that, it worked."

Marv, smiled and then said, "Well maybe I'll try that."

They walked back, turned in their parachutes and decided to wait for Charlie.

That night in the barracks, there was a lot of talking and hand flying describing the day's activities. Finally, Lowell reached in his footlocker and out came the writing kit.

Dearest Helen,

Well, today was the day! I actually flew an airplane today. Wasn't very far, maybe just a mile or so, but I had all the controls in my hands. I really like my instructor, his name is Mr. Cochran and he is a civilian instructor at the base and a very nice guy.

After writing a bit more about the day's activities, he turned to home.

How are things with you, how is school going? Do you see Betty often? What does she hear from Jew? What about my folks? Do you see them very often? Mom wrote that she had you and your folks over for dinner a couple of weeks ago.

Writing a couple more lines he closed his letter.

As always to you I give my love and life,
Lowell

Primary training went on and the cadets got more and more flying time. Physical training (PT) did not let up though, nor did the class work. They learned more about engines, navigation, weather, and aircraft identification. In the air, they learned how to recover from a stall, plus how to roll and loop the aircraft. As the men sat around the day room, the conversation usually centered on the day's lesson and how each had done.

Charlie said, "Boy, I thought I would loose my lunch when the instructor put that plane in a loop."

"Yea," said Marv, "But the rolls were more scary for me than the loop."

"Did you have any trouble bringing it out of the loop Low?"

"Well a little the first time, but I caught on okay."

As the weeks went on, none of them had any trouble with the various maneuvers. All three of them were at the head of the class in both flying and class work.

One day after several flights, Mr. Cochran announced that he was going to demonstrate to the cadets one of the things in flying that could not only end their flying careers, but also their lives. Again he told Lowell that he would be first and to get ready. Lowell suited up and climbed into the front cockpit. By this time in the training, the cadets who were advancing as expected were able to go through the pre-flight checklist and take-off without the instructor's control.

He told Lowell to climb to 8,000 feet and level off and then said over the gosport tube, "I've got the controls."

This was the signal for the cadet to release the stick. Mr. Cochran also told Lowell to watch the instruments carefully, particularly the airspeed and RPM. Suddenly the airplane began to climb and the RPM indicator began to rise, but the air speed was decreasing. Lowell had read enough to realize Mr. Cochran was putting the plane into a stall. The air speed was almost down to zero and the RPM were still high when suddenly the plane fell off on one wing. The instructor then decreased power and leveled off the plane.

Yelling into the gosport tube he said to Lowell, "That Mr. Andersen was a stall, not particularly dangerous unless you are close to the ground."

After landing, Mr. Cochran talked to Lowell about when a stall is dangerous. Usually on take-off or if you have to go around again, there is a tendency to pull back on the stick too hard, causing a stall and in most cases, death of the pilot.

Lowell was fairly sober that night during chow.

Marv asked, "What's wrong with you tonight?"

Lowell asked, "Did your instructor demonstrate the stall to you today?"

"Yea. Why?"

"Well, that was the first time I had thought of the fact that we might die."

"Oh bull shit!" said Marv.

The letter to Helen that night was much more subdued than before, but was signed with the usual loving phrase.

Primary flight training continued with much more physical exercise, running everywhere they went and some harassment from the upperclassman. One day after some eleven hours of dual instruction including many take-offs and landings, Lowell had made what he considered to be a very good take-off.

Mr. Cochran said, "Okay, Mr. Andersen, go around once and land."

Lowell thought he had done something wrong as they taxied up to the apron and cut the engine. Mr. Cochran climbed out of the rear cockpit and motioned for Lowell to go. It took him a moment to realize what Mr. Cochran meant; he repeated the gesture and smiled up at him.

A very cold feeling came over Lowell and he just stared down at his instructor until he climbed on the wing and said, "Do I have to dynamite you into the air?"

"Are you sure I'm ready?"

"As ready as I can make you; now either go or get out of the seat!"

With a smile, Mr. Cochran climbed down. Lowell went through the start up procedures, taxied out to the runway where he finally settled down, did the pre-flight checklist and when cleared by the tower, added power and took off. He flew around several circuits and then landed. His whole class was waiting when he landed. As the first in his class to solo, a special event awaited for him. When he climbed down, he was immediately picked up by the members of his class and carried behind the ready room to the recreation area, then unceremoniously thrown into the swimming pool. That night he was so excited he wrote not only to Helen but to Jew, his parents and even separate letters to both Diane and David.

Hi Squirt,

How is school? I really enjoy flying and I have some great news! Today I soloed. I think you know what that means. All I have to do now is work on some techniques and then advanced training and I will get my wings. When I do, I'll give you a set just like mine.

Did Mom sew those patches on your coat yet? I bet they really look keen. When I finish my training I think I will get a leave to come home and I am really looking forward to seeing those patches.

Love, Your Big Brother,

Lowell

To Diane he wrote.

Hi Darling,

How is everything with you? I am fine. I flew the airplane all by myself today. That is a very big thing for us cadets. It is the first step to becoming a real pilot.

Are you studying hard in school? If you plan to go to college, you have to have good grades. Mom says you and your Girl Scout troop are gathering tin cans and rubber for the war effort. Keep it up; we can use all the rubber and tin you can gather.

I can hardly wait to get home to give you a big hug. I'll bet you are so big by now that you won't want me to hug you any more, but I'm going to do it anyway.

All my Love,

Your big brother,

Lowell

As primary went on the cadets learned many more things about flying, navigating, compensating for wind drift, flying the radio beam, and of course take-offs and landings. One lesson they learned sent a scare through all the cadets. One day as Lowell and Charlie were lounging in front of the ready room, several instructors and Captain Peterson came running out shading their eyes looking across the field. Lowell and Charlie stood up and looked in that direction. They saw a trainer coming in very fast and steep.

Lowell asked, "What's going on?"

Captain Peterson answered, "Nothing, you cadets go inside until you are called!"

Just as Lowell and Charlie turned to obey, they heard a loud crash and then an explosion. Of course, they turned back toward the field and saw smoke rolling up in the air; a trainer had crashed. This was the first fatality for class 43-L.

The next day, the class was gathered in the classroom and Major Arnett came on stage to the appropriate "ATTENTION."

"At ease men, sit. Yesterday the hazards of flying were brought home to you in a most terrible but not unusual way. One of your classmates was killed in an accident. This will happen; you will never get used to it, but you must not let it affect your training.

"Training will continue today as scheduled and I want you men to learn from this accident."

The major turned and walked off the stage to the usual "ATTENTION."

The cadre then shouted "Attention, fall out in formation."

By this time every one in the class knew who was killed. He was on his second solo flight. His name was Eugene Christensen from Idaho. Lowell didn't know him well; he was in another barracks and had a different instructor. That night in the room there was little talk. Everyone was in his own thoughts.

Finally, Bill said, "I heard in the mess hall that he panicked and would not land."

"Yea, I can't imagine panicking that much," said Oscar.

"Well it happens I guess," said Bill. "I read that nearly one third of the Army Air Corps Cadets either wash out or are killed in training."

"That's a great thought Bill," said Lowell and he rolled over with his own thoughts vowing not to tell Helen about the accident.

Some weeks later Marv and Lowell walked into the room and found Oscar packing his bag.

"What are you doing?" asked Lowell.

"Well, I'm not going to be flying airplanes, I know that for sure," he replied.

Marv said, "You washed out?"

"Yea, I just can't get those landings down. My instructor has tried everything, but I bounce like a kangaroo. The captain called me to the orderly room and gave me the news today."

Lowell asked, "Where are you going?"

"I've got orders for bombardier training in New Mexico."

"Yea, one of the guys at pre-flight went there. Well, at least you'll be in a flight school," replied Lowell.

"Well, good luck fella, maybe we'll see ya in England," said Marv as he walked over and shook hands with Oscar.

Lowell did the same and asked to help with his gear.

Oscar said, "Nah, I can manage."

As he walked out of the room, Bill Minor came in looking confused and said, "Where's Oscar going?"

Then after a minute's thought, "Oh shit, did he wash out?"

"Yea," replied Marv.

Everyone in the barracks was pretty glum that night. Oscar had been one of the favorites with all the men. There had been twelve others before him and it almost always caused a down night in the barracks except when John La France washed out. No one liked him much and the only one who would even carry on a conversation with him was Lowell.

That night as they lay in their beds, Bill said, "I wonder if they will replace Oscar in the room?"

"I don't know – there are a lot of empty bunks in the barracks," said Lowell.

Bill went on, "Wasn't Charlie a friend of you guys in pre?"

"Yea, why?"

"Well, I was thinking that he's an okay guy and instead of waiting for them to put some knot head in here, why don't we see if Charlie wants to move over?"

Lowell said, "Yea, that's a great idea, but I don't know how that will make the guys in his room feel."

Marv said, "I think he would jump at the chance, he was telling me the other day that he sure wishes he could get away from Porter, whose snoring is about ready to drive him crazy."

Bill added, "Yea, and he is with Ramsey, the second most disliked guy in the class."

Lowell said, "Yea, well I'll ask him tomorrow and if he wants to, we'll find out how to do it. Now let's get some sleep. Tomorrow is a busy day."

*****

The next day was busy, PT first thing in the morning followed by two hours of classes, more PT, then lunch and the afternoon flying.

As they walked from the ready room to the flight line with their parachutes banging against their legs Lowell said, "I wonder what Mr. Cochran will have us doing today?"

He greeted the cadets with the respectful, "Good afternoon gentleman, this afternoon were going to see if you can keep your lunch down. We're going to do some snap rolls."

Lowell looked around at the other cadets and they were all looking wide-eyed and a little scared.

"Okay Cadet Andersen, you first."

Lowell followed the procedures, started the engine, taxied to the runway and took off. Mr. Cochran, through the gosport tube told him to climb to 12,000 feet.

When he reached altitude, Mr. Cochran said, "I'll take the airplane, you just hang on."

Lowell suddenly felt the plane roll violently to the left and stop momentarily with the wings in a vertical position, then roll to an inverted position for a moment, then roll in the vertical position and then back to level.

Mr. Cochran said through the tube, "Think you can do that?"

Lowell nodded his head affirmatively and the instructor said, "Your airplane."

The first attempt by Lowell was less than successful. He rolled the plane over on its back, then to about a forty-five degree angle and then in the level.

Mr. Cochran said, "You forgot one position. Don't push the stick so far and then correct sooner."

On the second attempt Lowell did better but still couldn't stop the roll with the wings in a true position. Mr. Cochran was very patient with him and on the fourth try, Lowell performed the maneuver satisfactorily and he told him to practice five more and then land.

After they landed and got out of the plane, Mr. Cochran said, "Well, you have just learned the snap roll. Very good."

"Well I thought I had a lot of trouble getting it right," Lowell said.

Mr. Cochran put his hand on Lowell's shoulder and said, "Cadet Andersen, you learned that in about half the time most cadets take. Don't be so critical of yourself."

Charlie was in the ready room when Lowell walked in and asked, "How'd you do with the snap roll?"

"Well not so good at first, but I seemed to satisfy Mr. Cochran after awhile. How'd you do?"

"I got the first two positions okay but had trouble leveling the plane," replied Charlie.

"Oh say Charlie, if we can arrange it how would you like to move in with Bill, Marv and me?"

"Say that would be swell. Do you think they would let us?"

"I don't know; let's find out."

When the day's training was over, Lowell, Marv, Bill and Charlie asked permission to speak to the barracks cadre and were granted an audience. They removed their hats, entered the room and hit a brace. The barracks cadre gave them an at-ease and asked what he could do for them.

"Sir, since Cadet Booker washed out, we have an empty bunk in our room," said Lowell. "We wondered if Cadet Smith might move in with us?"

"You guys want another body in there to get in the way?" asked the cadre.

The four man rooms had only one shower and one sink and each morning it was a bit of a hassle to get ready in the short time allotted. The three cadets just stood there not knowing what to say until Marv said, "Yes sir!"

The barracks cadre looked at them for awhile, smiled and said, "Yea that's okay, go ahead and tell him to move. Anything else?"

"No sir!"

"Dismissed!"

The three friends did a smart about face and left the room. "Well that was easy," said Marv.

"Yea, now all you have to do is talk to your former roommates, Charlie," said Lowell.

"Oh I don't think that will be a problem. We don't seem to get along too well anyway," replied Charlie.

"I don't know how anyone can get along with Ramsey; he is such a prick," said Marv.

That night, Charlie moved into the room with Marv, Bill and Lowell. Marv immediately began to harass him.

"Okay, as the newest guy in the room, you will be expected to shine our shoes, make our bunks, shower last and bring us cokes at night."

"Ya know Marv, if I wasn't such a good Christian I would tell you to go to hell!" replied Charlie.

Bill said, "Boy I am sure glad I suggested this; you guys seem like really good friends."

To which Lowell replied, "Oh, who ever said we were good friends?"

They all laughed and began to help Charlie get settled.

Primary training continued the very busy schedule for the cadets. They were flying about four hours a day and still had classes and PT. As the year wore on, it became a little cooler in California and the cadets were ordered to report to the supply room to draw fleece lined flight jackets.

Flying an airplane was still an awe-inspiring experience for Lowell. He now felt very comfortable doing spins, snap rolls, stalls and recovery. Landing and take-offs were second nature to him and he was able to set it down without a bounce. All in all, Lowell, Charlie, Marv and Bill were doing very well in the latter days of primary flight training.

After flying, Lowell liked the classes on navigation, weather and mechanics best. They all enjoyed the classes on Army Air Corps history. One day they were surprised and awed by a special guest to the class that gave Lowell the subject for his letter to Helen that night.

Dearest Helen,

Today, we had a guest speaker in class, General Jimmy Doolittle. I have never seen the cadets so attentive to a speaker. The general talked about flying, skills needed to be an outstanding pilot rather than just an average pilot, safety, how badly we are needed in the war effort, and the pride he has always felt in being an Army Air Corps pilot. It made all of us want to do the very best we can for the country and particularly for him.

After class, we changed into our flight gear and marched to the ready room. He was in there talking to Major Arnett and Captain Peterson. I thought just meeting him would be the highlight of my year, but when we walked in, Major Arnett called Charlie and me over and introduced us to the general as two of the top cadets in the class. The general talked to us for about ten minutes, wished us good luck and shook our hands. Boy, I don't think I will ever wash that hand again.

Enough about that; how is everything with you? Has Betty heard from Jew? Will he get home for Christmas? I still don't know if I will.

How's school going, are you staying away from those horny freshman boys? Mom wrote that she had you over for dinner a week or so ago. That's nice.

Lowell went on for a couple more pages and signed off in his usual way.

As always to you I give my love and life,
Lowell

*****

The cadets were given Thanksgiving off and many of the town's people who had gotten to know some of the cadets invited them to dinner. Attending the LDS church on Sundays, Charlie became acquainted with the Jensen family in Santa Maria. They had a daughter named Linda, who invited him to Thanksgiving dinner and told him to invite some of his friends. Of course, he invited Marv. Bill and Lowell.

It was a very nice day and gave Lowell more fodder for his letters to Helen. Linda Jensen was a sophomore at the junior college in Santa Maria and, except for Helen, was one of the most beautiful girls Lowell had ever met. They learned that beside the two younger brothers they had met when they came in, she had an older brother in the navy who was aboard a cruiser in the Pacific. Charlie was obviously taken by her and did a terrible job hiding it. Marv and Bill could hardly keep their eyes off her and Lowell admitted later it was a struggle for him as well. Dinner was the traditional turkey and dressing with all the trimmings. All four of the boys over ate and admitted later that they weren't sure they could get into their flight gear the next day.

After dinner, Mr. Jensen invited them into the living room. Linda's brothers asked about their training and the types of planes they flew. Both said they wanted to be pilots when they were old enough.

"Now boys, don't quiz our guests," said Mrs. Jensen as she and Linda joined them.

Linda added, "This isn't twenty questions!"

They asked Marv, Bill and Lowell about their families and their home towns. Of course they knew by now where Charlie was from. Then the conversation turned to Salt Lake City, the center of the Mormon Church and the Jensen boys asked Charlie if he had ever been in the Temple.

Mrs. Jensen, said, “What a silly question boys. He lives in Salt Lake City.”

Charlie just laughed as he looked at Linda and said “Yea, a few times.”

Mr. Jensen offered to drive them back to the field. They accepted of course and Linda was invited to accompany them. When they were getting in the car, Marv tried to jump in the front seat beside Linda and was unceremoniously shoved out of the way by Charlie who climbed in. Marv just laughed and climbed in the back to face his two friends rolling their eyes and shaking their heads at his brazenness. He just shrugged his shoulders as if to say *it was worth a try.*

That night in the room, everyone wanted to discuss Linda.

Bill said, “Okay, let’s hear about her!”

They all looked at Charlie and he raised his head and with a knowing smirk said, “Hear about who?”

Marv said, “You know about who. Where did you meet her?”

“Ya know, Marv, you are always making fun of me on Sundays when I go off to church. You ought to try it sometime; you never know who you might meet in church.”

Lowell laughed and chipped in with, “Well, that’s right! There are some very nice girls who go to church.”

“Well, I never met one; I only met big fat ladies who wanted to hug me,” replied Marv.

Bill said, “You mean you used to go to church?”

“Sure, until I was in about the eighth grade. Then my mother let me decide for myself and I decided to not go.”

“Yea, I know how that is. I used to go a lot as a little kid, but later only on holidays,” replied Bill.

Lowell said, “My uncle is a preacher so I went all the time.”

Marv said, “Damn it you guys. We want to hear about Charlie’s girl, not about how religious you are. How long have you known her and have you ever kissed her?”

“What a question!” said Lowell.

Charlie broke out into a large grin and said, “Well, as a matter of fact, I have.”

All three roommates looked at him in astonishment and then Marv said, “When? Tell us about it!”

"I'm not going to tell you about it, that's between Linda and me!"

With that Marv went over to Charlie and grabbed his head in a hammerlock and rubbed his hair saying, "Why you devil. I never thought you had it in you!"

They all laughed and went on talking for a few more minutes until Lowell got out his writing kit and the other three roommates groaned.

Bill said, "Well there he goes again!"

*****

The final weeks for primary training went much as the others: flying, classes, and of course the inevitable PT. Ten days before the end of primary, Marv was summoned to the orderly room. When he returned and walked in to the room, the roommates knew something was wrong. Marv was sullen and his eyes looked like he was about to cry.

He flopped down on his bunk and covered his eyes. Lowell asked, "Marv, what is the matter?"

"Major Arnett sent for me and told me they were going to set me back three weeks. He said, it was felt by the staff that I needed more hours of flying before I was ready to go on to basic. Damn it, I wanted to go on with you guys!"

After a strained silence in the room, Charlie said, "Well, it isn't like being washed out."

"Yea, that's right, you'll just be junior to us when we're commissioned," Bill said with a smile.

Marv sat up and said, "Gee, you guys sure make me feel better. Bastards."

"Aw come on Marv, it isn't the end of the world. You will still get to fly," added Lowell.

"Well, I'm going to buckle down and show these people that I am ready for basic and catch up with you guys!"

"That's the spirit Marv," Lowell said as he got up and went over and patted Marv on the shoulder.

On the fifth of December, they learned that their assignments for the next phase of their training would be posted on the eighth, two days before graduation. More importantly, it stated that after graduation on December 22 there would be a ten-day Christmas and transfer leave issued.

After training on the eighth, the boys hurried over to the orderly room bulletin board to find out their fate. Lowell looked on the list and saw that he had been assigned to basic flight training at Lemoore Army Air Base in Lemoore, California. He was very happy not to be going to another base in the Midwest or the South. He waited for Charlie and Bill to see what they got and they both had the same orders. By that time Marv had moved out of the room and joined the class behind them. They were able to talk freely without consideration of Marv's feelings.

CHRISTMAS LEAVE

When everything was ready, Lowell bid Bill and Charlie goodbye and said he would see them at Lemoore, caught a shuttle bus to the train station in town, was able to purchase a ticket without difficulty and waited on the platform. He was so excited that he had forgotten to open a letter he had received from Jew that morning. When he remembered, he reached in his pocket, brought it out and opened it.

Dear Low,

Well, by the time you get this I will be on my way home to tie the knot with Betty. Your note saying that you will be able to be my best man was very good news. I thought I might have to ask Vernon after all.

Betty and I decided that she would not go back to Texas with me until the end of the school term this spring. Boy, I don't know if I can stand it knowing she is going to bed alone without me each night.

I've given it a lot of thought and Betty and I have discussed it and I am not going to let our marriage stop me from requesting an overseas assignment. I've just got to get over there and bomb the crap out of those bastards.

Well, see ya in a couple of days.
Jew

The train ride home seemed to go on forever with all the stops; however, Lowell slept most of the way. When he woke, he looked out of the window and recognized the train station in Eugene, just forty-five miles to go and he would be in Salem. Sleep was not in the cards; his excitement grew and grew until he thought he would burst. To see Helen, Jew, his folks and even the twins made him feel so warm and cozy inside. He thought of how long it had been and it was only six months for his family and Helen, but nearly a year since he had seen Jew. Nevertheless, it seemed like a lifetime to him.

About an hour later, the conductor came through the train announcing "Salem next stop, Salem next stop!"

Lowell began to gather his stuff and get it ready. A man across the aisle asked, "First leave son?"

Lowell jumped, looked over at him and said with a sheepish grin, "Yea, I've been in cadet training since June."

"I know how you feel. I was in World War I and was gone for over a year," the man responded.

Lowell didn't want to appear rude, but he was so anxious to get off the train that he just smiled and picked up his stuff and walked down the aisle to the exit doors. When he got there, he saw the sign, "Salem Oregon" and thought his chest would burst with anxiety and tension. As the train passed the station he looked on the platform where there were many waiting and he saw his dad first, then the twins waving excitedly and then there she was, Helen, beautiful Helen looking even more beautiful than he remembered her.

He could hardly wait until the conductor opened the door and put down the steps. He jumped off the train, ran to Helen and grabbed her in a strong embrace that nearly took her breath away.

After a long kiss, he said, "Gosh darling, I missed you," and kissed her again.

His mother came up to them and reached out for him and he turned and gave her a big hug.

His father shook his hand and said, "Welcome home son!"

The twins stood off a little, seemingly in awe of him in his uniform until he reached out for them. Then he became aware of two other people standing in the crowd. It was Myron and Betty.

Lowell froze in mid stride and his eyes filled with tears and he said in a half whisper, "Jew, my God you look good!"

Myron stepped forward and hesitated for a minute, reached out and took Lowell in an embrace that nearly broke his ribs.

Lowell said, "Is it within regulations for an officer to hug an enlisted man?"

"Aw shut up cadet and welcome home!"

Betty looked at Helen and said, "They haven't changed a bit have they?"

They stood on the platform for a few minutes and Mr. Andersen put his arm around his son and said, "Myron drove over in his car and if you and Helen want to ride home with them it's okay. We'll see you when we get to Drayville."

Lowell looked at his dad and over his shoulder at his mother and said, "Thanks Dad. Is that okay with you Mom?"

"Of course son," she replied.

Lowell leaned over and kissed his mom and squeezed the twins again and said, "I'll see you when we get home guys."

To which Diane replied, "I'm not a guy!"

Lowell just smiled at her and patted her on the head.

As they got in the car Lowell reached over and put his arm around Helen and she melted in to his embrace and whispered, "Oh darling I have missed you so much."

That brought a response from Jew in the front, "Hey you guys, we're the ones getting married, and you've got to wait awhile so take it easy."

After taking Helen home and going in for a short visit with her folks, Lowell said, "Well I had better get home and spend some time with my folks. Why don't you come along Helen?"

"No, I think you said it. You need to spend some time with your family; besides, I hope I will see you tonight."

She walked him to the door and gave him a big kiss and clung to him saying, "My you feel good to me!"

It was quite cold and of course raining, but it was good to walk through Drayville again. As he came to Main Street, he decided to go down and say hello to George at the station.

When he walked into the lube bay, George was working under a car, hearing the footsteps he shouted, "I'll be with you in a minute."

Lowell answered in a pretend gruff voice, "Well I see the service at this station hasn't improved a bit!"

George recognizing Lowell's voice, pushed out from under the car and jumped up, "Well I'll be damned, the flyboy. How are ya Lowell?" grabbing and pumping his hand.

"I'm fine George, how are things with you?"

At that, George realized that his hands were very greasy and a lot of it had rubbed off on Lowell.

"Oh my God, I'm sorry Lowell," as he handed him a grease rag to wipe his hands.

"Seems like you're pretty busy around here. Guess I should go home and change clothes and come back to help."

"You had better not, your mom and dad would kill both of us!" replied George.

Lowell asked, "What do you hear from Bob?"

Bob was George's oldest son who had gone into the marines two weeks after Pearl Harbor.

"Oh, he's in the South Pacific somewhere; I'm not sure where, but he's aboard a ship and not making those landings on all those islands. I guess that's a little safer."

"Yea, I guess it is. Well, I suppose I should get on home, I've just dropped Helen off and haven't had much of a chance to talk to the family. See ya later George."

"Okay, take it easy," George reached out for Lowell's hand and remembered and pulled back as they both laughed.

*****

When Lowell entered the house, he was greeted by that familiar smell of the Oregon Douglas Fir Christmas Tree. He almost broke down with pleasure and took a minute before he walked into the living room. His folks were sitting there and they both got up. His mother came over, embraced and held him for several minutes.

His dad called up the stairs, "Kids, Lowell's home!"

David and Diane came bounding down the stairs and both grabbed

Lowell at the same time in a hug and immediately started arguing about who got the first hug.

Lowell laughed and gave both equal hugs saying, "Well I see you two haven't changed a bit."

Lowell took his jacket off and removed his tie and David immediately grabbed the jacket and put it on and reached over and got the hat and put it on as well. Diane crawled up on his lap and snuggled up while David marched around the room saluting everyone and everything in the room.

He turned to Lowell and said, "Did you bring me anything?"

To which Mr. Andersen said, "Why David, give your brother a chance to sit down at least."

Lowell chuckled and said, "Well let's see, bring me my bag and I will see what's in there."

David rushed over and Diane jumped off Lowell's lap and ran over with David who was dragging the bag over to Lowell.

Lowell opened it and said, "Well what do you know. Look what I have for you David."

Pulling a book of army paper dolls and handing it to David.

Turning up his nose, David said, "Paper dolls?"

Diane immediately reached over and grabbed them from her brother and said, "Those are for me, aren't they Lowell?"

"Oh yea, I guess I got a little mixed up."

David diverted his attention back to the bag and Lowell pulled out a box with pictures of airplanes on it.

"I guess this is all I have left, maybe it's for you," he said, handing it to David who took it with some reverence and a very wide-eyed expression.

"Oh boy a model airplane, will you show me how to put it together?"

"Sure, later," replied Lowell.

He continued to dig in his bag and came out with a small box and handed it to his father.

"Here Dad. Before I left I noticed that your old one was getting pretty worn."

His father took it and said, "Should I save this for Christmas?"

Lowell replied, "Well you can, it is kind of a Christmas present. I didn't have time to wrap it."

He dug deeper in his bag and came up with a smallish box and handed it to his mother.

Accepting the box, she said, "Well I'm not going to wait until Christmas!"

Opening it exposed a smaller velvet box, which she opened, put her hand to her mouth and said, "Oh Lowell they're just beautiful!"

She got up from her chair and came over to give her son a big kiss.

"Thank you dear."

Mr. Andersen looking quite perplexed said, "What is it?"

His wife showed him what was in the box and he said, "Earrings. Why those are beautiful!"

"Okay, I'm going to open mine," and he proceeded to take the top off. Blinking a few times he said, "A new pipe!"

He took it out and immediately put it in his mouth. "That feels just great; I'll smoke it after dinner."

Lowell had smelled something other than the Christmas tree when he came into the house.

He said, "Is that pot roast I smelled when I came in Mom?"

"Why yes, you don't think I wouldn't fix your favorite supper on your first day home do you?"

"Well it isn't even supper time yet. Are you folks eating a big meal for dinner or lunch now?" asked Lowell.

Dad said, "She's been saving up ration stamps every since we got the word you might be home."

"There wouldn't be mashed potatoes would there?" asked Lowell.

"Why yes, there would!" replied his mother.

Mrs. Andersen got up and said, "Well if we are going to have lunch or dinner or supper, I had better get it on the table. Diane you come and set the table for me."

"Oh Mom I just got the first doll cut out!"

"Go help your mother now and be quick about it!" Mr. Andersen said.

When they had left the room, he leaned towards Lowell and said with a very serious expression on his face, "How is it son, rough?"

"Well, the classes aren't bad, but the PT and running is a little tough in that heat."

"What's PT?"

"Oh, physical training; sorry I forgot you don't use those initials all the time like we do."

"How about the flying?"

Lowell smiled and said, "Dad, you won't believe how much fun it is. I soloed in ten hours, the first in my class, and had a lot of fun learning loops, rolls, and stalls. I even liked the mechanical classes; of course working in the garage helped me get through them much easier."

Diane came into the living room and said, "Dinner is ready."

The table looked just like Lowell remembered it: fully set, a big bowl of mashed potatoes, a platter of pot roast, cooked carrots, glasses of milk and coffee for his folks.

Scooping a large portion of potatoes onto his plate and adding several ladles of gravy he said, "Boy that looks good!"

With out even waiting for the meat, Lowell took a big bite of the potatoes.

He suddenly made a face and stopped chewing and his mother with a worried look said, "What's the matter dear?"

"Oh nothing, not a thing; they just taste a little salty that's all."

"Oh, did I put too much salt on them?"

"No, it's just that in the mess hall they never salt anything and I got out of the habit of eating anything very salty, but I'll get over it," he said as he put another large fork full of potatoes into his mouth.

As dinner finished and Mrs. Andersen and Diane were clearing the table, Mr. Andersen said, "The reason I took the afternoon off and Mom fixed such a big dinner is that we thought you would probably want to be out with Helen and your friends tonight."

Lowell responded, "Thanks Dad; that will be swell."

Lowell spent the afternoon visiting with his folks and playing with the twins but along towards evening he became restless to go see Helen. His father sensing this, reached into his pocket and took out the car keys.

"I didn't have time to get the '33 off the blocks so why don't you take the Pontiac," he said as he threw Lowell the keys. "It's full of gas."

Lowell went right to the phone and called Jew and told him he had the car for the rest of the day and why didn't they call Betty and Helen then do something. Myron said that Betty was at his house and to just come by and pick them up. After calling Helen and changing into some civilian clothes, he bid his family goodbye and hurriedly left with the car. He drove to the Rothstein's first, parked in front and ran up to the front door.

Jew answered the bell and said, "Come on in Low. Mom and Dad want to see you."

As he entered the living room, Mrs. Rothstein got up and came over to give him a big hug.

"Welcome home Lowell. It's good to see you."

Lowell thanked her as Mr. Rothstein came over and shook his hand and bid him sit down.

Myron said, "No Dad we haven't got time; he has to get over to Helen's and pick her up."

As the young people left, Betty went over to Mrs. Rothstein and gave her a little peck on the cheek and said, "Thanks for the supper mam."

Mrs. Rothstein pushed her away and held her by the shoulders and said with a warm smile on her face, "My dear if you ever call me mam again I'll disown you both, I am either mother, or Gertrude. Mam is something you call strangers."

Betty said with a big smile, "Okay Mother; thank you so much."

As they were going out the door, Myron said, "Well, I'm glad we got that settled!"

Betty punched him on the shoulder and said "Oh you!"

When they picked Helen up, they decided it would be fun to relive their high school days and go to the early show and over to Smith's for hamburgers and shakes. The movie was terrible and when they went to Smith's they found it full of high school kids and Myron said, "I don't want to remember that much about my high school days." Then Lowell said, "Why don't we drive over to Masonberg to that hamburger joint, the burgers are really good there." They drove to Masonberg and found a parking space right near the hamburger joint. They parked and entered the restaurant, found a booth near the window and began to look through the menu behind the napkin holder. The waitress came over and said, "What'll it be for you folks tonight."

Lowell said, "I want one of your great burgers with fries."

They all agreed and added cokes to the order. Lowell said, "So the big day is going to be the twenty-sixth, the day after Christmas?"

"Yea, only a few days of freedom left," said Myron.

Betty hit him on the shoulder and said, "Well, it isn't too late to back out you know."

"Nah, I can't do that, I've already made arrangements for our wedding night," Myron said with a leer.

"Oh you – is that all you ever think of!" replied Betty.

Lowell asked, "Where are you staying?"

"Well I thought we would stay at the Red Top Motel."

Betty said, "That's just at the edge of Drayville."

"Why, don't you think you can wait that long?"

Betty and Helen dropped their heads and laughed while Lowell and Myron winked at each other.

The waitress brought their food and Lowell asked if she had worked here for a long time.

"Yes, my dad owns this place and I've worked here since high school. My husband is in the navy and I can't think of a better place to work. Why do you ask?"

"Well, we were in here right after Pearl Harbor and met two guys from Masonberg and we talked. I just wondered if they are still around."

"What were their names?"

"I think Tagard and Brooks or something like that."

"Oh you mean Bill Brooks and Dick Toguard."

"Yea, that's them, are they still around?"

"Well Bill Brooks was killed on Guadalcanal and I think Dick is in the navy somewhere in the Pacific."

"Oh, that's too bad."

"Yea," Jew said, "I remember that day he said he wanted to join the marines."

"Yea, Bill didn't even finish high school; he quit in March and joined the marines. Say, I remember you guys, you were sitting with them and I had to come over and tell you to watch your language."

Lowell and Myron dropped their head and the girls caught their breath and both said in unison, "Oh!"

They finished their burgers, paid and left thanking the waitress and kidding her, saying she must have seen two other boys.

On the drive home, Lowell turned around and said to Myron, "What are you going wear for your wedding?"

"Oh, I think I'll wear my Levis and tennis shoes."

Betty said, "Oh Myron! I want you to wear your uniform."

Helen said, "Yea, why don't you both wear your uniforms; that would look swell."

"Oh, I don't know, any uniform with a brown bar on it doesn't look swell."

Myron said, "Better than one with a propeller on it!"

Helen said, "What are you talking about?"

The boys explained that a brown bar was the brass bar of a second lieutenant and a propeller was the emblem air cadets wore.

Lowell said, "What will your cousin wear do you think?"

"Oh I suppose he'll wear a suit, he's only sixteen you know," replied Myron.

"So we're meeting tomorrow night to rehearse for this fiasco, is that right?" asked Lowell.

"Yea if you can't make it, I think Vernon is in town. I'll call him."

"Oh you guys." Betty said.

"Well, with a Friday night wedding, I just don't know, I thought you Jewish people didn't do anything on Friday night."

"Well we're not that orthodox. I thought you Swedes didn't go to movies and eat hamburgers on Sunday either."

"Well we're not that orthodox, and besides I'm Norwegian," replied Lowell

"Same difference!"

"Oh you guys are really something, won't you ever get over doing that?" asked Helen.

Lowell looked around at Myron and said very seriously, "I hope not."

Myron looked into Lowell's eyes and nodded his head. The girls snuggled a little closer to their men.

"So you think you're going to wear your uniform are you?" asked Lowell.

"Yea, I guess so; nothing else fits me any more."

"Yea, me neither." replied Lowell

Helen said, "Yea, I thought you seemed a little bigger than when you left."

"How do you mean that Helen?" Myron asked.

Betty said, "Oh Myron get your mind out of the gutter!"

"I just remembered who Marv in primary reminded me of; you," said Lowell.

"Who's he?"

"Oh he was this character from Seattle I roomed with. He was always making suggestive remarks. My buddy Charlie Smith who was a Mormon met this real beautiful girl at the LDS church."

Betty asked, "What's LDS?"

Lowell explained, "It's the Church of the Latter Day Saints, another name for the Mormon Church. Anyway, her mother invited us for Thanksgiving dinner and when we got back to the room, Marv kept at Charlie about how far he had gotten with her until we all told him to shut up. Charlie was such a nice guy that he didn't seem to take offense."

Betty said, "See, Myron, you're just like Marv, who ever he is."

Lowell said, "Don't get me wrong, Marv was a great guy, just a jokester that's all. We all liked him."

"Yea, we had guys like that in training too." Myron said.

As the date drew closer, Lowell became more and more anxious about Myron and Betty's wedding. He wanted to talk to Helen about setting a date for theirs, but had yet to do so.

On Christmas Eve day, Lowell called her and said, "Would you like to go for a ride? There's something I want to talk to you about."

Of course Helen said, "Sure!"

Lowell picked her up in his father's car around two in the afternoon and started to drive out of town. He didn't say much when she got in the car.

"Hi," he said as he gave her a kiss.

As they drove into the country, Helen said, "What was it you wanted to talk to me about?"

"Well, you know how much I love you, I mean we have been going together for a long time and have been engaged for almost year, and I've been thinking, well – that is well – uh –"

Helen said, "Why don't we set a wedding date?"

"Okay."

She moved over closer and kissed him on the check.

"Is that what you wanted to talk to me about?"

"Yea, it was," Lowell responded with a silly grin. "I was thinking that a good time would be when I finish flight training and get my wings, what do you think?"

"When will that be Low?"

"Oh, if everything goes okay, it should be early this summer."

"Do you think you can get a leave?"

"They usually give you a leave before going on to another assignment or overseas."

Helen stiffened at that statement. She had never considered his going overseas and she knew what could happen if he went into combat.

Lowell and Helen decided to spend Christmas Eve with their families and meet later on Christmas Day.

After they had opened their presents, Lowell called Myron and when he answered Lowell said, "Well Jew, has Santa come to your house yet?"

"Sure and he brought me a bunch of great toys."

"Yea, I bet. Would you be able to walk down to my house for a minute, there is something I want to tell you."

Lowell told his folks that Myron was walking down to the house and he was going to meet him on the front porch. He put on his coat and went out side just in time to see Jew walking up the front walk.

"Hi, what is this big news you have for me?"

Lowell said, "Helen and I have set a tentative date for our wedding and I want you to be my best man."

"Well, it might be a good idea to tell me when this date is!"

"Oh well we don't have a firm date, just when I finish flight training and get my wings, it should be around June some time."

Jew said, "That might be possible, I plan to try to get leave and come up to get Betty about that time anyway. So you finally asked her to set a wedding date huh?"

"Well, I didn't exactly ask her."

"Oh no, not a repeat of your going steady question is it?"

"Yea, kind of."

"I'll tell you something, you Swedes have the damndest way of asking people things."

"I've told you, I'm Norwegian!"

"Same difference."

Christmas Day

Christmas had been somewhat of an anticlimax in the Speer, Rothstein, Andersen, and for sure, the Miles family. Lowell's Uncle Norwood and his family came over for dinner and they opened their gifts. After dinner, Lowell called Helen and they talked about what they'd received for Christmas. Helen was very excited to show Lowell how she looked wearing the pearl necklace he had given her. Lowell thanked her for the wristwatch and writing set.

He said, "I suppose you want me to write to you all the time now?"

"Oh Lowell, you sometimes drive me crazy!"

"Would you like to come over for awhile later this afternoon?" he asked.

"Well, I guess that would be okay, but why don't you plan to come over and pick me up and have a cup of eggnog with us?"

"Okay," he said. "How about 6:00?"

"That would be fine; I'll see you about 6:00."

As he hung up and looked at his new watch he thought, *three hours until I see her again, I guess I can wait.*

Back in the living room Uncle Norwood asked, "Well, Lowell, what do you think you will be flying?"

"Oh I don't know, our instructor said it depended on what they need at the time, but most of us guys want to fly fighters," replied Lowell.

"Yes, I suppose they are the glamorous thing to fly, but aren't bombers safer?"

Lowell's aunt said, "Oh for gosh sakes Norwood, let's don't talk about the war now at this time!"

The day wore on with David and Diane playing with their toys, Mom, Dad, Uncle Norwood and Aunt Vera talking in general terms about living back in Nebraska, the people they knew, Christmases they had known and of course the war. Lowell thought that 6:00 would never come.

Lowell said, "I think I will go over and get Helen, she wanted to come over and see everyone."

Mom said, "That will be fine son; we would all like to see her."

As Lowell drove to Helen's house he thought of the next few months, basic flight training, and if he made it, advanced. He wondered if he would make it, and what he would be flying. He also thought of Jew and

Betty's wedding. What a time this had been – Christmas, setting a date with Helen and Jew's wedding.

As he pulled into the Speer's driveway, the front door opened and Helen came out to greet him. He walked up on the porch, took her in his arms, said, "Merry Christmas darling," and kissed her.

"Merry Christmas to you too darling," she replied.

When they entered the house, Mr. Speer got up and came over to shake Lowell's hand and wish him a Merry Christmas then said, "A cup of Christmas cheer for you Lowell?"

"Yes, please sir."

"Now just one minute there soldier, I'm not your commanding officer so please don't call me sir, my name is George and maybe soon Dad."

Lowell could feel his face reddening and he looked at Helen who had diverted her eyes and said, "Well, I see miss blabber mouth has told you."

"Yes, and we couldn't be more pleased," said Mrs. Speer as she came over and gave Lowell a little hug.

The cup of Christmas cheer that Mr. Speer handed Lowell was heavy on the cheer. The first sip revealed to Lowell that it was generously spiked with whiskey.

Mr. Speer said, "Well, Lowell, have you talked to Myron today? I'll bet he is a nervous wreak."

"No, I haven't but I thought I would call him tonight."

They sat in the Speer's living room engaging in small talk for thirty minutes or so.

Finally Helen said, "Well, if we're going over to your house, maybe we had better get going, I don't want to be out too late tonight."

Leaving the house she took Lowell's arm as they crossed to the car parked in the driveway. Mr. and Mrs. Speer watched from the porch.

Mr. Speer said, "God, I hope that young man makes it through this war okay. It would kill Helen if anything happened to him."

"Oh George, don't even think like that," replied Mrs. Speer.

Myron's Wedding

Sunday, December 26 dawned chilly and wet after raining most of the night. It wasn't quite cold enough to snow with the temperature in the high thirties. Betty had hoped for a nice day for the wedding, but no such luck. She hadn't slept much that night, her mind jumping from one thing to another. *Have I finished everything for the wedding? I wonder how many people will show up? What will my wedding night be like? How will I react? I wonder if Myron will be as nervous as I am?* Then her thoughts raced back to the wedding and life after as a married woman.

Myron was experiencing many of the same thoughts and feelings. *How will I react on our wedding night? Will I perform adequately? Will I ruin how Betty feels towards me? Will I embarrass myself?* He kept telling himself that he was a normal young man and that he would fulfill his duties as a husband. He and Lowell had discussed this several times but always in a boyish joking manner and he would never admit that he was scared to death of what would happen on the wedding night.

Though it didn't make a lot of difference to him, Myron was glad the Methodist pastor of Betty's church had agreed to share the ceremony with a rabbi from the synagogue in Portland. It meant so much to his mother and father. Myron had arranged to hide his car at a friend's house to prevent any prankster from sabotaging it and Lowell would pick him up around two, an hour before the service.

At exactly two Myron heard his mom call, "Myron, Lowell's here, are you ready?"

"Yea Mom, have him wait, I'll be right down."

Jew and Low had succumbed to the girls request to wear their uniforms, though there wasn't much choice. As they left the house, Mrs. Rothstein watched them go down the walk and sobbed when she thought of all the times she had seen the two little boys in various outfits do the same thing. Her husband came up behind here and put his arm around her shoulders.

"It will be just fine dear; he is not our little Myron anymore, but he is still our son."

*****

At the church, Lowell drove around the back and they entered through a side door into the pastor's study. Myron flopped down on a small couch and Lowell took a chair across the room.

They sat in silence for awhile and Myron said, "Low, ya know, I thought about inviting you and Helen to go on our honeymoon with us."

"Are you crazy Jew; that's the stupidest idea you've ever had!"

"Yea I know, but we have always done things together, so I thought that might be okay."

"Well, you're on your own with this one fella. I won't be there to get you through it."

Myron just smiled and heaved a sigh and said, "I guess I can do it by myself."

They both laughed and fell silent again.

About ten minutes before the ceremony was to start, the pastor and the rabbi came into the office and asked if they were ready. Myron responded that he was as ready as he would ever be and they all laughed. After a few minutes of small talk, the pastor said, "Well, it's that time."

The four men walked into the sanctuary and Myron was somewhat overwhelmed by the number of people in the church. He immediately noticed all the young men in the various uniforms of their service. He had included many of his friends from school on his guest list, although he didn't know how many would come. As the ceremony began Myron's cousin joined them on the steps to the altar and the processional started with the flower girls and then Helen looking so beautiful that Lowell thought he would cry. Next came Betty's sister followed by Betty and her father. Lowell didn't remember much about the ceremony but did remember to give Jew Betty's ring in time. After being declared husband and wife and following the obligatory kiss, there was the traditional Jewish toast. Next came the breaking of the glass, the recessional, then out into the narthex and up to the social hall. Everyone was all smiles. There was a great deal of laughter by the men and many handkerchiefs displayed by the women.

At the reception, Myron and Lowell had time to renew some friendships with high school buddies. Lowell was surprised to see Gerald Olson there. He hadn't thought about him for some time. Gerald had joined the navy, had just finished boot camp in San Diego and had gotten home a few days before Christmas.

Lowell came up to him and said, "Well swabby, how are things in the navy?"

"Just fine fly boy! How are things in the air?"

They both laughed and walked over to the punch bowl and poured themselves a drink.

Lowell asked, "Where are you going next?"

"To the east coast for signalman's school," replied Gerald.

Lowell told Gerald he was heading to basic flight training, then suggested that they get together in the next day or so.

The next few days went by very fast and included visiting some more with Gerald and meeting his girl friend Norma Russell. December 29 came all too soon and he had to return to the Army Air Corps. Parting with Helen was so painful that he thought he would never survive, but survive it he did.

Myron enjoyed instructing the new cadets more than he thought he would. Much of the time he wondered if he was a natural born teacher and that after the war, maybe he should go into teaching. However, he still wanted to get into combat so he decided he would continue to request transferring to a combat unit as often as regulations permitted.

BASIC FLIGHT TRAINING

On the train ride back to Lemoore, Lowell could hardly think of any thing but Helen and when he would see her again. At one point he thought that he should have married her when he was home and realized what a crazy idea that was. Weddings took a great deal of planning, particularly for the women. When the train pulled into Medford, he wanted to jump off and catch the next train back, but he knew that was an even crazier idea. He knew he would get over it soon and must think of what was in store for him in the next few weeks.

Upon arriving at Lemoore, Lowell saw an army bus sitting at the curb. He walked up to the sergeant leaning against the fender and inquired as to whether the bus was going out to the field. The sergeant, pushing himself off the fender, replied in a very casual tone, "Yea, cadet, I'm waiting for a shipment in from Santa Ana, are you one of them?"

Lowell noticed that the sergeant had a double row of ribbons signifying he was a veteran of many campaigns and an air corps cadet did not particularly impress him. Lowell replied, "Yes sergeant, I'm probably part of that shipment, I just finished Primary at Santa Ana before Christmas."

"Well, I think there will be room. There's only supposed to be fifteen or twenty guys."

Lowell picked up his bag and walked over to a bench and sat down as the sergeant leaned against the fender again and continued to clean his fingernails. It became apparent that another train had just pulled in by the number of air cadets that came walking out of the station.

As he was casually looking them over, a falsetto voice said, "Are you looking for a good time soldier?"

Lowell turned and looked into the smiling face of Charlie and replied "Not from you fella! How are you Charlie?"

"Just fine, and how was your Christmas leave?"

"Swell, I got my friend Jew married and set a date for my wedding. How was yours?"

"Oh you know, family, a lot of food, presents and visiting friends. I did write to Linda and got an answer just before I left. We kind of talked about going steady, if that's possible when were so far apart."

"Far apart? Santa Ana isn't that far. Maybe you can get open post and go up and see her."

"Yea, we talked about that, but I'll bet we're going to be very busy down here."

"Have you heard anything of Bill?" Lowell asked.

"No, not since we left Santa Ana."

Charlie joined Lowell on the bench and they continued to get caught up. So much had happened to Lowell in just ten days that it seemed like months since he had seen Charlie. This was a different world all together than what he had just come from yet he had a feeling towards Charlie that was as close as some of the friends he had known since childhood.

As they talked, they observed many cadets boarding the bus and Charlie said, "I guess if we want a seat we had better get aboard."

"Yea, the sergeant said there should be room, but I guess you're right."

They got off the bench, picked up their bags and asked the sergeant if it would be all right if they came aboard and he just nodded his head.

Charlie said, "We don't get a lot of respect here I guess."

Lowell replied, "Did you see those rows of ribbons on his chest, I don't suppose much impresses him at all. He probably has seen it all and a bunch of air cadets are not a very impressive sight."

They both smiled as they walked to the back of the bus. About half way one of the seated cadets looked up and said, "Hi you guys; how's everything going?"

They looked down and recognized a guy from their class at Santa Ana.

"Fine," Lowell replied, "How's it going with you, did you have a good leave?"

"Yea, I got married when I was home and it was sure tough to leave."

"Boy I know what you mean," replied Lowell. "Although I didn't get married."

Charlie and Lowell found two seats across the aisle from each other and sat down.

"Well, tell me about this date you set," asked Charlie.

"Well, just before I left after Jew and Betty's wedding, I told Helen that we ought to think about doing the same thing and she agreed. Well, I didn't exactly say it, she said it but I agreed."

"So she set the date huh?"

"Well, kind of, but I was the one who brought it up."

Charlie laughed just as the sergeant started the engine and pulled away from the curb. The ride out to the base took a short time but Lowell and Charlie had time to discuss what they thought might be in store for them.

As the bus passed by the MP station at the gate, the sergeant yelled out, "Okay men, I'll call out the various classes as we get to the area."

After several stops where cadets got off, the sergeant finally called, "43-L."

Charlie and Lowell and the other cadet from their class yelled, "Here!"

The driver stopped and the three got off in front of the orderly room. Upon entering the orderly room and showing the corporal at the desk their orders, they were instructed to have a seat until the sergeant returned from taking two more cadets to their barracks and then he would take them to theirs. In a few minutes, a very tall sergeant came into the room, walked over to the desk, and picked up their orders.

Checking their names on a clip board he turned to them and said, "Okay Cadets Andersen and Smith, would you come with me please."

As they walked down the row of barracks Lowell asked, "Sergeant, has a Cadet Minor checked in yet?"

The sergeant consulted his clipboard and said, "Yes, this afternoon, he's in the same barracks as you gentlemen."

Charlie and Lowell looked at each other smiling.

Charlie said, "I hope he's in our room."

To which the sergeant replied, "No, he's just across the hall from you."

The sergeant led them into the barracks and down the hall to room A.

"Well, here it is, your home for the next few weeks. That is, if you make it for the next few weeks." Both Charlie and Lowell looked at him with some surprise and realized he was pulling their legs a little. They thanked him and entered.

The sergeant said, "Put your things down and go to the supply room and draw bedding. It's just next to the barracks."

"Thank you sergeant," said Lowell

After choosing a bunk and throwing their bags down, they walked to the hall just in time to see Bill coming in the back door. He broke out in a large smile seeing them.

"Hi guys, are you in this barracks too?"

Shaking hands with him Lowell replied, "Yea, well someone had to help you with your home work."

Charlie joined in the good-natured ribbing.

"Yea and they thought we might keep you from getting into too much trouble on open post."

After a few more minutes of good natured ribbing, Bill said, "Say, I don't think too much is going on tonight. When we're settled in, do you want to meet and go to the PX for a beer?" Looking at Charlie he added, "Or something else, in your case, Charlie."

"That sounds swell," they both responded.

Before going out, Lowell reached into his foot locker, took out his writing kit and began a letter to Helen.

Dearest Helen,

Well, we are here, I must say that it was the hardest thing I have ever done to leave Drayville and you, but I realized I had to. We are going to meet our instructors tomorrow and I suppose begin to fly. I'm in the barracks with Bill Minor and Charlie again, they are such great guys; I hope they make it.

I want you to know that our decision is the best thing that has ever happened to me. I wish we could go ahead with it now, but of course we can't.

I know basic will be very hard and will take a lot of my time and energy, but I promise to write as often as possible.

As always to you I give my love and life,

Lowell

*****

The next day started like all days in the army. The barracks cadre came through at 0500 blowing his whistle and yelling for the cadets to rise and shine. They fell out, were marched to the mess hall for breakfast and returned to the barracks to clean and tidy it up for inspection. After surviving the inspection they were marched to the theater for a greeting by Major Dennis, the training commander.

"ATTENTION!"

All the cadets jumped up to comply. Major Dennis came on stage.

"Rest; take your seats!" he said.

After the cadets were seated, he gave them what had become the typical pep talk and admonishment to do their best and they would all become United States Army Air Corps pilots.

"Men at this stage of your training, your chances of earning your wings are greatly increased. Most cadets who were destined to fail have already been washed out. Good luck. Carry on."

"ATTENTION!"

The cadets sprang to their feet again as the major left the stage and a captain came to the podium introducing himself as Captain Sanders, the training officer. He gave them a quick overview of what they would be doing in basic and then directed them to fall out in their class formation to continue with the day's training. The cadets were marched to the supply and equipment room where they were issued their flight gear consisting of leather helmet, coveralls, gloves, and boots. They were all aware that it seemed as if they were treated with a little more respect than they were in previous training sessions.

For the first few days of basic they were in the classroom again.

They learned about the Vultee BT-15 *Valiant*, which would be their basic training aircraft. They also reviewed basic navigation, take-off and landing procedures and basic radio procedures. It was time to report to the flight line for their first ride in the powerful Vultee BT-15. The *Valiant*, unlike the open cockpit trainers in primary, had a closed cockpit, was all aluminum and had a 450 horsepower engine. Unlike primary where the instructors were mostly civilians, the instructors in basic were air corps officers. Lowell, Bill and three other cadets were assigned to a Lieutenant Clark. Lieutenant Clark had finished his training in the summer of 1943. He was not happy about his assignment as an instructor; however, as training progressed, he proved to be one of the best instructors in the program.

The first day they reported to the flight line and Lieutenant Clark said, "You will continue to work on your basic flying skills including aerobatics maneuvers, formation flying, instrument flying and night flying. As Major Dennis told you, most of you will make it through this phase of your training. That is not to say it is impossible to wash out.

"You will be checked every few weeks by Captain Sanders and if you don't measure up, wash out you will! Who wants to be first for a check ride?"

Everyone looked at Lowell and he hesitantly raised his hand and said, "I'll try it!"

"All right, let's go."

Lowell fastened the leg straps on his parachute and climbed into the front cockpit. Lieutenant Clark, in the back cockpit, motioned for Lowell to plug in his headphones. He then went over all the instruments with Lowell.

Talking into the microphone he said, "I'll take her off and then let you fly her awhile."

With that Lieutenant Clark went through the startup procedures and taxied the aircraft out to the runway. Lowell could feel the added power of the BT-15 over the previous plane he had flown. Lieutenant Clark kept a running commentary of what he was doing.

At the end of the runway he said, "Okay, here we go."

After take-off, Lieutenant Clark said, "Okay Andersen, take it and let's see what you've got."

Lowell was not sure what he meant but he took the controls and flew a few minutes on a straight course,

The lieutenant said, "Let's see a stall."

Lowell pulled back on the stick without increasing power and the BT-15 started to climb. Suddenly the engine begin to scream in protest and the speed dropped off. Reaching stall speed the plane fell off on the left wing. Lowell pushed the stick forward and added power. In a few minutes the aircraft gained flight configuration again and leveled out.

"Very good Andersen," Lieutenant Clark said over the intercom.

They did a few more basic maneuvers and then he told Lowell to land. The in-class instruction continued in basic as well as the physical training. The cadets were expected to do push ups, run several miles every day, and be able to lift their body weight in barbells. This did not present a problem to Lowell because of his physical fitness, but several of the cadets did have a problem, including Bill Minor.

The first new flying challenge for the cadets was formation flying. This was one of the most dangerous aspects of cadet training. They were expected to fly in a two-plane formation and were always encouraged to fly as close to the other plane a possible. On the first day of formation flying, Lieutenant Clark told Lowell to climb aboard. Lieutenant Johnson took Bill Minor up for the first attempt at this maneuver. In the air, Lieutenant Clark told Lowell to climb up and level off just below the other plane, flown by Bill with Lieutenant Johnson in the back seat. When Lowell thought he was in perfect position he leveled off only to be told by Lieutenant Clark to get in closer.

"Come on Andersen, that's your buddy over their, don't you want to meet him?"

Lowell put in a little left rudder and stick and moved the aircraft a little closer.

"Get in tight Andersen!"

When Lowell thought the wings would surely touch the lieutenant said, "That's better, now hold that position."

The two aircraft flew in the tight formation and Lowell sneaked a quick peek at Bill who was looking straight ahead until he suddenly glanced over at Lowell, which caused the planes to lurch a bit, and Lowell jerked the stick to the right moving the plane off several feet.

"All right Andersen, you've taken a look at Minor, now get back in formation."

Lowell did as he was ordered but vowed never again to turn his head to look at his wing man. Lieutenant Clark was in contact with Bill's instructor by radio and when they decided both cadets had had enough for one day, he ordered Lowell to break formation and return to base.

When they had both landed and gotten their briefings, they walked back to the ready room and Bill said, "What in the hell were you trying to do up there?"

Lowell replied, "Me, it was you who jerked the stick and almost flew into me!"

"Yea, I guess you're right, but when I glanced over and you were looking directly at me, it startled me and I lost my concentration. Let's don't do that again."

When they entered the ready room, Charlie was sitting on the couch and he immediately jumped up.

"How was it?"

"Piece of cake," replied Bill.

"Yea I bet, how did you do Lowell?"

"Well, I did just fine until my wing man nearly flew in to me."

"Oh bull, you caused me to and besides we didn't nearly fly into each other."

Before Charlie could ask what that was all about, his instructor came in.

"Smith you ready?"

Charlie looked at Bill and Lowell with a very pained expression.

As he ran out the door they heard him say, "Yes sir, I am!"

Lowell liked the challenge of formation flying and with his depth perception and athletic skill, had no problem mastering it. Lieutenant Clark constantly complemented him on his skill and after one flight told him he was going to make a great pilot.

One night after chow, Charlie came in and said that he had just talked to Sergeant Miller and was told that they would be getting passes for the weekend. He said that he was planning to go up to Santa Maria and see Linda and would Lowell and Bill like to go along. Lowell didn't take long to accept his invitation.

Bill said. "No, I'm a little worried about instrument navigation and I think I'll stay in and study."

That night Lowell wrote another letter Helen.

Dearest Helen,

This weekend we will be getting passes and Charlie and I are going up to see his girl friend Linda Jensen. Remember I told you about her? She's a very beautiful girl just our age and a junior at the local college. I think Charlie is very much in love with her, and from the way she looked at him when we were there at Thanksgiving, it's mutual. I sure like Charlie a lot; sometimes it makes me feel guilty that maybe I have replaced Jew with him as my closest friend.

How is Betty getting along? I imagine she is missing Jew a great deal. Is school still going to your satisfaction? Watch out for those freshman and 4F boys, they've got the pick of the litter these days.

Lowell described his training at that point, how exciting it was to practice formation flying and the complement paid him from Lieutenant Clark. He signed off as usual.

As always to you I give my love and life,
Lowell

The weekend finally came and Charlie and Lowell caught the shuttle into town where they boarded the Greyhound for the three-hour ride to Santa Maria. The boys passed the time on the bus by sleeping and reading magazines.

At one point, Charlie put his magazine down and said, "Lowell, how did you propose to Helen?"

"Oh, so this isn't just any ordinary visit?"

"Well, no. I – well I – –."

Before he could finish, Lowell turned in his seat and said, "If you're going to ask Linda to marry you, why the devil did you want me along?"

"Well, I just thought you might give me moral support."

"Yea, I understand, it is a big decision. Have you talked about it at all, I mean have you, well you know talked about love and everything?"

"Oh Yea, we have professed our love for each other."

"My God Charlie, you talk like some sixteenth century poet, have you told her you love her and that you can't stand to be away from her and that you – –."

"Oh come on Low, I'm not going to tell you everything we talk about or that is written about."

Lowell looked at his friend and smiled and said, "I think you are going to be just fine buddy, but don't stammer like I did and make her propose to you."

"No worry about that; I think your Helen is a much more outgoing girl than Linda, or at least it seems that way from what you said."

"Oh I don't know. The few times I've met Linda, I think she is a great deal like Helen and I hope that some day they will get to meet each other."

Charlie replied as he laid his head back, "Yea, I hope so too."

After the weekend in Santa Maria, basic flight training went on as usual. Lowell enjoyed the flying, but also the class work, particularly the navigation. He was always good in math and navigation involves a great deal of math. As per the training syllabus it was time for the cadets to go "under the hood." This meant that they would be in the rear cockpit of a trainer with the windows completely blacked out and would have to take-off, navigate a course, and get into landing position back at the field without ever seeing the ground. Lowell was chosen by Lieutenant Clark to be the first to attempt to do so.

"Okay Andersen, here is what we're going to do. I want you to lower the hood, set the compass and after take-off I'll turn the controls over to you and you follow my compass settings on a course. Think you can do it?"

"Yes sir, I think I can!" Lowell replied.

Lowell climbed into the BT-15 that was specially equipped for this exercise and closed the canopy. Lieutenant Clark said over the intercom that he would taxi out to the runway and take-off and when they were at altitude would turn it over to Lowell. The engine was already running. The fact that Lowell's palms were very sweaty had nothing to do with the very warm day. As they taxied across the apron and onto the runway, Lowell felt a moment of panic and thought for a minute about telling Lieutenant Clark that he was not ready.

Just then the lieutenant said, "Okay Andersen, here we go!"

Lowell looked at the gauges one more time as the lieutenant increased the power, released the brakes and began the take-off run. At the proper speed the tail lifted off. Again at the proper speed, the airplane lifted off the runway and Lowell felt the slight turn and climb to get to the proper area. Watching the gauges, Lowell could tell the rate of climb and course.

After they had been airborne for some time, Lieutenant Clark said through the intercom, "Okay Andersen, take her up to 3,000 feet and set a course of ninety-five degrees."

Lowell followed the lieutenant's instruction to the letter and after twenty or thirty minutes of flying with several course and altitude changes he said, "That's good Andersen. I'll take it now."

When they landed Lowell's flight suit was almost completely soaked with perspiration.

Lieutenant Clark said, "That was very good Andersen, you're now qualified for the instrument card. It will be awarded at the end of basic."

As Lowell entered the ready room, Bill and Charlie were there and they jumped up and ran to him asking, "How was it? Is it hard?"

Lowell answered with "Nah, it was a piece of cake."

To which Bill responded with, "Then why is your flight suit soaked with sweat, or is that piss?"

When Lowell got back to the barracks, showered and got ready for chow, it was time for mail call. He went to the mailroom and in his box were two letters, one from Helen and one from the twins.

Of course, he opened Helen's first and read it.

Dearest Lowell,

It's such good news that your training is going so well. Well, maybe it isn't if finishing on time and at the top of your class means you might be going overseas sooner. I dread the thought of you going into the war, but I have faith in you and God that everything will be OK.

I am sorry I took so long to answer your last letter (it had been five days since he got a letter from her) *but we had those things we call finals last week and I had to study a bit. Betty was in the same boat; she didn't get a letter off to Myron for several days.*

I guess the big news from here is that Betty got a letter from Myron and he said there might be a chance he could get an overseas assignment in a few months. I guess that is what all you guys want, but believe me darling, those of us at home would be very happy if you didn't, in spite of what all the current songs say about how proud we are of our service men who are serving overseas. Of course we are proud, but I'm sure if you go overseas, I will be terrified all the time.

Helen continued several more pages telling him about seeing the twins down town and that his mother invited her to Sunday dinner this week before signing off with:

Dearest, I love you now and forever,
Helen

Lowell opened the letter from the twins and read:

Hi Lowell,

Are you still flying those PT-19s? I hope you get to fly P-38s some day. I saw a movie about them and they look really keen.

Love,
David

Hi Lowell,

Are you still in the Army Air Corps? I bet is it fun to fly an airplane. I wish I could see you. I hope you are OK.

Love,
Diane

Lowell leaned back and had one of those terrible lonely feelings sweep over him. He realized his eyes had filled with tears as he thought about his little brother and sister.

Suddenly a loud voice said, "Man! That was the greatest experience I have had in a long time."

It was Bill just coming in from his blind flying course. Looking down at Lowell he got serious.

"Is anything wrong Lowell? You look like you've been crying."

"Nah, I just read a letter from my little brother and sister and got a little home sick I guess," he replied.

Bill said, "Yea, I know what you mean, I got a letter from my little sister last week and kind of clouded up too. As much as we used to fight, I really miss her."

Lowell replied, "Yea, I do too. Well, better clean up and go to chow. Did you see Charlie? Did he do okay?"

"I don't know where he is, but when he came off the flight line, he gave me a thumbs up."

At that point Charlie came into the room. Both Bill and Lowell could tell something was wrong as he sat down on his bunk and stared at floor.

Bill and Lowell looked at each other and Lowell said, "What's wrong Charlie?"

He looked up and said, "My little brother Robert was hit by a car on his bicycle and is in serious condition."

"Oh no," replied Bill.

Lowell said, "Is he going to make it?"

"I don't know. When I came off the flight line, they called me to the orderly room saying the chaplain wanted to see me. He told me about it and said that if I wanted to, I could get an emergency leave and go home."

"What are you going to do?" asked Lowell.

"Well the captain let me call home and I talked to my dad. He said there is some improvement and that maybe I should consider not coming. I talked to the captain about it and he said he would approve a leave, but that if I did, I would be put back a class and have to repeat a lot of stuff we've done so far."

"Yea, I guess that would be the logical thing to happen," replied Bill.

"Anyway my dad said over the phone that I should stay here and he would call in the next day or so and tell me how things are going. The chaplain and the captain suggested I should wait and if things got worse, then consider going home."

"Well, buddy, we're here if you need anything."

With that Charlie got up and shook hands with them and said thanks. They noticed his eyes filling again and both Lowell and Bill realized their eyes were filling as well.

It was not easy for Charlie to concentrate on the task at hand with the load he had to carry. Every waking minute he was thinking about his nine-year-old brother lying in the hospital unconscious. Charlie was from a very large family with six brothers and sisters. Like most Mormon families, they were very close and Charlie, as the oldest, had been responsible for some of the rearing of the younger children. He had almost decided to ask the captain for an emergency leave and go home and take the set back. He thought he would talk it over with Lowell and Bill that night and see what they thought.

After a not so hot flight, Charlie had returned to the ready room when a sergeant came in and asked for Cadet Smith. Charlie was sitting with Lowell.

He rose and said, "Here sergeant!"

"Report to the orderly room on the double," ordered the sergeant.

Charlie just froze and Lowell rose and took a hold of his arm.

"You want me to go with you Charlie?" asked Lowell.

"Yea, would you?"

"Sure."

As they walked to the orderly room, Lowell said, "Maybe it's good news."

"Yea, maybe."

When they entered the orderly room, the captain's door was open and the chaplain was sitting in his office. Charlie froze in the door and Lowell had to push him inside. The slight disturbance caused the captain and the chaplain to turn and see him.

The chaplain rose and with a very happy smile came towards Charlie and stuck out his hand while saying, "Good news Cadet Smith. I just got a call from your father and your brother is going to be just fine."

Charlie just stood there for a minute and then said, "Are you sure chaplain?"

"Yes I am. Your father said he has regained consciousness and there doesn't seem to be any indication of any permanent damage. He has a broken arm and three ribs, but they'll heal in time."

Charlie took the chaplain's hand and shook it vigorously saying, "Thank you chaplain, thank you very much!"

"You're welcome son, but remember, I didn't do anything. The Lord is the one you should thank. Your father said there was no need for you to come home at this time."

"That's good news. Thanks again and I will thank the Lord Sunday at chapel."

As they left the orderly room, Charlie said, "Boy, am I relieved. Ya know, we have a big family, but every kid was raised as an individual and Robert is kind of special to me. He is the next oldest boy."

"Do you have other brothers?"

"Yes, the youngest is a boy. We have three boys and four girls."

They walked back to the barracks and told Bill and several of the other guys who were waiting on the steps. Charlie was well liked by all the men. He had helped several of them master complicated phases of their training.

Basic went on and with out the distraction, Charlie again dove in to training. As the end neared, they were all wondering where they would go for advanced training. The mystery was solved when with about ten days left, the orders were posted on the bulletin board. Lowell, Charlie, and Bill again lined up at the board and when they got close enough to read the names, Charlie turned around and said, "Well, Cadet Andersen, I guess I'm not done with you yet! We're going to Douglas."

Bill called to them, "Can you see my name?"

Charlie scanned the orders, turned around and said, "I can't find your name, but you are not on the list for Douglas."

When they could read all the orders, they discovered that they only had four days to report to Douglas. They found out that the train trip would take one day, leaving only three days travel leave. As they were walking back to the barracks, Charlie said, "Low, why don't we stop in Santa Maria and see Linda?"

"Oh, I don't want to interfere with your visit."

"No, that's okay. Linda would love to have you."

"Okay, I'll think about it."

Lowell knew he didn't have enough time to get to Drayville and see Helen and the thought of reporting early or sitting around the Lemoore wasn't very appealing to him.

The next day he said, "Ya know Charlie, I think I will take you up on your offer."

"That's great Low."

Basic ended with little ceremony except for the colonel's very short speech, a couple of pats on their backs by Lieutenant Clark and wishes for good luck.

*****

The boys picked up their new orders, shouldered the bags and headed for the bus that would take them to Douglas with a short stop in Santa Maria. In route, they slept some, talked some and read. However, Lowell thought that Charlie was acting kind of funny. He would break out in smiles for no apparent reason and seemed more animated than usual. He chalked this up to excitement in anticipation of seeing Linda. He thought he probably would feel the same if he was going to see Helen.

When the bus pulled into the station in Santa Maria, Charlie was squirming in his seat trying to see into the station. Lowell thought that seemed odd. He was usually a very reserved guy. The bus pulled in the loading area and Lowell looked out and saw a woman that looked so much like Helen that his heart jumped. He suddenly looked at the woman with her and it was Linda.

"My God, there's Helen with Linda!"

Charlie said, "Really?"

Lowell looked at him and he was grinning from ear to ear. "You devil you, what did you do?"

"Nothing, are you just going to sit here on this bus or get off?"

Lowell jumped up and followed the crowd down the aisle and off the bus. Helen came running into his arms and they kissed and held each other longingly. Linda and Charlie were engaged in a like activity.

Finally, Lowell asked Helen, "How did you get here?"

"What, you want me to go home?"

Lowell grabbed her in another long embrace until they became aware that the bus was getting ready to leave.

Charlie said, "Well, let's get out of here."

Walking to the car Helen explained that she had gotten a letter from Linda asking her to call and gave her the phone number.

"When I called her Linda suggested I come down and surprise you," said Helen.

Lowell turned to Linda and asked, "How did you know her address?"

"Charlie got it for me."

Lowell glanced at Charlie with a questioning look.

"When I had the idea and you agreed to come with me, I got it off a letter you had left on your bunk."

The three days, or more accurately, two-and-a-half, went all too fast. Helen was sharing Linda's room with her and Charlie and Lowell were sharing Linda's brother's room. They laughed about sharing a bed and promised they would not say anything to the guys. In the army, it was strictly against regulations for two men to sleep together.

The couples became very well acquainted and had a great time, mainly doing nothing except strolling in the park, going to a movie, and eating Mrs. Jensen's great food.

Finally it was time to leave for Douglas. Lowell had that empty feeling again and would not let go of Helen as they stood on the platform of the train station. Finally the conductor made the last call for boarding and he was forced to let her go. As the train pulled out of the station and the boys could no longer see their girls, they sat down.

Lowell said, "Boy that was one of the hardest things I have ever done. Even harder than when I left after Christmas."

"Yea, I know what you mean. Oh well, we will see them in a few weeks after we graduate," said Charlie.

They rode silently for some time and then Lowell said, "Come on, let's go to the club car and get a coke or something!"

"Okay," replied Charlie.

As they entered the club car, they noticed an officer sitting at one of the tables. He had on the wings and gold bar of a second lieutenant in the air corps. They walked by, both nodded and greeted him with a "sir."

He looked up at them and said, "You guys want to join me?"

Lowell looked at Charlie and they both nodded and said, "Yes sir, thank you."

The pilot moved his hand and said, "Oh drop the sir, I've only been an officer for about ten days."

They all laughed and Charlie said, "Are you going on leave or coming off?"

"Just coming off," replied the lieutenant. "I finished my training at Williams and I'm being sent to Roswell for transition to B-17s."

"We're going to Douglas for multi-engine training."

"Yea, I really wanted fighters, but with the war going the way it is, they seem to need bomber pilots."

Charlie said, "We were dumb enough to choose multi-engine."

"To each his own," replied the lieutenant.

Lowell stuck out his hand and said, "I'm Lowell Andersen and this is Charlie Smith, we just finished basic at Lemoore."

"I'm Victor Porter, that's were I did my basic."

Charlie said, "Can we buy you another beer?"

"No that's okay. I don't want to report in half stinko."

All three laughed with that knowing nod. Just then the steward came up and said, "Can I get you boys something to drink?"

Lowell and Charlie both ordered cokes, then Lowell turned to Victor and asked, "How was it at Williams?"

"Much more intense. You not only practice what you were taught in basic, but also begin learning a lot more about flying an airplane. But, if you guys have come this far, I imagine you will make it okay."

"Did they wash out very many?" Lowell asked.

"I think only two from my class. One was in my barracks. They washed him out because he failed the Naval Identification Test, twice."

"Really!" Lowell and Charlie responded in unison.

The boys visited with Victor for several hours and Lowell said, "Ya know, I think I'll go back to my seat and see if I can get a little sleep before dinner."

Charlie said, "That's a good idea, I think I'll do that too."

"Well, I'm too excited to sleep so I think I'll stay here and have another beer. To heck with my mom! I'm a big boy now."

They all three laughed and Lowell and Charlie left the club car and made their way back to their seats.

Lowell said, "It doesn't sound too tough, advanced I mean."

"Yea, I think we'll make it through," replied Charlie.

As the train rolled across the eastern California landscape, Lowell could not get to sleep so he reached into his bag, got out his writing kit and started a letter to his folks.

Dear Mom and Dad,

Well here I am on my way to Douglas for advanced. I sure had a good time in Santa Maria at Charlie's girl friends house. Boy was I surprised to see Helen! She said you guys knew all about it.

We are in Eastern California. Boy I never thought there could be so much deserted looking land. When you think of California, you sure don't think of desert. I guess Death Valley is in California.

How are things going at the shop Dad? With this rationing getting worse, I suppose the gas sales are really down. Oh well, maybe it won't last forever.

I got David and Diane's letter just before I left basic. I really laughed when they described their victory gardens. I can just see them fighting over what to plant and how to water it. Is it growing yet?

Lowell wrote a little more about the leave at Linda's and how much he enjoyed spending time with Helen before closing.

Give the kids a big hug for me. Helen said she would come by and see you as soon as she gets home.

All my Love,

Lowell

After he finished he laid his head on the back of the seat and closed his eyes for a minute. The next thing he knew, Charlie was poking him in the ribs.

"Do you want to go get something to eat?"

"Sure, what time is it?"

"It's 1230, chow time," replied Charlie.

They again made their way to the club car and as they entered, saw Victor sitting by himself again. He motioned for them to join him, sliding around to make room.

"Well, you guys get a little nap?"

"Yea we did," replied Charlie.

They asked for hamburgers and cokes and continued to pump Victor about what to expect at Douglas. As they ate, the conversation covered the whole spectrum from school, sports, girl friends, parents, and favorite teachers, non-favorite teachers and of course where they hoped to be sent after training.

Victor asked, "If it's not being too nosy, why did you guys choose multi-engine?"

Charlie and Lowell looked at each other and Lowell said, "Well, we thought that after the war there might be a chance that we could catch on with the airlines and that multi-engine would give us a better chance."

Victor thought about that for a minute and said, "I never thought of that. I enlisted in the air corps because I could not imagine being a ground-pounder and living in the mud."

The boys ate, talked and all of them had a beer after dinner. Time passed and the club car emptied without them noticing it. Finally the steward came over and asked, "Can I get you boys anything else, we're about to close for the afternoon."

They looked at him with some disbelief and checked their watches.

It was nearly 1500 and they had been visiting for nearly two and half-hours.

"Boy, the time really flew by," replied Lowell.

"Yea," said Victor, "I guess I had better get a little sleep too. What time do you guys get in to Douglas?"

They looked at each other and Charlie said, "I think it's around ten tonight."

They bid Victor goodbye and returned to their car and sat down.

Charlie said, "Well I'm going to try that sleeping thing again. Good night."

Lowell nodded and laid his head back, thinking about Helen and what lay ahead of him. He had soon fallen asleep.

Advanced Training, Douglas, Arizona

Upon arrival in Douglas after 2200 and arranging transportation out to the field, Lowell, Charlie and the two other cadets who had been on the train with them had some difficulty in finding a place to sleep for the rest of the night. They were finally able to locate the area where they were supposed to be housed. A very sleepy supply clerk issued them bedding and the sergeant in the orderly room asked them their names and gave them their barracks and room assignments. Charlie, Lowell and a cadet from basic, Homer Driscoll, were assigned to the same room. The rooms were much the same as those at Lemoore so it didn't take them long to choose their bunks and flop down. There wasn't much conversation that night. Lowell didn't even think about getting out his writing kit.

The next day started a little differently than other days in the army. A sergeant came into the barracks knocking on the doors of each room.

"Time to get up gentleman. Formation in fifteen minutes."

As they fell in a sergeant cadre came out of the orderly room followed by an officer, called them to attention, had them count off, turned to the officer, saluted rather lackadaisically, and reported that two cadets were missing.

"Stand easy cadets, I'm Lieutenant Chester. Welcome to Douglas Army Air Corps Training Base," he said. "I will be one of your instructors while you're here. Now, let's get first things first: chow. After chow, you will return to the barracks and do those things every man in the army does, and then we will march you to the theater for an official welcome from Colonel Gaelic. Take over sergeant!"

The sergeant called the cadets to attention, saluted the lieutenant, gave the men a left face command and marched them to the chow hall. As they were eating the men were permitted to visit with each other; this was a large departure from the first day in the other levels of their training.

Charlie said, "Boy this is different from basic isn't it?"

"It sure is," Homer said. "Where is the obnoxious cadre that usually yells and bangs to wake us up?"

Lowell said, "Well Homer, I bet we can find one if you really miss it that much."

They all laughed and asked questions of each other related to their arrival, how they got to the base, and so forth.

Another cadet from their Lemoore class asked, "Didn't you guys take a stop over somewhere on the way?"

"Yea, we went through Santa Maria and visited Charlie's girl friend," said Lowell.

"That's right, but Lowell's girl was there too. I thought he might go AWOL for a few days," said Charlie.

"Bull, I was the one who had to drag you onto the train," Lowell replied.

"Well I guess we had better finish this lovely meal and get back to the barracks," added Pete Tolson, another cadet from Lemoore.

The cadets finished their breakfast, walked back to the barracks and began to straighten up.

Dressing in the appropriate uniform they got ready to fall out when they heard, a loud "ATTENTION IN THE BARRACKS."

It was the sergeant who had marched them to chow and this was reminiscent of barracks inspections during other phases of their training. All the cadets stood at attention beside their bunks as the lieutenant walked through inspecting bunks, lockers and how they had displayed their uniforms on the clothing racks. When he was finished the sergeant called them all out into the hall where the lieutenant proceeded to give them a very good chewing out for being so sloppy. When he was finished he ordered them to fall out in the company street. As they were being marched to the theater to meet Colonel Gaelic, Lowell wondered about what had just occurred. Was it just to make a point or should they be ready for anything that might come along just as they had during other phases of their training?

They entered the theater, sat, and waited for the colonel. After several minutes, the expected command of ATTENTION was shouted from the back of the room and all cadets immediately came to a rigid attention. As the colonel mounted the stage he issued the "SEATS" command and the cadets took their seats.

Colonel Gaelic was a rather tall slender man in his early forties. Welcoming them to Douglas, he gave them a brief outline of what they would be doing in this phase of their training and wished them all good luck. Some one repeated the ATTENTION command as the colonel left the room.

A captain entered the stage and said, "Okay men, form up in the street. The sergeant will march you back to your barracks where you will change into flight gear. You will be taken to the flight line to meet your instructors and your new training planes. Take over sergeant!"

"Yes sir! ATTENTION!"

All the cadets again jumped to their feet as the captain left the stage. After changing into their flight gear, Lowell realized how hot it was in Douglas, Arizona even though it was early March. He had barely walked out of the barracks when perspiration began to run down his back. He couldn't imagine what it was going to be like with his helmet and parachute on.

"Boy, it is really hot here," he said to Charlie as they walked to the ready room.

"It sure is!" Charlie replied.

The sergeant commanded them to fall in, called them to attention, gave them a left face and a "Forward! March!" and proceeded to march them to the flight line. When they marched around the ready room, and got their first glimpse of the aircraft they would be flying in advanced training, they all hesitated a beat. It looked strange after the single engine planes they had previously flown. It was a short, high nosed twin-engine plane that had the look of a frumpy old lady. It was evident that they were all questioning themselves as to why they had chosen multi-engine.

The sergeant marched them to the supply room to draw their flight gear and then marched them to the flight line. He called out the various names to step forward and introduced them to their instructors. Lowell and Charlie along with another cadet had drawn a Lieutenant Paddock as their instructor, a short slim fellow with a continuous frown on his face. He bid them at ease and began to introduce himself and the trainer.

"Gentleman, this aircraft behind me is the Cessna UC-78 *Bobcat* in which you will be doing the majority of your flying here at Douglas. It is affectionately called the *Bamboo Bomber* by other cadets, but you will never refer to it as that in my presence. Is that understood?"

All the cadets answered in unison, "Yes sir!"

"All right then; who wants to be first to take a ride?"

The cadets looked around and Charlie said, "Go ahead Lowell. You were always first in basic."

Lowell gave him a dirty look and raised his hand.

Lieutenant Paddock said, "Okay cadet, get in your flight gear and climb aboard."

As Lowell complied with his direction, he thought, *Will I always be first?*

Lieutenant Paddock had Lowell climb into the right seat and began to explain the different instruments. He went through the engine startup procedures, started them, and taxied out to the runway. Lowell could feel the difference between the twin-engine aircraft and the single-engine craft he had flown. With two engines to control, it would take a lot more concentration. The ride was fairly uneventful except Lowell thought he would never be able to watch all the gauges, keep the throttles in the proper position for the engines to work together and still fly the plane. Lieutenant Paddock let him take the controls for a few minutes and the wheel felt so much different from a stick that he thought it was like starting all over again. The lieutenant assured him he would catch on and have no trouble flying the twin-engine craft.

That night as they turned out the lights, Charlie asked, "How did you do with the first ride?"

Lowell answered, "I think I have a lot to learn."

It was several days before the cadets got back in to the *Bobcat*. Most of their time was taken up with class work centering on multi-engine flight, navigation, formation flying and the inevitable Link Trainer.

The Link Trainer was a wooden structure with a hood over it and a steering wheel to control. There was a compass, a set of headphones and a microphone to communicate with the instructor who had control of where the cadet was going to be placed in relation to the destination, which was the airport. The instructor would set up a navigation problem centered on a certain line and instruct the cadet to follow a course back to base. The cadet was informed of how he was doing by a series of sounds over the earphones.

One night as they lay in their bunks Charlie said, "I think if I have to spend much more time in that dammed Link Trainer under the hood listening to all those dots and dashes and the instructions, I will ask to be washed out!"

Lowell and Homer rose up in their bunks and looked with some surprise at Charlie.

Homer said, "Why Charlie Smith, I didn't think you even knew any cuss word. Besides, I have never thought of you as a stupid person. What do you mean by asking to be washed out?"

"Yea, well I couldn't have lived around you guys for as long as I have without learning a few cuss words! You know what I mean though. I'm just frustrated with having to climb into that hot box and pretending to fly."

They all laughed and Lowell reached in to his footlocker and got out his writing kit.

Charlie looked over at him and said, "That's a good idea, I think I will write to Linda too."

Lowell replied, "I'm not writing to Helen, I'm writing to Myron."

Charlie just shrugged and reached for his kit.

Dear Jew,

How are things in the great State of Texas? I sure know what you mean about the hot weather. It has been in the high eighties every since we got here. Boy, do I long for some of that good old Oregon rain. I guess I didn't know how lucky I was to be in California all this time.

Well how is every thing with you? Are you still training good navigators? I hope to get a good one. Wouldn't it be funny if I got a navigator you had trained? That is if I make it through this phase.

Have you heard from Betty lately? I don't know if you knew, but on transition from basic to here, we stopped in Santa Maria at Charlie's girl's place and was I surprised to find Helen there. She says that she and Betty see each other nearly every day. The bad news is that she said they got word that Vernon Dickerson was missing in action. I guess he joined the air corps and ended up as a gunner on a B-24 in the 8th. I hope he comes through OK. I guess missing is better than killed although sometimes it ends up the same.

Have you had any better luck in getting an overseas assignment? On one hand I hope you do and on the other I hope you don't, though they read us some statistics on how many men are killed in training and I guess if your number is up it doesn't matter.

Well enough good news, it is almost lights out and I had better close. By the way, any luck on getting a leave in the next month or so? As you recall, there is a little function in Drayville I would like to have you attend. We haven't set a firm date yet, but I think it will be around the first week in June.

Hope to hear from you soon.

Your friend for life,

Low

Lowell put the letter in an envelope, sealed it and lay back on his bunk just as the lights out command was heard in the hall. He lay there awhile thinking about the great times he and Jew had when they were kids.

Looking over at Charlie, he asked, "Do you ever think about when you were a little kid and things you did?"

"Yea, all the time, I had a great childhood."

"Will you guys shut up with this *old times* discussion and go to sleep!" said Homer.

Lowell and Charlie both laughed and rolled over to sleep.

*****

Advanced training continued at a hurried pace with class work on navigation, formation flying, aircraft identification and more and more flying. The word around was that they would be cutting training a little short because of the need for bomber pilots. The air war in Europe was in full swing with daily bombings and the loss rate was climbing.

One day as they were walking back to the barracks after noon chow, Homer said, "Did you guys hear about that raid last week? They lost over a hundred aircraft. That's a thousand guys."

"Yea, no wonder they are hurrying us through. Well I'm ready, it seems we have been in training forever," said Lowell.

"I can't say I'm ready to get shot down or die, but I'm ready to have this training over," added Charlie.

On the day of their first attempt at take-off and landing in the UC-78 *Bobcat* the cadets were very excited but also very concerned. They had a few hours of flying the aircraft, but the instructor had taken off and then turned the controls over to the cadet in the right seat. Lowell had found that keeping the engines synchronized had not been as difficult as he had thought.

Drawing their flight gear and assembling in the ready room, they listened to Lieutenant Paddock.

"Okay gentleman, today we take-off and hopefully, land. Remember, take-offs are optional and landings are mandatory."

All the cadets laughed dutifully, but their hearts were not into joking at that point.

The lieutenant went on, "Well I suppose you want to be first again Andersen?"

Lowell hated that but nodded his head and answered, "Yes sir!"

They walked out to the flight line, it was a very warm morning, but Lowell still didn't think he should be sweating as much as he was. The interior of the *Bobcat* was very hot as he climbed into the left seat for the first time. He noticed that the lieutenant was also sweating. Maybe it wasn't all nervousness after all.

"Okay cadet, let's see what you have."

Lowell looked out the left side of the plane to see if the propeller was clear and that the ground crew was ready with the fire extinguisher.

He said, "All clear on the left."

Lieutenant Paddock did the same on the right. Lowell went through the start up procedure of setting the fuel mixture to rich putting in a slight bit of throttle, setting the flaps in the proper position and locking the brakes. He pushed the starter button for the right engine and listened for it to take. When it seemed to be running, he backed off the fuel mixture and reduced the throttle slightly. He repeated the process for the left engine and in a minute both engines were running smoothly. Lowell called the tower and requested permission to taxi to the runway for take-off. Permission was granted and a runway was assigned.

Lieutenant Paddock said, "Okay Anderson, let's see if any of my instructions took."

Lowell smiled, nodded and advanced the throttles. He guided the *Bobcat* to the assigned runway and advanced the engines to the proper revolution, the manifold pressure was within the take-off range and Lowell released the brakes. The *Bobcat* began to roll down the runway and Lowell added more RPMs to the engines and it gained speed. At the proper speed, Lowell eased the wheel forward. The *Bobcat* had a wheel control instead of a stick and the tail lifted off the ground. Again, at the proper speed, the aircraft lifted into the air.

Lieutenant Paddock said through the intercom, "Well now cadet, you see, if you have everything set correctly the airplane nearly flies itself. Nice take-off!"

Lowell felt very pleased with himself as the lieutenant gave him a heading to achieve. He gently turned the wheel while applying pressure on the proper rudder pedal and the plane turned onto the heading given him. They flew around with the lieutenant giving Lowell several course corrections and changes. After about thirty minutes of flying, Lowell was disappointed when he heard Lieutenant Paddock's voice over the intercom.

"Okay Andersen, take us home."

When they got within two miles of the base, Lowell called the tower for landing instruction and was informed that there was a twenty-mile an hour crosswind. He had never landed in a crosswind of that magnitude, but Lieutenant Paddock showed no concern. Lowell located the runway he had been assigned and lined up for the landing. The cadets had been instructed on how to adjust for a crosswind and Lowell hoped he remembered everything. As the aircraft got lower, the wind began to affect the path.

Lieutenant Paddock questioned, "You got it Andersen?"

"I think so sir!"

He found that he had to apply more and more rudder to keep the airplane centered on the runway, which was making his left leg, tense and he was afraid it might cramp. He also moved the wheel slightly to the left to compensate for the rudder. Finally just before touching down on the runway, Lowell let off the rudder and straightened the wheel to insure the plane would not veer off the runway. It hit with some force jarring them both but then touched down and ran straight until the reduced speed allowed the tail to drop. Lowell was somewhat mortified by the poor landing.

As they taxied up to the parking area Lieutenant Paddock said, "Andersen, that was one of the best first landings I have every seen. Nice going! You're going to make a fine pilot."

Lowell looked at him in astonishment until he smiled and punched him in the shoulder.

The lieutenant said, "Well, we'd better get out of the plane and give someone else a chance don't ya think?"

As he walked across the tarmac towards the ready room he met Homer who looked white and scared to death. He stopped a minute in front of Lowell.

"How was it?"

"Just fine, that wind gave me a little trouble, but it was okay."

"I hope I can do as well," replied Homer.

In the ready room several other cadets were sitting around including Charlie.

Looking expectantly at Lowell, one asked, "How was it?"

"Oh fine, a little rough on the landing in the wind, but just fine," replied Lowell.

He sat down beside Charlie and whispered, "I thought I would pee my pants with that cross wind."

"Yea, that makes an entirely different exercise doesn't it?"

Lowell looked at him and realized he had given Charlie something more to worry about.

He said, "Oh you'll do just fine; don't worry about it."

That night at evening chow there was a state of relaxation and euphoria. The cadets talked, laughed and retold the story of their first take-off and landing in a twin-engine airplane. Back in the room after an hour of studying, Lowell got out his writing kit and began a letter to Helen.

Dearest Helen,

Today I took another step towards being a bomber pilot. I took off and landed the twin engine "Bamboo Bomber." It was not a simple exercise because of a cross wind, but Lieutenant Paddock said I did the best of any cadet he had trained. This meant a lot to me. We all respect the lieutenant because he has actually flown in combat.

Well how are things in old Drayvilleeeeeee? How is school? What kind of a spring are you having? Wet I'll bet. Have you seen much of Betty? I wrote to Jew this week and asked about a leave in June but haven't heard.

Now, on to less important things. How are the wedding plans going? There's a rumor around here that we may finish sooner than we were suppose to. That would be great, but keep in mind it is only a rumor. I still believe that around the 5th or 6th of June will be just about right for the date.

Lowell wrote about several funny incidents that had taken place in training, leaving out the unpleasant part about a cadet washing out and that there was a crash on a landing that put the instructor and cadet in the hospital, then closed as usual.

As always to you I give my love and life,
Low

The classes on navigation, mechanics, map reading, aircraft and ship recognition and of course, physical training continued. One day the class was brought together and the captain announced that they would be flying with classmates instead of an instructor. He told them to choose the person they wanted to fly with and report to the flight line in full gear. Of course, Lowell and Charlie chose each other and after drawing flight gear, reported to the flight line.

Lieutenant Paddock told them to get aboard the *Bobcat.* He took a seat on the bench in the back and observed as they went through the pre-flight drill. Lowell was in the left seat as pilot and Charlie was in the right as co-pilot.

After the engines were running and the lieutenant was satisfied that they were going to be okay, he said, "Well good luck men, just take-off and fly three circuits, then land and we'll switch seats."

They were well aware what a circuit was as they had flown them many times. It merely involved flying a set pattern around the field and calling the tower for landing instructions.

Charlie said over the intercom, "Well Andersen, think you can get us in the air?"

"I think so. Let's give it a try!"

Lowell placed his hands on the throttles and Charlie put his hands over Lowell's to insure that the throttles couldn't be inadvertently reduced on take-off. They gained permission from the tower and proceeded to increase power for the take-off. The circuits were uneventful and after landing and changing positions, Charlie repeated the exercise.

That night in the room, Charlie said, "You know, I think flying multi-engines will be a lot of fun. We get to hold hands."

Lowell and Homer looked at him and he was just staring at the ceiling.

Homer said, "I didn't think you were that kind of a guy Charlie."

Lowell laughed and Charlie looked over at them and laughed as well.

He said, "How did you do Homer?"

"Oh I did okay I guess. The take-off was kind of rough, but the circuit was good. The instructor thought it was okay."

They visited for a little while and then Lowell reached in his footlocker and took out his writing kit.

Homer said, "Well, I guess the visit is over. There he goes again. Doesn't your girl get tired of opening those envelopes and reading all that bull?"

Lowell just laughed and said, "Well, at least my girl knows I can write!"

All three laughed while Lowell set about to the task at hand. He was not writing to Helen but rather to his folks.

Dear Mom and Dad,

Well, we had our first flight today without an instructor. Charlie and I are a team and they let us go up as pilot and co-pilot. I was the pilot on the first flight and Charlie on the second. They told us that after a few more circuits we would be given longer flights where navigation would play a larger part. I am not worried however because Charlie and I are both at the top of our class in navigation and I don't think we will have a problem.

How are the kids doing? I can't believe that they are both about to enter junior high school. When did they move the sixth grade to junior high? Tell them hello for me and that I will write when I have more time. They are really keeping us busy these days. When we get back to the room, we always have some studying to do and we are usually so tired we go right to sleep at ten o'clock when they call lights out.

Mom and Dad, I have been thinking of the next few months. I assume I will go on to graduate and become a pilot which means I will probably go overseas. I don't know what will happen but I want you to know that I love you both very much and feel very lucky to have parents like you. Also, I want you to know that I am doing exactly what I want to do.

Well it is close to lights out and I want to get a line or two off to Helen so I will close for now.

Love you both very much,
Lowell

Lowell laid back on his bunk and thought about his life with his folks. There were times that he thought they were too strict and didn't understand him, but all in all, they were very good parents. He wrote a short note to Helen about the day's events, signed off with the usual endearment, rolled over and immediately went to sleep.

Training continued on a hectic pace with flying in the mornings and classes in the afternoon. Of course, they were still in the army so daily routines also included KP (kitchen policing) and guard duty, cleaning the barracks and "police call," which involved picking up foreign objects found on the ground in the class area. The cadets were so close to getting those silver wings and that brass bar that they were very careful not to do anything that might wash them out.

It was painfully brought home to them one day when after evening chow they entered the barracks to hear a lot of banging around and cussing in the room next to theirs. Charlie looked in and saw Dick Saginaw throwing his things in a barracks bag.

"What's going on Dick?"

As he turned to look at the boys, they noticed tears in his eyes as he replied, "I've been washed out!"

Homer said, "Why?"

"Oh I just cannot get those landings right!"

They all fell silent for lack of what to say and finally Dick said, "I can't be too mad at Lieutenant Michaels, he gave me every opportunity."

"What happened? I thought you were doing okay," Lowell said.

"Yea, well I wasn't, I just didn't want to talk about it. I think if I had gotten fighters I would have been okay, but I just can't manage both throttles. This morning Lieutenant Michaels gave me another chance. I took off okay but when I came in to land, I almost drifted off the runway."

"Where are you going?"

"I've been assigned to bombardiers in New Mexico. I have to report day after tomorrow."

Lowell looked at him and said, "Well that still means you will be commissioned and get to fly."

"Yea, I guess that's right. Damn though, I wanted to be a pilot so bad!"

The three stood silent for a time and then Homer said, "Well, stop by and say goodbye before you leave, okay?"

"Sure, maybe we can go to the PX and have one last beer together."

"Yea," Charlie said with a smile. "I might even drink one with you."

"That might make my washing out seem okay," replied Dick with a smile on his face.

The three boys turned and crossed the hall to their room. They were all silent for a time.

Lowell said, "Well, I guess that shows us that we don't have it made. Washing out is still a possibility."

They all fell silent for awhile and Lowell reached in his footlocker and took out his writing kit to the groans of the other two roommates.

Dear Helen,

Hi darling, how are things at home? I suppose you are well into getting ready for finals. We are at that point as well. They told us that soon we would be doing longer trips with our chosen partners. As I said, Charlie is mine. We trade off as pilot and co-pilot.

We had a bitter lesson today. One of the guys just across the hall was washed out. I felt so sorry for him as I looked at the tears in is eyes; I guess I teared up a little as well. We have been together since basic and I thought he was doing okay, but I guess he had a lot of trouble landing the twin engine aircraft we are flying now.

How are the plans going? I sure feel bad that I'm not there to help you, but I must keep my mind on the events here so I guess the wedding is up to you to plan. I am still hoping that Jew can make it home, but Charlie said he is ready to be in the party, and if Jew can't make it, I'm going to ask him to be my best man. What do you think?

I think it is a good idea to have David and Diane in the party, but do you think they can come down the aisle without getting into a fight? HA, HA, I think they will do a great job as ring bearer and candle lighter.

I can't tell you how much I am looking forward to the wedding. I think that the greatest honor I could ever have will be to be your husband. When I think of us in our own house after the war, starting a family, and being together, I get goose bumps all over. I love you so much!

Lowell went on the tell Helen about how training was going and what they were doing. After another page, his eyes begin to blur and he thought it was time to sign off. He did so in the usual manner.

As always to you I give my love and life,
Lowell

As March gave way to April the weather got hotter and hotter. The only relief from the heat was when they were up in the air flying. There was more formation flying, navigation, and some emergency procedures. They got to spend some time in the powerful Curtis AT-9. They were not allowed to fly this aircraft with other cadets and had to go up with their instructor. The first time Lowell flew it, Lieutenant Paddock cautioned him about the added power and allowed him to start the engines and taxi out to the runway. Lowell realized that he had a much different breed of cat under him. He barely touched the throttles and the plane literally jumped forward. He glanced over at the instructor and noticed a slight smile on his face.

Lowell said, "I see what you mean sir. This is a hot airplane."

The take-off run was much shorter because the AT-9 got up to speed much sooner and when Lowell lifted the tail wheel, the plane left the runway almost on it's own.

Lowell exclaimed, "Wow!"

Lieutenant Paddock said, "See what I mean? This baby will jump out from under you if you're not careful. Now let's do a couple of circuits and then land and see how you handle that."

Lowell followed the lieutenant's instructions and lined up on the runway for landing.

"Now Andersen, this plane will come in much hotter than the *Bobcat* so remember everything has to be a little sooner."

Lowell crossed the outer marker and began to reduce power. The AT-9 began to loose altitude and settle onto the runway.

They ran a little further than he planned to, but Lieutenant Paddock said, "Nice landing Andersen, for your first."

It turned out that it was the only landing or take-off Lowell ever had in the AT-9. It was pulled from service that spring and did not return. There was more and more emphasis on formation flying. The cadets were now always teamed up in the Bobcat and were getting used to flying close to the other planes. Lowell and Charlie were a team and traded off in the left seat. Lowell was still very nervous when he came in too tight in formation with other planes. The heated desert below caused thermals that could toss a plane around a great deal.

One particular day the thermals were very strong and Lowell had a difficult time bringing the Bobcat in tight. It seemed they were bouncing up and down several feet. He kept looking out the left window at the other plane and edging into an acceptable distance. He knew that if he didn't, Lieutenant Paddock would give him a little talking to. When they were ordered to break formation and land, Lowell looked over at Charlie and discovered he was sweating nearly as much. They smiled at each other and shook their heads as Lowell banked the plane to line up for a landing.

*****

The time finally came for their cross-country navigation flight. This was where two cadets would be given a three-legged course covering several hundred air miles and they would plot the course, and fly the mission. Lieutenant Paddock explained that they would decide who would fly which leg and then lay out the course. He told them their destination for the first leg would be Yucca Auxiliary Field near Kingman, Arizona, a distance of nearly 300 air miles. The second leg would take them to Kirkland Field near Albuquerque, New Mexico and the last leg would bring them back to Douglas. They were told where auxiliary fields were located and that they should have them clearly indicated on their plot maps. Charlie and Lowell were again to fly as a team and they decided that Lowell would fly the first leg, Charlie the second and that they would flip a coin to see who flew the last leg.

The few days before the cross-country were very busy with preparations. They poured over maps of the route, identified the auxiliary fields as Lieutenant Paddock had instructed them to do, and plotted and re-plotted the coordinates. They calculated fuel consumption, tried to identify prevailing winds and worried a lot. The night before the flight Lowell came in just before lights-out, flopped on his bunk and reached into his locker for his writing kit. Homer groaned and Charlie just smiled.

Dearest Helen,

Well, tomorrow is the big test, a cross-country flight. It is to be one of the last big tests of our training and so we are all very tense. Charlie and I are again teamed up and we trade off flying and navigating. I wish I could fly all the way because I love to fly and I think Charlie is a better navigator than me.

How are things in Oregon? I guess by now the flowers are beginning to bud and you are seeing a little sunshine. As June draws nearer, I can hardly wait to get home and see those flowers. Oh yea, and that other thing we have planned.

Lowell smiled at his little joke as he imagined Helen going "Oh Lowell!" at the reference to their wedding.

How is school? What has Betty heard from Jew? Do you see the folks often? I guess I am pretty tired tonight, I can't think of much to say and have to resort to stupid questions. I think I will close now and not bore you with any more babble.

Finishing the letter, Lowell signed off in his usual way.

As always to you I give my love and life,
Lowell

The next day, at the end of training, Lieutenant Paddock called them together outside the ready room and reminded them that the following day they would be doing their long navigation flight; that they would have to land at other bases for refueling and go on to the next until they had completed the three legs and landed back at Douglas. As they walked back to the barracks, there was much speculation on how they would do. Charlie and Lowell thought they could handle it because navigation was not a problem for them.

They had been issued a little device called the E6B, which was a round navigation tool somewhat like a slide rule. They had both excelled in advanced math classes in high school and had learned to use a slide rule so using the E6B came fairly easy to them.

As they got their course, they walked to the plane and Lowell said, "Thank God for old Mr. Pearson."

Charlie said, "Who's Mr. Pearson?"

"Oh he was my math teacher in high school. As I look back, he was a very good teacher, but at the time we thought he was awful strict."

"Yea, I had a teacher like that. I think when I get home I'm going to go to the school and tell him how much I appreciate what he did for me."

Lowell answered, "Yea, I guess we just didn't appreciate any of our teachers at the time."

As they boarded the plane the next morning for the cross-country, Lowell took the left seat as he was chosen to fly the first leg. They went through the pre-flight check and began the startup procedure when Lieutenant Paddock stuck his head in the plane.

"You remember your call sign?"

"Yes sir, UC-785," they said in unison.

The lieutenant said, "Good luck guys, I'm really not worried about you two, but be aware all the time in any event!"

Lowell and Charlie again replied in unison, "Thank you sir."

They finished the pre-flight and start up procedures and requested permission to taxi to the runway. Lowell taxied the plane to the runway and requested permission to take-off. Permission was granted and he advanced the throttles of the UC-78 and began the take-off run.

"Here we go!" said Lowell as he deftly lifted the plane into the air.

After climbing to the appropriate altitude, Lowell looked at Charlie and said, "Okay navigator, give me the heading."

Charlie responded with the coordinates and Lowell put the plane in a gradual turn bringing the compass to the heading Charlie had indicated and they were on the first leg of their cross-country flight. They flew awhile and Lowell began to relax and asked Charlie how they were doing. He had been studying the compass and the map.

Charlie responded, "Just fine, I think Tucson is off to the West. That is, if I've given you the correct heading."

Lowell jerked his head around and looked at Charlie who was smiling at him. "Yea, well you had better or when I'm in that seat, I'll have you flying in circles."

"Well I just thought you might want to declare an emergency and land at Davis-Monthan Auxiliary," replied Charlie with a smile.

They fell silent for awhile and Charlie asked, "Low, how will you feel about dropping bombs on innocent civilians?"

Lowell thought for a minute and then picked up the intercom mike and said, "Well, if you could hear what my friend Jew said about his mother's family in Poland, you probably wouldn't think there were any innocent ones."

"Yea, that's kind of what I think, but I'm sure they're not all like the Nazis."

They both fell silent for some time as Charlie continued to check his compass and map. Finally he said, "I estimate we will be over Phoenix in about twenty minutes." Lowell nodded and looked down at his instruments to see that all was still okay. Air speed was as prescribed, heading was right on, and fuel was far in the green. Unless some strange occurrence happened, he should finish his leg of the flight with plenty of fuel remaining.

He relaxed a little more and then picked up the mike again and said, "Charlie, how do you feel about dropping bombs on innocents?"

Charlie picked up his mike and said, "Well, we were taught very early that killing was a mortal sin, but I guess even in the bible it was necessary on special occasions. I guess I just don't want to know about it. I'm sure that if we don't stop this war there will be many more civilians killed than we will ever kill."

"Yea, that's a pretty good way to look at it."

They flew on for some time and after checking the charts and maps several more times Charlie said, "Well, we should just about be over

Phoenix by now. That looks like a suburb coming up dead ahead."

Lowell rose slightly in his seat and looked out the windscreen. "Yea, it looks like some kind of settlement."

The city of Phoenix, Arizona began to spread out before the aircraft.

The boys became a little distracted and finally Charlie said, "Hey, watch your heading."

Lowell looked down at the compass and saw that he was several degrees off course. He quickly made a correction and said, "Sorry."

"Yea, I was distracted as well, we have never flown over a large city before."

Lowell replied, "It is kind of exciting isn't it? Okay, how much further is it to Kingman?"

"Let's see, I make it about 170 miles, another hour," answered Charlie.

"Yea, let's floorboard this thing and get there, I'm tired of flying and I would like to see some of the country like you've been doing."

"Ha, you'd better not! I want exact figures just like I gave you."

They flew along again in silence for a time and then Charlie picked up the mike and said, "Low, have you heard for sure if Helen is going to come down for graduation?"

"Well, I'm pretty sure she is. How about Linda?"

"Last letter I got she said she was, if she can get a train ticket."

Lowell thought for a minute, smiled and said, "That will be something else, won't it – pinning those Second Lieu bars and those wings? The lieutenant said they just hand them to us and we can get someone to pin them on. That's why I sure hope Helen can come down."

"Yea, that will be great," replied Charlie.

"I imagine my folks will come down too," Lowell said.

"Mine too, I hope," replied Charlie.

It was not so easy to talk over the intercom so there was minimal visiting. Mostly Lowell concentrated on flying the plane, the instrument panel and keeping on course. Charlie of course, had the navigation to worry about so he was quite busy.

After nearly another hour of flying, Charlie picked up the mike and said, "We should be about ten minutes out of Yucca."

"Thanks."

Lowell picked up the mike, changed the channel to radio, pushed the button and called, UB-785 calling Yucca tower, come in!"

After a short time the radio crackled and a voice replied, "Yucca tower to UB-785, over."

"UB-785 to Yucca tower, we are about ten minutes out and request landing instructions!"

"Yucca tower to UB-785, land on main runway south southwest, winds from the south west ten knots, over."

"UB-785 to Yucca tower, roger, out!"

Lowell released the button and looked over at Charlie who had such a stern look on his face that Lowell couldn't help but laugh.

Charlie turned and realizing why Lowell was laughing, joined him and picked up the mike saying, "Nice going."

His comment immediately brought another crackle of static from Yucca tower and the voice said, "Say again UB-785."

Lowell looked horrified and realized immediately that he had forgotten to switch the radio back to intercom and Charlie's response had been transmitted. He picked up the mike and said in his best-schooled radio voice, "Ignore last transmission, UB-785 out!"

Lowell switched the radio and they both had a laugh.

As he circled to get on the heading as instructed from the tower, Lowell was again the serious, concentrating cadet he always was when a challenge presented itself. He put in a little left rudder and turned the wheel, bringing the plane around to a south-southwest heading.

Charlie said over the intercom, "Don't forget the wind."

Lowell just nodded and began to adjust the throttles to slow the plane. He called for fifteen degrees flaps and the plane began to drop. When he felt it was in the proper alignment, he reduced power again and the plane began to settle down to the runway.

He said, "Boy, this wind is really pushing us." He called for less flaps and the plane settled more until they felt the expected bump and jerk as it settled on to the runway. Lowell kept it straight and called for flaps up and began to apply brake. The plane slowed and the tail dropped to the runway and Lowell gave an audible sigh of relief.

The tower instructed them to wait for the guide truck and follow it to the parking area. Lowell looked over at Charlie and smiled and Charlie returned the smile. Soon a pickup truck came pell-mell across the field and pulled in front of their plane with a sign saying FOLLOW

ME, which they did. After a short trip to the parking apron, a ground controller came out and motioned for them to cut the engines, which Lowell did after following the shut down checklist. Suddenly there was a loud banging on the cabin door and Charlie unbuckled his harness and opened the door.

A lieutenant climbed into the cabin and said, "Nice landing cadet."

Lowell answered, "Cadet Andersen sir, thank you."

"Well you guys disembark and stretch your legs while we top off your tanks. You can check in with the duty officer for any messages. We'll have you ready for take-off in about thirty minutes. There's coffee in the ready room and a latrine."

"Thank you sir." they both answered.

Lowell looked at Charlie and smiled as they walked across the apron toward the ready room and said, "Well it's too bad you don't drink coffee!"

"Well I might just forget I'm a Mormon for one day if you promise not to tell my bishop."

Lowell laughed out loud and said, "Okay."

As they entered the ready room, they both noticed how informal it was compared to theirs back at Douglas. They walked up to the desk and reported in with the proper salute.

The captain behind the desk returned the salute and said, "Stand easy! You boys ready for the next leg?"

"Yes sir."

"Okay, let's check your coordinates and time estimate; who's flying this leg?"

"I am sir," answered Charlie.

"Okay, let's see 'em."

Charlie handed his map chart to the captain who studied it for a few minutes and handed it back to Charlie.

"Looks fine cadet, better check your estimated time of arrival. We have a little tail wind on that leg."

"Yes sir, where can we get that information?"

The captain leaned around the two cadets and said, "Sergeant, call the tower and see what the winds are doing now!"

"Yes sir."

The sergeant picked up the phone and spoke into it for a few minutes and said, "They are still out of the west by southwest at about twenty miles sir."

"Okay cadet, figure that in and let me check it before you leave."

Charlie said, "Yes sir," and they both saluted, did an about face and walked over to the coffee bar.

Lowell poured himself a cup while Charlie sat down at the table, got out his slide rule and began to calculate. After a few minutes he handed the chart to Lowell.

"Check these figures will you?"

Lowell did and found that they were correct as far as he knew and handed them back to Charlie who immediately took them into the captain. In a few minutes Charlie came back in to the coffee room, went over to the urn and poured himself a cup.

"Well he agreed with my figures and said we could return to the plane and prepare to take-off for the second leg."

The two cadets climbed aboard the plane with Charlie taking the left seat and Lowell the right. They looked down at the ground crew giving the start up signal and Charlie ordered Lowell to start engine number one followed by number two. With both engines running, Lowell called the tower and requested permission to taxi in preparation for take-off. Permission was granted and Charlie told Lowell to follow the take-off procedures. At the assigned runway, Charlie again called the tower for permission to take-off. Once in the air, Charlie asked Lowell to set the course for Kirkland, their next destination.

Lowell gave Charlie the heading and settled back for the trip.

After a few minutes he picked up the mike and said, "Charlie, wouldn't it be something if we ended up in the same squadron?"

"Yea, I think that is a distinct possibility."

Lowell could tell Charlie was not in the mood to talk, he was concentrating on the task at hand so he did not discuss his thoughts further.

After nearly half an hour, Charlie picked up his mike and said, "What's the matter, you're so quiet?"

"Oh, I thought I would give you a chance to concentrate."

"Yea, I guess I was kind of tense. Would you take it for awhile? I have to go back to the tube; I knew I shouldn't have had that coffee."

Lowell reached out for the yoke with a laugh and Charlie unbuckled and climbed in back where the relief tube was located.

When he returned, Lowell asked, "Everything come out alright?"

Charlie responded with a laugh, reached for the controls and said, "I've got it!"

They flew on for some time with an occasional brief conversation over the intercom.

Finally Lowell said, "If I've figured it right, we should be only about twenty minutes from Kirkland. Think we should try to raise them?"

Charlie replied, "Let's wait five more minutes and then call."

Lowell nodded his agreement and they settled back for five more minutes of flight.

"Okay Low, I'm going to give 'em a call."

He picked up the mike, switched the channel and called, "UB-785 calling Kirkland tower. Come in. Over."

In a few minutes Kirkland answered, "Kirkland tower to UB-785, go ahead."

"UB-785 to Kirkland tower, we are fifteen minutes out on a heading of thirty-seven degrees south southwest requesting landing instructions. Over."

"UB-785, land on runway two. Wind from the southwest twenty miles an hour. Over."

"Roger, Kirkland tower. Land runway 2 with winds from the southwest at twenty."

"UB-785, be alert, the wind will be pushing you pretty good."

"Roger, Kirkland tower; we copy."

Charlie switched the radio back to intercom and asked Lowell if he heard all that. Lowell said he did and was ready. In a few minutes they spotted the field. It looked much smaller than either Douglas or Yucca.

Charlie located runway two, lined up, and brought the plane in just fine. He touched down slightly beyond the usual touch down point, but good enough to get a well done from the officer in charge. After trailing the FOLLOW ME truck to the parking area and shutting down, Lowell and Charlie climbed down from the plane and entered the ready room. The officer in charge asked if everything was okay and they reported no problem. He then offered them a bit to eat, which they quickly accepted.

When they had finished their meal, they got their charts and began to study the next and last leg of the flight.

Charlie said, "Oh, we forgot to flip to see who flies the last leg."

Lowell responded with "Yea, you got a coin?"

Charlie took a quarter out of his pocket and said, "Okay, you call it in the air," and flipped it with his thumb.

Lowell called, "Tails!"

Charlie caught the coin and slapped in on to the back of his left hand covering it with his right.

"Want to change your call, last chance."

Lowell responded with a negative shake of his head and Charlie uncovered the coin. It was tails.

Charlie said, "Well captain, it's your plane."

Lowell could see the disappointment in Charlie's eyes and said, "Why don't we do two out of three?"

"No, we agreed on a coin flip."

The boys got their charts, reported to the officer in charge, were warned again about the head wind, checked their calculations and were approved for the last leg. As they walked out to the plane, Lowell gave Charlie one last chance to flip again and Charlie refused, again. They climbed aboard, started the engines, followed the signals of the ground crew, taxied out to the runway and went through the take-off procedures. When they received clearance for take-off, Lowell called for engine run up, instrument check, and release of brakes. Then the plane began to roll and when the proper speed was reached the tail came up, Lowell eased back on the yoke and the plane lifted into the air. Lowell asked Charlie for the course to Douglas, which he provided, then swung the plane to that heading and settled back for the two-hour flight home.

Lowell and Charlie exchanged several bits of small talk over the first hour of the flight but spent most of the time in their own thoughts. Lowell let Charlie have the controls to get a little more stick time as he left the cockpit to stretch his legs. As they flew on, Lowell was thinking about the next few weeks: the wedding, seeing Helen, and getting his wings. Suddenly Lowell's reverie was disturbed by Charlie's quick movement to pick up the intercom mike and Lowell looked at him as he pressed the talk button.

"Lowell, look at the oil pressure gauge on the right engine!"

Lowell looked at the gauge and it indicated that the pressure was dropping.

At the same time Charlie said, "And check the manifold pressure and temperature as well!"

Lowell became alarmed as he followed Charlie's instructions and noticed the temperature was approaching the red zone, which indicated an overheated engine. He picked up the mike and told Charlie to try and contact Douglas to report the trouble.

"UB-785 to Douglas tower; come in."

After a brief wait, he called again and Lowell noticed a slight panic tone in Charlie's voice.

"Douglas tower to UB-785; over."

"UB-785 to Douglas Tower. We are experiencing a drop in oil pressure and a rise in heat on our right engine Over!"

"UB-785 from Douglas. Give me the readings on your gauges."

Charlie complied with the request as he noted, "The temperature continues to rise and the oil pressure continues to drop."

Lowell sensing a serious problem throttled back both engines and began to loose altitude when Douglas came back.

A familiar voice said, "UB-785 from Douglas tower. This is Lieutenant Paddock. Do you have a good fix on your location?"

"Douglas tower from UB-785. We are about an hour out of Kirkland but we have a twenty mile per hour head wind so we haven't made very good time," replied Charlie.

"This is Douglas tower. I estimate that you must be over an hour from Douglas and taking into account what you have reported, that engine will probably not make it. Can you see any smoke or fire? Over"

Charlie looked out at the offending engine and reported in the negative. Lieutenant Paddock asked who was flying at the time to which Charlie responded Cadet Andersen.

"UB-785 from Douglas. Andersen you're going to have to put it down or that engine will seize or catch on fire. What is your altitude? Over."

Lowell picked up the mike and reported they were at about 3,000 feet. Lieutenant Paddock instructed Lowell to go down to 1,500 feet and check the terrain for a flat smooth area and follow the in-flight shut down procedures on the right engines. Lowell did as he was instructed and began to lose altitude. They had some instructions and some flying time on one engine, but the cadets knew they had the other engine to depend on. This was different. The pull by losing an engine complicated the landing and Lowell hoped he was up to an emergency landing.

Suddenly Charlie tapped him on the arm and pointed out ahead. Lowell rose up in his seat and looked out seeing what he was indicating. There was a highway dead ahead running vertically to their course. He indicated to Charlie to report that, which he did. The response from Douglas was that the road they spotted was probably the Tucson Highway.

Lieutenant Paddock came back on the radio and told them that was usually a very busy highway and not to land, but look for any other possible landing sight. Lowell put the plane in a right bank and flew along the highway for a time until they spotted a farm road that ran parallel some 100 yards off and Charlie reported what they had found. Lieutenant Paddock asked them how the temperature and oil pressure was doing. Charlie looked down at the gauges and nearly panicked when he discovered that the oil pressure was nearly at zero and the temperature was approaching the red line.

Suddenly a different voice came on the radio. "Gentleman, get that airplane on the ground even if you have to dent it a little. This is Colonel Gaelic!"

Charlie and Lowell looked at each other somewhat taken aback that the base commander was giving them instructions.

The familiar voice of Lieutenant Paddock came back on and said, "Andersen, now listen to me. I want you to find a stretch of that dirt road that looks long enough and put it down. You are one of the best landers I've got so I know you can do it. Just remember, let the plane settle and don't be too quick on the brakes. You're not on a surfaced runway! Also, as soon as the tail wheel touches, cut the engines to prevent more damage or possible fire!"

Lowell just nodded as Charlie responded.

Lowell looked over at Charlie and shouted, "There's a good place, hang on!"

Lowell brought the UB-78 down as he reduced power. He yelled to Charlie to cut the engines as soon as the wheels touched. As they touched the ground, a large cloud of dust sprang up behind them but the road ahead looked fairly smooth. The plane bounced severely as it hit several chuckholes until finally it had lost enough speed to allow the tail to drop and Charlie did as Lowell instructed and cut the engines. Lowell applied the brakes and after a few more sudden jolts, the plane finally came to a stop. Lowell and Charlie just sat there for awhile until the radio crackled again with Lieutenant Paddock's voice.

"What's going on? Are you okay?"

Lowell picked up the mike and said, "UB-785 to Douglas Tower. We are on the ground and have cut the engines."

"Very well UB-785, see if you can positively identify that highway and report back. See if you can find any road signs. Over."

"Roger, Douglas. Is there anything we should do with the airplane?" asked Charlie.

"No, maybe one of you should stay with the plane. Over."

"Roger. Out!"

Lowell looked over at Charlie and said, "Should we flip another coin?"

Charlie laughed and said, "No, you're the plane commander. It's your call."

"Okay, I'll go look, you stay here."

Both cadets unbuckled, rose from their seats and climbed down from the plane. Lowell walked around checking everything out.

He said, "Boy, I'm glad we didn't hit anything harder than those chuck holes. These *Bamboo Bombers* don't take crashes very well."

"Yea, well you did a very good job on that landing," replied Charlie.

"Okay, well if I'm not back in an hour you will know that I got picked up by a good looking girl."

Charlie just laughed and patted Lowell on the arm.

"Well, if you run across a soda fountain, bring me a coke."

"I thought you Mormons didn't drink coke."

"We don't. I wanted to soak my feet."

Lowell set off for the highway some 100 yards from their dirt road. Walking through the rabbit brush and mesquite, Lowell thought about the Eastern Oregon stories he had heard about rattle snakes and he became vigilant. He finally reached the macadam highway and walked out to it. He looked both ways and saw a car coming from the east. He moved to the middle of the road and began to wave his arms. As the car came closer he moved to the side and continued to wave. The car slowed and pulled over to the side. A man in a business suit rolled down the window and asked with some surprise.

"What are you doing out here?"

Lowell laughed and said, "We're from Douglas Air Base and we've had to land with engine trouble. The base has asked us to find out where we are. Can you help us?"

"Well yes. We're about thirty miles west of Lordsburg on Tucson Highway number 80. Are you alone?"

"No, my co-pilot is back at the plane." Lowell motioned towards the plane and the man looked over.

"Are you going to be able to contact your base?" asked the man.

"Yes sir, we are in contact with our base by radio."

"Is there anything I can do for you?"

"No, I think the information was all we needed. Thank you sir."

Lowell stepped back from the car and gave the man a salute. When he got back to the plane, Charlie was sitting under the wing reading something.

"Did you find a library out here?" asked Lowell with a smile.

Charlie was known around the barracks as a constant reader. Charlie looked up and laughed somewhat embarrassed,

"No, I was just reading the tech manual on this aircraft we are stuck with here."

"Well, we are about thirty miles west of Lordsburg on Highway 80," said Lowell.

They climbed back into the plane and turned on the radio.

"UB-785 to Douglas. Come in."

An immediate response came back, "Douglas to UC-785; have you got a location?

Charlie responded with, "UB-785 to Douglas. Yes we are about thirty miles west of Lordsburg on Highway 80. Over."

"Roger UB-785. What I want you to do now is just sit tight and we will come get you. Do you have anything to eat or drink? Over."

"UB-785, nothing to eat but we have water. We ate back at Kirkland."

"Okay UB-785; it is going to take us awhile to get there. It might be dark, so at sundown turn on your navigation lights so we can see you. Over."

"UB-785, roger. Out!"

Charlie switched off the radio and looked at Lowell. They both displayed some concern but decided to make the best of the situation.

Lowell asked, "How far are we from Douglas?"

Charlie took out the map and studied it for awhile and said, "It looks like about 85 miles; that will take them about two hours of travel time after they get ready."

Looking at his watch, Lowell said, "Well it's obvious they won't get here before dark.

With that they both settled down, Charlie with his tech manual and Lowell with his thoughts. Helen immediately came to mind. He wondered if his thoughts about their wedding night were in some way sinful and an insult to her. He decided it wasn't, but he did wonder if she had the same thoughts and was as anxious as he was. After awhile Lowell dozed off and the rattle of a vehicle coming across the rough terrain woke him. As he jerked awake he realized that Charlie had been sleeping as well. They both jumped up and climbed down. As they walked around the plane they saw a small three-quarter ton truck led by a jeep. Lieutenant Paddock was driving the jeep and a mechanic crew was in the three-quarter ton.

Lieutenant Paddock pulled up and returned the boys salutes with a big smile.

"Well, you guys really know how to put obstacles in your training don't you?"

"Yes sir!" they both answered.

"Cadets, this is Sergeant Irons and Corporal Lawson; Cadets Andersen and Smith."

The sergeant and corporal nodded and went to the back of the truck to get their tools. They put a ladder up to the offending engine and removed the cowling and began to poke around. Because it was getting slightly dark they used a flashlight to look into the engine.

The lieutenant said, "Well men, let's leave the sergeant and corporal to their work. There's a small service station just down the road. Let's go have a coke and try to find you guys something to eat."

*****

Lowell and Charlie looked over at the men working on the engine and though they felt somewhat guilty about leaving them, climbed into the jeep. Lieutenant Paddock yelled to the sergeant and asked if they could bring them anything.

The sergeant yelled back. "How about a six pack?"
The lieutenant just laughed and turned the jeep around and started off toward the highway. They found the service station and enjoyed candy bars and cokes.

The lieutenant saw the beer cooler and said, "Wait a minute."

He went to the cooler, pulled out two beers and asked the clerk if he had anyway of keeping them cold. The clerk said he could take some ice and a paper bag.

With the beer and ice in a small bucket the clerk had given them and several bags of potato chips, they started back towards the plane. When they arrived, the mechanics were just putting the cowling back on the engine. Both Lowell and Charlie thought that was a good sign and the men confirmed it with their report.

Lieutenant Paddock said, "Well, what did you find out?"

Sergeant Irons said, "Well, the problem was a plugged oil line caused by a large dent in the line. We replaced it and checked the engine, we don't think there was any permanent damage done but won't know until we fire it up."

"Well, let's fire it up and see," said Lieutenant Paddock.

Corporal Lawson climbed into the plane as the sergeant walked around to the right engine. He signaled the corporal to be sure the switches were off and began to pull the propeller through. After several rotations, he nodded and signaled Corporal Lawson to turn on the ignition and push the starter button. The starter whined and finally the engine fired with a cloud of smoke being blown out of the exhaust ports followed by several back fires and more smoke before the engine finally started. Sergeant Irons listened intently and signaled the corporal to increase the throttle. The engine responded with an increase of RPMs until Sergeant Irons signaled him to reduce the throttle. After a few more minutes of listening, Sergeant Irons walked around to the door and climbed in to the cabin.

Lowell, Charlie and Lieutenant Paddock sat in the jeep not saying a word for several minutes.

Over the noise of the engine Lieutenant Paddock said, "Sergeant Irons is one of the best; he served in Africa until he was wounded at Caserne Pass. The engineering officer assigned him for that reason. If he says everything is okay, we will fly this plane out of here."

After a few more minutes, the engine throttled back and suddenly shut down. Sergeant Irons climbed down and walked over to the jeep.

"Well sir I don't think there is any problem with flying this plane, but I wish we could get it over to the highway for take-off, I don't like this rough ground."

"Yea, I know what you mean but look at the terrain we would have to cross to get there," responded the lieutenant. "Well, it's getting pretty dark so I guess we should wait until morning. Let's go in to Lordsburg and see if we can find some beds. You know though, some one will have to stay with the plane!"

They all looked around and finally Corporal Lawson said, "Oh hell, I'll stay. But I get both beers!"

The men laughed and Sergeant Irons handed him the sack with the beers and said, "Sleep tight."

The men arrived in Lordsburg around 2000 and were able to get two rooms with twin beds. Lieutenant Paddock and Sergeant Irons would share a room, as would Charlie and Lowell. Lowell had a little trouble going to sleep in a civilian bed again but finally sleep came. In the morning they ate breakfast at a local diner and climbed into the truck and jeep for the return to the plane. On the way back Lowell decided that if he got to fly home with the lieutenant, he would ask to fly the plane and finish his leg. They arrived at the plane but Corporal Lawson was nowhere around.

Sergeant Irons was livid and said, "That bug out; I'll kill him when he comes back. I bet he wandered off looking for more beer."

Just then they heard a shout and all looked down the road to see the corporal walking back towards the plane.

The sergeant said, "Where in the hell have you been corporal?"

Somewhat indignantly Corporal Lawson said, "I've been checking the road for rocks and pot holes."

Lieutenant Paddock, Charlie and Lowell laughed and a grin spread across the sergeant's face as he said, "Sorry corporal, I thought – –."

He let the rest go.

Lieutenant Paddock said, "What's it look like corporal?"

"Well sir, if you stay a little to the left and can get it off in under 1,000 feet, I think you will be okay."

"Fine, let's get at it then." He turned to Lowell and said, "I'll need a co-pilot, which one of you are going with me?"

Charlie and Lowell looked at each other and Lowell said, "Well, I guess we could flip again."

Charlie said, "No, this was your leg, you go."

"No, let's flip."

Lieutenant Paddock said, "Damn it men; I don't care who goes but get at it."

Lowell nodded at Charlie and then said, "Okay sir, I guess I'll go."

"Well get aboard!"

After they were in the plane, the lieutenant in the left seat and Lowell in the right, Lowell turned to the lieutenant and said, "sir, I would really like to fly the rest of my leg, including taking off from here."

Lieutenant Paddock stared at him for some time and said, "You know that if the colonel found out it would be my ass!"

"Yes sir."

The lieutenant stared at him for awhile longer and said, "Okay cadet, let's see your startup procedures."

*****

Lowell went through the procedures and finally called for the start of the right engine and when it was running smoothly, the left. Sergeant Irons climbed in the back of the plane and leaned between the two pilots and studied the gauges for a minute and then tapped the lieutenant in the shoulder and gave him the thumbs up.

He leaned down and yelled in to his ear, "Keep an eye on that oil pressure and temp on that right engine sir!"

Lieutenant Paddock indicated he had understood and the sergeant left the plane and closed the door. The lieutenant gave Lowell the thumbs up to begin take-off procedures. He advanced the throttles and released the brakes and the plane began to roll.

They had stationed the jeep with Corporal Lawson at the point that if they didn't get off they had to abort and stop because there were several pot holes just a few hundred yards further. Lowell increased the throttles and in checking the instruments, noticed that Lieutenant Paddock had a firm grip on his knees. Several yards from the jeep the tail came up and by applying backpressure on the yoke, the UC-78 lifted into the air. Lieutenant Paddock and Lowell as well as the men on the ground gave a collective sigh of relief.

They flew along occasionally exchanging comments. They talked over the intercom about many things. Lowell said at one point that he thought Sergeant Irons must be one of the best mechanics in the air corps. Lieutenant Paddock said he was and went on to explain that he was in Africa during the early stages of the war and was decorated for bravery at the battle of Caserne Pass. Lowell questioned how a mechanic got into combat.

"Well they needed everyone they could get and they activated cooks, clerks and mechanics."

"What did he do?"

"I'm not sure, but he has the Distinguished Service Cross for bravery above and beyond the call of duty. I heard that he single handedly rescued several men who had been cut off from their units."

"He must be quite a guy."

"Yea."

They both became silent for some time and then Lieutenant Paddock said, "I had better contact the tower." Picking up the mike, switching the channels, he said, "UB-785 to Douglas Tower, come in."

Immediately the response came, "Douglas Tower to UB-785; good to hear from you, over."

"UB-785, thanks; we are about fifteen minutes out. Request landing instructions. Over."

They received their instruction and Lowell looked over at Lieutenant Paddock and he just nodded indicating that Lowell should take her in. Lowell looked questioningly and the lieutenant picked up the mike,

"It's okay Andersen. I was just supposed to take it off that road; once up, it was fine to let you fly."

Lowell made an okay landing, not one of his best but satisfactory. After taxiing up to the parking area and shutting down, Lieutenant Paddock reached over and offered his hand to Lowell.

"Andersen, you are the best cadet I have ever trained and if I ever get out of here and get to the real war, I hope I get in your unit. I would be very proud to serve in your crew."

Lowell shook the lieutenant's hand, thanked him for his nice words then began to unbuckle and get out before the lieutenant could see the tears of pride well up in his eyes.

By evening chow Charlie and the two mechanics had arrived back at Douglas. Lowell and Homer were silently lying on their bunks having thoroughly discussed the "incident" with everyone in the barracks when Charlie came in.

Lowell looked up and said, "Well, welcome home fly boy, or should I call you truck driver boy? What kept you?"

Charlie threw his jacket at him and said, "Yea, thanks a lot. I don't think we missed a tavern between here and Lordsburg!"

Both Lowell and Homer laughed out loud and then got off their bunks and began to get ready for chow.

That night before lights out, Lowell took out his writing kit and started a letter to Helen.

My Dearest Helen,

You will never guess what happened on our cross country flight . . .

Lowell told her about the engine problem, the forced landing, the night in Lordsburg, and Charlie's truck ride home.

There was really nothing to worry about, but I can tell you, both Charlie and I were very worried. Something like that could have washed us both out if we had handled it wrong.

How are the plans coming? Have you guys checked on the trains to Douglas for graduation? It is coming much faster than I thought. Have you or Betty heard from Jew? Will he make the wedding? Charlie said he will try to come up, but I think he and Linda have plans and I wouldn't want to interfere with them, but I sure would like to have him in the wedding party.

Well, it's just a few minutes until lights out so I'll close.

As always to you I give my love and life,

Low

*****

By this time the story of Charlie and Lowell's flight had gotten all around the base. They had achieved something akin to celebrity status among the other cadets, although they felt it was undeserved. A day or two after the incident, they were called in to the colonel's office.

"You know that Lieutenant Paddock let me take-off and fly all the way don't you?"

"Yes."

"Well don't say anything to the colonel, Lieutenant Paddock said it would be his tail, so don't mention it, okay?"

"Don't worry; I won't if you won't say anything to Linda about my trip back with the sergeant and corporal."

Lowell stopped and looked at Charlie in an inquisitive manner and said, "What happened on that trip, did you join them in a beer?"

"Well, yes I did, they insisted so much I decided to try just one."

"Shame on you Charles Smith, what would the bishop say?"

Charlie punched him in the arm and they continued on to the colonel's office. As they entered, the sergeant at the desk told them to have a seat and he would tell the colonel they were there. In a few minutes the door opened and the sergeant beckoned them in. They entered the office, hit a brace and in unison reported to the colonel with their names and held the salute until he returned it,

"At ease cadets, I just wanted to say that we are all very proud of you boys for what you did in the emergency."

They both said, "Thank you sir."

"Yes and I wanted to personally congratulate you both and inform you that you will be receiving a letter of commendation for the way you handled it."

Again they both thanked the colonel and he said, "That is all."

They saluted, did an about face and left the offices.

Walking back to the barracks they were silent until Charlie said, "What is a letter of commendation?"

"Damned if I know; I guess it's like a merit instead of a de-merit."

"Well it can't hurt I guess," said Charlie.

Three days before graduation, Lowell was called to the orderly room.

When he entered the duty corporal said, "Cadet Andersen, I have a message for you."

He handed Lowell a slip of paper with note on it. It was from his father saying they had arrived, were staying in town at a small motor lodge and could he get in to see them. Lowell was so excited he forgot to thank the corporal and rushed out to tell Charlie and Homer that his family had arrived. By this time they knew they were going to make it and had in fact been issued their officers uniforms and insignias. Lowell insisted that Charlie and Homer come along, but they refused saying they could meet his folks at graduation on Friday.

On the way into town, Lowell was so excited he could hardly breathe. When he got to the motor lodge, he walked up the sidewalk until he found room number 6, where his folks were and decided to stop there first before going to see Helen and the twins in room 12. He knocked on the door and his mother opened it and let out a little scream and threw herself in to his arms. His dad put down the paper he was reading and came out and hugged them both. They went in and Lowell's mother wouldn't let go of his arm so he sat on the couch with her.

They exchanged updates and she said, "Didn't you go to Helen's room first?"

"No, I came to yours first so I just stopped."

His dad said, "Well you had better go see Helen and the twins. I don't know which is the most anxious to see you."

"Oh Dad, you know who is most anxious!"

Lowell got up, gave his mother another hug, shook hands with his father and started to leave.

His father said, "Son, send the twins over here after a few minutes, I'm sure you and Helen want to spend some time alone. When you're ready; we want to take you kids out for dinner."

Lowell left and nearly ran over to room 12. Knocking on the door he heard the twins arguing who would open it.

"I'll get it!"

When it flew open, Diane screamed, "LOWELL," and rushed into his arms followed by David.

Lowell gave them a hug and looked past their heads and saw Helen standing in the room smiling at the scene.

After a few seconds Lowell said, "Excuse me kids, there is someone else I want to tell hello."

He walked around the twins and up to Helen looking her in the eyes and said in a low voice, "Hello there soon to be Mrs. Andersen."

"Hello there fly boy," said Helen as she melted into his arms.

They hugged and kissed for a few minutes and then turned to notice that the twins were gone. Through the open door, they could see Mr. Andersen herding them into room 6. After some time lying on the bed, trying not to get to carried away, Lowell suggested that it might be time to go to his folk's room.

Helen said, "Give me a few minutes to straighten up and we can go."

That night was one of the most pleasant and warm evenings Lowell had ever spent. He talked incessantly answering all kinds of questions from not only the twins, but his folks as well. Helen asked about Charlie and Lowell explained that they would see him and Homer at graduation the next day. David wanted to know when he would get his wings and Lowell explained the ceremony and graduation. He asked if Lowell had gotten him any more insignias and was scolded by his mother.

They stayed in the cafe until the waiters began to look anxiously and his father suggested that maybe they should leave so the restaurant could close. Because the lodge where they were staying was only a few blocks, they walked back in the warm June evening. Mr. Andersen commented on how warm it was in Arizona in June, unlike Oregon where it could be cold and wet.

GRADUATION & COMMISSIONING

Several days before graduation, the cadets were gathered in the base theater and told how the ceremony would go. After the brief comments by Colonel Gaelic, the cadets would be called by name up to the stage and handed their wings by the colonel and their second lieutenant bars by Major Charles, the base adjutant. The cadet would salute the officers and leave the stage. If the cadet had family at the ceremony, the tradition allowed a family member to pin on the wings and bars after the ceremony. Receiving their officer's cap to wear with their pinks and greens, (the typical officers' uniforms) the cadets were instructed not to wear it until commissioned. Carrying the officer's cap to the ceremony they placed it under their chairs. At ceremony's end, the new officers removed their cadets caps, threw them in the air and put on their officer's caps upon dismissal.

They also received their orders. Lowell, Charlie and Homer were being sent to Blythe, California for transition to the B-17 *Flying Fortress*. All three would receive training as pilots and if successful, they would assume command of one of the big bombers. There was much backslapping in the room that night and they decided to go to the PX and celebrate.

After staying with his folks at the motor lodge, Lowell reported back to base at 0700 hours as instructed and made his way to the barracks. Homer was lying in his bunk but Charlie was not there.

"Where's Charlie?"

"Oh he just went up to the orderly room for something, said he'd be right back. How was your evening?"

"It was swell, really swell! How was yours?"

"Oh okay, I called my folks back home and told them I would be home in about three days."

"Well then, what's the matter?"

"Oh, I told them to let Virginia Meeker know. She was a girl I dated in high school. I thought I wanted to get more serious with her, but they said she had announced her engagement to a fellow she met at a USO dance."

"That's too bad Homer. Hey, cheer up; we're going to be officers and pilots in a few hours. That'll make her jealous."

"Yea, I guess."

Just then Charlie walked in and greeted them with a big smile and a slap on the back.

*****

Graduation went as expected with brief comments by Colonel Gaelic and a commencement address by some third assistant secretary of the army unknown to them all. When it came time to cross the stage, the cadets perked up a bit. Finally the class was called to attention and as the first cadet's name was called the colonel stepped to the table where the bars and wings were arranged.

"Cadet Andersen!"

Lowell stepped forward one step, did a right face and marched up the stairs to the stage. Colonel Gaelic handed him his wings and Lowell looked down at them stepped back and saluted. With another right face and two steps towards Major Charles he received his second lieutenant bars. Returning to his seat, he couldn't help but look down at them and smile. After all the cadets had passed over the stage, they were called to attention again and dismissed. On three, they all grabbed the bills of their cadet caps and threw them into the air after which they reached under their chairs and brought out their officer's caps, placing them on their heads.

With the completion of that little ceremony, the new officers moved out to mingle with their families. Lowell walked up to Helen and gave her an embrace and kiss.

Stepping back he said, "It is traditional that a loved one pin wings on new pilots for luck. Would you do me the honor Helen?"

With tears running down her face, Helen took the wings and after several attempts pinned them on straight.

Turning to his mother, Lowell said, "Mom, will you pin on my bars?"

Before she could answer, David said, "I want to do that!"

Mrs. Andersen smiled and said, "Okay David you can."

Diane said in a tearful voice, "What do I get to do?"

Lowell solved the problem, he thought, by saying, "Well, you know, I have two bars. Why don't you each pin one on?"

"Okay, I get the one on this side!" David shouted, then, changing his mind just as Diane started to move around Lowell, he said, "Oh no, I want the other side!"

Lowell, his parents and Helen all laughed as he knelt down so they could pin them on.

Diane looked over and said, "That's crooked David!"

"It is not, Lowell's just got his shoulder turned."

Lowell looked at Helen and said, "You sure you want them in the wedding?"

That night they went out with Charlie and Linda while Charlie's parents and the Andersen's went to dinner. Three of Charlie's younger siblings had come with his parents for graduation. Lowell and Charlie laughed about how they would do with all the kids. The two couples found a little restaurant, had dinner and went to a movie. It was such a beautiful June Arizona night that they decided to walk back to the motor lodge where they were all staying. On the way back they walked arm in arm and finally the subject of weddings came up.

With that opening, Linda made a big sigh and said, "Helen, I've been putting this off, but I don't think I'm going to be able to come up for your wedding."

Helen turned around and in an anguished tone asked why. Linda explained that the family had made plans to take a vacation together because her brother would be going into the service soon and they wanted to do something all together.

"I feel so bad about not letting you know sooner. I was hoping my father would change his mind, but he hasn't!"

Helen took Linda's hand in hers and told her that it was okay. She understood. Linda and Charlie then announced that they had decided to wait until they found out where Charlie was going to be assigned. Lowell asked again if Charlie was sure he wanted to come up for their wedding and Charlie assured him he did. Helen repeated how much she would like to have Linda in the wedding, but understood completely. The two couples relationship, particularly the girl's, was one born of the times. People who had not known each other very long became fast friends very quickly because of the war situation. Helen felt true friendship for Linda though they had known each other for only a few days.

Myron's Request

It was only three days before he started his leave to go home, see Betty and help Lowell get married. He was very anxious to do both. As Myron and his student walked across the apron towards the ready room, a corporal came up and saluted.

"Lieutenant Rothstein, you're requested to report to the major's office."

Returning the salute Myron said, "Very well corporal. Thanks."

Most of the enlisted men liked Myron; he was fair and treated them as humans, unlike some of the officers. Myron finished filling out the report on his cadet, filed it and left the ready room heading for the major's office. When he entered, he told the sergeant that the CO had requested to see him and he was told to have a seat. He couldn't figure what it was all about; he hadn't screwed up as far as he knew, but one was never sure in the army.

The major's door suddenly opened and the major came out.

"Come on in lieutenant."

Myron stood up and followed the major back in to his office. He started to salute but the major motioned him to sit.

"Have a seat Rothstein."

Myron had never seen the major act like this before. He was quite informal and wore a big grin. As he sat down, the major rounded his desk and took his seat. He looked at Myron for awhile then picked up a piece of paper.

"Guess what this is?"

Myron looked dumb founded and said, "I have no idea sir."

"Well, it is a large levy calling for twenty navigators to be reassigned to combat crews," replied the major. "And, it says all personnel qualified may be considered."

Myron began to get the picture and broke out in a large smile.

"Does that mean that you will accept my request for transfer?"

"Yes, that is exactly what it means."

Myron sat looking at the major for a minute as the realization sunk in. Then it dawned on him why the big smile was on the major's face.

He said, "Does that mean that the orders might include a certain major?"

"You damn betcha it does! I got permission from the colonel this morning. I will be assigned in a few weeks. So if you're still interested, have your request on my desk by morning."

"Thank you sir! I'll get right on it."

Myron rose from the chair and gave the major one of the snappiest salutes he had ever presented to any officer.

"Oh, just a minute Rothstein. When could you be ready to go on leave?"

"I'd like to leave Thursday morning, if I can make train connections."

"Why don't you call the flight line over at the field and see if they have anything going that way."

"Thanks a lot major. Can I do that from here, now?

"I don't see why not."

Myron made the call and found out there was a flight of three B-24s going to San Francisco on Thursday around 1000 hours and asked if he could catch a ride. The duty sergeant said he would put him down and that he needed to be at the flight line by 0800 at the latest.

As he walked back to the barracks, Myron could not help but smile to himself about the transfer, but he wondered how Betty would take it. It surely meant an overseas assignment and he knew that would be a problem for her. He was glad she had decided to finish the term at college and had not moved down with him. He would not have to face her when he broke the news.

That night after training, Myron sat down at his desk and filled out his transfer request. He sat and thought for a minute about what the future might bring and decided that he should not worry about it. He had wanted to get a combat assignment for so long that he wondered why he was even reconsidering; however, it was only a brief hesitation. He finished the transfer request, read it over, put it in an envelope, sealed it and turned out the light. Tomorrow he would begin a process that might, just might, get him killed.

The next morning as he drove the jeep loaned to him by the major he thought of how he would tell Betty. He decided he'd talk to Low; Low always had a good way of talking to girls. At the airfield he was issued a parachute, helmet and oxygen mask and introduced to the pilot.

"Where are you headed lieutenant?"

"I'm going to Oregon to see my wife and be best man at my best friend's wedding. Where you guys going?"

"I'm afraid that we don't have such a happy trip. We are flying the first leg of an overseas assignment in the Pacific."

Somewhat shocked Myron asked, "You flying all the way?"

"No," the captain said with a slight laugh. "We're loading the planes on a transport for shipment and it is a very slow boat I'm afraid."

"Oh, well I really appreciate this hop."

"Glad to help, let's get aboard lieutenant, I wouldn't want you to be late for that wedding."

The Trip Home

On the train ride home, Lowell asked about the wedding plans and Helen assured him they were on track. Lowell had received a letter from Myron and he thought he could get home okay.

Lowell asked Helen, "Are you very disappointed that Linda won't be in the party?"

"Well yes I am, but I understand."

"Who will you get to replace her?"

"I was thinking about Vera Freddricks, a friend from college, what do you think?"

"Yea, would she look okay with Charlie?"

Helen leaned forward and looked into Lowell's eyes, "Lowell, she won't be in the wedding party, that's my sister Linda and Betty, Vera will be doing the guest book!"

"Oh that's right, sorry I forgot. So Betty will walk with Charlie and Linda will be with Myron?"

"No," responded Helen, "Linda and Betty will come down before me. Just remember which girl you're going to marry."

Lowell reached out and pulled Helen to him again and said, "When will Charlie and Jew come down the aisle?"

Helen pulled away from him, looked him in the eye and said, "Myron will be in the back and will enter with you; Charlie will come down before the processional begins. You'll see how it all works at the rehearsal."

"Oh," and Lowell leaned back and brought Helen closer to him again.

As the train rolled across Arizona towards California Lowell looked out the window for a long period.

Helen reached up and turned his face towards her and said, "Penny for your thoughts?"

"Oh, I was just thinking what the next few months are going to be like and what surprises they might bring."

"Well, I like that, what surprises are you thinking about?"

Lowell laughed saying, "I don't mean us. I'm thinking about the war, where I'll be sent and what might happen."

"Don't you even think like that Mr. Lowell Andersen! Everything is going to be just fine, you wait and see!"

With that Lowell leaned over, kissed her and held her until they heard a young voice say, "Are you guys smooching again?"

They turned to see David standing behind them. Lowell reached out, grabbed him around the neck, wrestled him into the seat and gave him a knuckle rub on his head until he let out a loud yell. Mr. Andersen immediately got up from his seat and came forward.

"Come David, let's go to the club car and have a coke or something."

Diane immediately jumped up and said, "I want to come too."

"Okay, come on both of you."

Lowell and Helen just laughed and she said, "I think I'll go back and sit with your mother for awhile, okay?"

"Sure, that will give me a chance to think what I want to."

Helen gave him a loving punch on the shoulder as she got up and walked back the three rows to where Mrs. Andersen was sitting.

Later, as the train came into Salem, it was raining quite hard.

Lowell said, "Boy does that rain look good."

"Well it might to you, but we have a little activity soon and I want it to be a beautiful sunny day for that."

"It will be, even if it is raining."

The next few days were a blur of activity before the big day. They finalized the plans for the the wedding ceremony and honeymoon. Myron arrived in Salem on Thursday and at 4:00 that afternoon Lowell, Helen, Charlie, who had arrived the day before, and Betty, were waiting at the station. They asked the stationmaster if the train was on time and were told that it had been held up for a troop train in California, but would arrive within the hour. As they waited, Helen asked Charlie if he was disappointed about postponing their wedding.

"No, I'm sorry to disappoint Linda, but I think it is for the best. Remember, we haven't known each other as long as you two have; besides you never know what might happen."

A look of concern passed over Helen's face and Charlie immediately realized what he had done.

Later as the boys went in to the rest room, Charlie said, "God I'm sorry Lowell, I really put my foot in my mouth didn't I?"

"Nah, that's all right, I don't think Helen caught on. You know, I thought about it a long time when I thought of Helen as a twenty year old widow, but I don't think the girls ever consider what might happen to us."

After they had finished Lowell touched Charlie's arm and said, "There is something I must warn you about before Myron gets here."

Charlie looked confused and said, "Oh."

"Well, every since we have been little kids, Myron and I have this standing joke about our religion; I call him Jew and he calls me Swede. I hope it won't offend you."

"I don't think it will. One of my best friends at home was a Baptist."

Lowell laughed and said, "Oh really, where is he now?"

"He was killed on Guadalcanal."

"My God, Charlie, I'm sorry!"

"That's alright. You didn't know."

Suddenly they heard a train whistle and both rushed out toward the arrival platform. Betty and Helen were nearly jumping up and down as the train pulled in to the station. Charlie and Lowell approached and said, "Come on, let's go get Myron."

Betty could hardly control herself until she saw Myron in the door of train and all constraint went out of her as she screamed and ran to him nearly knocking him down. The rest of the welcoming committee stood back for awhile and let them have a moment. Finally they separated and Myron walked over toward Lowell and suddenly turned to Charlie.

"You must be Charlie, the guy that got my friend Lowell those little silver wings!"

Charlie laughed and offered his hand, which Myron took with a warm shake, then turned to Lowell and said, "Hello buddy, how are things?"

Lowell reached out and grabbed Myron and held him in an embrace for several seconds. "Good to see you old friend."

As they turned to the girls, who were standing with tears running down their faces, Myron gave Helen a big hug.

Looking toward Lowell he said, "Are you sure? I think I can find another guy. It isn't too late you know."

They all laughed as Betty said, "They haven't changed a bit. You might get used to this bantering this week Charlie but we never have and we've know them for nearly fifteen years."

Charlie laughed and said, "I like it. I've had a little sample over the last year so it isn't a surprise."

They all piled into the Lowell's '33 Ford, which his dad had prepared for him, and headed for Drayville. Lowell, Helen and Charlie were in the front and Myron and Betty in the back.

Lowell said, "Now listen Jew, we have a guest here so please wait until you get home will you?"

Betty reached up and punched Lowell in the back just as Helen punched him in the ribs. Charlie just laughed again, but there was a twinge of embarrassment in the laugh.

Next morning, the day before the wedding, Helen called Lowell and told him that he should stay out of her way this day because she had a lot to do and she needed Betty to help so they were sending Myron over to him. Mrs. Andersen fixed a big breakfast for the boys and served it with hot steaming coffee. Lowell and Charlie just smiled at each other but didn't say anything as Charlie picked up the cup and took a drink.

About 10:00 o'clock the back door opened and Myron came in asking if breakfast was ready. Mrs. Andersen said it was almost over but that she would fix him some.

He laughed and grabbed her in an embrace and said, "Do you think my mom would let me get out of the house without a big Jewish breakfast."

Lowell said, "Come on sit down, we've go plenty of ham left."

"Lowell, shame on you, Charlie might not understand you two."

"That's okay Mrs. Andersen. He's always trying to get me to drink coffee and coke."

When a blank look crossed his mother's face, Lowell said, "Charlie is of the Mormon faith. They don't consume anything with caffeine in it although I did get him to drink a coke once or twice."

"Lowell you should be ashamed of your self; I'm sorry Charlie, I didn't know."

"It's alright Mrs. Andersen, since I've known your son I've done several things that my mother probably wouldn't approve of."

"Well your mother is a very nice lady and I offer my apologies to her for anything Lowell has done to lead you astray."

"I'm sure Myron will agree with me that there is no better friend than Lowell."

"Well, I don't know about that," replied Myron.

"Well thanks a lot. Are you guys ready to go?" said Lowell as he turned to Myron. "We've got to show Charlie around town."

They got up and Lowell and Myron noticed that Charlie picked up his dishes and took them to the sink. They looked at him and both shrugged. They had never thought of doing anything like that. They climbed into the '33 and started off on their day's activities. They took Charlie to the high school and showed him where they achieved all their teen-age greatness. As they were getting into the car, the principal, Mr. Vernon came out of the building and yelled to them.

"Lowell, Myron! How are you boys?"

"Hello Mr. Vernon. How are you?"

"How is the army boys? Lowell, I hear you and Helen are getting married this week. Congratulations! She's a wonderful girl."

"Yea, I know. How's school going? I heard that the football team won the league this year! Finally beat old Willamette."

"Yes, and we had a very good basketball and baseball season as well."

"Oh, this is a friend of mine, Charlie Smith. Charlie, this is Mr. Vernon, our principal."

"Glad to meet you Mr. Vernon," said Charlie.

"What are you boys up to?" said Mr. Vernon.

"Oh we're just showing Charlie around the old town."

"Do you have any idea where you will be stationed next?"

"Well, Charlie and I go back to California for transition and somewhere for crew training. Myron, you're going back to Texas aren't you?"

"Well, I haven't mentioned it yet, but just before I left my CO told me that my transfer will be coming through soon after I get back."

"No kidding, that's great Myron. Any idea where you're going?"

"No, I will probably join a crew for further training, I don't know where."

"Hey, wouldn't it be great if you joined my crew?"

"Or mine," replied Charlie.

Saying goodbye to Mr. Vernon they continued the tour of Drayville stopping at various points of interest such as the river where they used to hang out. They pulled up on Main Street and walked down to Andersen's Garage where Lowell had a short visit with George and then walked further down the street. As they passed the bank, Mr. Dickerson came out. He greeted the boys and was introduced to Charlie.

"Oh, Mr. Dickerson, what do you hear about Vernon?"

"Well, he is still listed as missing and I guess that's something. We pray every day and I'm in touch with the army, but they have no new information."

"I'm sorry Mr. Dickerson; I hope you'll get word soon."

"Yes, thank you boys. Oh, and congratulations Lowell. You're getting a very fine girl."

"Yes, I know I am."

They continued their tour stopping at Rothstein's Furniture store and at Speer's Lumber Yard. They had lunch at the soda fountain. Several high school kids were there and Myron commented on how loud they were.

"It's hard to believe that we were just like that less than two years ago."

Charlie laughed and said, "Yea, I thought I was the most mature and sophisticated man in the world. Boy was I wrong. I think I'm that now!"

They all laughed and continued eating their lunch. After lunch, they walked back to the car and drove home.

There was a rehearsal at the church that night with Lowell's Uncle Norwood officiating and Lowell and Helen merely acting as participants. Uncle Norwood had met with them earlier in the afternoon and talked about the seriousness of what they were about to do. He mentioned the importance of being in love, about which neither Lowell nor Helen had any doubt. He also discussed that the affair the next day was just the tiniest part of a marriage and that devotion, respect and loyalty was very important in making a good marriage.

That night Lowell didn't sleep very well. All he could think about was the wedding the next day and the honeymoon. They had planned four days at the beach and then home. Lowell had only nine days leave then he had to report in to Blythe. They had decided that Helen would stay home until he could find a place to stay and get permission to live off base. After transition training, they didn't know what to expect, but they really didn't care. Lowell thought the chances of getting a crew training base on the West Coast were pretty good and Helen could go with him. After that, who knew?

WEDDING DAY

Saturday, June 5, 1944. The day of the wedding dawned clear and bright. There was a little nip in the air as always in early June. Lowell woke up but lay there for some time thinking of what was in store for the day. He and Myron had talked a lot about marriage and the doubts that come to one about to enter into that state. Myron assured Lowell that it is probably the ceremony and not the marriage that scares most men. Lowell surely hoped so because as he lay there he was more scared than when he took his first solo flight.

When he came downstairs, Charlie was already sitting in the kitchen talking to his mother. "Well, we weren't sure you were going to get up in time for the wedding."

"Oh, I was just laying in bed thinking about the day's events."

His mother said, "What would you like for breakfast?"

"I'm not really hungry this morning Mom, maybe just some coffee."

Just then the twins came in from outside and David was yelling, "Mom, Diane won't let me ride the bike."

"I will too, you rode it for a long time and now it's my turn."

"Okay you guys, I might have a solution for the problem," said Lowell.

"What's a solution?"

"A solution means to solve the problem," replied Lowell.

"What is it?" both twins asked in unison.

"Come with me."

Lowell took them downstairs to where he had hung his bicycle and took it off the hooks. Both tires were flat, but other than that, it was in reasonably good shape.

"Let's take it down to the garage and have the tires pumped up and you can use mine."

"Really? Oh boy, I get it."

Diane said, "Who says?"

"Well it's a boy's bike and I'm a boy."

"So is our bike," replied Diane.

Lowell said, "Yes, but your bike is newer and slightly smaller and David is bigger and probably he will be able to ride mine better."

"Oh that's right. Okay, I get the newer bike."

David didn't quite know if he had received the best of the deal but he was getting Lowell's bike so that made it okay. Lowell looked at Charlie who had followed them down to the basement.

"Do you have to go through this with your little brothers and sisters?"

"I sure do! This makes me feel right at home."

Lowell yelled up to tell his mom that they were going down to the garage to pump up his bike tires and that they would be right back. On the way, David kept trying to jump on the bike and Lowell had to keep yelling at him. In their excitement the twins, pushing the bike, were nearly a block ahead of him and Charlie. When they arrived at the garage Mr. Andersen had the bike out at the air hoses and was just finishing pumping up the tires. Lowell took David around the back and helped him on the bike and shoved him off. He had no trouble riding the bike.

Diane took off on her bike and yelled, "Wait for me!"

Mr. Andersen, Lowell and Charlie just stood there laughing as the twins rode out of sight.

Mr. Andersen turned to Lowell and said, "That was very nice of you. I had thought of giving them your bike a dozen times, but I remember how hard you worked for the money to buy it and wasn't sure that would be okay. I'll be sure he takes good care of it for you."

"That's Okay Dad. I probably won't use it after I get home anyway."

"Well, what have you boys got planned for the day?"

"Oh I have a little shopping to do and I might go see Helen."

"Oh no, you can't see the bride on the wedding day! It's bad luck," Charlie said.

"Well we will probably go get Jew and hang out down at the soda shop or something."

*****

Lowell came downstairs in full uniform and his parents stood up and stared for a minute. His mother walked over and put her arms around him and gave him a big hug. His father shook his hand and the twins for once didn't have a thing to say. Charlie stood in the background; he was about as excited as Lowell. They walked out to the '33 and got in just as Myron came down the sidewalk.

"Well, it still isn't too late you know."

"Just get in and shut up, will ya!"

Charlie laughed; Myron got in the car and Lowell started it up. They drove to the church and Lowell and Myron walked around the back while Charlie went in the front. He was going to act as an usher until it was time for the ceremony. As they entered the church office, they were greeted by Uncle Norwood who shook hands with both boys.

The wedding ceremony was a big blur to Lowell except when he saw Helen and her father coming down the aisle. She was the most beautiful thing he had ever seen. She walked like an angel with a very large smile on her face as she nodded to people in the pews. He really hadn't noticed anyone before but as he watched Helen, he realized that many people were present that he knew. Diane, acting as flower girl, was leading the procession and gently dropping rose petals. Then Linda, Helen's sister, came down the aisle, followed by Betty. A smile crossed Lowell's face when he saw David carrying the pillow with the ring on it. He looked so serious and he marched like a soldier. Charlie, who had joined them at the altar, stepped next to Myron.

The ceremony went off as scheduled, ending with Uncle Norwood saying, "I now pronounce you man and wife,"

Lowell just stood there looking at him until he said, "Go on Lowell, kiss your wife!"

Among much laughter, Lowell gave Helen a slight peck on the lips just as the recessional started. Helen took his arm and they walked down the aisle as man and wife followed by Linda and Myron, Charlie and Betty, and finally Diane and David. The processional went out through the narthex to the social hall for the reception. They formed a line with Myron, Betty, Linda and Charlie. Many old friends came through, mostly the girls they had gone to school with because many of the boys were away in the service.

One surprise was the pitcher from the baseball team, Gerald Olson. He was in his navy uniform and looked very handsome. He had a girl on his arm and when Lowell greeted him, he introduced her as his fiancée, Ruth Carlson. He and Lowell exchanged a few recollections from high school.

"Gerald, I'll talk to you later," said Lowell. "Stick around will you?"

"Yea, I've got two weeks home before I ship out."

Later after all the guests passed through the line, Lowell and Helen cut the traditional wedding cake and each had a piece. Lowell spotted Gerald Olson over in the corner talking to Jew and Charlie.

He walked over and said, "Well Gerald, how are things with you? Last time I saw you was at Jew's wedding and you were heading to signalman's school."

Myron said, "Remember how this guy pulled our bacon out of the fire in that Mitchell game?"

"Yea," Lowell responded. "You had just struck out and Gerald stepped up and drove me in for the winning run."

"I don't remember that!" Myron exclaimed.

Lowell turned to Gerald and asked. "Where are you going next?"

"I'm on my way to the Pacific," he replied. "I don't know where but we get to spend a month in Hawaii." Looking down at Myron's chest he asked, "How come your wings are different than Lowell's and Charlie's?"

"Oh they're just airplane drivers, I tell them where to go; I'm a navigator."

Lowell taking all this friendly banter in said, "Well I guess I should move around the room a little. Catch you guys later."

As he walked away Charlie watched him go and said, "Lowell was the best pilot in our class. He and I had to make an emergency landing on our final cross country flight and he brought the plane in on a dirt road. They gave us both a letter of commendation, but I felt I didn't deserve one."

"Oh come on Charlie, you were crew and I'm sure you contributed just as much as Low did." Myron slapped him on the back and turned to Gerald, "How long are you going to be home?"

"Well I've got ten days, but we're going to Albany to visit Ruth's parents, so I guess I'll be around here for a week or so."

"Charlie, how long are you staying? I thought we might get together and do something."

"I'm leaving tomorrow morning if I can get a seat on the train."

"Where do you live?"

"Salt Lake City."

"You shouldn't have any trouble; there aren't many bases in that area are there?"

"Just a couple. I'm going to try to get to Santa Maria, California to visit my fiancée."

"Oh, that could be another matter. Say, Betty and I are going out tonight, why don't you guys join us, maybe a movie and hamburgers."

Both Charlie and Gerald agreed that would be great. Suddenly there was a disturbance at the door of the social hall.

"They're trying to sneak away."

Everybody ran to the door grabbed little cups of rice and headed for the front of the church where Lowell and Helen were trying to get through amid flying rice. As they got to their car, they discovered someone had wired several tin cans to the rear bumper and filled the front seat with rice and wadded up newspapers. Myron ran up to Lowell as he shut the door on Helen's side of the car, grabbed his hand and whispered something in his ear. Lowell looked up, punched Jew in the shoulder and ran to the driver's side where several men were trying to get the door open but it was still locked. Lowell pushed his way to the door, Helen opened it from inside and Lowell got in, started the car and they were off in a hail of rice and rattle of tin cans. Mr. and Mrs. Lowell Andersen, taking their first ride as man and wife.

Transition, Blythe, California

As the bus pulled into the base at Blythe, California, Lowell had never seen any place so desolate and barren. The wind was kicking up dust swirls and there did not seem to be any living vegetation in sight. If there was anything that could make him feel more depressed than leaving Helen it was his new duty station.

He reported in and was told he would be quartered in Bachelor Officers Quarters number fourteen, several yards down the street from the orderly room. A corporal said he would help him, picked up his duffel bag and bid him to follow. As they walked down the street, Lowell could see into several of the barracks windows, and didn't find them to be much different from other barracks in which he had lived. So much for being an officer and a gentleman.

When they entered number fourteen, several fellows he knew from advanced greeted him. There were individual rooms housing two men each.

The corporal looked on a sheet and said, "This is your room, sir."

As Lowell entered a familiar face looked up at him and said, "Well, look who's here," as he got up and extended his hand.

"How is every thing Homer?"

"Just fine and with you? Say weren't you going to get married?"

"Yea I did and it was, I mean is great! Who else is in here with us?"

"Well, I'm not sure, but Charlie's in the next room."

"Oh that's swell."

While he was unpacking, Charlie walked in and said, "What, you're staying in the barracks? I though you might have a different room mate down here."

"Yea, well, we decided to wait until I looked over the situation and found a place to rent. I guess they will give me enough time to look around."

"Well, I suppose they will."

The next day started like many except that no cadre came into the barracks yelling. They were told to fall out. The first day was merely an introduction to what they would experience during the transition training. There would be some class work and a lot of flying including night flights, flights on three engines, and maybe even short flights on two engines. They would sharpen their navigation skills and work a lot on formation flying, but mainly, they would learn how to fly the Boeing B-17 *Flying Fortress.*

That afternoon Lowell got a pass and went into town to look for an apartment. Checking the local papers he found four advertisements. The first was a one room shack out in back of a very old and not very well kept house. They wanted fifty dollars a month rent. The second was a single room upstairs in a house with kitchen privileges after 5:00 at night for forty dollars a month.

The third place was in a much better neighborhood and Lowell went up to the front door of a very nice house. He knocked and a middle aged woman answered. She reminded him of Mrs. Cooper who lived just down the street from him in Drayville.

"May I help you lieutenant?" she asked in a very pleasant voice.

"Yes, I was wondering, is the apartment still for rent?"

"Why yes it is. Would you like to see it?"

"Yes I would. I am looking for a place for me and my girl friend."

Lowell immediately realized what he had said and corrected himself. "I mean my wife!"

The lady smiled and asked, "Haven't been married for long huh?"

Red-faced Lowell responded, "About two weeks."

"I'm Mrs. Yocum," she said extending her hand."

"I'm Lowell Andersen, glad to meet you."

"I'll show you the apartment but I have to get the key first."

She went in the house and came out with a key in her hand.

"Right this way," she said as she pointed off the porch.

She led him around the back of a building that looked like a garage. There was a stairway up the back which she climbed, unlocked the door, and beckoned him in. As Lowell entered he was hit with a blast of hot air, but the apartment looked clean and he noticed a door towards the back.

Mrs. Yocum said, "This is of course the living, eating area and kitchen and in the back is the bed room. The bath with shower is on the back porch of the house, but there is a separate door that you would have a key to."

Lowell walked around the living area and then opened the door and looked into the bedroom. There was a small wardrobe in the corner, a bedside table on one side and the bed looked fairly new. He took a deep breath and though he was almost afraid to ask, he said, "How much rent?"

"Twenty-five a month."

Lowell almost choked and with open mouth he said, "Twenty-five a month?"

Mrs. Yocum laughed slightly, and said, "Too much?"

"Oh no, that's not it."

"Well, my husband and I fixed this loft for you service boys. We have two sons in the service and wanted to do something to help."

"I'll take it!"

"Okay, I would like to have the first month in advance. Also we do not allow parties past 10:00 P.M. No drinking and another thing I guess I might tell you, my husband is in Los Angeles working in the aircraft industry and only gets home on week ends so I might call on you or your wife to help me with an occasional chore."

"Oh that would be just fine." Lowell reached in his pocket and took out his billfold removing two tens and a five and handing them to her.

As he walked back towards town with a quick step he found a pay phone and called Helen. He told her of his good luck and she said it would take a few days to make arrangements but she would come as soon as possible. Lowell gave the address of the apartment, told her to hurry and that he loved her and missed her.

The next few days as outlined in the syllabus, were mostly classroom work, including instrumentation, fuel mixtures and a myriad of other technicalities of the B-17. Lowell was somewhat distracted as he tried to imagine what Helen was doing at that moment. He hoped she was on the train on her way to join him.

He had submitted a request and had been approved for off-base living. He packed his B4 bag and with help from one of the pilots who had a car, Charlie and Homer, he moved into the apartment. Homer made several suggestive comments about the workbench (bed) where little engines for tricycles are made but they all agreed it was a find.

Several days later after a shortened training day, Lowell took the bus in to town and walked the few blocks to the apartment. When he turned the corner near the Yocum house, he saw someone sitting on the porch with Mrs. Yocum. He quickened his pace until he was running. When Helen spotted him she ran off the porch into his arms.

On their first night, Mrs. Yocum had invited them for a marvelous supper of fried potatoes, hamburger and a green salad. As they finished dinner, she began to ask them about their lives. They told her they had known each other since grade school and had only been married a few weeks. She told them about her family. The Yocums had two sons in the service and a daughter whose husband was also serving. Mr. Yocum had been a local businessman but when the war started, he wanted to do more so he turned the business over to his brother for the duration and went into essential war work. He worked at the Lockheed plant in Burbank building B-17s. Lowell related that that was the plane he was learning to fly.

"Where are your boys?"

"Well, Victor is in the navy serving in the South Pacific and David is in the air corps some where in England. Gloria's husband is a supply officer in the air corps in India."

"Oh that would be the Ninth Air Force."

"Yes, I guess, I don't pay much attention to those numbers."

"What business was Mr. Yocum in?"

"He was in partnership with his brother in a car dealership."

Lowell said, "My dad owns a service station and garage in Drayville, kind of the same thing I guess."

"My folks own a lumber yard," added Helen.

After a very relaxing evening, Lowell and Helen excused themselves and went to their apartment. As they reached the door, Lowell reached down and picked Helen up.

"Our first home, I have to carry you across the threshold."

Helen gave him a kiss and snuggled up to his shoulder as he carried her into the apartment. They immediately opened the one window and left the door open to cool it a little. "Boy, we don't need a heater in here."

"Well maybe this winter."

"I hope we're not here this winter."

Helen gave him a worried look and said, "Yes, I wonder where we will be this winter?"

Lowell, realizing he had upset her, took her in his arms and said, "Wherever I am, I will be okay and still in love with you."

"Oh you. I know that!"

*****

As outlined, the first weeks of transition was mostly classroom work, but finally they were told to report to the flight line. Lowell was assigned Captain Compton as a transitional instructor. He had drawn his flight gear including a parachute and walked out inquiring for the captain. A sergeant pointed him out and Lowell walked up to him, saluted and reported in. Captain Compton was a fairly short stocky man who looked several years older than Lowell although he learned later that he was only two years older. He also learned that he had completed thirty missions with the Eighth Air Force out of England and he was waiting to be re-assigned.

The captain greeted him and said, "Come on over here and meet the rest of the flight crew."

The flight crew for transition consisted of only a radio operator, a navigator and a flight engineer.

"Gentleman, this is Lieutenant Andersen, our pilot for today. Lieutenant this is Lieutenant Casey, our navigator, Sergeant Noble, the flight engineer, and Sergeant Towner, our radio man."

Lowell greeted each one as he shook hands all around. They boarded the 17 and Lowell was instructed to take the right seat for the first few flights. The captain went over the instruments and had Lowell repeat them all. He called the rest of the crew on the intercom to see if they were ready and then turned to Lowell and asked if he was ready. Lowell responded that he was and the captain began the start up procedures. With all four engines running, they taxied out to the runway. The captain called the tower and gained permission to take-off.

"Okay Andersen, put your feet on the brakes and you will have your first lesson in flying the B-17. Now as I run up the engines, we both have to stand on the brakes, got that?"

Lowell nodded his head and did as he was told. As the captain ran the engines up the aircraft seemed to want to go and they had to press harder and harder on the brakes to hold. Finely Captain Compton told him to release the brakes and the 17 began to roll down the runway. Lowell was surprised at the power he felt with the four big Wright cyclone engines running at near full RPMs.

After they were airborne at about 3,000 feet, Captain Compton said, "Okay Andersen, take it."

The 17 flew considerably easier than the UB-78. The extra two engines made a great deal of difference in power and rate of climb. The captain told him to climb to 5,000 feet. Lowell advanced the throttles and was pressed back into his seat. He then realized why Captain Compton had told him to climb.

"Climbs pretty good doesn't it?" he heard the captain say over the intercom.

"Yes sir, it sure does."

"You have just had your second lesson on the difference between a training aircraft and a combat one."

After a few circuits and several more climbs and dips, the captain said he would take it and land.

"Tomorrow we'll see how your take-offs and landings are."

That night during supper, Lowell was very quiet and pensive. Helen asked if there was anything wrong.

"Captain Compton said that tomorrow I'm going to try my first take-off in the 17," he said. "I guess I am just thinking about what if I mess up."

"Lowell Andersen, why would you think that? Haven't you managed to do everything so far in training with out messing up?"

"Yea, I guess; but you know, there is always a first time."

"You'll be just fine, so quit worrying about it and eat your supper."

"You sound just like my mother when I was worried about a game or a test."

They both laughed and Helen reached over and kissed him on the cheek.

The next day was, as most days in Blythe, very hot and dusty. Lowell was in a full sweat before he even got to the flight line – mostly from his nervousness. Captain Compton greeted him in his usual cheery way and asked if he was ready. Lowell responded with a sigh and was told to climb aboard. When they got to the cockpit, he motioned Lowell to the left seat. With some hesitation, he slid into the seat and began to adjust his straps and chute.

"Okay lieutenant, let's see what you've learned."

Lowell began to go through the checklist as the captain answered each inquiry he presented to him. When they finished the pre-startup list, Lowell said, "Clear on the right?"

"Clear."

"Start number three engine."

The whine of the starter engine filled the airplane as the propeller on the number three engine began to turn. Number three, the right inboard engine, was always started first because it powered the hydraulic and electrical systems for the entire aircraft. Suddenly in a cloud of smoke the engine sprang to life with a roar. Lowell repeated the process until all four engines were running. He scanned the instrument panel to be sure all gauges were in the proper position, ordered the captain to stand on the brakes and ran the engines up. He again scanned the instruments and when he was satisfied that everything was normal, backed the throttles down to the idle setting.

He called the tower for permission to taxi to the strip for take-off and was given permission. As he advanced the throttles, the plane failed to move and he looked with horror at Captain Compton who said with a slight grin, "Don't you think you should indicate to the ground crew to remove the chalks?"

Lowell was mortified. To forget such a basic step as that was unforgivable. He immediately opened the window and gave the ground crew the signal to remove chalks and grinned sheepishly at the captain.

When they taxied to the strip, Lowell ordered the take-off checklist to be read. When it was complete, he called the tower again and requested permission to take-off. The tower gave him a wind direction and speed and replied that he was clear for take-off. Lowell turned and told Sergeant Noble to take station for take-off, then picked up the intercom mike.

"Pilot to crew, take stations for take-off."

He called for take-off engine mixture, proper flaps and prop pitch then began to advance the throttles. At the recommended RPMs he released the brakes and the big ship began to roll down the runway. The take-off was very smooth and he was again amazed at the power the four big Wright engines put out as the B-17 lifted effortlessly into the air.

The weeks passed with more and more flying and several lessons that caused many of the pilots some consternation. The night flying was the most difficult to master. Being unable to see the ground was difficult even though they had been exposed to it in advance training.

One day as Lowell and Charlie were sitting in the day room drinking a coke, Homer walked in and said, "Did you guys hear about Bracken?"

Tony Bracken was a classmate from advanced.

"No, what?"

"He and his crew are missing. They didn't return from the exercise last night and they have no idea were they are."

"Wow, that's awful. What route were they flying"?

"I'm not sure," replied Homer.

They were silent for a time until Lowell said, "Do they think they crashed or maybe just made a forced landing some where."

"I guess they don't know. They have search planes out but the guy who told me said they haven't located anything yet."

"Let's go over to the ready room and see if they know anything yet," said Charlie.

"I just came from there and they won't tell you even if they know," replied Homer.

Because they were scheduled for more night flying, Lowell did not go home that night. He wanted to call Helen so much he hurt but he did not want to worry her. She had gotten a part time job working in a Five and Dime store in town and would just about be getting home. Besides, he didn't want to bother Mrs. Yocum.

The night exercise went well for Lowell, but the thought of Tony Bracken was on his mind and detracted from the complements Captain Compton gave him for a good flight. As they walked from the plane to the ready room, the sun was rising.

Sergeant Noble caught up to him and said, "Lieutenant, excuse me, but I just wanted to say you are one of the best pilots I have ever flown with and if I have to go over seas again, I would like to be in your crew."

Lowell was somewhat taken aback by the sergeant's comments since he had completed thirty missions over Europe and was a master sergeant.

He smiled and said "Thank you sergeant. I can't believe that with your experience, but thanks so much."

"Well, some of us enlisted men were talking the other day and we decided that you and Lieutenant Smith would be our choice to fly with if we have to go over again."

"I really appreciate that sergeant, and if I have a choice, I would like to have you in my crew also. Thanks again."

That complement helped Lowell take his mind off of Tony somewhat but mainly he was so tired that he just wanted to get home to Helen and go to sleep. After an all night exercise, the trainees were given a day off. He entered the supply room, turned in his flight gear and walked over to the ready room to meet with Captain Compton for his debriefing on the flight. When he opened the door, he was shocked to see Tony standing there.

With out thinking he yelled, "Tony, how did you get here?"

Tony turned around and said, "By truck."

They both laughed and slapped each other on the shoulder. Charlie entered at that point and had nearly the same reaction.

After they were done, Lowell said, "Come on, let's go to the day room, I want to hear all about it."

As they settled into the chairs with their cokes, Homer came in with two other pilots and joined the group. They all were firing questions at Tony until he said, "Come on you guys, shut up and I'll tell you."

"Well, I was of course flying the left seat and my flight engineer was standing in his usual place when he asked Captain Fowler if he could smell anything.

"The captain said yes he could and I could also. We were only about 4,500 feet and we hadn't turned on the oxygen yet. We began to check the instruments and suddenly everything went dark. No instrument lights, no running lights, nothing. Then the engines started to run rough.

"We'd had a total electrical failure. Captain Fowler said he would take it and began to circle with the power we had left. Lucky for us it was a moonlit night. We spotted a flat and tree free piece of land and he put it in. Of course, we couldn't lower the gear so it was a wheels-up landing. He did a great job, except it wasn't totally tree free, we caught the right wing on a little tree and it spun us around. We jumped out and ran, though without electricity, there was little chance of fire."

"What did you do?" asked one of the pilots.

"Well, we made sure everyone was out of the plane and we sat down and began to discuss what to do next. Of course, the power went out so suddenly, the radio man didn't have a chance to send out an SOS so we knew no one was aware what had happened."

"Yea, all we heard was that you guys were missing," added Homer.

"We sat there for a little while and Sergeant Toliver said that he would start walking and try to find a road. Captain Fowler said not to go off half-cocked, that we had better develop a plan."

"Boy do I know about that! When we were in basic, Charlie and I had an engine failure and had to land on an old ranch road," Lowell said.

"Yea well, we all decided to wait until daylight and see what the situation was like and go from there. Now this is where it gets funny. We went back into the plane, got some blankets and seat covers and bedded down for the night. Kind of like Low and Charlie did."

"Yea, you have to remind us of that do you?" replied Charlie.

"Anyway, when it began to get light, we discovered there was a road about 200 yards from where we were, so we all started to walk and came across a farm house about four miles from where we landed. They didn't have a phone but the farmer said he would drive us to the nearest one and we called the base, and you guys know the rest."

There were the appropriate caustic and smart remarks and then the group broke up. Lowell walked up to Tony and reached out and touched his shoulder and said, "You really had us worried fella. Welcome back."

"Thanks Low. I'm glad to be back."

Training went on through July and into August. There were several more incidents, some much more serious than Tony's. There was a crash at the end of the runway with a first time pilot, which caused much concern among the men. It was explained that the pilot had panicked and lost control of the aircraft. One of the crew perished but the rest survived. The pilot was washed out and sent to a different program.

Helen had settled into her new life as a working wife. She enjoyed being able to have something to look forward to each day, going to work at the Five and Dime. She had met the wives of two of the other pilots and because they had many night exercises, was able to have companionship during part of those lonely nights. Of course Mrs. Yocum was also a wonderful help. She would often invite Helen for dinner or just for a visit when Lowell was gone.

Helen and Lowell did some entertaining as well inviting other couples over for dinner or a night of Monopoly. Of course Charlie and Homer spent considerable time at their house when they weren't flying. One weekend Linda came over from Santa Maria to visit and the two couples had a marvelous time. As officers, the boys were making considerably more money than as cadets so they were able to eat out and take in a movie now and then.

A day or so later as they were waiting in the ready room for their flight, Charlie said, "You know, when I saw Linda and thought about how happy you and Helen are, I kind of regret that Linda and I didn't get married."

"Yea, it's just great, in more ways than one!"

They both laughed and settled back to wait for their flight.

Formation flying, navigation, night flying, as well as more class work kept the boys very busy and Charlie didn't have a great deal of time to lament not marrying Linda. Finally as the middle of August approached, they were told where they would go next for crew training. Again it was revealed in a list posted on the Orderly room bulletin board. Homer came in to the barracks and announced that the list was up. They all jumped up and ran to see where they had been assigned.

Lowell was elated when he read, Spokane Washington. "Wow, I'm going to Spokane!"

Charlie read and said, "Well, I guess this is goodbye for awhile. I'm going to Luke Field in Arizona."

Lowell looked at him and experienced a moment of sadness when he thought that they had been together for over a year and now they were parting, however Homer had also drawn Spokane so that was something. He could hardly wait to get home to tell Helen.

Myron's Transfer

Several weeks after returning to Texas and his duties as an instructor navigator, Myron was beginning to wonder if his transfer had been side tracked and that he may not be getting a combat assignment. After completing his daily obligations he was laying in his bunk when there was a knock on the door of his BOQ room.

Myron yelled, "Come!"

The first sergeant entered. Myron noticed that he had an envelope in his hand and a smile on his face.

He said, "Well sir, I think this will interest you."

He handed the envelope to Myron, saluted then turned and left the room. Myron tore open the envelope and read the paper. There was the usual military jargon at the beginning and further down the page he read:

SECOND LIEUTENANT MYRON ROTHSTEIN WILL REPORT TO FAIRCHILD AIRFORCE BASE, SPOKANE WASHINGTON FOR CREW ASSIGNMENT NOT LATER THAN 22 AUGUST 1944. LIEUTENANT ROTHSTEIN WILL BE RELIEVED OF DUTY AS INSTRUCTOR NAVIGATOR NOT BEFORE 15 AUGUST 1944 AND A FIVE DAY TRAVEL TIME WILL BE GRANTED.

Myron jumped off his bunk and let out a yell that brought several of his fellow instructors to his room to see what all the fuss was about. Myron excitedly explained that he not only got his transfer, but that he was going to Spokane, Washington for crew training. "How far is it from where you live?" asked Vic Raney.

"Oh, I guess it's several hundred miles, but it's a lot closer than Texas."

"You lucky dog."

"Yea, I guess you just have to know someone in high places," commented another of the instructors.

Myron checked the calendar to be sure of the date and realized that he had little less than a week before he had to leave. He immediately got out his writing kit and wrote to Betty that he was coming home for a few days and that he got his assignment and would be joining a crew in Spokane. He got a quick note off to Lowell and decided he would invite a couple of his closest buddies to the Officers Club for a small celebration.

The next morning because he did not have to fly, he went to the Orderly Room to see if he could catch another hop to the Northwest. He called the flight line and learned that there was a lone C-47 transport flying to the Sacramento area on the thirteenth of August. He asked permission to see the major and the first sergeant knocked on his door, stuck his head in, exchanged a few words with him and told Myron the major would see him.

Myron entered, saluted, was given an at-ease and told to have a seat.

"What can I do for you lieutenant?" asked the major.

"Well sir, I suppose you know I got my transfer orders and I'm going to Spokane, Washington. I checked with the flight line and there is a C-47 going to Sacramento on the thirteenth, but my orders are that I am to be released from duty on the fifteenth, and I was – –."

The major interrupted and said, "Oh that won't be a problem, we're kind of between classes now and I can change that."

He pressed a button on his desk and the first sergeant came in and the major told him to change Myron's releases date to the twelfth of August. Myron thanked him and asked, "Did you get orders too, sir?"

"Yes, I'm going directly to England and will assume the responsibility for all squadron navigation in the 346th of the Ninety-Ninth Bomb Group."

"When do you leave sir?"

"The same day you do, I plan to spend a couple of days at home in Ohio and then report to New Jersey for shipment."

The door opened, the first sergeant entered and handed Myron his newly typed orders. He started to leave, but closed the door instead and said, "May I speak frankly sir?"

"Of course; what is it?"

"Well, I just wanted to say, Bill that I have really enjoyed working for you and I wanted to wish you good luck." The sergeant reached over the desk and extended his hand to the major.

The major rose, took his hand and shook it saying, "I wish you were going with me."

"Thank you sir, but I've been there."

The sergeant had flown thirty-five missions with the Eighth Air Force.

Turning to Myron he said, "And likewise to you Myron, you are one of the best and most respected officers on the line. All the enlisted men, myself included, will miss you."

The major said, "Okay, that's enough. Now get out of here sergeant before you have us all bawling."

Myron did feel a slight swelling in his eyes and was surprised at feeling so emotional about getting what he had always wanted, a combat assignment. The sergeant reached over and extended his hand to Myron who took it warmly. He smiled, saluted, and left the office.

*****

As the C-47 droned over the desert of the Southwest, Myron tried to get some sleep, but the cold and noise made it nearly impossible.

The crew chief came over to him and yelled, "Do you want some coffee lieutenant?"

"Yea, thanks, I would."

"Where are you going, sir?"

"Washington. I'm being transferred to crew training."

Myron sipped his coffee and like all air corps coffee, it was strong and hot, but little else could be said for it. He thought about Betty and how glad he was going to be to see her again. He hoped that she had received his letter in time and that Lowell had as well. He wondered were Lowell would go for his crew training. He hadn't heard from him for some time and did not have any idea.

After landing in Sacramento, Myron caught a ride to the train station and purchased a ticket to Salem. He called Betty and told her when he was arriving and that he could hardly wait to see her.

Lowell's Visit Home

Unlike advanced, where they received their commissions and wings, the finishing of transition was very informal. There was a short speech from the school commander. He wished them luck and gave them a few words of encouragement. They were then told to report to the orderly room to pick up their orders and dismissed.

As they left the theater, Homer said, "Boy that was short and sweet."

"Yea, I guess they have a lot to do to get ready for the next class," said Lowell.

Saying good by to his close friend Charlie was a down time for Lowell, but any sadness was off-set by the fact that in a couple of days, he would be home and heading for a new adventure. Getting ready to move in such short notice gave him and Helen some anxious moments, but happy ones. They decided that they would go to Drayville and that Helen would stay there until they found out what the situation was like in Spokane. Once that was settled, they purchased their bus and train tickets for travel from Blythe on August 13 and arrival in Salem the following day.

Mrs. Yocum said that she was sorry to see them go, but knew everything was going to be just fine. She said that she had heard from her son in the navy. His ship was coming into San Francisco the following week and he would be home for a few days.

Lowell asked, "How can he tell you that? I thought that sort of thing was against regulations?"

Helen said, "Oh Lowell, don't ask such things!"

Mrs. Yocum laughed and said, "Well, we came up with a sort of code that both our boys can use to tell us where they are and so forth. You kids might want to do the same."

Helen looked at Lowell and they smiled, "Yea, maybe we can do that," he replied.

That last night Mrs. Yocum invited them for dinner and to sleep in her house because they had packed all their things getting ready to move. Both Lowell and Helen woke early to the smell of bacon. Mrs. Yocum was already up and fixing breakfast for them. When they came down stairs, she greeted them with a very warm smiling face. Asking them to sit down and eat, she said that she planned to drive them to the bus station and would not hear of any objections.

Arriving at the bus station, that old feeling brought on by departures came across them as they said good-by to this marvelous, generous woman. In the short time they had lived with her, they had established a warm relationship. As they got out of the car, they wished each other good luck and climbed aboard the bus. Mrs. Yocum stood by the car and waved good-bye as the bus pulled out of the station.

The bus ride to the train station only took about an hour. Upon arrival, Lowell went in and bought them both cokes while they sat and waited for the train. It finally came and they climbed aboard. They looked around for two seats together but saw none. A sailor offered to move so they could sit together. Lowell thanked him and said maybe he would buy him a beer in the club car later on.

As the train pulled out of the station the conductor announced that the next stop would be Bakersfield, but they would ride this train to Sacramento where they'd catch another for the remainder of the trip.

Lowell slept most of the way to Sacramento while Helen read and worked a crossword puzzle. True to his offer, Lowell later invited the sailor to the club car for a beer, then learned he was only eighteen and couldn't drink.

Laughing, he purchased two cokes and asked. "Where are you going?"

"I am being transferred to Astoria, Oregon."

"Oh yea, I'm from Oregon; I know Astoria well. Where are you from?"

"Tucson, Arizona, sir."

"Oh drop the sir. We're just a couple of servicemen traveling together. Astoria will be somewhat of a surprise for you. It rains a great deal there."

"Yea, I heard that, but at least I'm not going to the Pacific yet."

"That's right."

They finished their cokes and returned to their seats. Lowell found Helen asleep and tried not to wake her as he sat down, but that was impossible.

"Did you have a nice beer?"

"No, he was only eighteen so we had cokes instead."

"That's nice." Helen replied somewhat sleepily and then closed her eyes and dozed off again.

In Sacramento they gathered up their luggage and departed the train. The schedule on the wall of the station listed the times and destinations of all trains. They found they had nearly an hour to wait.

"Do you want to get something to eat?" Lowell asked.

"I'm not hungry," replied Helen. "I'd like a coke though."

"Yea, that's about all I want anyway," said Lowell.

After their refreshment break the train arrived and they boarded. Most of the seats were full in every car they walked through. Lowell was busy trying not to bump people with their suitcases and yet trying to find a seat when he heard a familiar voice.

"You can't sit down, but I would be glad to share mine with the good looking lady."

Turning around and irritated by the brazenness of the comment, Lowell saw the impish smiling face of Myron "Jew" Rothstein.

"Jew, you son of a B----," Lowell stopped himself just in time as most everyone in the car turned to see what the shouting was all about. Myron jumped up and started to shake hands with Low, but decided to embrace him instead.

From her position behind Lowell, Helen didn't see what was going on at first, then she recognized Myron over Lowell's shoulder. He reached out for her hand and squeezed it. After the initial shock of seeing each other, they found seats and sat down. Helen insisted that Lowell take the seat beside Myron and she went several rows further up where a soldier offered her a seat.

"What are you doing here Jew?"

"Well, I'm being transferred to Spokane for crew training, I got my transfer, I wrote you, but I guess you didn't it."

"I can't believe it, that's where I'm going. No I didn't get it."

Lowell jumped up and went to where Helen was and told her.

Returning to his seat, he asked, "When do you report?"

"I have to be there by the twenty-second, how about you?"

"Same day! Say, remember when we were home and talking about ending up in the same crew?"

"Yea."

"Well, what do you think about requesting it, if we can?"

"That would be just swell. Say, can you fly an airplane all by yourself?"

"Admit it Jew. You haven't changed a bit have you?"

"I guess not."

When the train pulled into Salem, they saw a crowd on the platform that was made up of all their folks.

Myron said, "You'd think they've never heard of gas rationing."

"Well, you must remember that one of them owns a gas station!"

They all laughed and prepared to disembark the train. As Myron stepped down, Betty ran into his arms and his warm embrace. The twins were the first to reach Lowell. Helen's parents gave their daughter a warm hug and kiss. After the appropriate time of discussion, Mr. Andersen suggested they leave and go home. Mrs. Speer announced that everyone was coming to their house for a meal. This sounded good to the three who had been eating either mess hall food or simple fair.

Helen's mother looked at her and commented, "You've lost weight dear!"

Lowell looked at Jew and said, "Don't you dare make a comment!"

All the older people looked at Lowell and then at Myron as Betty punched him in the shoulder. Of course the twins wanted to know what Lowell had brought them and they were chastised by their mother.

Lowell said, "Well, I brought a little bit of the Mojave Desert."

David said, "Oh boy! What's it like."

Diane was skeptical and asked, "What's that?"

"Well, you know what a desert is. I brought you some sand."

"Oh Lowell, you don't mean it, do you?" asked Diane.

Mr. Andersen said, "Come kids, let's be on our way. Get in the car."

There was some organization to be accomplished before they could all get in the cars. It began to look like either Lowell and Helen or Myron and Betty would have to ride in separate cars.

Lowell said to Helen, "Why don't you ride with your folks and I will ride with mine."

"That's sounds okay with me."

"On second thought, why don't we ride with Betty and her folks and Myron can catch a bus, when the next one comes. As I remember there are two a day between Drayville and Salem!"

With that both Betty and Helen reached out and punched him on the arm.

Myron added, "Yea, that's a great idea. Low kept me talking on the train and I could use a nap."

Again, both Betty and Helen punched him on the arm.

For dinner, Mrs. Speer had asked some of her church friends if they would provide potluck dishes for all the families, and what a dinner they provided: Fried chicken, two different roasts, a ham, (which Lowell kept trying to get Myron to eat) mashed potatoes, rolls and many, many pies.

As they were sitting around tables in the back yard, Mr. Rothstein asked, "Is there any chance you boys could end up in the same crew?"

Low looked at Jew and they both shrugged.

Lowell said, "Well, I guess you can request crew members some times, but I have no idea if we will be able to."

Myron said, "Well, I want to see him fly before I make up my mind. If it is anything like driving a car, never mind. I'll take my chances with anyone else."

Of course, Betty punched him in the arm for that remark.

One of the church ladies asked, "Lowell, when do you have to report?"

"We have to report in on the twenty-second."

"Oh, you will have a few days at home?"

Suddenly a familiar voice came from the side of the house.

"Did you leave anything to eat?"

Lowell looked up to see his Uncle Norwood and Aunt Vera coming around the garage. He immediately got up and went to them giving both a big hug. Helen came over and hugged them as well.

Mrs. Andersen got up and said, "Well, your meeting got over sooner than you thought."

"No," Vera said. "Norwood handed off the reins to the chair of the trustees and we just left."

Lowell's father said, "Well, that is the first time I've every heard of that."

"Why little brother, do you think I would miss a chance to get a free meal and see my nephew."

Everyone laughed and Ethan said, "Do you know everyone here?"

Mr. Miles rose and said, "I don't believe we have met, I'm George Miles, Betty's father and this is my wife Nora."

"Glad to meet you folks, I'm Norwood Andersen, Ethan's big brother and this is my wife Vera."

Mr. Rothstein rose and greeted Lowell's uncle with, "How are you Norwood."

"Fine Aaron, how is everything with you?"

"Now that Myron is home for a few days, just fine."

After the greeting, the other members of the Andersen family sat down and were served by the ladies.

Norwood, always the cutup said to Mrs. Pollard, "Say how would you like to becoming a member of my congregation? It would be easy. Only drive a few minutes and you'll be there. Of course you would have to bring these other ladies with you. This is some of the best food I have ever eaten. You would have to change from that secondary Methodist church to a real one."

To which Lowell's mom said, "Now Norwood, no recruiting is allowed here."

Mr. Rothstein said, "I was thinking about asking them if they would like to join our synagogue in Portland, they could go to Friday service and still make Sunday at your church."

"Say, that's a very good idea Aaron. It wouldn't be a problem at all."

Aunt Vera said, "Would you men behave yourselves! You're embarrassing her!"

They both offered good-natured apologies and Mrs. Pollard nodded and said, "That's okay, my husband is always kidding with someone. I'm used to it."

That night the boys decided to stay home with their parents. Lowell and Helen walked over to her parent's house and visited for awhile and walked back to Lowell's. His parents were still up so they visited with them for some time and finally Lowell said, "Well, I'm really tired, I think I'll go to bed. I promised the twins I would take them around to some of their friends so I could meet them."

His dad said, "Yea, they want to show you off."

Helen said, "I think I'll join you too, it has been a busy day."

They bid Mr. and Mrs. Andersen good night and climbed the stairs. The twins were again sharing a room so that Lowell's old one was available for him and Helen. As usual, Lowell was ready for bed first and he lay down and watched Helen get ready. When she came back from the bathroom he was smiling to himself. She climbed in on top of the covers and started to tickle him.

"What are you laughing about anyway?"

Lowell said, "If you knew how many times I dreamed of getting you in this bed!"

"Oh you! Is that all you ever think of?"

"Pretty much!"

With that she tickled him again until he grabbed her and held her arms down. In a few minutes she quit struggling and they both settled down. It didn't take long for Lowell to fall asleep. Helen leaned over and turned off the light.

The next few days flew by. They visited friends and family and went to the movies with Jew and Betty. One night they drove down to the river where they used to spend summer nights on the beach. Myron, up to his usual tricks said, "Say Lowell, did I ever tell you about the night Betty tried to put the make on me here?"

Lowell laughed and Betty said, "Oh Myron you dirty dog you, I never ever did anything like that. It was always the other way around."

Helen covered her mouth to hide the laughter and Lowell was somewhat embarrassed as well.

"Oh, was that the way it was, I'd forgotten."

"Let's drop the subject shall we," Betty replied with some firmness.

Myron laughed and said, "Okay, I'm sorry. I didn't mean to embarrass everyone."

"Yea, like hell you didn't buddy," retorted Lowell.

"Come on you guys, watch your language. There are ladies present."

They all laughed and Myron said, "We need to talk about whether you girls are going to come up or not."

There was a long silence and Betty said, "I would really like to if you want us to."

"Want you to, of course we do. How do you feel Helen?"

She thought for a minute and said, "Well, I also want to very much, but I think you guys better find out the situation first. I don't think we will be lucky enough to find another Mrs. Yocum."

"Yea, that's true, but I think there must be some place for wives to stay."

Myron let out a sigh and said, "Tell you what, why don't we go up alone, then have you girls come up the first weekend we get off and look around for a place to stay."

Lowell responded with, "Yea, that sounds like a good idea. What do you think Helen?"

"Well, Dad could use me in the lumber yard. I think that would be just fine."

"We can talk more tomorrow. It's getting late."

Lowell started the car, backed away from the river and turned for home.

Early the next morning, the bedroom door flew open and Diane charged in yelling, "Lowell, make David give me back my ribbon!"

"I haven't got your ribbon!"

Both Lowell and Helen rose up from bed with a start and Lowell said in a not to friendly voice, "Come on you guys, don't bust in here like that, Helen is not used to yelling kids."

Helen, awake by now smiling said, "It's okay kids."

"Alright, what's this about a ribbon?"

Just then their mother called up the stairs, "Kids, you're not bothering Helen and Lowell are you?"

Diane turned and ran out of the room yelling to her mother about the ribbon.

David stayed in the room and asked, "What's it like to be married?"

Lowell's mouth kind of dropped open and Helen let out a little giggle as her face flushed.

Lowell said, "Well David, you're a little young to know everything, but I can tell you that it is just great, if you find a girl like Helen."

Helen reached out and took Lowell's hand and said, "That's right David, if you can find someone as nice as Lowell."

As he turned to leave, he said, "Oh you guys, I know a lot more about marriage than you think I do."

A look of astonishment crossed their faces and they both burst out laughing.

The week went by all too quickly for both Myron and Lowell. It was time to leave. They had finalized the plans with the girls about coming to Spokane. They would report in, find out what had to be done to allow their wives to come up and be in touch with the girls.

Both the Rothstein and the Andersen families drove their boys to Portland to catch the train. The goodbyes on the platform of the station we're painful and long. The parents bid their goodbyes and went into the station to wait for the girls. Lowell held Helen very tightly for several minutes and said, "Be sure and write me won't you?"

"Of course I will dummy, and you had better write me, too."

Finally they heard the "ALL ABOARD" being called and broke apart. Betty held Myron's hand until the train started to leave. Both girls were crying without shame and the boys had some difficulty holding back the tears as well.

Though it was crowded, they found seats together and flopped down. Myron said, "God that was hard."

"Yes, it seems to get harder each time."

"Well, on to our next great adventure, huh?"

"Yea I guess."

CREW TRAINING

The train ride up the Columbia Gorge was beautiful, but the boys had more on their minds than scenery. They dozed, went to the club car for a beer, and talked to two other airmen who were going for crew training. One had just finished Transition in Texas and had sneaked a visit home. He was from Vancouver, Washington.

They arrived in Spokane around noon and inquired about transportation to the base, and learned that a shuttle bus met every train. They walked out of the station and saw the usual olive drab painted bus sitting in a loading zone. The boys boarded along with several more airmen, both enlisted and officers. The ride to the base was mostly in silence except for one lieutenant who kept talking to the driver.

Arriving at the base they received directions where to report and when they reported in, they learned they'd been assigned to any room they liked in barracks 4723. Deciding to try and room together, they walked down the hall checking each room. Finally they found one with only one bunk occupied.

Lowell stuck his head in and said, "Got room for two more?"

"Yea, come on in," said a lieutenant who was making up one of the bunks. "I'm Robert Winceck."

"Lowell Andersen."

"Myron Rothstein."

They all shook hands and the boys threw their gear on the empty bunks.

Lowell asked, "Are the crew lists up yet?"

Robert replied, "I don't know, I'm sure curious. You want to go over and ask?"

"Sure, why not. I see you're a pilot too."

Robert looked down at his wings and said, "Yea, it took me two tries to make it."

Myron asked, "What do you mean?"

"Well, I washed out on my first try back in forty two."

"How did you get back in to the program?"

"I just kept applying and finally they accepted me again."

Lowell and Myron looked at each other knowingly.

Myron said, "I kept trying but they said they needed navigators more."

They walked over to the orderly room and entered.

The duty sergeant asked, "May I help you gentlemen?"

"We were wondering are the crew lists up yet?"

"The major is still working on them," the sergeant replied.

"Is it possible to request a someone as a crewman?" Lowell asked.

"I don't know, I'll ask the major."

The sergeant entered the major's office and came out a few minutes later.

"The major will see you," he said.

Lowell entered, reported to the major and was given the at-ease command.

"What can I do for you Lieutenant Andersen?"

"Sir, is it possible to request a particular individual as a crew member?"

"Well, not usually, but I'm just beginning to make up the crews, so who would you like to request?"

"Sir, I request Lieutenant Rothstein be assigned to my crew as navigator."

The major looked down his list and looked at Lowell saying, "No problem lieutenant, he is already assigned to your crew. Any particular reason you want him?"

"Well, yes sir. We are from the same town and I have known him for a long time."

The major frowned looked down at the list again and Lowell thought for a minute that maybe he shouldn't have said that. Maybe there was some regulation prohibiting people who know each other from being in the same crew.

He finally looked up and said, "Well, you got him."

"Thank you sir!" Lowell came to attention, saluted, did an about face and left the office.

On the way out he thanked the sergeant who looked surprised but said nothing. Jew and Robert were waiting outside and Lowell decided to play a little game. He just walked by and started down the sidewalk.

Myron said, "Well?"

"Oh, yea I've got to put up with you. Couldn't do anything about it. You were already assigned to my crew."

"Hot dog!"

Robert shook his head and said, "Something tells me you guys have known each other for a long time."

They told him about their friendship and he gave an understanding nod. That night in the barracks, Lowell and Myron found themselves alone in the room. Robert had gone out to look for a buddy with whom he had gone through training.

Myron looked over at Low and said, "I want to tell you that I really appreciate being in your crew and that I will never let our friendship stand in the way of getting the job done."

He paused for a moment and added, "And I want you to promise me you won't either. I have not changed my mind about getting into combat and bombing the crap out of those Nazi bastards."

Lowell looked hard into his friends eyes and said, "Thanks Jew, I really appreciate that, I know you will do a good job; you've always come through when the going gets tough. I must admit that having you in my crew has been a slight concern of mine and I want you to know that when we're in the air, I will treat you just like any other crew member, and if you screw up, I'll come down on you just as hard."

Myron smiled at him they looked into each other's eyes and Jew extended his hand and they shook.

Just then Robert came in and Myron asked, "Did you find your friend?"

"No, I guess he hasn't reported yet."

Suddenly Lowell heard a familiar voice.

"Is there a Lieutenant Andersen in this barracks?"

"Homer, in here!"

Homer entered and said, "Boy you guys have it soft, I had to make up my own bunk."

Homer and Lowell shook hands and Lowell said, "When did you get in?"

"This morning, how about you?"

"Around noon."

"Oh Homer, this is Myron Rothstein, that friend from home I've told you about, and Robert Winceck, this is Homer Driscoll, we have been together since pre-flight."

Myron extended his hand to Homer as did Robert and they exchanged greetings as they shook hands.

Myron said, "How have you put up with this guy for all these months?"

Homer looked a little perplexed but caught on and replied, "Oh I don't know, I guess we just ignored him at times."

Lowell laughed and asked, "I wonder how Charlie's doing?"

"I don't know, I know I would rather be here than in Texas."

They all nodded in agreement and decided to see if they could get some chow.

*****

That night Lowell reached into his footlocker and took out his writing material.

He said, "Okay you guys, you might as well know I write a letter to my girl friend every night."

Myron looked up and asked, "Does Helen, your wife, know you're writing to your girl friend?"

Robert laughed and said ,"I remember my brother-in-law used to make that mistake for almost a year after he and my sister were married."

They all laughed good-naturedly and then returned to their thoughts.

Myron reached into his footlocker and said, "Yea, I guess I had better write to my *girl friend* also."

The next day they were told to report to one of the large theater-like buildings to meet the rest of their crew members. As they entered, the room was about half full. There were long bench type seats that reminded Lowell of church pews. A captain was at the door with the always-present clipboard and asked Lowell his name. He replied and was told he was in row twelve. Lowell turned as he asked Myron his name and told him row twelve as well. There were several enlisted men already in row twelve as well as one officer.

Lowell said, "I guess this is our row."

The enlisted men jumped up to let him in. He indicated to them to take their seats and started to move in to the row.

One of the enlisted men, a master sergeant said, "Sir, I think you're supposed to sit on the aisle."

Lowell looked somewhat embarrassed and said, "Oh, okay," and sat down.

After a few minutes, a captain came on to the stage and yelled, "Atten Hut!"

All the men jumped to their feet as a full colonel came up on the stage and said, "As you were men! I'm Colonel Materson and I command this base. It is my job to see that you all become a crew in the best sense and that you work together to perform the task you have been trained for up to this point. This is your last training base in the United States. From here, it is overseas and combat."

The colonel let that sink in for awhile before continuing.

"Pay attention to your instructors . They've been in combat. They know what they're talking about. That is all!"

Again the call for attention was given and all the men jumped to their feet as the colonel left the stage. A captain then came up and instructed them about what was going to happen in the next few days.

"If you don't have a full crew, stay in your rows and wait for the officer to contact you. Of course, you need to find out if you have full crew."

Lowell realized he had better check his crew status, so he leaned over and said, "Sound off with your name and assignment."

Myron sitting beside Lowell sounded off, "Rothstein, navigator."

The man sitting next said, "Bracketts, bombardier."

In order they called out, "Wright, flight engineer."

"Martinez, waist gunner."

"Risen, ball turret."

"McDonald, waist gunner."

"Miller, tail gunner."

Lowell did a quick count and found they were short a co-pilot and a radioman.

When the captain came down the line he looked at his clipboard and said, "Andersen, do you have a full crew?"

"No sir, I lack a radio man and co-pilot."

The captain turned around to the next man in line and said, "Okay lieutenant, this is your crew."

To Lowell he said, "You'll have to wait for awhile for a radio man."

As the captain moved down the aisle, Lowell turned to the lieutenant and extended his hand and said, "I'm Lowell Andersen, welcome to the crew."

Lowell was taken back by the lieutenant's response as he said, "I'm Vern Stewart," in a very surly tone.

Lowell went on, "Well, take a seat."

Lowell conducted an informal informational meeting with his crew. Before being dismissed, the captain asked for silence and announced that the pilots should go to the desks in the back of the room and pick up profiles of their crews. They were then dismissed to return to their barracks and take some time to settle in.

In the BOQ, Lowell spent most of the evening going over each man's profile until he finally decided he needed to stop and write the nightly letter to Helen. From the profiles, he thought he had a very good crew. Most, like him, were just out of training except the flight engineer, Bob Wright who had been in combat in the Pacific.

The next day each crew was assigned a small group meeting room where they could get better acquainted. To be sure that they were in the right place, Lowell and Myron left early enough to be there when the remainder of the crew arrived. When the boys entered the room, a sergeant was leaning against the wall by the door.

When he saw the officers approach, he came to attention and said, "Lieutenant Andersen?"

Lowell answered, "Yes."

"I'm Sergeant Ellingston. I've been assigned to your crew as radio-gunner."

"Very good sergeant. We're about to have our first crew meeting so come right in."

As the crew filed in to the room, Lowell walked to the front and welcomed them to be seated.

"Sit anywhere you want men, we are now a crew and I hope one big family."

Regardless of his admonishment, the officers sat in the front and the enlisted men in the back. This bothered him somewhat because he was determined to have a well-rounded and close crew. Discipline was very important of course and vital in the air, but for the get-acquainted meeting, he wanted to impress upon them that friendship was also very important.

To solve that problem, Lowell said, "Okay guys, pickup your chairs and follow me."

He came off the stage and carrying a chair, went to the back of the room, put it down and instructed the men to form a circle with their chairs.

"Now this is what I want from this crew, a circle of support that needs to be joined to function and if broken, will allow us to fail. Is that clear?"

The men nodded and Lowell noticed a sneer on Lieutenant Stewart's face that gave him a moment of concern.

"Okay men, let's talk about ourselves. I'm Lowell Andersen, I come from Drayville, Oregon. My friends call me Low. I played sports in high school and had one year of college before entering the Army Air Corps. I'm married to my high school girl friend and no matter what anyone says, and I mean anyone," he said looking at Myron, "I'm Norwegian."

He looked at Lieutenant Stewart and said, "Okay lieutenant, tell us about yourself."

Vernon Stewart looked at him for a minute, lowered his head and said, "Well, there isn't much to tell. I'm from Tulsa, Oklahoma and I thought I was going to fly fighters."

He dropped his head again and everyone looked at him in anticipation but nothing more was forth coming. Lowell thought for a minute, looked around the room and realized he was going to say no more.

Lowell nodded to the next man in the circle and he began to speak.

"I'm Wayne Ellingston and I'm from Tyron, Nebraska. Because of my initials, my friends call me WE. I graduated from high school and immediately joined the army hoping to become a pilot, but washed out in basic. I guess because I used to spend most of my free time hunting, they made me a gunner/radio operator. I'm not married but have a steady girl and hope to marry her when I get home. I will do my best to keep those ME-109s away from us."

"Thank you. That would be great. Who's next?"

"Well, I guess it's me. I'm Vincent Bracketts the bombardier, and I usually go by Vince. I'm from Denver, Colorado or at least near there. I graduated from high school and had two years of college at Colorado State. I played a little baseball, but wasn't very good. I'm not married, but hope to be someday. And, if Lieutenant Rothstein gets us to the target, I will try to hit it each time or at least they will hit the ground every time."

A chuckle went around the crew and then Lowell motioned for the next man.

Myron looked up at him in some surprise and realized Low meant for him to say something.

"I'm Myron Rothstein, navigator," he began haltingly. "I am also from Drayville, Oregon and my very close friends call me Jew, with love of course."

Catching hold of himself he reverted to his usual humor.

"I am in this crew to make sure Lowell takes off right and lands with the wheels down. I have been taking care of this guy since we were in the second grade, and I don't think there is any difference between a Swede and a Norwegian."

All the crew laughed except Vern and Lowell said, "Okay lieutenant, continue."

Myron went on, "I am also married to my high school girlfriend and I hope to never get you guys lost. And yes, I am Jewish."

Lowell gave Jew a slight smile and looked at the next man.

"I'm Bob Wright from Monroe, Connecticut. I have been in the Army Air Corps for five years. I'm the flight engineer and top gunner. I'm married and have two children. I'll try to keep the ship running and hope to protect the topside."

He paused and looked at Lowell, but when Lowell didn't call on the next man, a puzzled look came over Wright's face.

Lowell said, "Isn't there something else you would like to tell us?"

Wright continued to look puzzled and Lowell said, "Tell us where you were on December 7."

Wright's face flushed and he looked down, "Well, I was in a B-17 trying to land at Hickum Field during the Jap's attack."

The whole crew including Vern looked up at him with surprise and some awe.

Lowell added, "Gentleman, Sergeant Wright is the only one in the crew who has seen combat. I believe it was in the Philippines wasn't it?"

"That's right sir."

"Well, let's go on, who's next?"

They all looked at the next man in line.

He cleared his throat and said, "I'm Lorenzo Martinez from Pierre, South Dakota. My friends call me Zo. I'm the left waist and I will try my best to protect the left side of the plane."

Lowell said, "Thanks Zo. By the way, how did you get up to South Dakota?"

"Well that's kind of an interesting story. As you probably know, there aren't many Mexicans in South Dakota. My dad was in World War I and he became friends with a fellow from Pierre whose life he had saved in a fight on the Marne. After the war they both went home. My dad was from West Texas. He married my mom and a couple of years later, the friend, his name was Bill Museen, wrote my dad and asked him if he would come up and help run the ranch. My dad was doing ranch work in West Texas. So after a couple more letters, the folks decided to try it and moved up to South Dakota where my sister and I were born. After a few years, Bill made my dad foreman of the ranch, and he still is."

"Thanks. Oh, I didn't mean to pry into your private life."

"That's okay, sir. A lot of people ask me about that."

"Okay, now who's next?"

"I guess I am sir. I'm David McDonald from Lewiston, Idaho. I'm the right waist. I was also selected for gunnery school because of my experiences with a shotgun. I spent a lot of time hunting when I was a kid, and Wayne, if we could get some shot guns, I would like to show you how to hunt pheasants."

They all laughed at that and Wayne said, "Maybe I can show you a thing or two."

Zo spoke up and said, "Wait a minute, I'm from the pheasant hunting capital of the world. Can I get in on this and show you both how to hunt?"

That brought laughter from everyone including Vern Stewart.

"Okay, who's next?"

"Well I guess that's me. I'm Nigel Risen; my friends call me Niggs. I'm from Brooklyn, New York. I'll be protecting your bellies in the ball turret, and I've never even seen a pheasant or what ever you call them. I'm single but have a steady girl I hope to marry when we get home."

"You know Nigel, we would have never guessed you were from Brooklyn."

This brought another round of laughter from the crew and Lowell said, "Who's next?"

"Well, that would be me seeing ya'alls have finished. I'm Clark Miller, my friends call me Gabe. I'm from Cold Springs, Alabama. I'm the tail gunner and will do my level best to protect ya'alls behind. And I wouldn't mind being invited to that hunting party ya'alls talking about; I've done my share of hunting. I am single but plan to change that as soon as I get home."

The men all laughed and Lowell said, "Okay men, we seem to be a mixed bag of people from all parts of the country. And I want you all to know that my method in this informal introduction and background of each of us is to get better acquainted. It is not to have any effect on discipline in this crew. If we all learn our jobs and do them, we will be a successful crew and that informality has nothing to do with what I will expect in the air. Every one will obey without question orders given during flying missions or they will be removed from this crew. Do I make that completely clear?"

There was a smattering of yes sirs and head nodding.

"Okay men, you know that for next few days, we will be divided up into our prospective assigned groups and given ground school," said Lowell. "So, let's all concentrate on the ground schooling we will receive so that we're ready when it's time to fly. You're dismissed to fall out to your barracks."

As the men left, Myron hung back and came up to Lowell and said, "Jesus Low, you've grown up. I hardly realized who I was listening to."

Lowell looked at his friend, smiled and said, "Thanks Jew."

That night Lowell wrote to Helen:

My Dearest Wife,

Well, we had our first crew meeting today. They seem like a very good bunch of guys. Only one has seen any combat and he has been in a training command for the past two years. He is the oldest man in the crew and was on one of those B-17s that tried to land in Hawaii during the Jap's attack.

My only concern is my co-pilot; he was all set to fly fighters when he was transferred to bombers. He does not show any indication of wanting to be in our crew. I don't know what to do so I'm going to talk to our instructor for advice.

Lowell went on to tell about the other crew members and told Helen to let him know when she and Betty could come up. He closed the letter in his usual way:

As always to you I give my love and life,
Low

The training was divided into various sections. The pilots were trained on everything from local flying regulations to take-off and landing procedures. There was considerable time spent in the Link, with charts and maps, reviews of the aircraft itself, and navigation and bombing. The bombardiers spent many hours over the Norden Bombsight to refresh themselves on it as well as learning techniques for the local bombing range. Gunners were also further trained at the shooting range. They were put in backs of trucks with a shotgun and driven at a very rapid speed past targets. Most of the men thought it was fun. The flight engineers spent most of their class time reviewing the engines, startup and shutdown procedures as well as emergency procedures. They were also expected to practice on the gunnery range. The navigators spent considerable time in class learning about the local areas. They also spent time in their version of the Link training for night and adverse weather flying. Because of his instructing experience, Myron had little trouble with this and was able to help several of the men.

One day after class, the captain said, "Oh Rothstein, could I see you a minute?"

"Yes sir, what is it?"

"With your experience in training I'd like you to be an assistant instructor for me. Some of the guys need a little more help."

Myron had a moment of concern with the question and it showed on his face. The captain asked, "What's the matter lieutenant?"

"Sir, may I speak frankly?"

"Of course!"

"It took me nearly a year to get assigned to a combat crew and I don't want to be pulled out as an instructor again."

"Oh don't worry about that, when you've gotten this far, nothing like that is going to happen."

"Thank you captain; in that case I would be glad to help."

"Fine, I'll get together with you later."

*****

One day Myron came into the room all excited and said, "Did you see the announcement on the bulletin board?"

"No, what announcement?"

"They are giving us a two-and-half day pass over Labor Day!"

Lowell broke out in a big smile and said, "Great, let's call the girls."

"Well, what ever made you think of that?"

Home, Speer Lumber

The phone rang in the office of Speer Lumber and Helen answered, "Speer Lumber."

Her dad liked that answer with the unspoken meaning.

"Helen, I just got a call from Myron, they have Labor Day weekend off and they want us to come over!" exclaimed Betty.

"Oh that's wonderful, lets meet for a coke at Smith's and plan. I'm kind of busy now; we just got a big order in for Camp Adair."

"Okay, say around three?"

"That's fine. See you there."

The rest of the morning was a blur to Helen, she made three mistakes on invoices and her father became impatient with her.

"Honey, I know you're excited, but we have to get these orders out first thing in the morning."

"I'm sorry Dad. Oh, will my being gone over the week end create a problem for you?"

"No, I think we will close for the weekend and if we get these orders out before then, I don't think we will be very busy. Besides, your mom can come down and help if need be."

"Thanks Dad."

Finally at 2:30 all the invoices were finished and the men were loading the trucks for Adair. Helen went looking for her dad and found him in the yard.

"Dad, I'm going to meet Betty at Smith's. I'll be back around 4:00."

Mr. Speer said, "That's okay honey; take the rest of the afternoon off. You and Betty have a lot of planning to do."

Helen reached up and gave her father a peck on the cheek and hurried back through the office and up the street to Smith's. When she arrived, Betty was already there studying a sheet of paper. Hearing the bell on the door jingle, she looked up and rose to greet her friend.

"Hi, did you have any trouble getting off?"

"No, Dad was very nice about it; did you?"

"No, I didn't work today. I was just helping Mom around the house. It's canning time you know."

"Okay. What have you got?"

"I called the train station and there is a train leaving for Spokane Thursday morning at 9:15 and it arrives in Spokane really late that night."

"Well, I hope the boys think to get a place for us to stay. When did Myron say they could get off?"

"I think it's Friday night at 5:00."

"Are they going to let us know if we have a place to stay?"

"Yes, he said one of them will call either tonight or tomorrow to find out when we can get there and they will try to get a place," Betty replied.

True to their word, Lowell called that night. They had a short talk and then were reminded that their three minutes were up. Helen told him that they would arrive in Spokane some time late Thursday night so they would need a room. Lowell said okay just as they were cut off.

Lowell and Myron inquired about vacancies and only found one, so they reserved it.

Myron said, "What are we going to do with only one room?"

"Well, I guess we'll just have to take turns."

They smiled at each other and started to walk towards the bus station for a ride back to the base.

The week went very slowly for the boys and their concentration was short of perfect, but they got through it and Friday night they took off for town to meet the girls. When they arrived at the Motor Lodge, they asked at the office if their wives had checked in and were told they were in Room 14. They hurried over to the room, Myron knocked on the door and it flew open as Helen burst out and nearly threw herself into Myron's arms.

Lowell yelled, "Hey, wait a minute you've got the wrong guy!"

Helen rectified the mistake and repeated the action with her husband.

Of course Myron began to make cracks about which couple got to use the room first, causing the girls to look at each other with slight smiles. The boys not knowing what the smiles meant, looked quite perplexed.

Helen finally said, "Well, we don't have to share; there was a cancellation and we were able to book another room. You and Lowell will be in Room 23."

They responded with, "Oh funny!" as they grabbed their wives in a tight embrace, and planted kisses.

The two couples went out for dinner that night and talked about seeing a movie. Myron, of course, made several lewd comments that embarrassed the girls, but they decided to return to their motel rooms and call it a night.

Saturday was spent having meals together, walking around downtown Spokane and talking about their training. Lowell asked how things were going at the lumber yard and if Helen saw much of his folks. She reported that the twins were still arguing over everything but his folks seemed to be okay. They had dinner and went to a movie but, if questioned later, none of them could report what it was about. They all turned in early that night.

The boys had arranged a picnic in the city park for Sunday and invited all the crew who wished to join them. Lowell had made that announcement Friday after their crew meeting. The girls had agreed to put together some sandwiches and drinks. Lowell was somewhat concerned about Vern, but he said he would like to join them. This gave Lowell hope that maybe he was beginning to come around.

The picnic went very well and all the men seemed to dote on Helen and Betty. They were perfect gentleman and the girls thought a lot of them as well. There were a lot of comments about taking care of the officers and such. After the picnic, Lowell and Myron told the guys to go ahead and leave - they would clean up. However, Vince stayed behind and helped. Lowell noticed that Vern made no attempt to do so.

Saying goodbye again to Helen was painful. The girls train left Tuesday morning so the farewells were Monday night. Helen asked the boys if they would get a leave before going overseas. They didn't know, but thought they had all the leave they were going to get.

*****

Crew training resumed the Tuesday following Labor Day with more instruction for the pilots, including sessions on take-offs, landing patterns and formation flying. Navigators concentrated on dead reckoning, foul weather navigation and using the radio signal. Gunners were still practicing from the back of trucks, but were told they would have some sleeves to shoot at soon.

Although the pilots had been exposed to formation flying, they were expected to hone their skills in much closer formation. They had to keep their wing tips no further than fifty feet apart and fly no further than fifty feet below the plane above them. The first attempt was with Captain Nelson in the right seat and Vern in the jump seat. Though he was sweating profusely, Lowell had little trouble maintaining the prescribed distances. Only once did the captain have to remind him. When it became Vern's turn, he did not hesitate but climbed into the pilot's seat and with no comment, was able to maintain the distance very well. When the captain and Lowell congratulated him, he just grunted and got out of the seat.

Vern's attitude was really beginning to wear on Lowell. One night when they were alone, he brought it up to Myron, who agreed that Vern had a very bad attitude. Something had to be done.

Lowell said, "I don't know, do you think I should talk to Captain Nelson or talk directly to Vern?"

"Well, if you talk to the captain, I think he will do something. Why don't you have a little talk with Vern first? Then, if it doesn't change, talk to the captain."

"That's a good idea. I think I will if it doesn't change over the next few days."

After one particularly long flight, Lowell had had it with Vern's attitude. Though he hadn't talked to the instructor, he was sure the captain was well aware from looks he had given Vern. Captain Nelson was a good guy who had flown thirty-seven missions with the Mighty Eighth and he knew what he was talking about.

When Lowell parked the plane, he called for the magnetos to be shut down.

Vern said "What?"

Lowell had to reissue the order and as he looked at Vern, out of the corner of his eye he saw Captain Nelson shaking his head.

Lowell said, "Vern, hold up a minute, I want to talk to you."

"What about?"

"Wait until the crew has de-planed."

Finishing his checklist, he waited until he was sure all of the crew had departed.

"Okay Vern, let's go for a little walk," said Lowell.

They both climbed down and walked a few paces from the plane. Lowell noticed the crew chief walking towards them and he held up his hand for him to stop.

"Vern, I want to talk about your attitude."

"What's the matter with my attitude?"

"It stinks! I know you're unhappy about not getting fighters, but you didn't. You were assigned to my crew and by your attitude, I'm not sure I could count on you if I needed to. You might someday have to bring this crew home," said Lowell. "If it doesn't change I am going to request that another co-pilot be assigned and you be transferred from the crew. And, I don't think you will get fighters either. You will probably be assigned as supply officer somewhere in Greenland, or at best be flying transports!"

Vern was staring at Lowell with anger and hate in his eyes and suddenly they filled with tears. Lowell had a moment of indecision as to whether he was doing the right thing or had he gone too far. Just as he was about to soften his approach, Vern spoke up.

"It's just that nothing I have tried to do in my life ever worked out. Oh, that's not quite true, but most things."

He looked Lowell in the eyes and Lowell noticed tears running down his checks.

Softening his approach he said, "You want to tell me about it?"

Vern's Story

There was a long pause then Vern sighed and began. "It seems like I was meant to be disappointed. My mother died giving birth to me and I think my dad resented me for it. He was not a very good man. He drank and brought women home while my sister and I huddled in our bedroom. If we ever said anything he would slap us around. Finally when I was about five and my sister nine, he just disappeared."

"What happened to you?"

"Well we were taken to a state home for orphans until they found a foster home for us. We were in and out of several foster homes until my sister quit high school and got a job. We found a small apartment and moved in. I was an eighth grader at the time and picked up small jobs to help out. My sister met a guy where she worked and they began to date. He was a pretty good guy and I think they were planning on getting married. One night as they were coming home from a movie in the next town, a drunk hit them head on and they were both killed."

This brought tears to Lowell's eyes. What a terrible story.

He said, "That's all right Vern you don't have to go on."

Vern cleared his throat and said, "No, I want to, I have never told anyone this story and I think you deserve to know."

He looked at Lowell and turned looking off toward the distance, then continued.

"I became somewhat of a discipline problem in school. I was trying to make it on my own, and still go to school. One day during PE we were playing softball and the baseball coach came out to the field. It was the start of the season. I was at bat and hit a ball clear over the center fielders head. The coach came up to me after class and asked if I wanted to go out for baseball.

"Well, with my attitude, I started to give some smart answer until I realized I really wanted to play ball. But, I answered that I had to work and wouldn't have time. He just nodded and said, 'We'll see.' His name was Ken Palmer, he was also the science and math teacher and I was in his algebra class. I really liked math and science.

"The next day I was called to the principal's office and he and the coach talked to me for a long time about my situation. It seems the coach's son had left for college and he had a spare room at his house and they wanted me to move in."

Lowell just nodded and Vern went on.

"Well I did and I lived with him for the rest of my high school years. I played baseball, basketball, took every math and science class I could and got mostly A's. My grades in the other subjects also improved.

"I graduated in 1942 and started college with the help of Coach Palmer. When the draft board started breathing down my neck I knew I would be drafted so I joined the Army Air Corps. You know the rest."

They stood out there on the apron for a few minutes.

"Vern, I really appreciate you telling me this; it explains a lot. However, what I said to you still goes. You need to decide."

"Thanks Low, I think I have," he said, pausing for a moment before adding, "Could I talk to the crew tomorrow?"

"Yea sure, just before we take-off."

They stood there for a minute more and then Lowell said, "Well I guess we had better get changed."

They both turned and walked towards the ready room.

*****

The next day before they went to the flight line, Lowell said, "Just a minute men, Lieutenant Stewart has something to say." Turing to Vern he said, "Lieutenant."

Vern stood up and shuffled a little and said, "Ah, I want to apologize to you guys for the way I've been acting. Low pointed out to me that I have a large responsibility to this crew and I haven't been fulfilling it. I promise I will from now on and if it ever becomes necessary to get you home, I promise I will do my damnedest to do so."

The men looked at him for a few moments, then someone started to clap and the room filled with applause. Vern looked embarrassed until

Lorenzo punched him on the shoulder.

"That's okay sir; we know you will."

Lowell said, "Enough of this stuff, let's go fly!"

True to his word Vern's attitude did change. There were a few times that the old surliness showed up, but all in all, he did become a member of the crew. Lowell realized he was a very good pilot and had no doubt he could bring them home, God forbid, if the need arose.

The next week they received word that they were going to fly their navigation-training course. Myron had the route, which would take them northwest almost to the Canadian border, south over Seattle at night; then due west out over the Pacific for approximately 250 miles, turn South again for approximately 100 miles and then turn east taking them over Oregon and back to Spokane. The total trip would take most of the night and some of the next day covering nearly 1,200 miles total. Though Myron had taught many navigational cadets celestial navigation at night, he was somewhat nervous. He expressed this to Lowell in a serious manner but Low merely slapped him on the shoulder.

"Come on Jew, you've been teaching this stuff for over a year, you'll do fine."

Myron just smiled at him in that unspoken communication that indicated their feelings for each other.

The crew had been briefed about this mission as to what their jobs were and what to take. Lowell met them at 1900 hours in the ready room and went though the checklist for each crew member. They were taken out to the flight line and boarded the aircraft. After take-off, Lowell called Myron and asked for the course.

Because this was basically a night flight, much of it would be by celestial and radio navigation meaning Myron and Ellingston had to work closely together. They flew over the darkened state of Washington for some time and then Myron came on the intercom and announced they would be getting a new course heading in fifteen minutes. Lowell responded appropriately and asked Vern to be ready. Vern nodded his understanding and began to check the compass on the control panel.

After the allotted fifteen minutes, Myron again came on the intercom.

"Okay guys, new course."

He gave them the new heading that would take them south over Seattle, adding "If you've never seen a foreign country, just look out the starboard side. That, gentlemen, is Canada. That is, if I have navigated correctly."

That brought smiles to the whole crew who were getting used to his humor and enjoyed it a great deal. Vern and Lowell looked at each other and smiled.

Vern said, "I've never seen a foreign country before."

"Well just take a look."

Vern turned his head and said, "It's dark, how can I see anything?"

Lowell responded, "Well, if our navigator is any good, it's down there."

The flight continued on the prescribed course for a time and then Myron called for the change in course that would take them out over the Pacific for their third leg.

When the new heading was achieved, Lowell said, "Take it awhile Vern, I need to stretch."

Vern nodded and Lowell unhooked his headphones and got out of the seat. He was quite stiff and the thought crossed his mind that if he was stiff in this short time, how could he manage a five or six hour flight to Germany? He stopped at the radio station and WE offered him some coffee, which he accepted. He checked on the gunners, visited that famous tube, and returned to the cockpit, but still let Vern fly for awhile.

After making the next course change that would take them back to land over the Oregon coast, Lowell said he would take the controls and that Vern should take a break.

Vern responded, "That's okay Low, I don't need one."

Lowell reminded him that was not a request but an order. Vern smiled and nodded his head, unhooked his belt and headsets, got out of his seat and made his way to the rear of the plane.

Myron had realized when he first saw their course that they would be very close to Drayville. He decided to go up and ask Lowell if they could make a little course change and fly over their hometown. Lowell said that maybe they could get a little wind drift, just let him know.

After reaching the Oregon coast, Myron called Lowell and gave him the new course that would take them over Drayville. When they were over the city, he called the crew and told them to look out the right side of the ship and they would be looking down on the greatest town in America.

This resulted in a round of comments that they must have really been off course to fly over Alabama, New York, and Minnesota.

The next course change took them north toward Spokane. Several minutes later, one of the crew came on the intercom and told them to look east; they could see the sun rise. After several more minutes, Myron reported that they were about thirty minutes out of Spokane.

When they landed and shut down procedures were completed, Lowell turned to Vern and said, "You did a fine job Vern."

"Thanks Low, I really enjoyed flying this big ship; I didn't think I would."

They de-planed, turned in their flight gear and proceeded to the theater for debriefing. It went well and they were given the appropriate congratulations.

The next big flying assignment was formation bombing. For this they flew down to the bombing range on the Columbia River, which was named after the town nearby: Boardman. It took some time to form and achieve their altitude. For this mission, they would drop their load at thirty thousand feet.

When they got to the IP (inspection point), Vince called it out and Lowell said, "It's your airplane."

With the Norden Bombsight, the bombardier would take over some of the control of the airplane and fly it until the bombs were dropped. The Norden could not control vertical changes, so the pilot would still have to maintain altitude.

As they approached the drop point, Vince kept calling out, "Steady, steady, bombs away!"

Lowell felt the aircraft surge up with the loss of weight and said, "I've got it!" and took total control again.

When they got back to the base and went to debriefing, the instructor bombardier told them that everything being equal, it was a very good bomb run. Lowell patted Vince on the shoulder as they got up to leave.

As training continued with much more formation flying, more night flying, and less and less instructed flying, Lowell felt that they were coming together as a crew. The gunners had displayed their skills during aerial gunnery, Vince had been successful with the bomb runs, and Myron had kept them on course. The best measure of this was that after every flight, the crew all seemed to be joshing each other over some imagined mistake.

This reminded him of how the team members would kid each other in high school after a good game.

At the end of the day on a Monday just two weeks before completion of training, the crews were assembled in the theater and addressed by the colonel. He told them that some crews would be shipped to Kearney, Nebraska and from there they would ferry new B-17s over to England. The remainder of the crews would be shipped to Camp Kilmer, New Jersey for transport overseas. He went on to tell them how proud he was of all of them and that the combat squadrons would be lucky to have each and every one of them. The announcement that brought the most reaction was that they would all be getting three-day passes at the end of the week.

After being dismissed, Myron asked, "Shall we call the girls and see if they want to come over?"

"My thought exactly."

They made their way to the phone center and Lowell placed a call to Helen's home. While waiting for the call to go through, he said to Myron, "We better try to find a hotel or motor lodge close."

"Yea, when we finish here let's see if we can borrow Duncan's car and go into town."

"Good Idea."

Just then the operator called, "Lieutenant Andersen, your call is ready."

As Lowell rushed toward the booth the operator reminded him, "Remember, lieutenant, you only have three minutes."

Lowell nodded as he opened the door of the booth, picked up the phone and heard the operator say, "Go ahead."

"Helen?"

"Yes Lowell, is everything okay?"

"Oh yes, we just got word that we have a three-day pass next weekend and wondered if you gals wanted to come up?"

"Oh yes, I'm sure that Betty will too. I'll call her as soon as we hang up and if you can call back tomorrow I'll let you know."

"That sounds swell; Jew and I are going into town tonight to try and find you a place to stay. Why don't we wait until we find a place and can fill you in on that."

"That would be just fine. How are you darling; how is the training going?"

"Oh just fine, you know, we only have about two weeks to go and the rumor is that we will not be getting any delay in transit leave this time."

"Oh, Lowell that means you're going directly overseas."

Before he could respond the operator came on and said, "Time is up."

"Good by darling, I love you so much." Lowell said,

But all he got of Helen's response was "I love – –." Then the line went dead.

Lowell walked back to the BOQ thinking about Helen and how much he missed her. What would it be like when he was overseas? He had no idea how long it would be before he could take Helen in his arms and love her.

Borrowing Duncan's car, the boys drove into town and were able to get two rooms at a respectable but not fancy motel.

Driving back to the base, Lowell said, "I don't care what the room looks like, I just want to be alone with Helen for a few minutes."

Absent of his usual reply, Jew just looked up at him and nodded. It seems that both boys were thinking the same thing.

The next few days were torture for Myron and Lowell. They only had one flying mission, but it was night formation flying that took a great deal of concentration and physical skill. Lowell could not stop thinking about what Helen was doing and he could hardly keep his mind on the task at hand.

At one point Vern looked over at him and asked, "Low, what is the matter; you're all over the sky tonight. I suspect that we will get a good chewing out from Captain Nelson."

"Yea, I'm sorry Vern. I keep thinking about my wife and that she will be here tomorrow."

"Would you like me to take it for awhile?"

"Sure, go ahead; maybe if I take a little walk, I'll be better."

Lowell turned over the controls to Vern, got up and started down the narrow aisle to the waist.

Sergeant Wright asked, "Everything all right sir?"

"Yea, I guess I'm just a little distracted tonight; Lieutenant Stewart is going to take it for awhile."

"Just relax Low; I've flown with a lot of men who can't hold a candle to you as a pilot."

Lowell looked at him and smiled, then tapped him on the shoulder saying, "Thanks Bob, coming from you that means a lot."

Friday finally came and the boys picked up their weekend passes and headed for town and their wives. When they got to the motel, they found the office and inquired as to which rooms their respective wives occupied.

Walking down the row of rooms, Lowell looked around and said, "Boy, this is no Ritz, is it?"

"It is a heap of junk, but the rooms seemed clean and they looked good to me after five places with no rooms available."

Lowell looked at him and smiled, "Well, I hope they have good strong beds."

"Yea, that's all that counts."

Lowell came to his room first and knocked on the door while Myron continued down the row. Lowell knocked again but there was no answer. When he turned to look, he saw Helen come out of Betty's room and start to run towards him. Lowell dropped his bag and ran to meet her and they met in a Hollywood embrace in the middle of the sidewalk.

Myron, not wanting to pass up an opportunity like that said, "Wait a minute, can't you at least get to your room!"

Lowell looked over his shoulder and gave him a one-finger salute and led Helen toward their room. Later, as Lowell and Helen lay on the bed, there came a soft tap on the door. Lowell got up and opened it to see Jew standing there.

"You guys want to go get something to eat and maybe try to take in a show?"

Lowell looked into the room at Helen; she nodded and answered, "That sounds great, give us a few minutes and we'll be ready."

In a few minutes Lowell and Helen walked out of their room and down to the Rothstein's. Lowell knocked on the door.

"Are you ready?"

From in side the room Jew answered, "Just give me a few minutes to get my pants on."

They heard Betty say, "Oh Myron, behave yourself," just then the door opened and they came out fully dressed.

They stopped at the office to inquire about a good place to eat and how far the theaters were from the motel. The clerk recommended a place downtown but they would probably want to take a cab as it was several miles and he offered to call them one. The two couples agreed and he went to the phone and called.

It took nearly thirty minutes for the cab to arrive and when it did, it was an old model Plymouth and was not the cleanest car they had ever ridden in, but it got them downtown. They asked the driver if there were cabs available for a ride back to the motel and he said usually they're around the bus depot just up the street. They found the recommended restaurant and had a very good meal.

While they finished their coffee, Helen asked, "Do you think you will get a plane to fly over to England."

"I hope so; three weeks on a ship is not my idea of fun," replied Lowell.

"Yea, I've heard of crews going to Kearney and when they get there, there are no planes available and they still have to take a ship," said Myron.

"Well, I hope it doesn't happen to us."

After dinner they found the theater but the movie didn't seem like one they wanted to see, so they found a soda fountain and went in for a coke. They stayed downtown for another hour and then walked to the bus station and found that there were, indeed, cabs available. They hired one to return them to the motel and settled in for the night.

As they lay in bed, Lowell and Helen began to talk about the future.

Helen asked, "Will you go back to college when you get out?"

"Yea, I think so, but I'm not sure what I want to do."

"Weren't you thinking about teaching?"

"Yea, but right now I'm not sure. I do know that I want to return to Drayville or at least the county after the war."

"Gee, that's good news honey!"

They rolled into an embrace and held each other until sleep set in.

*****

Returning to the field that Sunday night was again one of the most difficult things the boys had ever done. They promised to call when they knew more about what was going to happen, but told the girls not to expect to see them again. They had been told that when the orders came down, there was usually no leave allowed.

The next day started as usual, reveille at 0530, breakfast at 0600 and classes at 0700. Lowell and Myron were walking to the theater after breakfast when Homer called, "Hey you guys, wait up!"

They stopped and waited until Homer had caught them and Myron asked, "What's up?"

"I just talked to a corporal from the orderly room and he said the orders should be up by tonight after training."

"Boy, that's good news!" Lowell responded.

"Yea, I sure hope I get to ferry and not take that slow boat; I tend to get a little sea sick."

Myron with his usual humor said, "Well, just think, you won't have to keep that awful navy food in your stomach very long."

"Oh very funny."

That weekend, with pheasant season just open, some shotguns were found and Dave, Lorenzo and Wayne had gone hunting. Much of the talk with the crew later centered on who shot the most birds and who the best shot was. Niggs Risen had a lot of fun kidding them about shooting a defenseless bird. Lowell liked hearing the good-natured kidding; it meant they were coming together as a crew.

The days of training that remained involved more formation flying, some gunnery practice and navigation exercises. By 1800 each evening they had completed the day's entire syllabus. Over the intercom Lowell would say, "Well done men. We have completed our assignment so let's head for the barn."

The last week of crew training seemed to fly by. There were several short hop missions. One in particular caused Sergeant McDonald to become very excited because they flew over Lewiston, Idaho, his hometown. Lowell was able to drop down to just under 3,000 feet and Dave narrated the tour of his hometown although he could not spot his house. Over the intercom the crew asked several questions.

"So, do you have toilets and runnning water?" Niggs asked.

Gabe said, "Do they speak English in Lewiston or Idaho?"

Dave took all the ribbing with a good attitude until Lowell came on and said, "Okay you guys, that's enough chatter."

One day after landing they taxied up to the assigned parking space,

Lowell and Vern went through the shut down procedures and they deplaned. A three–quarter ton truck arrived at the apron to pick them up. Homer and his crew were already aboard and helped them to climb over the tailgate. As they rode toward the ready room Homer asked if they had heard anything yet about the orders. Lowell shook his head.

As they climbed down from the truck, they saw that the orders must be up. There was a large crowd around the bulletin board. Lowell walked up and, looking over the heads of several men he could just make out the orders.

THE FOLLOWING CREWS WILL DEPART FOR KEARNEY, NEBRASKA ON OR ABOUT 25 SEPTEMBER 1944 BY PUBLIC TRANSPORTATION WHERE THEY WILL RECEIVE THEIR OVERSEAS INOCULATIONS AND BE PROCESSED FOR OVERSEAS SHIPMENT.

SECOND LIEUTENANT LOWELL ANDERSEN AND CREW
SECOND LIEUTENANT HOMER DRISCOLL AND CREW
SECOND LIEUTENANT PETER SIZEMORE AND CREW

Lowell turned around with a big smile and raised his hand towards where his crew was waiting. Homer looked anxiously towards Lowell and he gave him thumbs up, which caused Homer to let out a little cheer.

The crews assembled later in the theater. Colonel Materson mounted the stage to a loud ATTENTION and he immediately gave the command of at ease and seats.

As the crews sat down, he said, “Men, we have done all we can to make you come together as crews. You have all done a fine job of it, which indicates to us that we have succeeded. Your next assignments will be in a combat unit in the Eighth Air Force in England. Some of you will fly directly to the British Isles and some of you will be transported on troop ships for which I offer my apologies.”

This brought some laughter from the assembled crews.

“As I was saying, we here at Spokane have done all we can to make you combat ready; the rest is up to you. Good luck men and may God be with you in the coming months.”

As the colonel left the stage to another command of ATTENTION,

Lowell and Myron looked at each other with winsome smiles, then Myron reached out and slapped Lowell on the arm.

That night, their last in Spokane, several of the men from Homer's crew and Lowell, Myron, Vince and Vern decided to take one last look at the Pacific Northwest. They caught a bus into town and Lowell, always the 'den mother', cautioned them about imbibing too much in celebration. This went for naught with several of them, including Myron.

When they arrived back at the barracks around 1230, Myron flopped on his bunk and said, "Boy am I tired."

"No, you're not tired; you're drunk!"

"So be it; I think I will go right to sleep."

Lowell, who had more to drink than he planned to, smiled at him and stretched out on his bunk. Then he reached in his footlocker and took out the writing kit.

Dearest Helen,

Well, this is our last night in Spokane. We got our orders but won't know if we got the orders we were hoping for a few days. I will try to call you tomorrow, but tonight I don't think I should. We went out on the town and I am really tired.

Lowell went on a few more pages and signed off as usual.

As always to you I give my love and life,
Lowell

*****

The next day was spent with packing for travel, arranging for train tickets and saying goodbye to all the guys they had met. Lowell tried to call Helen, but could not get through. Late that afternoon they boarded busses to the railroad station.

At the station they boarded the train and looked for seats. There were several close together and Lowell's crew took them. Lowell and Myron sat together and the rest of the crew was dispersed within a few seats.

As the train pulled out, Myron said, "Boy, I'm going to try and get some sleep."

"Yea, you probably need it after last night's episode."

"Aw shut up, will you lieutenant!"

The train rumbled on towards Kearney. The boys slept, read and talked. About mid-day Lowell decided to take a walk to stretch his legs and he got up and walked toward a door that led to the end of the train. Bob Wright was out there having a smoke and when Lowell entered he stood up.

Lowell said, "Oh don't bother with that Bob."

Bob reached into his pocket and took out his cigarettes and offered one to Lowell. He realized what he had done and somewhat embarrassed said, "Oh sorry sir, I forgot you don't smoke."

"Yea, that's one bad habit I haven't acquired yet."

After a short silence Lowell said, "Bob, what is combat really like? I mean, I have been very worried about whether I will live up to the responsibilities I'll have as pilot."

Bob looked at him for awhile and said, "Listen Low; don't worry about that one bit. I've flown with many pilots and you're the best. I mean, you can kind of tell about a man and what he will be like and I have no concern about you."

"Thanks Bob, but I worry a lot about it."

"Well don't. To answer your question, It's hard to say what combat is really like. Each man in the crew experiences it little different. Of course, I was not in the kind of combat we'll be facing in the European theater. In the Pacific, we didn't fly those large formation attacks, just three or four planes and we usually attacked shipping or a small naval base."

At that the door opened and Jew and Vern came out.

Jew said, "We're going to the club car for a beer, you guys want to join us?"

Bob said, "Yea I will."

Lowell said, "I think I'll go back to my seat and try to get a little more sleep."

They parted and as Lowell walked up the aisle, he noticed Vince sitting and looking out of the window. He said, "Mind if I join you?"

"Not at all Low, have a seat."

As Lowell sat down he said, "What are you doing, enjoying the scenery?"

"Yea, some scenery, sage brush and sand."

"I thought you were from this part of the country?"

"Not far, but the countryside was a lot different."

"You did four years of college, didn't you Vince?"

"Yea, but I didn't know what I wanted to do. My folks wanted me to be a doctor, but I really didn't want to."

"Isn't your dad a doctor?"

"Yea, both my folks are doctors. Dad's a surgeon and Mom is a pediatrician."

"Wow, you must be rich."

"Well, we lived pretty good."

"My Dad's a mechanic and Mom's just a house wife. I always thought it would be good to be rich and get anything you wanted."

"Boy are you wrong. My folks thought my sister and I shouldn't be brought up to have everything we wanted so if we wanted something other than food, clothes and shelter, we had to earn it."

"Yea, well we all had our crosses to bear."

After a moment of silence, Vince said, "Your dad was a mechanic?"

"Yea, he owns a garage and I had to work there when I was in high school and my one year in college."

"Boy, I would have given anything to have a dad that knew something about cars."

"Yea, my dad was pretty good that way; when I was eighteen, he fixed up a '33 Ford and gave it to me for my birthday."

"What? You got a '33? Man I had a 1927 model "A" and that was all I ever got. I don't mean to put my dad down. He's a very nice man and a great father, but I would have killed to have a father who understood cars. When I used to work on my "A" and Dad would come out and ask if he could help I would have him hand me wrenches; I knew more about cars then he ever will."

"Yea, my dad is a great guy."

There was a moment of silence. Myron and Vern came down the aisle and sat down across from them.

Myron said, "Boy, there are a couple of good looking girls in the dining car; you ought to go check that out Vince."

"Maybe I will, you want to go Low?"

"Sure, I'll go with you, but not to look at the girls."

Lowell got out of the seat and followed Vince and Myron up the aisle to the club car. When they entered, there were several service men, two businessmen, and two ladies of undetermined age. Lowell looked at Myron and said, "Boy buddy, you haven't been away from Betty three days and you think these women are good looking?"

"Well, those aren't the ones we saw, are they Vern?"

"Heavens no, these were very good looking and about fifteen years younger."

"I don't know about you two."

Myron looked at Lowell with disgust and said, "Let's have a beer."

As the train rumbled on the rest of the day and into the night, the crew settled down to sleeping, reading or just talking. Wayne, sitting up the aisle several rows from Lowell, got up and walked to Lowell's seat.

"Sir, you know I'm from Nebraska and we live only a few miles from North Platte where all the trains stop for water and coal. There is a canteen there and all the service men can get off the train and have a bite to eat."

Lowell nodded, and Wayne went on, "Well my folks will be at the North Platte station and I wonder if you wouldn't mind meeting them. I'm sure they will be there because my mom and sister work at the canteen on most week ends."

"Certainly WE; I'll be glad to meet your folks. What do you mean a canteen?"

"Well the Union Pacific allowed the townspeople to turn the train station into a canteen for the soldiers who stop there. Almost all the troop trains that travel across the nation stop there. I worked there some when I was in high school."

"What do they do at the canteen?"

"Oh they serve coffee, sandwiches, milk, pass out magazines and such."

"Oh, that sounds swell; I'm looking forward to it."

As Wayne went back to his seat, the man across the aisle from him, whom he supposed was a businessman, leaned over and asked, "You headed overseas son?"

"Yea, were going to Kearney."

"You're a pilot I see by your wings."

"That's right, we're a B-17 crew," Lowell looked around and thought he shouldn't have told him that.

The businessman said, "Well, I flew during the Great War. It was very different with open cockpits and that castor oil smell permeating every thing. I don't suppose the modern planes have that do they?"

"No, they don't use castor oil anymore I guess."

"Where are you from son?"

"Oregon, a little town called Drayville, just South of Portland."

"Yes, I know it; I sell automotive parts in Oregon, Washington and Idaho."

"Really, have you ever sold anything to the Andersen garage in Drayville?"

"Oh yes, Ethan Andersen is one of my best customers."

"No kidding; he's my father. He owns the garage and I worked there all through high school and college."

"I'll be darned. You know, I thought you looked kind of familiar. I'll bet you were there when I called on your father. Small world."

Lowell and the salesman discussed automotive parts for a few more minutes and the conversation died. Lowell turned and looked out the window and noticed it was getting dark. He leaned his head back, closed his eyes and drifted off thinking about his folks back in Drayville, wondering what the twins were doing and of course what Helen was doing at that very minute. The conductor woke him with the announcement that they were coming in to North Platte and there would be a fifteen-minute stop. He said the soldiers could get off and visit the canteen but must be back on the train when they hear the whistle blow for all aboard.

As the train pulled in, Myron came up the aisle and said, "What's going on?"

"They have a canteen here and we can get off and get something to eat and drink."

As their car passed the station platform, the boys saw women with baskets of fruit, magazines, cases of milk bottles and coffee standing on the platform. When the train came to a complete stop, the boys made a mad dash for the station. Entering it was quite a shock; it was nearly full of troops, ladies and a few men. There was a sailor from another train playing a piano and several of the men were dancing with the younger women. Lowell heard his name being called and turned to see Wayne signaling him accompanied by what were probably his parents and a very attractive young woman.

Wayne approached and said, "Sir, this is my father and mother, Mr.

and Mrs. Ellingston and my sister Ruth."

As Mr. Ellingston reached out to shake Lowell's hand he said, "Glad to meet you sir. Wayne has written about you several times, he seems to think you are a pretty good pilot."

Lowell was somewhat taken back, but managed to say, "Glad to meet you sir; we think Wayne is a pretty good radio man as well."

Just then Myron, Vince, Zo and Gabe walked up and Wayne introduced them to his family. Gabe and Zo were much more interested in Wayne's sister than his folks, but they were courteous. Just then the whistle calling the men back to the train sounded.

Vince turned to Lowell and handed him a sandwich and a bottle of milk saying, "We didn't think you had time to get one."

Wayne's mother gave Wayne a hug while his father shook his hand. His sister gave him a hug while keeping her eyes on Zo and Gabe. They all ran for the train and jumped aboard.

As the train pulled out of the station, Myron said, "What a marvelous thing."

"Yea, Midwestern people are like that."

Kearney was only about 100 miles from North Platte so the rest of the trip only took about an hour and a half. When the train pulled into Kearney Station it was the middle of the afternoon. As the crews disembarked, they all commented on the heat. Lowell had forgotten how humid the Midwest could be.

Myron came up to him and slapped him on the back saying, "Welcome home Low."

"Yea, thanks, I don't remember it being this hot."

"Well, when you're five or six you don't notice those things."

Homer came up and told them that the bus was out in front. They all picked up their bags and proceeded to the front of the station. One of the crew asked the driver, a sergeant, how long a ride it was to the base.

"Oh about twenty minutes if there isn't some farmer on the highway."

They both laughed.

The sergeant stood up and said, "Gentlemen, welcome to Kearney. We will be out at the base in about twenty minutes and get you men settled in, so sit back and smoke if you've got 'em."

There was a small titter of laughter. The driver sat down and started the engine. Lowell noticed that he had two rows of ribbons on his chest indicating he had probably completed his required missions and was now relegated to driving a bus. He thought about that a minute and decided that wasn't such a bad job after all.

Lowell reached into his pocket and pulled out the last letter he had gotten from his mother. She had written about her sister who lived up in O'Neil. *I sure hope you can get up to see Aunt Bertha while you are there.* Lowell smiled to himself with the thought that his mother was forever the family organizer; however, not only could he *not* travel to O'Neil, but he couldn't even call his aunt because of security.

As the bus pulled up to the orderly room, the driver shut off the engine, stood up and said, "Okay gentleman, this is it; everyone off."

Lowell and the crew gathered their belongings and dismounted from the bus. Another sergeant met them, instructed them to report in and said they would be told where to draw their bedding and shown where to bunk. Lowell, Vern and Myron were assigned a room together with the rest of the officers next to them. After making up their bunks, the men flopped down and with their hands behind their heads looked up at the ceiling and to a man, their thoughts were much the same; *What was ahead for them?*

Lowell thought of Helen and reached into his bag and took out his writing kit.

Myron looked over and said, "My God, he's at it again!"

Everyone laughed just as a corporal stuck his head in the door and said, "Formation in ten minutes sirs."

With a smile on his face, Lowell closed his kit, got off the bunk and said, "Come on boys, duty calls."

As the crews formed, they were called to attention as a major came out of the orderly room and gave the command to at-ease.

"Gentleman, welcome to Kearney. You will be given your overseas shots, and some of you may be chosen to shuttle aircraft. We have several ships to ferry and we will soon choose and notify three crews for that purpose. Now, go back to your rooms and get settled in. Chow will be at 0530."

As he turned, the command ATTENTION was again called and the men struck the pose until they heard DISSMISSED!

Lowell spotted Bob Wright, Zo and Dave McDonald and walked over to them.

"Hi men. How are things going?"

"Fine sir, do you think we might get a shuttle?"

"Well, I sure hope so, but I have no idea."

"We do too," answered Zo.

"Well, I guess we better do what the major said, see you later."

When he turned to go, Homer came up and said, "Boy I sure hope we get a shuttle."

"Yea, I do too."

Just then he thought he heard someone calling his name. He looked around into the sea of khaki uniforms but did not recognize anyone he knew. He turned to leave when he heard his name called again and turned to look into Charlie's face. For a minute Lowell didn't realize who he was looking at but then realization hit him.

Moving towards him, he shouted, "Charlie!"

When they met, they gave each other a short embrace and looked around somewhat embarrassed. Lowell turned towards the door and called Homer who apparently didn't hear him greet Charlie.

"Come on, Homer just left. Let's catch him!"

When they caught up with Homer they stood for several minutes catching up on the past few months and found that Charlie was housed two streets away from them and that he ate in a different chow hall. They decided to get together after chow, go over to the Officers Club and really catch up on each other.

When Lowell entered the room, Myron was already there and said, "Some of the guys are going to a movie tonight, want to go?"

"No, guess who I ran in to after the meeting today?"

Jew looked at him like he used to in grade school when he would pull that quiz game on him and said, "Well, I really don't know since there are probably several thousand men here."

"Charlie Smith!"

"Oh, that's really swell."

"Yea, we're going to go over to the Officer's Club and renew old times. Want to come along?"

"Nah, you go ahead Low; he was your friend and I only knew him for a little while. I think I'll go to the movies with the guys."

When Charlie, Homer and Lowell met at the Officers Club that night, Homer and Lowell ordered beers and Charlie ordered a soft drink.

Homer said, "Still the pure Mormon are you?"

"Yea, pretty much, though I have had a couple of beers with my crew on occasion."

"How is your crew?" asked Lowell.

"They're just great. By the way my navigator was trained by Myron down in Texas. That's some coincidence isn't it?"

"Oh, you know that Myron is my navigator?"

"You don't say. How did you swing that?"

Homer piped in with, "Well you know, those Swedes have to stick together."

"You had better not let Jew hear you say that Homer."

All three laughed and Homer ordered another round of drinks and the discussion turned to the possibility of getting a shuttle. All three men thought they had a very good chance of doing so, but it was only hope. They discussed how much fun it would be to end up in the same squadron or at least in the same group. The conversation then turned to the other men they had gone through the various stages of training with and whatever happened to them.

Finally as the evening wore on, Charlie said, "You know, I just got in today and I'm very tired, so I think I'll turn in."

They all rose together and agreed it was time.

Lowell managed to get off a few lines to Helen before he got so tired he couldn't see the paper anymore. He was hoping to wait until the other three men returned from the movie because he knew they would probably stop off at the club on the way home and have a few drinks, which would increase the noise they would make getting settled down.

When the men returned to the barracks, Lowell was fast asleep, but it didn't take them long to wake him.

Low said, "You guys sound and smell like you stopped off at the Officers Club on the way back from the movie."

Jew responded, "We didn't get to the movie, we spent the entire evening at the club. Old Vince here kept buying rounds until I had to stop him."

"Oh sure, I can just imagine you stopping him. We were at the Officers Club, but didn't see you guys."

"We went to the one on the main post. It's much better than our local one."

As Myron flopped down on his bed with out undressing Lowell had to get up and turn off the light.

ON TO ENGLAND

Kearney was a transition base but reveille still occurred at 0530. Breakfast was much the same, including scrambled eggs, greasy bacon, and cold toast. The coffee was very hot, however, and for that the crew was thankful. Lowell tried to pile some bacon on Myron's tray, but he didn't touch it. It wasn't so much a matter of his beliefs, but more the activity of the night before.

After morning chow, the men assembled in the theater and went through the ritual of jumping up and sitting down as officers entered.

"Welcome to Kearney gentlemen," said the major. "Today you will receive the first of a series of shots that will be given over the next three days."

He continued talking about the day's activities then announced, "You will find a posting of the shuttle crews tomorrow, which will be followed by separate navigators' and pilots' meetings."

Lowell looked at Myron and they both smiled as they read each other's thoughts: their crew would be one of the chosen. The men jumped to their feet as the major left the stage and Lowell realized how many men gathered in the theater. Most of the crews heading for the European Theater went through Kearney. He had assumed it would only be those crews selected for shuttle services.

The next day after they received their second series of shots, they went by the orderly room to check on the posting of shuttle crews. Sure enough, the list was up.

Myron ran up to the board and let out a whoop, "We got one!"

Lowell came up and ran down the list of several crews until he found Charlie's crew but not Homer's. He felt good for Charlie but sorry for Homer. At the bottom of the list were instructions for the navigators to report to building number 2007 and the pilots to number 2003 at 1000 hours.

In the pilots' meeting, Lowell learned that they would ferry the third ship. A pilot he didn't know, Sam Clark, would fly the first and Charlie the second. During the first leg of the trip they would fly to Bangor, Maine then on to Gander, Newfoundland. At that point they would receive orders and the flight plan for their destination in the United Kingdom. The navigators learned of their first leg destination and the charted courses. Both groups were surprised to learn that they would not fly together as assumed; instead they would fly spaced one hour apart. They were provided with information about first leg weather patterns they might encounter and restricted areas to avoid.

Saying goodbye to Homer and his crew, Lowell packed his bags and stowed them in his assigned aircraft. Impressed by the newness of the airplane he hoped it had been gone over with a fine-tooth comb to make sure everything was in its proper place.

Looking at Vern he smiled and said, "Let's don't bend this plane. It's very new."

"Yea, I guess we better be careful," Vern replied with a smile.

The third ship to depart, Lowell went through the start up procedures, called the tower and requested take-off clearance.

Speaking into the intercom Lowell said, "Okay Jew, this is where we find out if you are any good as a navigator. As soon as we're wheels up, I want the course."

Jew responded and Lowell detected an air of professionalism in his tone that made him feel that Myron was very much up to the task. He turned to Vern and said, "Okay buddy, ready to go?"

"Yes sir, I'm more than ready!"

"Okay, pilot to crew, ready for take-off?"

Each crew member answered from his station and Lowell nodded to Vern as he put his hand on the throttles. Vern covered them with his as a back up. They watched the RPMs and when they were at take-off revolutions, Lowell released the breaks and the B-17 began to roll down the runway.

As the plane lifted off the runway, Lowell was aware of how differently it handled with a near full load of fuel. He called Myron and asked for course directions, which he received without hesitation. Lowell still had the plane in a climbing attitude to gain the required altitude for their first leg.

Reaching cruising altitude, Lowell went on the intercom and said, "Pilot to crew. We're at our cruising altitude and headed for Bangor, Maine. We're going to be up here for a long time, so relax. You can remove your chutes but keep your harnesses on."

A familiar voice came on and said, "Why, do you think you might forget how to fly?"

Lowell didn't respond but looked at Vern and they both grinned at Jew's response.

Lowell began to relax and he loosened his harness. Vern looked over at him and asked if he wanted some coffee, Lowell responded that he would wait awhile but for him to go on.

Vern said, "Oh, I can wait too."

After a minute of silence, Vern said, "Lowell, I have been thinking a lot these past few weeks about that conversation we had in the early days of crew training."

Vern saw that Lowell had a puzzled look on his face and he continued, "I've decided you might just have saved my life."

"What do you mean?"

"Well, I was so intent on being a hero and flying fighters that I probably would have done what I have done all my life and that is to take unnecessary chances doing stupid things just to prove that I'm better than everyone else."

"Why would you need to do that?"

"Well, you know, I told you about my family. Every kid in school used to talk about their moms and dads and I just got angrier and angrier when I heard that, so I made up my mind I was going to show the world I didn't need a family to be good."

A wave of compassion swept over Lowell and he didn't know how to respond. Lowell thought for quite awhile about how to answer but couldn't come up with a very plausible response. He was rescued from having to, however, when Bob Wright came into the cockpit.

"We're burning fuel at a normal pace. I think we will have more than enough to reach Bangor."

Somewhat relieved at not having to respond to Vern, Lowell asked, "How are the engines, Bob?"

"Oh they're just fine. I haven't seen such beauties for a long time. Most of the ones we had in the Pacific were nearly run-outs."

"Well, keep an eye on 'em Bob. New engines can cause trouble as well."

Bob left the cockpit and only the very loud drone of the four Wright cyclone engines powering the B-17 interrupted the silence.

Finally Lowell said to Vern, "Well I don't know what I had to do with it, I think you did it yourself."

"Yea, well thanks anyway."

After a few more minutes Vern said, "I have never had friends like these crewmen. If I'd had the opportunity to fly single-seaters, I wouldn't have had such close friends."

Lowell looked over at Vern and said, "Well for my part, I can't imagine a better pilot than you. Now, I think I'm ready for that coffee."

"You bet. I'll be right back!"

As Vern was leaving the cockpit, Lowell thought about all the friends he had in school and wondered what they were doing at this moment. He knew that Vernon Dickerson was missing in action. Although he never considered him to be a particularly good friend, he was indeed a friend. Vern returned with the coffee and Lowell thanked him. He sipped on the hot strong liquid and his thoughts turned to home. He wondered what his folks were doing that minute and the twins. He thought of Helen, what she was doing, how much he missed her, and realized that this was the first time since he entered the service that she didn't know where he was.

Home

Diane came running down the stairs yelling, "Mom! David hid my shoes."

David followed Diane, yelling, "I did not, they're right under your bed where you left them."

Their dad said, "Now David we've told you to stay out of her room."

Although Lowell had turned his room over to David when he left for the service, Diane also wanted the larger room. It took several weeks to resolve the situation. Their dad came up with a plan that made the decision easier. They would draw straws and the one with the longest straw could chose to either move or stay in the old room. In addition, their Dad said that the one who would remain in their old room would get Lowell's radio. This was not a perfect solution, but it worked. David drew the long straw and could have chosen Lowell's room, which he desperately wanted. However, if he had the radio he could listen to his adventure serials right in his room without having to go down stairs. He chose to stay in the old room and have Lowell's radio.

"Come on kids, get dressed for church. We're going to pick up Helen. She's going with us today."

Diane let out a yell of excitement and David's face broadened into a large smile. Both twins liked their sister-in-law very much and always liked to spend time with her.

"Are we going to have dinner at Uncle Norwood's?"

"No, the Rothstein's have invited us over for Sunday dinner."

On To Bangor

Suddenly Lowell was jerked out of his thoughts by Myron's voice on the intercom saying, "Navigator to pilot, we've just passed the point of no return."

"Thanks Jew. Pilot to radio, can you get a weather report from Bangor, Wayne?"

Lowell had directed the crew instruction not to use Wayne's nickname of 'WE' on the intercom. It could cause confusion that might be dangerous.

"Radio to pilot, I haven't picked up anything yet; I've been trying but there seems to be some interference."

"Well keep trying Wayne."

They flew on in silence for some time and then Lowell said, "Vern, you want to take it awhile, I want to stretch my legs."

"Got it."

Lowell unhooked his harness, climbed out of the seat and started through the aircraft. He was surprised at how stiff he was and again thought about what it was going to be like when they flew combat missions, some lasting as long as ten to twelve hours. This flight was going to be close to that.

As he entered the roomier part of the fuselage, he noticed that several of the crew were stretched out on the floor asleep. He used the tube, poured himself another cup of coffee from the thermos bottle and went over to Wayne's position.

"Anything yet, Wayne?"

"Negative lieutenant. I'll keep trying."

"Fine. Let me know when you get through. I guess we're quite a ways out yet, aren't we?"

"Well, yes but the short wave should pick up something."

"Okay, just keep trying."

After several hours more flying time, Myron came on and reported they were approximately one hour out from Bangor. Lowell thanked him and said to let him know when they were about thirty minutes out.

Wayne came on the intercom and reported that he had just reached Bangor and that the weather was good with a little northeast wind.

Lowell did not respond, but waited some minutes more and called Myron to keep him updated on their estimated time of arrival (ETA).

After a time, Myron came over the intercom, "Low our ETA is fifteen minutes. Better try to reach 'em."

"Bangor tower from B-17 2730, inbound from Kearney," called Lowell. "Come in!"

In a short time, which seemed like hours, a voice came on.

"B-17 2730 from Bangor Tower. Over."

"Bangor tower from B-17 2730 we are about fifteen minutes out. Request landing instructions. Over."

"Roger B-17, land on runway three four, wind is in the northeast twenty miles an hour so be careful. Over"

"Roger Bangor Tower, landing on runway three four, winds northeast twenty miles an hour."

Lowell said to Vern, "If the wind is out of the northeast why are they having us land towards the northwest?"

The runway number three four indicated the landing pattern would be on a heading of 340 degrees or in a northwesterly direction.

"Pilot to crew, get ready for landing, there is a northeast wind at twenty so it might be a little rough."

By the numbers given him from the tower, Lowell knew the direction of the runway was northwest and that he should approach from the southeast. Watching the compass, he swung into the landing pattern. He did this without any problem.

Vern called out, "There's three four."

Lowell made a few minor adjustments and said, "Vern get on the rudders but don't apply pressure unless I call for it!"

The landing went off without a hitch, but Lowell was bathed in sweat. A "Follow Me" vehicle came out and led them in to a parking area. As they shut down Vern looked out the window and said, "Isn't that Sam Clark's plane they're working on over there?"

Lowell rose up in the seat and said, "Yea, I think it is; I wonder what's wrong."

"There's Smith's plane on the apron and no one is working on it."

"Yea, that's odd."

As they entered the ready room, Sam and his crew were sitting around looking very dejected.

Lowell went over and introduced himself again to the pilot and asked, "What's going on?"

"Well, we developed a tremendous oil leak at about an hour out and almost lost an engine. They say they may have to do an engine change and that we might be shipped to Kilmer for overseas transport."

"What are they going to do with the 17?"

"I don't know," said Lieutenant Clark. "Bring in another crew I guess. I'm going to go see the colonel this afternoon and see if we can't just wait."

Myron came up and said, "Boy that's awful. I hope you make it."

"Yea, thanks."

Most of Lowell's crew had come up by then.

Niggs noticed one of the other guys and said, "Well I'll be damned, Ty Larson, how the hell are you?"

The other crew member rose up and said, "Niggs you SOB, how are you?"

Niggs turned to Lowell and said, "Sir, this is Ty Larson. We went through basic together down in Texas."

Lowell reached over and shook the gunner's hand and said, "Glad to meet you sergeant."

As they turned to leave, Lowell said, "Well good luck lieutenant. I hope you make it."

The lieutenant nodded his thanks and said, "Yea, good luck."

A sergeant came up to Lowell and said, "Lieutenant, if you will follow me I'll show you where can report in."

"Thank you, sergeant."

Lowell told the men to relax and he would be right back. He followed the sergeant out of the ready room and down a few doors to the orderly room. As he entered, the sergeant said, "Here's Lieutenant Andersen."

A master sergeant looked up from his work and said, "Welcome lieutenant. Please wait a minute."

He opened the door to the colonel's office and announced Lowell, then turned and motioned for him to enter. Lowell entered, reported with the appropriate deportment and was given the command to relax.

"Lieutenant, your crew did a great job and I understand you hit your ETA right on the nose."

"Thank you sir. I have a very good navigator."

"Any problems you want to report?"

"No sir."

"Okay then lieutenant, the sergeant will show you where to bunk tonight. We'll go over your ship and have it fueled and ready for you in the morning."

Lowell thanked him, rose, saluted and followed the sergeant out of the office, then returned to the ready room and his crew. As Lowell came into the ready room again he said, "Okay men, grab your stuff and follow the sergeant here."

After they drew bedding and were shown to their quarters, Lowell made up his bunk and lay down.

Jew said, "I wonder what there is to do here on this base?"

Lowell raised up and looked at him and Vince said, "Well, I've got what I need, a bed."

Lowell and Vern agreed and Myron said, "I didn't mean I was going out, I just wondered."

Just then a familiar voice said, "Well, you finally got in huh?"

Lowell looked up and saw Charlie standing in the door. "Yea. Did that cross wind give you any trouble?"

"Yea, a little but we made it. You guys going to chow?"

"Yea, as soon as we get settled."

That evening while eating they talked mostly about what they saw during that day's flight and what the next leg would be like. After chow, both crews were so tired they all agreed that it was a good idea to go back to the barracks.

Charlie said, "Yea, I suppose you need to write to Helen tonight."

Lowell just laughed and said, "You remember, huh?"

They parted at Charlie's barracks and agreed to meet for morning chow, saying good night although it was only a little after 1800 hours.

*****

At 0500 hours, a sergeant came into the quarters and shook Lowell, Myron and Vince.

"Time to get up sirs. Your aircraft awaits you."

As the officers entered the mess hall, the crew was already eating. Lowell went over to his men and asked about their night. They all answered with a less than enthusiastic response. Lowell smiled in understanding, then noticed that Bob was not with them.

He asked, "Where is Bob?"

Niggs said, "Oh you know Wright sir, he had to go look after his baby, even though we only have it for a few days."

"Well, let's don't be too critical about someone who is taking care of something that will get us home everyday."

After chow, Myron went to the ready room to get the course directions and altitude while the rest of the crew packed their equipment into the plane and got ready for the next leg to Gander, Newfoundland.

Off To Gander

The take-off was much simpler than the landing. No cross wind. When they reached their cruising altitude, Lowell asked Jew for the course and swung the big ship to the coordinates for the next leg to

Gander, Newfoundland. Lowell realized that this would be the first time he had flown over a foreign country.

Several hours into the flight, Lowell noticed that the countryside was changing dramatically. He had never been to the Northeast and was unfamiliar with that part of the country. It was certainly different. Bob came up to the cockpit and reported that number three was running a little hot.

Lowell asked, "Is it controllable?"

"It's not a problem yet," Bob answered. "But if it gets any hotter, we'll have to feather it."

"Thanks Bob, but let's see what happens when we land," said Lowell. Then, looking at Vern he added, "If necessary, talk to me before you report it. We don't want to end up like Sam's crew and have to go by ship."

"Yes sir, I'll keep you informed."

Vern said, "Damn, I knew everything was going too well."

"Ah, don't get excited until there's good reason."

They flew on for some time with a watchful eye on the temperature gauges and they held their breath that it would stay the same. After a few minutes, Bob came up to the cockpit again and reported that number three was running normal again.

"I don't know what caused it but I'll look into it when we land," he said.

The landing at Gander was far less exciting than at Bangor because there was no crosswind. Lowell brought the plane down and again proceeded after the 'follow me' vehicle to the parking apron.

After they de-planed, a sergeant told Lowell he would take him to the colonel for instruction on the next leg.

The procedures were similar to Bangor except that Lowell received a sealed envelope with instructions not to open it until one hour out of Gander. This reminded him of a movie where sailors received orders that were not to be opened until well out to sea. He couldn't help but smile.

The colonel looked stern and said, "Do you find something funny lieutenant?"

"No sir. I just was remembering, oh well, ah, no sir!"

Lowell saluted the colonel, did an about face and left the office. As he returned to the quarters assigned to them, Myron was just entering and he asked Lowell if he had any information on course direction and altitude. Lowell responded that they were all very secretive and orders would be opened after they were in flight.

When Lowell was back with the crew he told them, "Well men, let's get to our quarters and to bed. We've got another eleven or twelve hours of flying to do tomorrow."

The crew gave no resistance to the suggestion. They were very tired after two long days in the air. When they entered their quarters, Charlie's crew had already made up bunks and were waiting to go to chow. As in Bangor, there was not much socializing between the crews, partly because they really didn't know each other but mostly because they were very tired.

Even though Lowell was awfully tired, he reached into his bag and took out his writing kit.

My Dearest Wife,

I don't know when I will be able to mail this, maybe when we get to England. By then I guess it will be OK for us to tell our families where we are. So far we have had a very good flight with only one minor problem. One of our engines began to over heat, but Bob Wright is such a good flight engineer, he was able to do something and it never really became a problem.

Charlie has joined us again. We ran in to him at Kearney. We sure hope that we can end up in the same squadron or at least the group. Homer did not get a plane so he and his crew are being shipped. I don't know when we'll arrive or where, and couldn't tell you if I did, you know, military secrets and all that.

Lowell wrote another page before he signed off due to fatigue.

As always to you I give my love and life,
Lowell

As he folded the letter, he had no idea when he might be able to mail it. Just writing it made him feel closer to her.

The next morning brought a familiar routine. The men got up, went to morning chow, and proceeded to the ready room for final instructions. Lowell sent Vern to get the weather and Myron to get his navigation data.

Because there were only two ships, the meetings were quite small.

When they got to the plane, Myron said, "I don't know what all this secret stuff is all about. Everyone knows we're headed for England.

Lowell responded, "Well I suppose there are several bases and they don't want the enemy to be waiting for us."

Because they were flying into a combat zone, the gunners were all issued ammunition, which gave most some pause. When Lowell climbed aboard, Niggs was storing his ammo.

Looking up he said, "Gosh sir, this really brings it home doesn't it?"

"Yea Niggs, it certainly does. Are you ready?"

"As ready as I will ever be."

Lowell continued forward and asked Bob if they found anything that would have caused the engine overheating.

"No sir, they didn't. The base maintenance checked it over and said it must have been just one of those gremlins."

"Well, I hope he got off here and hasn't decided to go on over with us."

They both smiled as Lowell continued to the cockpit. Vern was already in his seat.

"You do have those sealed orders, right?"

"Right here," said Lowell as he patted his chest indicating they were in his inside flight jacket pocket. "Has Charlie left yet?"

"Yea, about forty minutes ago."

"Well I guess we had better get this thing warmed up then."

They went through the pre-startup procedure as Bob came up and said, "Ready to turn propellers sir?"

"Turn away!"

Final Leg to England

They finished the startup check list, cleared the ground crew away and pushed the start button on the number three engine. The familiar whine of the Wright engine came to their ears and then the backfire and smoke as it caught and smoothed out. They repeated the process until all four engines were running and Bob reported everything was normal.

Lowell gave the engines a few more minutes to warm up, looked at his watch, and called the tower for permission to taxi, which was granted. At the end of the designated runway, he picked up the mike again and requested permission to take-off. Permission was granted.

Lowell looked at Vern and said, "Well, next stop somewhere in England."

Vern responded with a somewhat strained smile and shook his head. Lowell picked up the mike and switched to intercom.

"Pilot to crew, prepare for take-off; next stop, somewhere in England."

Several "rogers" came over the intercom as Lowell reached for the throttles. Vern reached over and covered Lowell's hand on the throttle as he began to advance them to take-off RPM. This was done as a caution in case the pilot's hands might slip and cut the power at a critical time. They released the breaks and the B-17 began to roll down the runway. At the proper speed, Lowell pushed the controls forward and the tail came up to the take-off position. Again at the appropriate speed, Lowell pulled back gently on the yoke and the big aircraft lifted into the air.

After a few minutes Lowell said, "Gear up!"

Vern reached down and pulled the wheels-up control, The satisfying whine of the hydraulic system lifting the gear was followed by a bang as the wheels locked in the up position.

Vern said, "Gear up!"

Lowell kept the aircraft in a gradual climbing mode until it reached the prescribed altitude for cruising and then called Myron to ask for the proper heading. Myron responded and Lowell gave a slight push on the left rudder pedal and an ever so slight turn of the wheel until the compass swung to the heading provided by his navigator.

After a few minutes Lowell went on the intercom with, "Okay guys, just settle back and enjoy the ride but don't neglect your duties. It's fine to take a little nap, but keep your head phones on. I don't think it is necessary to man your stations, but be ready in case of an emergency."

Again there were several "rogers" and then everything was silent except for the drone of the four Wright cyclones. After some time, Bob Wright came in to the cockpit from his position in the top turret, leaned between Vern and Lowell and tapped several of the gauges.

Vern asked, "Is every thing okay Bob?"

"Oh yea, I was just checking on everything. Better be safe than sorry.

"Bob, when you're flying over the ocean do you tend to get hypnotized by watching the waves," asked Vern.

"No, not really, but of course I was always pretty busy."

"Yea."

Lowell said, "It's time. Take the controls Vern."

Lowell reached into his pocket, took out the envelope and tore the end off. He blew the sides open and pulled out a folded piece of paper, unfolded it and read.

"Well, this is a surprise, we're ordered to fly on to Nuts Corner, Belfast, Free Ireland, by way of Greenland and Iceland."

Picking up the mike he said, "Pilot to crew, I have read the orders and we are to proceed to Nuts Corner, Free Ireland."

Hearing several "rogers" again Lowell said, "Pilot to navigator, I've got some new headings for you."

"Roger, I'll be right up."

Myron's head popped up through the trap door and reached up for the orders. He studied them for a short while.

"This shouldn't be a problem. I'll work it out and let you know."

They flew along for some time and then the trap door between the nose compartment and the cockpit opened. Myron stuck his head up and handed Lowell a piece of paper with the new headings written on it.

He made a few small adjustments to the controls and handed the sheet to Vern.

"I think I've got it, check me out."

"Looks good to me Low."

Myron then asked, "Anyone for a cup of coffee?"

Vern said, "I don't think yet, why don't you two go on back and I'll take a break when you're back."

Lowell responded with, "Yea, that sounds good. Let me get on this new heading first."

"Thanks Vern, it's your airplane," said Lowell as he proceeded to unbuckle and get out of his seat. Myron squeezed up through the opening and they moved to the back of the plane. As Lowell walked by the radio compartment he asked Wayne if he was picking up anything.

"Yes sir, I have a very good swing station from Boston."

"Why don't you pipe it over the intercom?"

"Okay."

All the gunners were lying around the waist compartment. Niggs was sleeping, Zo and Dave were playing cards and Gabe was re-reading a letter he had received from his girl friend just before they left Spokane.

Myron asked him, "Haven't you read everything in that letter yet?"

"Oh yes sir, I just love to read her words."

Jew reached down and patted him on the shoulder and said, "Yea, I know what you mean."

Lowell and Myron both used the relief tube and then poured themselves a cup of coffee. Lowell took a swig.

"It sure doesn't taste like Mom's."

Myron asked, "Did your mom let you drink coffee?"

"Sure, my grandmother used to give it to me when she would come out to visit after my grandpa passed away."

"Yea, I kind of remember coming over in the morning and you were sitting at the table drinking some. Boy, I thought that was the weirdest thing I'd ever seen."

"Well, I still don't drink as much as you do now."

"Yea, I guess you're right."

It was a little difficult to talk over the sound of the engines, but it was much better than in the cockpit. The boys didn't talk much. They sat on the floor and went into their own thoughts. Lowell wondered what Helen was doing and how she might react if anything happened to him. He shuddered at the thought. Myron looked over at him.

"Are you okay?"

"Sure. I guess I should go back up front."

Both boys got up, stepped over the legs of the rest of the crew and made their way through the bomb bay into the cockpit. Lowell opened the hatch to the nose compartment and asked Vince if he needed a break. Vince replied that he did and crawled up through the hatch, working his way through the cockpit, which was no small task with the crowd. Lowell took his place in the left seat and told Vern to go take a break with Vince. When he had gotten out of the seat Lowell motioned for Myron to sit down. Sitting down, Myron looked over the control panel with all its dials and gauges.

Shouting to Lowell he said, "Boy, I really wanted to do this."

Lowell nodded and then said, "Can you believe where we are?"

"Well, I hope so. I'm supposed to know all the time."

"No, I mean you and me. Just think, a couple of years ago we were sitting in a duck blind talking about how to win basketball and football games and how to get girls."

Myron laughed and said, "I never thought of that. Do you remember the Mitchell game when you broke through the line and had only that big line backer between you and the goal?"

"Yea, I remember you threw a great block on him."

"Well I knew that if you scored you would beat me for touchdowns and I thought for a minute that I would let him tackle you."

"Oh crap Jew, you never thought that in your life!"

"Well maybe, but I think you still owe me buddy."

They were both silent for awhile and then Lowell looked over at him and saw that impish grin on his face. Then it disappeared as they both had that look again that showed how much they cared for each other.

"Jew, I want you to promise that if anything happens to me, you will see that Helen is cared for."

Myron looked at him with a look of concern and mild shock on his face. Lowell expected some sort of sarcastic retort but instead Myron just nodded.

"I expect you to do the same for Betty."

Suddenly they were aware that Vern was standing in back of them. Myron jumped out of the seat and offered an apology.

Vern merely said, "That's okay."

Somehow Lowell realized that it wasn't okay and said.

"Vern I'm sorry about that little scene, it's just that we've know each other for so long that some times we forget that we are just crew mates."

Myron stood there dumb struck for words and then Vern said, "Guys, I would like to be a part of that pack. I don't have folks or a wife, but if anything should happen to me, would you contact my old baseball coach and make sure he gets my stuff. I'll get you his name and address when we get to our base."

Both Lowell and Myron nodded their heads and then Myron said, "Well I'm glad that little scene is over. Now, let's get back to what we're supposed to be doing."

With that he slipped through the hatch again and in a few minutes Vince came from the rear of the plane and followed him into the nose. They flew on for some time. Then suddenly the headphones crackled and

Myron's voice came on.

"Navigator to pilot."

"Go ahead nav."

"Small course correction for you."

"Go ahead, I'm ready."

Both Vern and Lowell noted the new heading and made the correction.

Lowell called, "Pilot to navigator, any estimation of our position."

"Nav to pilot, we're about three hours from the point of no return."

"Roger, navigator. I wish there was another term for that."

A slight chuckle came back and then Lowell called pilot to crew, "Did you read that?"

Several "rogers" came back from the crew.

After several minutes Vern leaned over and said, "You know I remember a baseball game when I was a junior. We were playing Prairie City, our chief rivals, and we were down two runs. I drew a walk and the coach called for a bunt from the next batter. He was a tough kid from one of the ranches and a bit bullheaded. Instead of bunting, he swung away and drove the ball over the left fielders head for a homer and we both scored, tying the game. The next inning was scoreless and we scored in the last inning, winning the game seven to six. The coach took us in the dressing room and gave us a very long talk about following instructions and doing what he tells us to do. Apparently the victory was less important than following instructions. I have never forgotten that."

Lowell thought for a few minutes and wasn't quite sure what response was appropriate.

Vern followed up, saying, "Even though I was a real idiot when I first joined this crew, I never once considered not following orders or instructions and I want you to know I never will."

"I know that Vern."

"Unless they are really stupid instructions."

Lowell looked over and Vern was smiling and he reached out and gave him one of those friendly punches on the shoulder like he and Myron were always doing.

Vern sobered and then said with a very serious expression, "Thanks Low. Thanks a lot!"

"Now mister co-pilot, I'm giving you an order. Get some sleep if you can because I will want you to take over after while."

As they flew along, Lowell's mind began to wander back to his childhood. He remembered the time he and Jew sneaked cigarettes from his dad and went out to the park at the edge of town and smoked several, one right after another. It was then that Lowell decided he would never pick up the habit although Jew had. He always wondered why he didn't get sick like everyone said he would. He never considered smoking. Maybe it was Coach Roberts insisting that as athletes, they should never ever abuse their bodies with cigarettes.

His thoughts then wandered to Helen. He almost teared up with the thought that it might be a year or more before he would see her again. Maybe he would never see her again. He shook his head and decided that he would never think that again.

Looking at him, Vern asked, "Are you okay Low?"

"Yea, sure. I was just thinking about home."

"Yea, I know what you mean. Even though I didn't have such a happy childhood. I still miss home."

Lowell nodded and they both fell silent into their own thoughts.

Suddenly their reverie was interrupted with, "Navigator to pilot."

"Go ahead Jew."

"Small course correction. Are you ready?"

Lowell motioned for Vern to write it down and then replied, "Give it to us."

"Come south twelve degrees to a heading of zero nine four degrees south."

"Roger, zero nine four degrees south."

There was no other response as Lowell began to turn the plane on to the new heading.

He then called, "Pilot to nav, what is your estimated time of arrival?"

"Ah, about five hours or so."

"Roger, thanks Jew."

Lowell had decided when they were in the air and on intercom, a certain amount of informality would be permissible, but when things were tough, he would not tolerate unnecessary chatter.

"Pilot to radio, picking up anything Wayne?"

"Negative sir, just static."

"Okay, let me know if you do."

"Roger."

Lowell settled down again and flew on for a short time.

Vern looked over at Lowell and said, "You want me to take over for awhile Low?"

"Yea, I've got to visit the tube again."

Lowell undid his harness, got out of the seat and made his way back to the center of the plane. After taking care of his bodily needs, he sat down with the crew and Zo asked him how it was going. Lowell responded that everything was just fine and that he wished he could keep this airplane.

After a few moments of silence, Dave McDonald said, "Sir, will we be able to stay together when we get to our permanent base?"

"Yea, I think so, otherwise all this crew training would be for naught."

After several minutes of shouting to be heard above the drone of the engines, conversation usually stopped, and thus it did now. Lowell rose and bid the boys goodbye stating there were only a few hours left. About two hours out, they would man their stations and check guns. This caused some stir among the crew even though they had been briefed on this before leaving the States. The realization that they were about to enter a war zone caused them to tune up their alert level.

Lowell took his place in the left seat and motioned for Vern to go ahead and take a break. Vern unhooked his harness and got out of the seat and proceeded to the rear of the plane. As Lowell flew along he began writing Helen a letter in his head.

Dear Helen,

Well here we are out in the middle of the North Atlantic Ocean. Did you ever think that any of us from Drayville would ever be able to say that? We are making good time and when I get to my station I will put this down in writing and send it off to you....

"Radio to pilot."

Jerked out of his composing, Lowell jumped and responded, "Go ahead Wayne."

"Sir, I've picked up a signal from Nuts Corner. It's quite weak, but definitely from them."

"Okay, Wayne. Jew, are you reading this?"

"Nav to Pilot, affirmative."

Just then Vern came hurrying back to his seat with an apology, which Lowell ignored. "Get this Vern."

"Pilot to Nav, go ahead."

Myron gave them a new course, which took them a little further south, southeast.

"Roger Nav, thanks a lot. Pilot to crew, man your stations, gunners load and check your guns."

Receiving several "rogers," Lowell felt a big rush of adrenaline and a heightened sense of alertness though they were still more than two hours out of Nuts Corner.

"Pilot to radio, keep me informed on that signal Wayne."

"Roger."

Lowell relaxed a little after the excitement of Wayne picking up the signal from Nuts Corner. Suddenly Jew called again to report that they were right on course for the base and that they were about an hour out. Lowell thanked him and looked over at Vern and smiled. Vern smiled back and they both settled in for the last few miles.

"Jew, let me know when we're about twenty minutes out will you?"

"Roger, I will."

Bob Wright came into the cockpit then and leaned over to check the gauges.

He said, "You guys have done a great job. We could fly several hundred more miles with the fuel you saved."

Both Vern and Lowell chuckled at that and Vern said, "You want to spend more time in this thing Bob?"

"No, not really, I just wanted to let you know that you did a great job on fuel consumption."

"Thanks Bob, better take your station."

"Yes sir."

In a few more minutes Jew came on to report they were about forty miles out.

"Thanks Jew."

Lowell asked Wayne to switch him to the frequency they were given in the sealed order that was the Nut Corner tower.

Wayne reported that the radio was on the right frequency and Lowell picked up the microphone.

"B-17 2730 to Nuts Corner come in."

Lowell waited what seemed like an eternity before hearing "Nuts

Corner to B-17 2730. Over."

"Nuts Corner from B-17, we are about twenty minutes out, requesting landing instructions."

"Nuts Corner to B-17 2730, descend to 1,500 feet on your heading."

Lowell did as he was instructed. Several minutes later the tower called again.

"Nuts Corner to B-17 2730, come fifty degrees south and descend to 500 feet. Prepare to land on runway two seven. Do not answer anymore transmissions."

"Roger, Nuts Corner."

Lowell switched to intercom and said, "Pilot to crew, prepare for landing. We'll be landing in about twenty minutes." He added, "Vince and Jew keep an eye open for number two seven and sing out when you see it."

"Roger," they replied.

In just a few minutes Vince yelled, "There it is!"

Lowell chuckled and then said, "Thank you."

He swung the plane a little more towards the south and then began to throttle back for the approach. On the ground he could see several aircraft sitting on the apron and parked around the field. Lowell was very busy trying not to mess up the landing, after having a very successful trip over the last nearly twelve hours of flight.

As they neared the appropriate altitude, Vern looked at him and said, "You want me to lower the gear?"

Lowell shook his head and said, "My God yes, sorry."

"No one will ever know."

Lowell stole a look and saw a slight smile on Vern's face. In another few minutes the wheels touched the ground. The ship bounced slightly and then settled as Lowell allowed the tail wheel to touch. The usual "follow me" vehicle appeared and Lowell swung in behind it to their parking area.

Lowell went on the intercom and said, "Welcome to England men. We are here."

Vern reminded him that they were in Free Ireland and not exactly England.

Lowell just shrugged and said, "Let's go through the shut down, okay?"

ENGLAND

As they de-planed a three quarter ton pulled up, a sergeant leaned out and said, "Jump in sirs and I'll take you to the orderly room."

When they were in the truck, the driver said, "Have your guys gotten everything out of the plane that belongs to them?"

Lowell leaned out and told the crew to go through the plane to be sure they had removed everything. The sergeant then gunned the truck and they were off. Arriving at the orderly room, Lowell and Vern entered and were told to have a seat and the major would be right with them. Just then the door opened and Charlie and his co-pilot came out. They greeted each other and asked about their respective flights.

After touching base with Charlie, the sergeant told them to go on in. They stepped in and saluted. The major returned their salute and told them to take a seat.

"Well men, welcome to Free Ireland."

"Thank you sir."

"Okay. You'll spend a few days here while we arrange transportation to your permanent assignment. When we're done here, the sergeant will take you to the supply room to draw bedding and then to the barracks."

"Sir, can you tell us where our base will be?"

"No, I haven't received the most recent replacement requests yet."

"How long will it take sir?"

"Why? Are you anxious to get into combat?"

"Oh. No sir, just curious."

"Well, you'll be here probably three or four days."

After a pause the major asked, "Are there any more questions?"

Lowell looked at Vern and they shook their heads in the negative.

"Okay then, you're dismissed."

Lowell and Vern jumped up and saluted, did an about face and left the office. When they came out of the major's office, the rest of the crew had arrived and were waiting outdoors. Lowell asked the sergeant about the location of the supply room.

" Sergeant Goodwin will show you sir."

Sergeant Goodwin had driven them from the ship. They went outside and the sergeant said, "Ready to go sirs?"

"Yes, let's go," said Lowell.

After drawing bedding, they were taken to their barracks. The officer's barracks was divided into rooms sleeping four men. When they started looking into the rooms, they noticed that there were only two bunks available in the first room.

"Okay, who's for this one?" Lowell asked.

Vern and Vince said that they would take them and they found two more in the next room that he and Myron would take. Lowell noticed that one of the B4 bags was labeled with Charlie's name.

Lowell threw his gear on the floor and started making up an empty bunk. When he was finished he said, "I think I'll go over and see how the men are doing. The enlisted men's barracks was across the street and down a few buildings."

As he entered, someone shouted "ATTENTION!"

Lowell said, "Oh, forget that! How is everything men? Does everyone have a bunk?"

Niggs responded, "I don't need a bunk sir. I think I will just sleep on the floor."

Bob Wright laughed and said, "Yea, we've got enough."

Zo asked, "When is chow sir?"

"Well I don't really know, but I'll check. Seems like something is going on because no one is here."

"Oh that's alright sir, I think I'll just go to sleep for awhile."

Lowell asked, "WE, what time is it here anyway?"

Wayne looked at his watch and said, "I think it's about 0800."

"Well then, guess we missed morning chow. I'll settle in and then go see if I can find out anything."

*****

After he unpacked a few necessities, he said to Jew, "Want to go with me?"

"Nah, I think I'll hit the sack for awhile."

Lowell left and started to walk down between the rows of barracks until he spotted some men walking toward him. As they got closer, he recognized Charlie. He approached them and greeted Charlie who introduced his co-pilot and navigator.

"Where have you guys been?"

"We just came back from the mess hall. Did you guys get anything to eat?"

"No, but we're so tired most of the guys just wanted to sleep. When is the next chow call?"

"Oh they serve twenty four hours a day because there are so many crews coming and going at all hours. I'm afraid its only warmed up C rations, though."

"By the way, Myron and I moved into your room. I hope that's okay."

"Sure, that'll be neat. Are you going over to the mess hall now?"

"Yea, I thought I would, but I want to go tell the men. Why?"

"Well if you don't mind, I'll go back with you. We've got a little catching up to do."

"Great."

After informing the men of the chow schedule, they started to walk back towards the mess hall. Lowell asked about Linda and Charlie asked about Helen.

Then he said, "Where's Myron?"

"Oh, he sacked out. Say, have you found anything to do around here? The major said we'd probably be here three or four days."

"No, I thought this afternoon we could go down to the Officers Club and ask someone."

That afternoon Lowell, Charlie, Myron, Vern, Vince and Charlie's co-pilot, Dale Prichard, found the Officers Club. It wasn't much as officer clubs go in the States, but they had comfortable chairs, pool tables, a ping-pong table, and a bar. As they walked in several officers were playing pool and several were sitting at the bar having a drink.

Myron said, "You guys grab a table; I'll stand for the first round of drinks. Let's see, beer around and one milk for Charlie."

They all laughed.

They laughed even harder when Charlie said, "Oh I'm up to cokes now."

Myron raised his eyebrows, stared for awhile and said, "Okay."

Lowell explained to Dale about Myron and they all smiled.

Vern said, "Yea, you should be in his crew."

Vince spoke up with, "Crazy as he is, he sure hit the center of the runway here."

They all nodded their heads. Many crews had to have radio directions to find the base.

As Myron came up to the bar and ordered five beers and one coke, an officer turned and said, "Well I'll be God damned if it isn't Rothstein."

Myron turned and saw who made the comment, "Major Sanders, what in the hell are doing here. I thought you were going to Foggia?"

"Well so did I, but you know the army. There was a change."

"What happened?"

"After my leave at home I reported to Kearny and found they had canceled my orders. They nearly hooked me for another training command, but I ran into a bird colonel I knew and he TDYed me to his command until a levy came up. He stuck me on it and here I am in England instead of Italy. Do you know where you're going?"

"Not yet, we just got in today. Say why don't you join us, it looks like you're alone."

"Oh I don't want to horn in."

"Nah, come on sir. Join us."

"I will if you'll promise to drop the sir."

They walked over the table where the rest of the boys were and Myron introduced Major Sanders to them.

"Low this is the major I wrote you about who held me against my will in Texas for all those months."

Lowell and the rest of the guys stood up and the major bid them to sit.

"Rothstein, if you had been a screw up like a lot of the guys you could have gone right overseas."

Lowell spoke up, "Sir, are we talking about the same Myron Rothstein?"

"Well first of all I only agreed with Rothstein to join you if there were no sirs and secondly, I think he finally found something he could do."

The major turned to Myron and said, "Is this the friend that you used to talk about? The one that did everything so perfectly?"

Lowell laughed and Myron said, "Please don't bring that up. I don't want him to know I liked him."

More laughter ensued and then Myron introduced the rest of the men.

Major Sanders said, "Well, I guess we got what we asked for."

Myron passed the beer around and Vince took a big swig and nearly spit it out.

Coughing he said in a strained voice, "This beer is warm!"

Major Sanders laughed and said, "That's all you'll get around here, but it is very strong and after a couple you won't notice."

After another round of laughter, Lowell said, "Sir, oh I mean major, do you have any idea where we might be going?"

"No lieutenant, I don't even know where I'm going."

Charlie asked, "Will you be a lead navigator?"

"I don't know, most field grade officers end up in the headquarters unit, but I hope I can get a little air time."

Lieutenant Prichard asked, "Have you had any combat experience?"

"Yea, I was in a squadron in the Philippines and just barely got out before we surrendered. That's when I was assigned the training command."

Vince spoke up with, "Our flight engineer was in the Philippines, probably about the same time."

"Oh, what's his name?"

Lowell spoke up saying, "Sergeant Wright, Bob Wright."

The major thought for a minute and then said, "There was a Sergeant

Wright in our squadron, but I don't know his first name."

"What squadron was that sir?"

"The 527th."

"I'll asked him tomorrow," replied Lowell.

After more discussion about possibile destinations, the evening ended with Vern saying, "I don't know about you guys, but I'm very tired and I've had about as much warm beer as I can stand. I'm leaving."

They all agreed that it was probably about time and stood to go.

Lowell said, "Major do you have any idea how long you're going to be here?"

"No, I don't but they usually don't keep crews very long. Don't forget to ask Wright about his unit, okay?"

"Oh yea, I will."

Every one said good night to Major Sanders and they left.

On the way back to the barracks, Myron said, "You know, I would like to see if we can get passes to go into town tomorrow night."

"Good idea. I'll check."

*****

The next day Lowell went down to the orderly room to see if anything had been decided about where they might be going. The sergeant at the desk told him they were expecting replacement levies any day and that would determine where they would go.

Lowell asked about passes and he said, "Oh yes sir, all you have to do is sign out."

"How about the enlisted men?"

"Them too."

Lowell thanked him, returned to the barracks and reported what he had learned. They all decided they would like to go into town.

"What about transportation?" Vern asked.

"I'm going over to see if any of the crew want to go first. Then I'll go by the orderly room and ask about transportation," said Lowell.

He walked over to the enlisted men's barracks and as he entered, someone called attention.

Lowell said, "Oh just forget that guys I just came to tell you that there are passes to town available. All you have to do is sign out and hop a bus ride."

Zo said, "Thanks sir. I think we'll probably try tomorrow."

"Oh say Bob, we ran into a Major Sanders at the Officers Club. He was Myron's commanding officer in Texas. He said he was in the Philippines about the same time you were. We wondered if you might know him."

"Yea. Captain Sanders, a navigator. Do you know his first name?"

"No, I didn't get it. Maybe tomorrow we can meet and find out."

"Yea, he was an okay guy. All the enlisted guys liked him."

"Well, don't forget about the passes, I don't know what time the buses leave so you had better check."

Home

The phone rang at the lumber yard office. Helen reached over and picked it up, "Speer Lumber Yard."

"Helen, would you have time for lunch today?"

Helen recognizing Betty's voice said, "Sure, what's up?"

"Oh nothing, I just wanted to talk. I'm feeling a little blue today."

"Sure, where do you want to meet?"

"I don't know. What do you think about Marshall's?"

"Oh that's good. Around noon?"

"Swell, I'll meet you there at twelve."

Helen hung up the phone and sat for a minute trying to figure out what Betty was talking about. Betty was working just up the street in Mrs. Belmount's dress shop. Neither girl needed to work. They didn't need the money. Most girls whose husbands were in the service and couldn't be with them worked just to keep their minds busy.

At a few minutes before noon, Helen went out to the yard and told her father she was meeting Betty for lunch.

"I'll be back around one Dad."

Mr. Speer said, "That's fine honey," and leaned over to give his daughter a little peck on the cheek.

Helen got her coat and left the yard for Marshall's. It was one of the better restaurants in town; one they very seldom frequented as kids, but as married women they visited whenever they got the chance. As Helen entered, she gave her eyes a minute to adjust and then looked around for Betty. There were several businessmen eating and talking and a few families. She heard her name and spotted Betty waving from one of the back booths.

Helen approached the booth, then slid in across from Betty and said, "How are you feeling now?"

"Oh I don't feel bad, I just like to talk to someone about the boys and the women in the shop are not much into talking about boys."

They both laughed and then Betty asked, "When did you get the last letter from Lowell?"

"Just before they left that base in Nebraska."

"Yea, me too. Myron wrote that he tried to call, but couldn't get through. Do you think they're overseas yet?"

"Yes. Lowell's last letter from Spokane said that they would only spend a few days in transition and if they got a plane to fly, they would be in England in about three days."

"I wonder what they think of England. I've heard that those English girls think a lot of the Americans."

Again they both laughed as the waitress came up to get their orders. Betty ordered a chicken salad and Helen a small open face sandwich.

Betty said, "Are you sorry you didn't get pregnant before Lowell left?"

"In a way, but I think that would have put a lot more strain on him. He'll have enough to worry about without worrying about me and a baby."

"Yea, I kind of felt like I was being selfish, but I really did want to, though I never told Myron that."

As their lunches came, they visited about this and that and made plans to go to a movie on Saturday night. Helen said she would like to invite the twins to come along and Betty thought that would be a good idea. The film playing at one of the local theater was one that children would enjoy and adults seem to like too.

Belfast, Ireland

As the bus from the base pulled in to Belfast, the boys fell silent. They had never seen a city with such old buildings. When they disembarked from the bus, they noticed the people as well. They all looked tired. Their clothes were worn and for the first time, they realized what the war had done to these people.

Myron said, "Look at these people; I didn't realize how much they've suffered."

"Yea, they all look so tired and sad."

Besides Lowell, Myron, Vince and Vern, Charlie and his co-pilot, Dale Prichard were also along. They walked up the street looking at the old buildings and the tired looking people. As they rounded a corner, they spotted a pub and Vern suggested they go in and get a drink. They all agreed and crossed the street to the pub.

When they entered, they observed several older men sitting at tables and at the bar. The place was very dark and smelled of smoke and several other scents no one could identify. They found a table and a middle-aged woman came over and asked what they would like. Of course everyone except Charlie ordered beer.

While waiting for their drinks, Vince leaned over and said, "Can you imagine this bar in the States?"

"Yea," replied Myron, "It wouldn't stay open five minutes in Oregon. The state health inspectors would close 'em down."

"Well they have different standards over here I guess," responded Lowell.

The beer, when it came, was very dark, very strong, and very warm. They had learned about warm beer at the officer's club, but their second experience was just as shocking. They continued to talk among themselves and drink their beers.

An old man at the next table, smoking a pipe and looking every bit the epitome of the typical Irishman, said, "You Yanks just get here?"

Lowell answered with, "Yes sir, a couple of days ago."

"Where are you from?"

Myron spoke up with, "Well, everywhere."

"Any of you from New York?"

"One of our crew members is," said Vince.

Lowell asked, "Have you been to New York?"

The old man removed his pipe and said, "Yes, many times. When I was a Merchant sailor I made many trips to the US. I visited New York, San Francisco, Seattle and other ports."

Lowell said, "Did you ever get to Portland, Oregon?"

The old man thought for a minute and then said, "I think only once. That's the one up a river isn't it?"

"Yea, the Columbia. I live only about thirty miles from Portland."

"Oh," the old man responded nodding, "Well, welcome to Belfast."

He then picked up his beer and turned away. The boys all looked at each other and smiled, wondering why he had started the conversation and then ended it as abruptly as he did.

They continued exploring the town until they found a building with a sign posted in the front window that read WELCOME YANK FLYERS. They decided to go in and look around. As they entered a very large middle aged woman greeted them with a hearty welcome. She asked if they had just arrived and asked them to sign a guest book. As they all signed, she pointed out the amenities of the club. There were biscuits, coffee, some soft drinks and comfortable chairs to relax in.

Lowell said, "Anyone for a biscuit?"

"Can we get gravy on em?"

The lady looked very perplexed and said. "Well now, why would you want gravy?"

Myron said, "You know, I don't think biscuits over here are the same as biscuits at home."

This brought on a jolly laugh from the woman and she said, "Oh, excuse me. I forgot you're Yanks! I mean cookies."

The boys all laughed at that and Lowell said, "Sure, we'll have some biscuits."

Their first lesson in British terminology being a total failure, the boys decided that they would have a couple of biscuits and coffee, then continue their exploration.

That night in the barracks, Charlie said, "You know, I don't think I will go into town again while we're here. It was very depressing."

"Yea, me neither," replied Myron.

"I agree," said Lowell.

*****

On the third day, a sergeant came into the barracks and asked for Lieutenant Andersen.

Lowell said, "Here."

"Lieutenant the major wants to see you in the orderly room."

"Thank you sergeant."

As Lowell got off his bunk he looked at Myron and raised his eyebrows. "Maybe this is it."

"Yea, I hope so."

Arriving at the major's office, he asked Lowell to take a seat and handed him a sheet of paper that turned out to be their travel orders and assignment. Lowell looked down and read it quickly.

"Sir, where is Sulensborne?"

"Oh, it's down in East Anglia in the United Kingdom."

"Is the 315th a new group sir?"

"No, they came over in forty three. They've had a bunch of tough missions and need a lot of replacements."

"Oh, it says by train, how long will it take us to get there?"

"I don't know, several hours I guess. You will take the ferry across the North Channel of the Irish Sea to Liverpool and then you'll travel by train to Sulensborne."

Lowell stood up and said, "Yea, I forgot there was water between Ireland and England."

He thanked the major, saluted, did an about face and left the office. When he got back to the barracks, he showed Jew, Vince and Vern the orders and answered what few questions he could.

"I'm going to go talk to the crew. You guys better get packed. We have to be at the train station at 0800."

As he walked over to the enlisted men's barracks, Lowell thought, *Well, this was what we trained for, but am I ready to lead a group of men into combat? Do I have what it takes to do that? Will I live up to my crew's expectations*?

When he entered the barracks, no one called for attention even though that was a common courtesy afforded an officer when he entered enlisted men's quarters. He didn't mind however because it was always a little embarrassing when that happened.

He found Bob Wright lying on his bunk writing a letter and said, "Bob, will you get the rest of the guys and meet me out side, we have orders!"

Bob jumped up and said, "Yes sir, right away. Oh by the way sir, I did run into Major Sanders, and he is the same one I knew in the Philippines. We had a nice visit."

Lowell smiled, turned and went out and sat on the barracks railing.

It didn't take long for the crew to assemble. They were all very anxious to find out where they were going.

Lowell said, "Well guys, we have our orders. We're being assigned to the 247th Squadron of the 315th Bomb Group at Sulensborne. I don't know exactly where that is, but it's in East Anglia somewhere. We go by ferry across the North Channel of the Irish Sea and then by train. We leave at 0800 tomorrow. The major says it will take several hours, but we should be there for evening chow. Any questions?"

The crew looked at each other and shook their heads so Lowell said, "Get packed." Pausing for a moment he added, "You probably shouldn't go into town tonight. I would hate to see any of you miss that ferry."

There was a little ripple of laughter and they all agreed that would not be good. When Lowell returned to the barracks, he asked Charlie if he had gotten his orders.

"Yea, we're going with you."

They both smiled at each other and then Charlie said, "We aren't in the same squadron, but at the same base."

"That's very good buddy. We can see each other occasionally then."

*****

That night after packing, Lowell reached into his bag and took out his writing kit.

My Dearest Wife,

Again, I don't know when you might get this, but I am writing it anyway. Well, today we got our orders. I can't say where but we are going to England. I have learned a lot of English history in just the few days we've been here. If only us kids in Mr. Black's history class could have known what was ahead for us, we probably would have paid better attention. I think he was probably a very good teacher although as you remember, not many of us liked him. Well Charlie and his crew are also going with us, but to a different squadron.

Our short time here has also given us a little taste of what this country has been going through for past four years. As I wrote you in my last letter, the people look so worn. Their clothes are shabby and they just look tired. They are very friendly and I like them a lot. There is a lot of conflict here, however, between the Catholics and Protestants. We Americans don't understand that at all.

Lowell went on to describe the town, a little about the base and then closed.

I hope to be able to mail this letter soon along with several others I've written since leaving you know where.

To you I give my life and love forever.

Your Husband,

Lowell

The next morning the wake up call came very early. After showering and shaving, they rolled up their bedding and went to breakfast. The mess halls were not segregated so Lowell was able to check on his crew. They all looked excited and anxious to get to their base.

Sulensborne

The short ferry trip from Nuts Corner across the Irish Sea to Liverpool and the train ride to Sulensborne was very exciting, yet very tense. As they stood on the deck of the ferry, Lowell said to Myron, "I hope there are no subs out here."

"Yea, wouldn't it be hell to get sunk before we even get to our base."

"I don't think subs come into the St. George Channel," said Vince.

Myron looked at him and said, "How do you know what they call this?"

"Oh, I wrote a report on the English and Irish relationship one time in history class."

Lowell and Myron looked at each other, both reflecting on their history class.

Lowell said, "Well, I guess I was sleeping in that class."

"No, this was in college. I really liked history and thought about majoring in it."

They all fell silent and watched the bow waves break away from the ferry.

Landing in Liverpool was somewhat of a shock to the boys. It was their first time to see a city so touched by the war. Entering the harbor, they were awestruck by the devastation. Partially sunken ships, destroyed buildings and warehouses, and the stench of burned material was evident all around.

Lowell said, "Boy, I didn't have any idea of the devastation the war brought to these people."

"Yea, you think all the destruction has been to the Germans."

Vern said, "I just can't guess what Germany must look like."

After a few minutes thought, Myron said, "I don't care what it looks like. They get everything they deserve."

They all looked at him, but only Lowell knew what he meant.

They were met at the dock by an Army bus that took them to the train station. Boarding the train, they were shocked by the condition of it compared to what they had ridden on at home. The seats were just plain wood, the paint was scratched off in many places, and the windows were so dirty one could hardly see out.

"Boy, this train is a bunch of junk," said Vince.

"Yea, it could use a little fixing up."

"Well, it's better than walking. Settle in, it's going to be a long trip," replied Lowell.

The train rumbled through the English countryside. It reminded Lowell of parts of Oregon, but without the mountains. It was quite pretty yet very tired looking. Several times they were shunted off to a siding to let a military train pass. They saw flat cars with tanks, trucks, and general supplies.

"I guess the war is still on," commented Myron.

There wasn't a club car, as they knew them on the train in the States. There were stations in some of the cars where they could get a light snack and all the boys took advantage of those. Several of the men tried to sleep, but the seats were so uncomfortable that it was very difficult.

As Lowell walked down the aisle, Zo looked up and asked, "Lieutenant how far is it to our base?"

"Well, about 300 kilometers; I think that's just under 200 miles."

"Oh, so we'll be on this train for awhile?"

"I think so," replied Lowell.

He continued down to where Charlie was sitting and stopped to visit for awhile. One of Charlie's crew offered his seat but Lowell refused saying he was going out on the platform for a little air. Charlie got up and joined him as he walked down the aisle. When they went through the door to the platform, several soldiers were standing outside smoking. They immediately moved over so the officers had a place to stand.

Charlie said, "That's okay men. We just came out for a little air."

A conductor came by and they asked him how much longer it was to Sulensborne. He responded that they should be there in two more hours.

Lowell and Charlie talked a bit longer and then, even though the seats were hard and the train was a little on the smelly side it was warmer. They went inside again.

Taking his seat beside Myron Lowell said. "The conductor says we'll be at Sulensborne in a couple hours."

"None too soon for me. Boy my butt is crying out for some relief."

In just over an hour-and-a-half, the conductor came through the cars announcing that they would be in Sulensborne in fifteen minutes. The boys began to gather up their gear and anxiously looked out the windows. They had passed several towns with Army Air Corps bases. They also saw many US soldiers at the town's train stations so they knew they were in East Anglia.

Arriving in Sulensborne they began to unload. Walking out of the station they saw the usual army bus that would take them to the base, which was located three miles outside the town.

As they rode through the countryside, Zo said, "Boy this makes me home sick, all this farm land."

Dave McDonald responded with, "Yea, except no mountains."

Wayne said, "It looks a lot like the land around St. Cloud."

The men grew quiet then and just watched the fields pass by. Soon they began to see aircraft in the air and knew they were getting close to the field and their anxiety and excitement increased.

315th Bomb Group, 247th Squadron, Sulensborne, England

The routine of reporting in, drawing bedding, and being taken to their barracks was much the same as it was in the States. When Lowell, Myron, Vern and Vince entered their barracks, or more accurately the Quonset hut or even more accurately, the Nissan hut, they found several empty bunks and threw their gear on them. They felt fortunate that they were all in the same hut. They were told that this might not happen.

Lowell said, "I'm sure glad that we get to stay together."

Vern responded with, "Yea, I would hate to be with strangers."

They all agreed and began to make up their bunks.

The hut or barracks they were assigned to held sixteen men with whom they would become friends in the next few weeks. In situations like these, you make friends quickly and in some cases, lose them just as fast. Lowell and Myron would learn later that next to them was Larry Bishop, a pilot who had flown twelve missions and Dave Lampson, another pilot with several missions.

After the bunks were finished, Lowell said, "I think I'll go over to the crew's barracks and see how they are doing."

"Wait, I'll go with you," said Myron.

"Okay, hurry up."

The boys walked out of the hut and started toward the enlisted men's location. Myron said, "I guess we should get used to calling our residence a hut and not a barracks."

"Yea, you're right."

As they entered, no one yelled for attention, which pleased Myron and Lowell. They saw Wayne and Dave sitting on their bunks and when they approached, both stood up but with less formality than they would have in the States.

"How are things going men?"

"Fine, lieutenant."

"Where's the rest of the crew?"

"Oh they're in the next hut. There wasn't room for them here."

Lowell looked around and saw several empty bunks and pointed them out.

Dave said, "We were told they belonged to guys who haven't returned from a mission and not to take them until their stuff has been packed."

Lowell and Myron looked at each other with surprise and alarm.

Myron said, "Oh, I see."

As the boys left the enlisted men's hut, Lowell said, "Boy, have we got a lot to learn about a combat unit."

"You aren't kidding!"

*****

The next morning as instructed, they all met in a large theater-like building. Six new crews besides Lowell's joined the squadron. As they sat there waiting, Lowell looked around and recognized several faces of men he had met somewhere during his training, but could not come up with names.

He leaned over to Myron and said, "Funny, there are several faces I recognize here but I can't put a name to them."

"Yea, I thought I recognized several also, probably from the training command."

Suddenly someone yelled ATTENTION and the men all jumped to their feet. A major and a captain climbed the stairs to the stage.

"At ease, take your seats. I'm Major Fisher, the assistant squadron commander and this is Captain Eagleston, the squadron training officer, welcome to the 247th."

Several voices responded with, "Thank you sir!"

Major Fisher looked up from his notes with some surprise and said, "You don't have to respond men. Before you are allowed to fly a mission as a crew, we want to be sure you are all ready. To that end, you will fly several training missions and the pilots and co-pilots will fly with experienced crews on scheduled missions. Now, I'll ask Captain Eagleston to take over and give you more details. Captain."

As the major left the stage, the captain stood up, thanked him and began, "I too would like to welcome you all to the 247th. Let's see, we have seven new crews. As I call your pilot's name, each crew will stand up."

With the introductions over and a briefing on what to expect for the next few days the crews were dismissed and told to return to their barracks. The next day began the formal orientation that included a tour of the base and a visit to the flight line.

Orientation not only included familiarization with the base, but physical exams, lectures on proper prisoner procedures if captured and possible escape procedures. This gave Lowell some consternation. The next step in this phase caused them the most concern when taken to a photo studio, given civilian clothes and photographed for their escape pictures. The fact that they were photographed in civilian clothes made them feel quite strange until they learned the purpose of the photographs.

They learned that they were to carry them on all missions. If shot down and if they made it to friendly people, such as the underground, these pictures could be used to make civilian identification papers.

The pilots and co-pilots had to attend radio class that lasted for several hours followed by a visit to squadron operations. Then all the crew members were taken to supply for their flight gear and parachute harness fitting. The flight gear consisted of leather helmets, fur lined leather suits and headsets, as well as heated underclothes.

"Okay men," the major said as he mounted the stage at the next session, "You will fly several training missions and then the pilots and co-pilots will fly right seat on a combat mission with another crew. While they're doing that, you navigators will be in session for familiarization with the geography of the area. The bombardiers will also be in classes to learn how to arm and fit the bombs as well as target areas and procedures for making drops. Are there any questions so far?"

A gunner from another crew raised his hand and was recognized by Captain Eagleston.

"What do us gunners do sir?"

Eagleston looked sternly at him and said, "Be patient sergeant, I'll get to you."

The captain went on and then looked at the sergeant who had asked the question.

"Now sergeant, while your officers are learning all about flying a combat mission, you gunners will be on the range honing your skills so that you can protect your ship."

The sergeant's face was very red and he tried to slide down under his seat as everyone laughed.

The captain said, "Okay men, flying combat is not funny and I want you all to realize that right here and now so we don't have to pack your belongings and send them to your families!"

A silence spread over the group as the reality of combat was again brought home to them. Lowell thought about the empty bunks in the enlisted men's hut and was overwhelmed with a cold feeling of fear and foreboding.

After the captain finished and instructed the men about what came next, he left the stage to the usual ATTENTION. From the back of the room, another captain stood up and told the men they were dismissed and to return to their huts.

As the men assembled for the next meeting, Captain Eagleston sat down on the edge of the stage and began to describe what the crews would do over the next few days to get ready to fly combat. As he outlined the activities, there was a lot of looking at each other by the various crews. After about an hour, he asked and answered a few questions from various crews.

Lowell asked "When will we fly our first combat mission as a crew?"

"Probably in about a week; Watch the bulletin board for schedules," the captain responded.

Leaving the theater, there was much talk. Lowell walked along with Clarence Dawson, another new pilot to the 247th.

"I sure didn't think we would be given so much more training."

"Yea, it's like we haven't had any."

"Oh I suppose they know what they're doing."

"Yea, I suppose."

"I don't know if I could fly with another crew."

Lowell said, "Well, you might as well expect it. You know what they said in orientation."

"Yea, but I sure hope we don't have to," replied Vern from behind Lowell.

As they walked Lowell said, "Do you think they would let us go down to the flight line and watch the planes come in?"

"I don't know, but I'd like to."

Lowell turned around and waited for Myron and the rest of the crew and asked them if they would like to go. They responded they would just as Captain Eagleston came out of the theater. Lowell walked over to him.

"Sir, some of the guys would like to go down to the flight line and watch the planes come in. Would that be possible?"

"Sure, it's quite a walk and I can't promise you any transportation. Just stay out of the way."

Lowell thanked him and returned to the group. Going by the orderly room they found out the planes were suppose to be returning about 1800. They decided they would go down about 1700. As they were walking along the road to the flight line, a three quarter ton truck came by and offered them a ride. They gladly accepted and climbed aboard. In addition to Lowell's crew, there were several men from the other crews.

Arriving at the flight line, they thanked the corporal driver and unloaded. They walked over to the fence separating the road from the tower area. There were several of the ground crews doing various time killing activities. Some were playing catch with a baseball; several more were playing a little game of pepper with a bat and ball, but most were lying down reading or just sleeping.

The onlookers talked in hushed tones, feeling like outsiders and not wanting to disturb. After some time the speaker on the tower came to life.

"Leader to Sulensborne tower. Over."

With that call, all activity of the ground crews ceased and their attention was focused on the southern sky.

"Sulensborne tower to leader come in."

"Leader, we are about twenty minutes out with three damaged and two with wounded. Over."

The visitors looked at each other with shared thoughts. The word "wounded" brought the shock of reality home very suddenly. The flight was given instructions on where to land the damaged planes and where to land the planes with wounded. The boys watched the planes come in with great anticipation. The first damaged one to land was flying on only three engines and a piece of the tail was flapping in the slipstream. They noticed that another one was coming in with only one wheel down and the third was streaming smoke.

With the announcement of wounded, the medic crews dropped their activities and ran to the ambulances. They knew by the runway assigned where to go to meet the planes.

After all the planes were down, their crews began to un-load right next to the gate where the visitors were standing. The crews began to file by and they all looked very tired. Their shoulders were hunched, eyes down cast, and with the flight boots, their walk was more of a shuffled gate. Some of them would look up briefly at the men standing by the gate, but others merely walked by heading for the debriefing hut.

One airman walked by, lifted his eyes, glanced at Lowell and passed him by. Suddenly he stopped, backed up and said, "Low?"

Lowell looked at him and after a few minutes said, "Oscar?"

Oscar Chadwick reached out his hand and said, "I'll be damned, what are you doing here?"

"Well, I've joined the squadron and I think I'm going to fly B-17s."

"Well I'll be damned!"

Lowell realized the rest of the crew was looking somewhat perplexed and he turned around and said, "Guys, this is Oscar Chadwick, we were roommates in training."

Myron stepped forward and said, "Hi, I'm Myron Rothstein."

Oscar took his hand and looked at Lowell and said, "Is this the guy you used to talk about, the one who did everything so perfectly?"

"No that's not him. I just made that guy up."

They all had a good laugh and Lowell introduced the other members of the crew and then Oscar said, "Well I've got to get to debriefing; why don't we get together tonight. We can meet at the officers club."

"You know, Charlie is here in the group as well."

"Why don't you try to get a hold of him and see if he can meet us?"

"That sounds swell."

Oscar explained where the officers club was located and they set a meeting time. As he walked away, Lowell said, "You know, I thought he would eventually get his pilot's wings, but I guess he ended up either a bombardier or navigator. We'll find out tonight."

As Lowell and the crew walked back to the barracks, he said, "I'm going to go to the orderly room and find out how I can get in touch with Charlie. See you guys at chow."

*****

Lowell walked into the orderly room and asked the duty sergeant if there was any way to contact someone in the 275th squadron.

He said, "Sure, I'll just call and leave a message for them to call us and then I will come and get you."

Lowell thanked him and told him where he was quartered.

"Yea, I know," said the sergeant.

Lowell somewhat embarrassed, thanked him and left. He returned to his hut and decided to write a letter to Helen. He had barely gotten started when a corporal came in and told him he had a phone call. Lowell jumped up and ran to the orderly room. The sergeant handed him the phone and told him not too be to long.

Lowell took the phone and said, "Hello."

"Lowell, this is Charlie, what's up?"

"Hi Charlie, you will never guess who I ran into today."

"Who?"

"Oscar Chadwick, remember him?"

"I sure do, he washed out in basic."

"Well he's here in a crew. I think he's a bombardier. Anyway, he wants to get together tonight in the Officers Club. Can you make it?"

"I think so, although I start flying tomorrow."

"On a mission?"

"No, no just a training flight."

"Oh yea, I think we will start in a day or two. Well, hope to see you around 1900."

"That sounds swell. See ya then."

Lowell invited the officers in his crew but only Myron accepted. The Officers Club was not typical of most officers clubs they had visited. The base had been an RAF fighter base but when the German invasion threat no longer existed and the Army Air Corps began to build up, it was taken over by the Americans. Consequently, it was very British. The boys looked around, Lowell spotted Oscar at one of the tables and walked over. He rose and greeted them and Lowell re-introduced him to Myron.

"I just wanted to come along to hear more about what Low said about me."

They all laughed and then Oscar said, "What are you drinking?"

They both said beer and asked if it was warm. Oscar responded that here they have cold beer. He went to the bar, bought three beers and returned to the table.

"Did you get a hold of Charlie?"

"Yea, he thought he could make it."

Just then Myron said, "There he is now."

Oscar said, "You know Charlie?"

"Yea, he came up to be in Low's wedding."

"Wedding! You got married?"

"I sure did and that is the best thing that has happened to me."

As Charlie came over to the table they all rose and Oscar reached out his hand and greeted him.

Charlie said, "Oscar, how the heck are you."

"Oscar grinned, looked at Lowell and said, "He hasn't changed a bit has he."

Lowell said, "Oh yes, he drinks coke now."

"Well if I had known this was a meeting about my life I wouldn't have come."

"Oh, sit down and have a coke Charlie," Myron said.

As they sipped their drinks, Oscar told them about what had happened since washing out of primary training. He went to bombardier training in New Mexico. It was a little shorter course than pilot training so he had finished in the spring of 1944 and shipped over in June just after D-Day. He only had twelve missions to go to complete his thirty, but thought he would extend to thirty-five.

Myron asked, "Why would you extend?"

"Oh I don't know. I just thought that I would like to stay through until the end. You know, the war won't last forever."

Myron responded, "Well not me. As soon as I can, I'm heading for home."

Lowell and Charlie both nodded their heads in agreement and Oscar just shrugged his shoulders.

*****

That night in the hut, Lowell took out his writing kit and began a letter to Helen.

My Dearest Wife,

Well today we went down to the flight line and watched the planes come back from a mission. It was quite impressive, but the strangest thing was that I ran in to Oscar Chadwick. I don't know if you remember me mentioning him, but I was with him from indoctrination until primary. He washed out of pilot training and became a bombardier. I was able to get a hold of Charlie and we spent a couple of hours together.

Tomorrow we're going to be assigned a plane. We were told it would probably be a new one just ferried over from the states. It will be a brand new airplane and I sure hope I don't dent it or anything, HA, HA. We haven't seen it yet, but they said we could name it. I asked the crew to think on it awhile and then we will discuss it before our first mission, which should be in a couple of weeks.

Tomorrow we get to take the whole crew up for our first training mission. I am very excited about it and hope I don't foul up.

Lowell went on with more about the base, what England is like and then signed off with the usual closing.

As always to you I give my love and life,
Lowell

*****

The next morning, the day of their first training flight, the crew was up early, went to morning chow and reported to the theater along with the two other new crews. Captain Eagleston came in and the usual ATTENTION was sounded as the men jumped to their feet.

The captain said, "At ease men. Today we are going flying. I want to take each crew up for about three hours to see how you function and then you can go up yourselves. There are no missions today, so we don't have to worry about other planes.

"I'll take Lieutenant Stowell's crew first followed by Andersen's and then Carson's. There is a truck outside that will take you to the flight line. I want you all to go out to your ships and check them over thoroughly. Any questions?"

Hearing none, the captain said, "Okay then, lets go fly."

The men left the theater and boarded the truck. As they approached the flight line, the captain stuck his head out of the cab and said, "Okay Andersen, here's your ship."

They jumped from the truck and walked over to their ship. They were all somewhat awed by having their own plane especially a new one, although they were told that they might not always fly that particular plane or that they may not be the only crew to fly it. Nevertheless, it was theirs. They all stood for a minute and just looked at *their* airplane.

A minute or two later, a sergeant walked up and introduced himself as Sergeant Goldstein, the crew chief. Lowell shook his hand and introduced him to the rest of the crew. Lowell asked him if everything was ready for a flight.

"As ready as I can make it sir."

Lowell had been told in transition training that there was an unwritten law that the plane belonged to the ground crew chief and he only loaned it to the flight crews.

Keeping this in mind, Lowell said, "Well sergeant, we'll always try to bring your ship back in good shape."

The sergeant looked at him and then smiled, "So, you've heard whose plane this really is, huh?"

They both laughed and Lowell patted him on the shoulder. He then turned to the rest of the crew and told them to check their stations and then meet under the left wing. He turned to Goldstein and asked about naming the plane. Goldstein told him that it was okay for the crew to name it because that was usually a good luck thing.

After the crew had finished the airplane check, they began to assemble under the left wing.

Lowell asked, "Does everything look okay guys?"

They all answered in the affirmative and then Lowell said, "Well, we are lucky. We get to name our plane. Anyone have a suggestion?"

Several were made such as "Flying Trapeze" and "Pile of Tin" and "Superman's Home." The guys laughed and rejected them.

Then Niggs said, "Sir, didn't you and Lieutenant Rothstein go to a high school that had a grizzly for a mascot?"

"Yea, we did."

"Well, why don't we call our plane Grizzly?"

Dave McDonald said, "Yea, my high school mascot was the Grizzly too."

Lowell thought for a minute and then said, "Well, what do you think men?"

And then Gabe said, "Well I agree with you all, but it seems to me that just Grizzly is kind of dumb, what about *Grizzly's Roar*? That would include us all."

There was a moment of silence and then Wayne said, "Ya know, I think that is a very good idea Gabe."

Lowell looked around the group and they were all nodding their heads.

He turned to Bob Wright and said, "Bob, do you think the artist can do a grizzly bear roaring?"

Bob turned to Sergeant Goldstein who shrugged indicating that would be okay.

Lowell said, "Well then, our plane is officially *Grizzly's Roar.*"

The crew all responded with clapped hands and nods.

They re-entered the plane and just sat around until nearly 1100 hours when a jeep pulled up. Captain Eagleston jumped out and approached the ship. Lowell was waiting for him by the left wheel and stepped out and saluted. Captain Eagleston asked if everything was ready and Lowell reported that it was.

He said, "Okay lieutenant lets go for a ride."

*****

They boarded the plane. The captain told Vern he would sit in the right seat and Vern should go back, strap in for take-off and after take-off, come up to the cockpit. The captain then led Lowell through the start up procedures and seemed impressed with Lowell's ability and knowledge. He then told Lowell to notify the tower that they were ready for take-off and to request a runway.

Following the captain's directions, Lowell went through the start up procedures and had all four engines running. He asked Bob if everything was okay and got an affirmative response. He then called the tower and requested take-off runway assignment and clearance for taxi, which he received. He cut the two outboard engines and taxied with only the two inboards running. This was the standard procedure when taxiing out to the runway for take-off. Captain Eagleston watched with much interest and gave away his feelings as to how Lowell was doing with affirmative nods at everything he did. When they taxied to their assigned runway, Lowell called the tower again and asked for permission to take-off.

Home

Diane came running down the stairs shouting, "David has a girl friend. David has a girl friend!"

David was following and screaming at her, "I have not!"

"Yes you have!"

Diane waved a piece of paper around and laughed uncontrollably. David grabbed it out of her hand and wadded it up.

"Will you two please calm down!" Mrs. Andersen exclaimed. "What is this all about?"

Diane said, "David has a girl friend!"

"I do not!"

Mrs. Andersen said, "Diane what are you talking about?"

"David wrote on his paper DA + EJ"

"I did not!"

"Yes you did!"

Helen was visiting that day and said, "Diane, you shouldn't snoop in David's room. So what if he has a girl friend."

David responded with, "I don't have a girl friend!"

"Oh yea, EJ stands for Elsie Jensen."

"It does not!"

"Yes it does; I've seen you talking to her at recess."

Mrs. Andersen stepped in at that point.

"Now you kids settle down, and Diane, as Helen said, you should not snoop in David's room. Go on up to your rooms and finish your homework. Helen and I would like to visit."

Diane asked, "Helen, are you staying for dinner?"

Mrs. Andersen answered. "Of course she is. Now get upstairs."

As the kids left the living room, Mrs. Andersen looked at Helen and said, "Isn't David a little young to be thinking about girls?"

"I don't know, but I believe boys think about us a lot sooner than we think."

"Well I suppose, but I can't imagine my nine year old thinking about girls."

"I kind of remember a time in grade school," Helen responded. "Probably around fourth grade, when Lowell used to hit me and throw balls at me during recess."

"Oh no! He didn't did he?"

"Don't worry, us girls found out later that they did it to get our attention, though we used to report it to the teachers anyway."

Mrs. Andersen thought for a minute and then a smile crossed her face and she said, "Yes, I remember boys doing that to us as well."

England

Lowell increased the power of the aircraft with Captain Eagleston's hand over his to insure the throttles were advanced without a problem.

The four engines roared and the plane began to shake with anticipation. Lowell released the brakes and the ship began to roll down the runway. At the prescribed speed, the tail lifted and when the plane reached take-off speed, Lowell pulled back on the controls and the B-17 lifted from the runway.

Captain Eagleston again nodded his head in approval though Lowell was so engrossed in the take-off procedure he didn't notice. The captain gave him a course to follow and Lowell checked the compass and turned the big ship to that heading. He called Jew to confirm the heading and settled down for a flight.

The check ride called for a flight some 200 miles up to northern England, a turn to the west to avoid any problem with other aircraft coming back from a mission or the possibility of enemy interference, and then running south to the base. After the turn to the northern heading, Lowell began to relax some. He looked over at the captain who seemed to be preoccupied.

"Captain, is everything okay?"

Captain Eagleston looked at Lowell and said, "Yea, everything is just fine. You're doing a good job lieutenant."

They flew on for awhile and then Bob Wright came into the cockpit. Lowell turned and asked if everything was okay and Bob responded with, "Yes sir, just fine."

The flight continued without incident.

Captain Eagleston said, "Okay Andersen, I think I've seen enough, let's head for home."

This confused Lowell because they had completed only about half of the mission.

He asked, "Is anything wrong sir?"

"Oh no. You have complete control and I don't think I need to waste your time going any further."

Lowell called Myron and got a bearing for the base and began to turn the plane. He looked over his shoulder at Vern who was smiling. Lowell nodded to him and then settled down for the short flight back to Sulensborne. When he was about fifteen minutes out he called the tower and requested landing instructions, which he received. He lined up on the runway and brought the ship down in a near perfect landing. He looked over at Captain Eagleston who nodded and a slight smile crossed his face.

When they had taxied up to the parking area, the captain said, "Well, shut down then come on into the briefing room and I'll give you a run down."

"Should the whole crew come sir?"

"Yes, of course."

With that he unhooked and climbed out of the seat. Vern moved back to let him have room to pass and then slapped Lowell on the back.

"Nice going buddy."

Myron stuck his head up through the hatch and said, "What the hell. Did we fail or something?"

Vern answered, "Hell no, we passed with flying colors."

Lowell got on the intercom and reported to the crew what had happened and told them they were all to report to the briefing room for a critique. With that Lowell and Vern finished the shut down procedures and climbed out of the plane. Sergeant Goldstein was waiting on the ground with a puzzled look on his face.

He asked, "What's wrong, did the ship have a problem?"

"No, the captain said we would not need to complete the mission and told us to turn around."

The sergeant still looked puzzled and said, "That was the shortest first training mission I have ever seen."

That night Lowell wrote to Helen.

My Dearest Wife,

Today we had our first flight over England. We had a check ride with the squadron training officer and I think we did pretty well. He didn't even have us finish the mission, which was to go north for about 200 miles, turn west for about forty miles and then turn south for the base. Well, at the turn he told us to return to base, that we did fine.

Jew is doing well with the navigation and the rest of the crew is just great. I don't know how I was so lucky to draw a crew like I did. The only one who is a little weird is "Niggs," Sergeant Nigel from Brooklyn, Remember? You met him in Spokane. He will not get aboard the plane until he flips his lucky nickel and gets three out of five heads. I don't know what I will do to him if he ever holds up our take-off.

The country around here is very much like Oregon except the mountains. It is very flat with a lot of farmland. I heard that because we built so many bases in this area, the food production is way down in England. What a shame.

Lowell went on for several more pages and then signed off as usual.

As always to you I give my love and life,
Lowell

The next two days were taken up with more navigation for Myron, Link trainer sessions for Lowell and Vern, and more gunnery practice for the gunners.

After the second day of that schedule, Myron said, "Are they ever going to let us go on a mission?"

Lowell responded with, "Just be patient Jew. You'll get your chance to bomb those SOBs."

Two days later the crew was told that they would have a flight that day and to report to the briefing room at 0630. The flight consisted of some low level formation flying and more familiarization with the area around the base. The formation flying didn't give Lowell any trouble, but several of the aircraft in the formation did. One pilot panicked and pulled back on his controls nearly causing his plane to collide with the plane above. At the debriefing that day, Captain Eagleston had a few harsh words for him and the boys heard later that he had been grounded indefinitely.

The classes, training missions and pure boredom went on for nearly a week and then one day Lowell, Vern and Myron were told to report to operations. Being concerned as to why, they walked over discussing the situation.

"Do you think we fouled up somewhere Low?"

"I can't imagine where."

"No, neither can I, we seem to be getting good reports."

They entered the operation building and told the sergeant on the desk their names and were told to have a seat, the major would see them in a minute. They followed his instruction and sat in silence until they heard the buzzer on the sergeant's desk and the major's voice asking him to send them in.

They reported to the major, were given an at-ease and told to have a seat. The major started by telling them their training up to now had been very good and then announced that tomorrow they would fly their first combat mission with other crews. Lowell was to fly with Lieutenant Buckner's crew as co-pilot, Vern with Lieutenant Cushman and Myron would fly as navigator in Captain Waldon's crew, the assistant squadron leader.

As they left the operations office, Myron put forth the question that was on all their minds, "Are we ready for this?"

"I don't know, but I guess we have to be."

"Yea, I tell ya, I hope I don't mess up."

"Oh come on Low, you have never messed up in your life."

Lowell looked at his friend and his eyes teared up and he looked away.

Jew touched his arm and said, "You know Low, I don't know if I have ever told you how much influence you've had on me during our life together. I don't think you'll mess up tomorrow and don't worry about it. Besides, who could mess up worse? What would happen if I navigated the assistant squadron leader to France or something?"

Vern walked along listening to this exchange and had a moment of sadness thinking that he had never had a close friend like these two.

"Jew, you're really something. Why do you make me feel good with those stupid remarks you've always made?"

All three laughed as Lowell and Myron looked at each other with that look that expressed feeling that could never be verbalized between two men.

That night Lowell took out his writing kit.

My Dearest Helen,

Well, tomorrow I fly with another crew for my first combat experience. The pilot is very experienced and I am told one of the best in the squadron. I will fly as his co-pilot. It seems like kind of a mild run so don't worry.

This last week we have flown every kind of practice mission we can get. We did close formation, emergency landings, everything. I've told you about Niggs' lucky coin flipping, I wish he were going with us, but I am sure that Lieutenant Buckner has someone like him in the crew.

We went into town last night and sat in the pub for about an hour and decided it was just as much fun in the base so we went home and hit the sack early.

Well, we have an early call in the morning so I better try to get some sleep.

As always to you I give my love and life!

Lowell

*****

The next morning Lowell, Vern and Myron were awakened at 0400, and they knew they had an hour to dress, eat chow and get to the briefing room. Lowell found Lieutenant Buckner's crew and slid in beside them. Lowell didn't know Buckner, though his hut was just down the line and Lowell had seen him on occasion. Buckner's greeting was less than warm and Lowell did not know if it was because of the hour or that he was a stranger.

As Lowell poured himself a second cup of coffee, the bombardier, Lieutenant Case, leaned over and said, "I wouldn't drink too much of that. It becomes a problem at thirty five thousand feet."

Lowell understood what he meant and thanked him. Lieutenant Case just smiled and nodded his head.

Crews became like family with the officers being the older kids and the enlisted men the younger siblings. Lowell understood this and did not resent it in the least. He had made up his mind he was going to do the best he could on this mission.

The briefing started with the meteorologist giving expected weather on the route as well as over the target. The 315th's commander required that all members of the crew attend the briefing. However, after the initial introduction to the mission, the navigators and bombardiers left to go into another room for a specialized briefing.

Finally the curtain covering the large map of Northern Europe was drawn back and Lowell got his first glimpse of the red ribbon, which marked the route they would take. The target for the day was a factory in Southern Germany. The briefing officer outlined the routes the various groups would take, where the rendezvous of the groups would take place, the bomb load they would be carrying and fuel. Then the bombardiers and navigators were dismissed and Lowell spotted Myron across the room. He looked very serious which made Lowell almost laugh, knowing how few things Jew took seriously. It did give him comfort that Myron would take this seriously, although Lowell never doubted it.

The briefing went on through several more officers. They described the weather to the target, over the target and on the way home. They told the men what to expect from enemy resistance to the target, over the target and on the way home. This caused a visible alertness of every man in the room. They were all very attentive to this phase of the briefing and Lowell noticed that most of the pilots were taking notes. They were shown on the map where enemy fighters might be expected although at this stage of the war, fighters were becoming less and less a threat. This was not true of the antiaircraft artillery, however. They were told to expect very heavy fire at about twenty-five miles out from the target, over the target, and the same twenty-five miles away from the target.

Lowell knew from talking with many of the experienced pilots on the base that antiaircraft fire was the most dreaded. You didn't know when it would hit, unlike enemy aircraft, which you could see coming, and they were as big a threat. The men were also briefed about where they would lose their fighter escort on the way to the target and where to meet it on the way home.

When they were dismissed from briefing, Lowell walked out with Lieutenant Buckner who was looking down at a sheet of paper that told all the particulars, including where their plane was parked, when to start engines and the take-off order. Lieutenant Buckner turned to him and asked if there were any questions.

Lowell thought for a minute and said, "No, everything was pretty clear."

"Okay, let's get our flight equipment then."

The flight equipment consisted of flying suits, Mae West vest, flotation devises, the parachute harnesses, and the flak helmets. The crew members also drew flak vests, which came in two pieces, one for the front and one for the back. Lowell learned that the pilots usually only wore the front because of the armor plating around the seats. Likewise, he learned that the pilots usually didn't wear the electric underclothes because of the heat from the engines; it was quite warm in the cockpit. Lowell thought the helmets and the flak suits were very interesting and that he looked kind of funny in them. The helmets were like the infantry wore except they had a section around the ear area with a hinged flap that allowed for earphones. The parachutes were issued and the harnesses were worn over flight suits that were like the coveralls he had worn when working in his dad's garage, but with many zippered pockets. The flight suits were worn over the regular uniforms.

One of the items issued to flight crews that gave Lowell some consternation was the escape kit. It consisted of a silk map of France and neighboring countries, some French money, a small compass, first aid kit, several hard candy bars, a sewing kit and other items to help a crew man who had been shot down. To these items Lowell added his escape picture. Lowell's job as co-pilot was to draw and distribute the kits to the rest of the crew. He thought for the first time that it was possible that he might not return from this mission.

As they left the equipment shack, Lieutenant Buckner said, "Let's get on board the truck, we're supposed to be turning engines in forty five minutes."

Lowell knew that was a way of saying that they were to have the plane's engines running and warming up in forty-five minutes.

They boarded the truck to the flight line. The way the driver drove, Lowell thought that they might not live to fly; he must have been going forty miles per hour. As they approached the aircraft, the driver only slowed down a bit for them to jump off. Lowell jumped, stumbled, but regained his balance just as one of the gunners caught his arm.

Lowell was embarrassed and apologized.

The sergeant smiled and said, "That's okay sir, it took me several missions before I could jump and not fall."

Lowell noticed that the bombardier was already at the plane arming the bombs. The ground crew greeted them and Lieutenant Buckner walked up to the crew chief asking if everything was ready. The chief replied it was and the lieutenant beckoned for Lowell to come with them to conduct the walk-around inspection. Lowell took note that the lieutenant was not casual with the inspection. He checked the control surfaces, the tires, looked up in to the wheel wells. He finished his inspection by walking around and doing a visual check of the skin of the aircraft.

When he finished he turned to the crew chief, patted him on the shoulder and said, "Nice job sergeant."

Turning to Lowell he said, "Lieutenant, you can never be too thorough with the ground inspections. It would be terrible to have an accident and injure a crew man just because you didn't check everything."

Lowell nodded agreement and then the lieutenant said, "Well, let's get on board."

They boarded the plane and took their seats, putting on earphones as they did. This procedure was familiar to Lowell, being the same whether it was a training mission or combat.

Lieutenant Buckner switched on the intercom, "Okay men, let's do a thorough pre-flight check."

Lowell realized why he was assigned to this crew. This lieutenant was very thorough with everything and especially the safety aspect of the mission. The inspection and startup procedures took about thirty minutes. When the crew all had checked in with "ready," Lieutenant Buckner slid open the window on his side and motioned to the ground crew that they were ready to pull the props through. Lowell remembered that this exercise was very important because it helped vent any foreign matter that might be in the cylinders. The mixture was set to full rich and then Buckner nodded to Lowell who opened his window, looked out to be sure the ground crew was clear and pushed the starter button for the right out-board engine. He heard the familiar whine of the starter, then the small explosion of the cylinders firing and the blue-white smoke burst from the exhausts as the engine started. Looking out the window, he got the okay sign from the crew chief and turned to the lieutenant giving him the same okay signal.

The startup procedure went on as prescribed until all engine gauges registered normal. They made sure the brakes were set and Lieutenant Buckner signaled out his window to remove chocks as Lowell did on his side. When the command came to taxi, Buckner released the brakes and began to roll towards the main runway. Lowell kept a close eye on the gauges. This was the assignment of the co-pilot, but he couldn't resist a peek out the side to observe all the aircraft lining up for take-off. The squadron commander was in the lead and their aircraft was number five behind him. There was another short delay and all eyes were glued on the control tower looking for the flare that would signal the take-off. Finally it came.

As they began to roll, Lowell thought he had never been so tense. He remembered high school games when he thought he was tense, but nothing he had experienced in the past, even his wedding ceremony, came any where near the feeling now. Lieutenant Buckner reached over and gave him a little punch on the shoulder and winked and smiled at him. It helped a little to know that the lieutenant had faith in him, but not much.

When the plane lifted off, Lieutenant Buckner yelled to Lowell to keep an eye out the side for other aircraft. Lowell knew that one of the most dangerous times on a mission other than when they were over the target, was while climbing to altitude and joining other ships in the squadron.

Lieutenant Buckner called the radio operator and asked if the ADF was on and got a positive response. Each plane had a radio device called the Automatic Direction Finder or ADF. This instrument had an arrow on a 360 degree calibrated circle. An instrument on the ground called a Buncher Beacon sent out a signal. The ADF on the aircraft showed the direction the plane was flying, either away from or toward the beacon. After take-off, the planes flew a looping course over the Buncher Beacon climbing until they reached formation altitude.

When they reached 10,000 feet, Lieutenant Buckner said, "Pilot to crew, it's time to put on the masks."

Lowell did so as they continued to climb and he was on constant watch for the rest of the planes coming into formation. When they were fully formed and at altitude, they headed for the Channel. Lieutenant Buckner called the gunners to get to their stations and test their guns. Even though Lowell expected it, when all the guns begin to fire, he jumped and was embarrassed by the motion. No one seemed to notice, which pleased him a great deal.

The formation continued on toward the target.

Lowell was beginning to relax a little when one of the gunners called, "Left waist to pilot, I see a bogy at ten o'clock high!"

"What's he doing Mike?"

"Just flying above the high formation, he doesn't seem to be attacking."

"Okay, just keep your eye on him and report if he attacks."

"Roger that."

Lowell tried to see the enemy plane but the angle from his right seat wouldn't allow him to see that high.

The lieutenant said over the intercom, "They're probably reporting us to the antiaircraft batteries up ahead."

They flew on for some time and Lowell noticed small black puffs up ahead and realized it was antiaircraft shells being shot at the lead formation.

The lieutenant said over the intercom, "Okay guys, flak ahead, put on your helmets."

Lowell reached for his removing his headset and cap. He replaced the headset and put on the steel helmet. He had never worn one before and found it heavy and uncomfortable. It pushed the headset down hard on his ears and put pressure on the top of his head. He wondered how long they would have to keep them on.

The formation continued to fly toward the target. Flak became thicker and thicker as they got closer. Lowell could now see the black puffs much plainer, hear the explosions and feel the jarring of the plane. The explosions and the turbulence from the other aircraft buffeted around the plane.

As he was thinking about it, he heard the navigator call over the intercom about the approaching inspection point, the location of the site they would bomb.

"Nav to pilot. IP in five minutes."

Lieutenant Buckner said, "Roger." over the intercom.

Turning to Lowell, he said "Okay lieutenant, here is where that close formation training comes in handy."

He again told Lowell to keep an eye on the plane next to him as they closed the distance even more.

Lowell thought, *How can we get any closer?*

Suddenly the navigator called that the IP was reached.

Lieutenant Buckner said "Pilot to bombardier, you on target?"

"Roger."

Lowell then realized why the pilots did not wear the electrically heated underclothes. He noticed sweat running down Lieutenant Buckner's face and he could feel it under his helmet as well. The bombardier made several small adjustments and the pilot responded appropriately in order to keep the plane level.

The bombardier kept calling out "steady, steady," and then he almost shouted, "Bombs away!"

Lowell could feel the surge of the plane when it suddenly became several thousand pounds lighter and seemed to leap upwards. The lieutenant motioned for Lowell to take the yoke as well and started to turn the plane to the right in a broad turn to get them on course for home. Suddenly a much louder explosion shook the whole plane and a tearing noise was accompanied with the strong odor of cordite filling the plane.

He knew that it was close when Lieutenant Buckner said over the intercom, "Crew, report damage!"

A voice came on saying that Billie had been hit. Lowell knew that Billie was the right waist gunner.

Lieutenant Buckner said, "How bad is he?"

The answering voice reported that he had been hit in the left shoulder and was bleeding badly. Buckner told them to try and stop the bleeding and asked if he was conscious. They reported that he was.

They continued to make the turn until the navigator reported that they were on the proper course for home. Lieutenant Buckner told Lowell to take the controls that he was going back to check on the wounded man. Lowell nodded consent. He was surprised to find that he was not shaking anymore and was quite calm although the sweat was still running down his head and face.

Lieutenant Buckner unhooked his head set and oxygen mask, picked up the portable bottle they used when moving around the plane, unhooked his harness and moved between the seats to the rear of the plane. Lowell held the yoke in a firm grip and scanned the instruments and on occasion the horizon for any enemy aircraft. He kept a close surveillance of the aircraft around him as well and tried to keep the plane at the correct distance. The flight engineer came into the cockpit and plugged his intercom into the system and reported to Lowell that all the engines were running smoothly and that the damage to the plane should not affect their ability to fly. This gave Lowell some relief and although he had never thought of the hit as anything but a minor scratch, it struck him that any damage to a plane could be fatal no matter how minor it may look or seem.

Just then a frantic call came on the intercom, "Tail to pilot, a plane has been hit; one wing is almost blown away."

Lowell was not sure what to do but was saved from a decision by another voice that said, "How many chutes?"

"I see four, five – six, seven, eight, that's all!"

The voice came on again and said, "Anyone else see more than eight?"

There were no other responses and Lowell knew that only eight chutes meant two men had probably died in that plane. He flew on maintaining position and thinking about what he had just heard when Lieutenant Buckner returned to his seat, plugged into the ship's oxygen system and his intercom.

"Pilot to crew, Billie will be okay if he doesn't loose any more blood. I think we've got it stopped so all we have to do is get home and he'll make it. Gunners keep your eyes open for enemy aircraft. We're getting into their area."

He then leaned over and touched Lowell's arm, gave him a thumbs up and took control of the plane again. Lowell sat back and relaxed a little and again started to scan the sky for any enemy. He took the lieutenant's motions to mean he had done well. He vowed then always to put his crew above anything else.

They flew along and occasionally flack bursts were seen but none too close. After some time, Lieutenant Buckner touched his arm again and pointed to the steel helmet indicating he could remove his. What a relief that was to be shed of the weight and the pressure on his head.

The lieutenant said over the intercom, "Channel coming up."

Lowell looked out the window and, indeed, there below was the Channel. He also became aware that they were losing altitude.

Soon Lieutenant Buckner said, "Pilot to crew, you can take 'em off now."

Lowell looked down and saw that they had reduced altitude to under ten thousand feet as he removed his mask.

When they were within radio range, they heard the leader call the tower. The tower asked about damage and wounded and the leader ordered any plane with wounded to report. Lieutenant Buckner reported that they had a wounded man on board but was not declaring an emergency. They received the landing instructions and circled until their time to land came up and the lieutenant lined up on the runway and brought the plane in very smoothly. They taxied up to the parking area and were met by an ambulance but the wounded man refused and chose instead to ride to the hospital in the truck. Lieutenant Buckner just shook his head and approved his request.

As they walked to the truck, Lieutenant Buckner said, "Andersen, you did a good job up there today. I am going to recommend you take your own crew up on the next mission."

Lowell said a weak thank you but did not feel he had done anything unusual and wondered if the lieutenant was being a little too complementary.

As they arrived at the debriefing hut, Lowell spotted Myron and walked over and asked how it went.

Myron looked up, smiled and said, "Just fine, how about you?"

Lowell responded with the report that he had flown for some time and about the gunners wound.

Myron looked serious and said, "You guys were close then; we didn't even feel any jarring."

The debriefing hut was one of the big ones like the theaters, long and low with tables along both sides. Lowell and Myron ran into Vern as they entered and asked him how it went. He responded with the usual okay.

Along the walls of the hut, officers were sitting on one side of the tables and crews on the other. All crew members were required to go through debriefing and tell what they saw and experienced. The information was first entered on a form and then the debriefing officers would go over it with them asking questions as they went.

As Lowell and the crew entered, they were given a shot of whiskey that they could either accept or reject. Lowell accepted it and gulped it down in one shot. It burned all the way down, but as he was filling out his form, it began to relax him a little, which was the purpose for the shot. When he got to the table of officers, a captain looked over his form, then referred to a list.

"Andersen, you were flying co-pilot?"

Lowell nodded and the captain continued reading the report.

Looking up at Lowell he asked, "Well, what did you think of your first combat mission?"

Lowell thought for a minute and then said, "Well I hope they all aren't that exciting."

The captain smiled and then dismissed him. Lowell stood, saluted and walked away.

Walking out the door he saw Vern who greeted him with, "Boy, that was exciting, but I think I did okay."

Lowell said, "Oh, I'm sure you did just fine Vern. Don't worry about it."

They decided to wait for Myron whom Lowell had seen just sitting down for his debriefing so they knew it would be a little while. As he came out he said, "I wonder if they have seconds on the whiskey?"

Lowell laughed and said, "Jew, will you ever change?"

"I hope not."

They looked at each other with warmth, Lowell reached over and patted Vern on the back.

"Let's get back to the barracks and shower."

That night, the men asked if Lowell wanted to go to the Officers Club for a beer but Lowell didn't feel like going anywhere.

"No, I think I will write to my wife and parents and just turn in. We have another training mission tomorrow."

"Okay, we'll see you later."

After they left, Lowell got out his writing kit and after some thought, began to write.

My Dearest Wife,

Well, how are things with you? Is the lumber yard busy? What have you been up to? I hope you haven't been accepting those invitations to movies from the guys who come in. HA, HA!

I flew my first combat mission today and everything went well. I flew as co-pilot on Lt. Buckner's crew. Lt. Buckner was on his twenty-third mission so he has had a lot of experience; he sure is good. I learned a lot about being a combat pilot from him on just one mission. I sure hope that I can be as good a leader as he is.

He is from Nebraska, not far from where I was born and attended the University for three years before joining the army. I can't imagine what it must be like having only seven missions to go before completing his thirty.

Lowell decided not to mention the gunners wound or being hit by flak. Both he and Jew decided they would only write about daily stuff knowing that whatever either one wrote to their wives, both would know in a matter of minutes of receiving the letter.

I am really tired tonight, though I didn't actually fly the plane much; it takes a lot of concentration and some physical strength to maintain formation.

Lowell went on talking more about the mission but only the highlights. He knew that he couldn't mention where they had gone or how successful it had been. After another page he closed.

Like I said, I am really tired tonight. I nearly fell asleep on the last

page so I think I will close for now.
As always to you I give my love and life,
Lowell

*****

The next day, Lowell got the crew together before the training mission and talked to them a little about how it went yesterday and about the things they would be doing today. He asked Jew and Vern if they had anything to add. Vern shook his head in the negative.

Jew said, "Guys, I found out there are a lot of good pilots in the outfit, so if you want to shop around a bit, I bet you could."

Lowell just stood there with a disgusted look on his face and when Jew finished, said, "Are you through?"

The crew laughed and he broke out in a smile. Lowell then said, "Okay guys, let's get aboard."

They rode the truck out to the *Grizzly's Roar.* Upon arrival, Lowell walked over to Sergeant Goldstein and asked, "Everything ready sergeant?"

"As ready as we can make it sir."

"Okay, let's do our walk around."

The two men, whom by now had formed a mutual respect alliance, did the walk around, checking the controls, tires, up in the bomb bay, all the small protrusions and holes that are necessary for a B-17 to fly properly.

Finally Lowell said, "Looks good sergeant. Nice job."

He climbed aboard and he and Vern began the pre-flight checks, which took about twenty minutes. All the pilots and crews were required to view a film about the hazards of not pre-flighting an aircraft before take-off. In the film, the pilot was sure everything was okay and didn't pre-flight but as they were making the take-off run and he tried to lift the tail, the controls were still locked and they crashed into a building. What a building was doing at the end of the runway, no one ever explained. The point was well taken, however, and most pilots were very thorough with the pre-flight.

The *Grizzly's Roar* would fly with two other ships and practice high level close formation navigation as well as climb out procedures using the ADF and Buncher Beacon. The two other 17s were flown by Dave Lampson and Larry Bishop, two men who shared the hut with Lowell and Myron and with whom they had become very friendly. Lowell learned that in the army, it doesn't take long to make good friends.

As they received their permission to take-off, Lowell and Vern advanced the throttles and the ship began to roll. At the correct speed the controls were cycled and the tail wheel came off the ground. As the speed increased, the ship lifted gently into the air.

Lowell called for wheels up and the familiar whine and bump assured them that all the wheels were in their proper configuration. The three ships climbed in the prescribed manner to the prescribed altitude and closed to a tight formation.

An instructor riding in Lampson's ship kept calling out to "Tighten it up!"

Lowell always felt very nervous at this point of their training; it was the tight formation that caused the accident in transition training back at Blythe and caused the death of six men. He told Vern to keep an eye on the ship to his side and sing out if he thought they were getting too close. He had established complete trust in Vern over the past few months. Unlike the beginning relationship he had with him, Vern had proven himself to be a skilled pilot and completely trustworthy. Lowell had no doubt that he would some day command his own crew, although he would hate to lose him.

They flew on following their assigned course until the instructor said over the radio, "Okay guys, I think we can turn back now and head for the barn."

Lowell looked at Vern with a questioning look and Vern just shrugged. They were supposed to fly a three-leg course and they had barely completed the first.

The other planes opened up allowing more room to make the turn. Lowell began the turn to the course that would take them back to Sulensborne. He told Vern to take it for awhile, unbuckled and crawled through the seats to the back of the plane. As he entered the radio compartment, Wayne said that he had just received a weather report and that a storm was forming over the Atlantic. Lowell said that was probably why the mission had been cut short.

After landing, the crew went by the operation room to check the mission board. Lowell's heart skipped a beat when he saw that they were scheduled to fly a mission the next day. It would be their first as an intact crew. He turned around and looked Myron directly in the face and noticed that he had somewhat the same look.

Vern said, "Guess we're going tomorrow."

"Yea, it looks like it," replied Lowell.

As they turned to leave, Captain Eagleston came out of the hut.

He saw the looks on their faces, smiled and said, "Don't worry men, you'll do just fine, you have a good pilot here," as he tapped Lowell on the shoulder.

Lowell looked embarrassed and lowered his head, but Jew came to his aid with one of his smart remarks and they all laughed.

In the vein of jest, the captain said, "The first one is always the hardest, but don't worry; it doesn't get any easier."

A round of tense laughter from the crew followed and then they all turned toward their respective huts.

After chow that night, Lowell admonished the crew to get to bed early to be ready for the next day's mission. When they had settled down, Lowell reached in his footlocker and got his writing kit.

My Dearest Wife,

Well, tomorrow is the big day, our first combat mission with our crew. I think I told you that the crew voted to name our ship Grizzly's Roar because of our Drayville Grizzlies and that was also the mascot of Dave McDonald's high school. Well tomorrow the Grizzlies are going to roar.

We ran into Captain Eagleston, our squadron training officer and he told us not to worry because we had a good pilot. That made me feel really good; of course Jew had a smart remark to make about that. Anyway, I pray that I will not foul up or do something dumb. They all seem to have faith in me, so I guess I shouldn't worry.

Well, do you see much of Betty? Jew is sitting across from me right now writing a letter to her, I guess. We laughed that maybe we could just take turns writing because we know that you two will share everything. Well we hope not everything.

Lowell went on to tell a little more about the base and some of the new men he had met. He then thought he had better follow his own advice and turn in so he closed with the usual.

As always, I give my love and life to you.
Your husband,
Lowell

After finally falling asleep, Lowell woke with a start and noticed that it was daylight outside. Fearing he had overslept, he jumped up and looked over at the other bunks where Jew, Vern and Vince were and they were all still sound asleep. He shouted to them and leaped out of bed, put on his pants and shoes and started out when he noticed that it was very foggy out. This made him realize that probably the mission had been scrubbed.

Myron asked, "What's going on?"

Lowell said, "I don't know, but I think the mission has been scrubbed; look outside."

Jew walked over to the window and noticing the fog, agreed.

Lowell finishing dressing and putting on his jacket said, "I'll walk over to operations and see what is going on."

As he climbed the steps to the operation building, he noticed that there was another bulletin up on the board. He read the posting and it did state that all missions for that day had been canceled due to bad weather. Being much relieved, he turned to leave when the duty sergeant came out with another posting. Lowell asked him if the mission had been rescheduled and he replied that it had for two days hence due to weather. This front was expected to last for next two days.

Walking back to the hut, Lowell had a mixture of emotions. He was relieved that they did not have to fly although a small degree of disappointment accompanied that feeling because of not getting to fly their first combat mission. When he entered the hut, Vern asked what was up and Lowell related what he had found out.

Lowell removed his clothes and crawled back in bed. After a few minutes he got up because he could not sleep. He started to leave and Jew call out to him.

"Where you going Low?"

"To the mess hall to see if they're serving breakfast."

Wait a minute and I'll go with you."

Everyone else in the hut seemed to have gone back to sleep.

As they walked over to the mess hall, Jew said, "When do you think we will fly?"

"The duty sergeant said the front was supposed to hang on for a couple of days and the next mission is scheduled for Thursday."

"I suppose we will have more training flights."

"I don't think so in this weather."

"Yea, you're probably right."

The boys entered the officer's mess and found that several men were sitting around finishing breakfast or just drinking coffee and smoking. Lowell spotted Lieutenant Buckner.

He walked over, greeting him and asked, "Lieutenant, does this happen often?"

"In the winter it does, but this is the earliest fog we've had since I've been here."

Lowell introduced Myron to him and Lieutenant Buckner introduced the men at the table. Lowell knew two of them because they were in Buckner's crew. The Lieutenant invited them to join the crew at the table. Lowell and Myron said they would as soon as they got something to eat.

Getting their food, they sat down and listened to the talk, which involved the weather and the possibility of flying on the following day.

"I remember a time during early spring when we didn't fly for a week," said Lieutenant Buckner.

Myron asked, "Wasn't that just before D-Day?"

The lieutenant said that it was but reminded them that D-Day was slipped in between some pretty big storms. Both the boys nodded in agreement. Then Lieutenant Smith, Buckner's bombardier, asked them where they were from. Both Lowell and Myron answered in unison that they were from Oregon. Lieutenant Smith said with some astonishment, "Both of you?"

Lowell explained that they were from the same hometown and had grown up together. The response was one of light-hearted laughter and the question of how they ended up in the same crew.

Jew answered, "Well, the Army Air Corps knew that Low couldn't find his way around Europe alone and asked if I would mind showing him. I've been leading this guy around all our lives so I said I thought I could handle it."

That brought another round of laughter and more comments about how odd it was.

Lieutenant Buckner said, "Oh I don't know, you remember Pritcher's crew, two of his gunners were from the same town some where in the Mid-West."

They all nodded as they remembered. Just then, Vern and Vince came into the mess hall and walked over to the table. Lowell introduced them around the table. Vern asked if there was anything good to eat and the answer was the usual, "Nothing new."

With that, Lieutenant Buckner said he had some letters to write and he thought he would go, which caused the rest of his crewman to agree and they bid the fellows goodbye, leaving the table.

Myron said, "He seems like a nice guy. How many missions did you say he's flown?"

"I think he said he he'd flown twenty six."

"Wow, he only has four to go."

Lowell asked, "What do you want to do today?"

"Oh I don't know – why don't we see if we can find Charlie and go in to town or something."

"That's a good idea. Ya know some of the older men said you could ask the mess sergeant for extra rations and take them into the church for the orphans. Maybe we can do that."

"Yea I've been thinking about that. I wonder where the closest synagogue is."

Lowell looked at his friend and Jew just pierced his lips and shrugged.

The boys changed in to their class A uniforms, went to the mess hall where the sergeant had prepared several boxes of food, gathered them up and headed for the bus stop. It was a cold cloudy day with a very low ceiling.

Lowell said, "Ya know I am disappointed at not flying today, but in a way I'm glad."

"Yea, me too," replied Jew.

Vern spoke up and asked, "Do you think we will fly tomorrow?"

"I don't know, they said this front might last a couple of days."

They boarded the bus to Sulensborne and rode in silence. When they got to the bus station, they got off and began to walk around looking for the church that was housing orphans. They asked several people along the street and, following all the instructions they received, finally arrived at a church.

When they entered, the pastor was sitting in the front pew reading something from a piece of paper.

Lowell said, "Good morning pastor."

The pastor jarred out of the revere, spun around in the pew and got up greeting them in his very warm fashion.

"Good morning boys, come right in."

They entered the little church and Lowell said, "We understand that you have orphans here and are always in need of food."

"Oh my, yes we do and we always need food. Everything is in such short supply these days."

"Well we brought some."

Lowell turned and went out to the steps where they had left the boxes. The pastor, with some embarrassment but much gratitude showed them where to put the food and then offered them some tea, which they accepted.

The boys asked about the orphans and the pastor explained that they were not all orphans. When the major cities were under such heavy attack, the residents evacuated many of their children to the more rural areas.

Myron then spoke up and said, "Pastor, I'm Jewish and I was wondering where the closest synagogue might be?"

"Oh my, it's quite a ways from here, down in London."

"Oh, I just thought I might like to attend a service."

"I'm sorry lieutenant, I can't help you."

Lowell was looking at his friend with such pity and sadness that when Jew turned to him he laughed and said, "Come on now, it isn't the end of the world."

Lowell laughed and reached out and gave Myron one of those *I love you* taps on the arm but neither would have ever admitted that was what it meant.

When they had just about finished their tea, the pastor's wife came in with a small dish of "biscuits." They each had one and she encouraged them to take another. They did. When finished, they thanked her and the pastor, then left.

As they walked down the street, Charlie said, "My God, can you imagine being taken from your family and placed with total strangers."

Lowell looked at Vern knowing that was exactly what had happened to him. Vern was nodding his head and looked up to catch Lowell's eye. He just smiled and nodded some more.

They wandered around the town for awhile and bought some lunch from a sidewalk vender. It was the typical fish and chips: sliced fried potatoes and fried fish wrapped in newspaper. When they first arrived in England and saw the typical English meal served, the newspaper part put them off; however, after trying it several times without getting sick, they now enjoyed the fare without thinking about the wrapper. Paying the vendor, they crossed the street to a small park and sat on a bench, eating in silence. They watched the many US service men wandering the streets.

Lowell said, "I wonder how all of us will affect the country when the war is over and we all go home."

"I don't know, but I'm sure it will change a lot," Charlie responded.

Suddenly a drizzling rain interrupted their thoughts. Slight at first, it began to increase and Myron said, "Let's get out of here."

The boys returned to the base and their huts. They all took naps, wrote letters and then it was time for chow. After chow, they went by the mailroom to check on mail. The boys had not heard from their wives since arriving in England. At the introduction to their assignment, they learned that it would take a couple of weeks for their mail to catch up with them. Lowell and Myron had continued to write to their wives. Although Jew had always kidded Low about writing so much, he had written nearly every night to Betty. As they entered the mailroom, Lowell stepped up and gave them his name.

The sergeant looked and said, "Yes lieutenant, you've got several letters."

Lowell took them and looked at the three V-mails; two were from Helen and one from his folks. V-mail or Victory Mail consisted of letters that had been reduced in size to allow more mail to be shipped over seas than the usual paper and envelopes used in the States.

Handling them with some reverence, he turned to meet Myron's anxious eyes. Lowell nodded and walked to the back of the line and waited for Jew. Although Lowell wanted to see if Myron had any, he could hardly wait to open Helen's letter. Jew finally got to the window and when he turned around Lowell noticed that he had a big smile on his face indicating he had also gotten some mail.

As he walked up to Lowell, he said, "I got two from Betty and one from my folks."

Lowell said, "So did I!"

"You mean you got two letters from my wife and parents?"

"No, you dummy. I mean I got two from Helen and one from my parents."

The boys went back to the hut and the seclusion of their bunks to open their mail in private. Although a single bunk did not provide a lot of privacy, the rest of the men in the hut did not interfere.

Lowell looked at the post date on the letters and opened the first mailed.

My Dearest Husband,

Darling, I got your first letter from England today and was it wonderful to again see your handwriting and know you actually had touched the paper. I can't believe you are so far away from me. I know you are doing what you want and I am so proud of you for that. When I go to bed at night, I think about the few nights we had together and pray that there will be many more. I reach over and touch the side of the bed where you will be sleeping when this terrible war is over and you are home again to me. I don't want to even think about not having you home, because I know you will be here.

I hope my thoughts don't depress you, because I want you to know that you are doing what is necessary and important for people all over the world. The men who come into the lumber yard always ask about you and when I tell them, they say, "Well, you must be proud of him." I can't tell them how proud I am.

Your folks have been wonderful; they invite me over for dinner at least once a week. The twins are such a comfort to me. David is looking so much like you did when you were his age that it makes me shudder. Your father is having some trouble getting parts to repair the cars and trucks he gets into the shop. One of our trucks had a clutch problem and Dad took it to him. It took three weeks to get a new clutch! That is sure different from before.

Helen told him about meeting Betty for lunch several times a week and going to an occasional movie together, then she closed her letter:

I will love you forever and ever.
Your loving wife,
Helen

Lowell folded the letter and realized he had tears in his eyes. He wiped them away and looked over at Jew who avoided his stare. Lowell realized he struggled with his emotions too. Lowell opened the second letter from Helen and read about what had been going on in Drayville and with the family. She again expressed her love and devotion to him as she signed off.

Next, he opened the letter from his folks. His mother of course wrote it, but there were some inserts from the twins.

Dear Son,

We got your first letter from England and were so glad to hear from you. Your dad and I have tried not to worry too much but I have to admit, we have. He is keeping busy at the garage and I am still volunteering with the Red Cross and helping at church. Uncle Norwood and Aunt Vera were over the other night for supper and we had our usual good time. Helen and her folks came as well. Helen seems to be keeping busy and she looks great, but I'm sure in her quieter moments she misses you even more than we do.

Lowell's mother went on to tell more about what was going on in Drayville, which he dearly loved to hear, then she closed:

Your loving parents,
Mom and Dad

Lowell then unfolded the short note from the twins that renewed his humor. They both told what they were doing in school and David complained that the bike had a flat tire and they couldn't get a new one. Diane said her class was still collecting tin and rubber for the war. One of her lines made Lowell laugh out loud: *How do you soldiers use all those tin cans we save?*

He shared that with Jew and they both had a laugh.

Lowell said, "I think I will go see if there is a mission on for tomorrow."

"Yea, I'll go with you."

As they started to leave, the door of the hut opened and Vern and Vince came in somewhat wide-eyed.

Vern said, "We're on for a mission tomorrow."

Lowell thought about their training in putting a mission together. Bomber Command selected the target and notified Division, who in turn notified Group and down the line to the 247th and to them.

Lowell looked at Myron and that feeling of tense excitement passed over him.

He said, "Well, I hope we get to go this time."

FIRST MISSION

Lowell did not sleep very well again, but when the orderly came in at 0500 and called them, he was fast asleep. He jumped up as if on springs and started to wake the other crewmen. However, they were already getting up.

Lowell said to Vern, "I wonder if we will ever get used to this?"

"I guess it will become routine the more we do it."

They dressed and went to the officers mess for breakfast which consisted of pancakes, bacon, ham, eggs and all the coffee they could drink. Lowell remembered what Lieutenant Case had said about not drinking too much coffee. At thirty thousand feet, the relief tube froze and became very difficult to use for the intended purpose.

Vince, Vern, Myron and Lowell attended the briefing for officers while the enlisted men went to a much shorter version. The boys sat together in one of the back rows as expected of new crews. They also knew that they shouldn't ask a question unless it was vital and very important to the mission. Held in a large single hall in one of the bigger buildings, the briefing room contained rows of seats not unlike the auditoriums in schools, divided by an aisle in the middle. There was a stage in the front with steps on each side and a large map in the center. The map usually remained covered until the conclusion of preliminaries.

After a short time, the door to the briefing room flew open and there was the usual ATTENTION, followed by the crews jumping to their feet. The colonel and his aides came striding purposefully down the center aisle and onto the stage.

The colonel called, "AT EASE, SIT DOWN MEN."

He smiled down on the seated crews and Lowell thought he just did that to kill time and it irritated him.

"Good morning men, did you sleep well?"

There were a few murmurs and he continued, "Today's mission is a long one."

He turned to the officer standing by the big map and nodded. The officer reached up and pulled the curtain back revealing a map of Northern Europe with a red streamer going from the base to Hamburg, Germany. There was an audible moan from the room and the colonel turned again with a serious look on his face.

"Today's target is the oil refinery in Hamburg. It will be about a seven-hour flight with much of it over water. Good luck."

He then left the stage and Major Booker took over. The major was the briefing officer, charged with planning the mission, bomb load requirements, and route to target. He began with telling the crews they would be carrying six 500 pound REX bombs.

He went on to describe the route and then said, "Okay men, navigators and bombardiers are dismissed to their briefing."

The navigators' briefings consisted of further detailed routes and altitudes. The bombardiers sessions provided information about the IP and target description.

Pilots stayed in the original briefing room and received information on taxi instructions, forming up, and weather. Each pilot, along with his co-pilot, received two sheets of paper. On one, Lowell reviewed a roughly printed small map of the field with their taxi route. It also provided the order of aircraft taxiing to the runway. They would take-off in the order in which they would fit into the formation. The sheet also listed the take-off time. Each pilot's name was hand written at the top and the taxi route was just a line drawn on the taxiways.

The second sheet was a list of all the planes by number, the pilots or aircraft commanders' names and the time schedule including when they were to start engines. Flying near the end of the formation, Lowell's plane was one of the last to taxi and take off. He would not start the engines as soon as some of the other planes scheduled to take-off earlier. Lowell leaned over and showed it to Vern and they both smiled.

When the briefing was over and pilots dismissed, they left to board the trucks. Lieutenant Buckner came up to Lowell and said, "Well, are you ready for this one?"

Lowell looked at him and said, "I sure hope so."

"Well I think you are Andersen. One good thing about Hamburg is the over-water -light; no ack ack."

Lowell looked at Vern and they both smiled. It was a small relief to know that the Germans probably wouldn't shoot at them for most of the flight.

Vern said, "That's sure good news."

"Yea that makes it a little better."

Myron was waiting for them at the truck. Vince had already gone out to the flight line to help and supervise the arming of the bombs. They had barely gotten in the back when the driver gunned the engine and took off. The first stop was the armor room so that Myron could pick up their guns and ammunition. The next stop was the equipment room where they all picked up their heavier clothing, flak helmets and vests, parachutes and harnesses. Vern, as was the system, also got the escape kits to distribute to all of the crew.

As they pulled up to the *Grizzly's Roar* the rest of the flight crew and the ground crew were waiting for them. They all were anxious to know where they were going and when Lowell told them Zo asked, "Is that very far?"

They had a little laugh at his expense and Lowell gave a few more details of the mission.

Bob was standing beside the crew chief, Lowell walked over and asked if the *Grizzly* was ready to fly and Sergeant Goldstein said, "As ready as I can make her sir."

"Well, let's have a look."

Lowell, Bob and the sergeant started the walk-a-round inspection. The plane was indeed ready for flight as near as Lowell and Bob could tell. Lowell congratulated Sergeant Goldstein and thanked him.

The sergeant said, "Okay lieutenant, you take good care of my air plane now."

Lowell looked at him and noticed the smile in his lips. He patted the sergeant on the arm and said, "We will sergeant, and we'll see you in about seven hours."

He then reached up, grabbed the frame of the open hatch in the bottom of the plane and swung his legs up pulling himself into the vessel. Bob followed and they both went to their stations. Lowell asked Vern if everything was ready and he said it was.

He looked at his watch and said, "Well, we don't have to turn engines for another 20 minutes, so let's double check everything to be sure."

Vern nodded and picked up the clipboard with the pre-flight checklist. He began to read the list and Lowell answered each question with the proper answer. Finally, it was time for the pull through to start the engines. Lowell told Vern to open his window and be sure that all the ground crew was clear of the props. The first engine to start was the right outboard that supplied electrical power to start the remaining engines. Sergeant Goldstein gave him the thumbs up indicating the ground crew was clear and ready. Vern turned to Lowell and gave him the okay to push the starter button engine. The familiar whine of the starter motor and then the cough and the cloud of white smoke signaled the engine was running. They started the other three engines in the same manner until all four were running.

Bob was at his station between the two pilots, carefully monitoring all the gauges, as were Lowell and Vern. When they were satisfied, Lowell reduced the throttles allowing the engines to reduce the RPMs.

As they sat on the apron with the engines idling, Lowell focused on the plane in front of him on the taxiway. Finally, it began to move and Lowell announced over the intercom that they were off. He could hear a slight cheer from back in the plane and though he was very nervous, he couldn't help but smile. The planes took off at thirty-second intervals and Lowell watched the time carefully.

It was time for them to take-off. Lowell motioned to Vern and they both put their hands on the throttles. They pushed them forward to full RPMs for a few seconds and then backed them off for take-off RPMS. They released the brakes and the *Grizzly's Roar* began to move down the runway. At the proper ground speed, Lowell pushed the controls slightly forward lifting the tail wheel off the ground. Bob kept calling off the speed and when they reached take-off speed, Lowell pulled back on the control and the plane rose into the air. Lowell was again shocked at how heavy it felt with a full bomb load.

"Pilot to radio, is the ADF on?"

"Radio, roger."

At about 500 feet, Lowell turned the airplane until the needle on the Automatic Direction Finder showed the signal was coming from directly ahead and they were flying toward the Buncher Beacon. He continued to climb until they flew over the beacon and the needle swung around 180 degrees indicating they were flying away from the beacon. Wayne noted the time they flew over the beacon and Lowell noted the altitude. They flew away from the beacon for three minutes and then turned again circling around in a figure eight until they were flying towards it again. This process continued until they reached the formation altitude and joined up with the rest of the aircraft.

When they reached formation altitude, Lowell called "Pilot to crew, keep an eye on the aircraft around us and sing out if it looks like we're either pushing them or they are getting too close to us!"

In a few minutes, Vern tapped the altimeter and Lowell noticed they were reaching the altitude where oxygen was required.

Lowell nodded to Vern who triggered his intercom and called, "Co-pilot to crew, time for masks and if any of them are not working, sing out immediately."

There was no response from any of the crew so Lowell knew that all oxygen masks were functioning properly. Lowell flew along watching the needles on the various gauges and continuing to climb toward the bomber stream at 25,500 feet. He realized again why the pilots didn't need electric underclothes. He was sweating profusely. Lowell's assigned position in formation was in the low element of the second squadron, which meant they were stacked high left and *Grizzly's Roar* was the outboard plane of the element. Lowell instructed Vern to keep an eye on the planes on his side and above just as Lieutenant Buckner had instructed him.

He looked over at Vern who was also concentrating on the instrument panel and sweating. It was very hard to keep the plane level and within the prescribed formation distance with all the turbulence caused by the many planes in the formation.

Lowell called to Bob. "How are we doing on fuel use?"

Bob replied, "We're right on target."

Lowell looked down and realized they were approaching the channel just as he heard in his ear phones, "Navigator to pilot."

"Go ahead nav."

"Coming up on our first course change in five minutes."

"Roger, navigator, let me know the heading."

"Roger."

Lowell tensed up a little more with the thought that in a few minutes the whole formation would be turning.

"Navigator to pilot, come to a heading of forty-eight degrees on my mark. Five, four, three, two, one, mark."

Lowell and Vern applied slight right rudder and turned the wheel until the big plane swung to the left and the compass needle showed forty-eight degrees. The whole flight made the turn without mishap but with a little less formation discipline; however, crews made corrections as the turn was completed. The route took them out over the North Sea where Denmark extends toward Germany. Lowell remembered from the briefing that they would turn south toward Germany near this point. They flew on for some time more and Lowell occasionally sneaked a look down at the sea. It was a very clear day and the sun was well up by now.

Lowell thought. *What a beautiful sight. I sure would like to show Helen this view some day.*

Jerked back to reality by a crackle in his headphones he heard a voice say, "Left waist to pilot, request permission to test our guns."

Lowell looked over at Vern and kind of shrugged his shoulders indicating he had forgotten that little procedure.

"Roger waist, okay gunners test your guns but be careful not to shoot down any of our own and remember the 'bursts of five' rule."

He smiled under his oxygen mask at his little witticism. During training, the gunners learned to shoot in bursts of five rounds to avoid damaging or burning out the barrels of the guns. As the gunners fired test shots, Vince prepared the Norden Bombsight so it was ready and to insure he would not forget when the excitement of the bomb run might distract him.

After flying for more than an hour, Lowell was beginning to relax which may not have been a good thing. His arms were killing him and his back was stiff and worst of all, his feet were freezing. He looked over at Vern and he was lost in his own revere. Lowell thought of what he was like when he first joined the crew and how concerned he was about Vern fitting in. The little talk they had that day in Spokane changed Vern's attitude completely. He had kept his promise. Lowell was thoroughly convinced that if the need arose for Vern to bring the crew home, he would do everything in his power to do so.

As they got closer to Germany, they began to notice the black puffs of smoke up ahead, which signaled the beginning of flak. Lowell called the gunners and told them to keep an eye out for enemy fighters although if flak was present, there probably wouldn't be any fighters. He knew from his mission with Lieutenant Buckner that they would probably experience more and more flak the closer they got to the target. True to his comments, the flak increased and several explosions shook the craft severely. Suddenly a very panicked sounding voice came over the intercom.

"My God they've hit that plane right in the middle."

Lowell recognizing the voice of Dave McDonald.

Lowell said, "Which plane, give me the number!"

After a short pause, Dave came back on with, "It's number 2754 sir!"

"Do you see any chutes?"

"No I don't, I don't know how there could be. The whole plane blew up!"

"Okay, Dave, take it easy and get back to your station."

Vern checked his sheet listing the crews' location in formation and held out the sheet pointing to 2754. It was Waldo Beckham's plane. Lowell didn't know Waldo at all, but felt sorry never the less and a bit relieved that it wasn't their plane. They both resumed their concentration to keep in formation and on course.

Home

As Betty got off work, she decided to walk over to the lumber yard and see if Helen wanted to go to a movie that night. When Betty entered the yard office, Helen was still busy at the desk typing and Betty startled her.

Betty laughed and said, "Hi, don't worry this is only a social call."

Helen laughed as well and said, "Aren't we something? Every moment we worry about our husbands and though I try not to, I think anytime someone comes in the office it might be bad news."

"Yea, I'm the same way at the store. Anyway, what I wondered is would you like to go to a movie tonight? There's a new Betty Grable musical showing. It might be fun to see something light for a change."

"That sounds swell. What time?"

"Oh we could meet at the theater around seven. We'd miss the newsreels that way."

"That sounds good."

The girls had decided that they didn't like the newsreels that were mainly about the war because they didn't like the reminder.

Betty said, "You can invite the twins if you want."

"Well, David has decided he doesn't like any movie that does not have either a cowboy or soldier in it, but Diane might like to come."

"Okay, see you around seven."

"Goodbye."

Betty was leaving just as Mr. Dickerson was entering. He greeted her warmly and asked, "What do you hear from Myron?"

"Well, I got my first letter from England this week. They're getting ready to fly their first mission soon."

"Well next time you write, tell him hello for me will you?"

"I sure will."

As Betty left the yard, she thought of the many people who had asked about Myron and Lowell. They were two of the most respected boys in town and everyone liked them. She prayed that when this war was over, they could live in Drayville and raise a family. That haunting wish that she had tried to get pregnant before Myron left, again, made her feel very sad.

The movie was just what Betty and Helen needed. It was a fun picture with a lot of music and dancing in it and nothing to remind them of the war or their husbands so far away. Diane liked it although she fell asleep towards the end. She was wide-awake and excited to go to the ice cream store for a treat afterwards though.

Walking down the street to Smith's, Betty asked Helen if she and Lowell had ever talked about starting a family before he left.

Helen said, "Why Betty, we've talked about this before and I said yes we did. Are you okay?"

Helen noticed that Betty had tears in her eyes and she reached out and put her arm around her shoulders. Betty began to sob and Helen held her for a minute and then had a terrible panicked feeling and leaned back to look her in the face.

"Betty, have you had some bad news?"

"Oh no! I guess I'm just lonely tonight."

"I know, sometimes I think I can't make it with all this worry and the loneliness."

Over Denmark

Myron's voice came through the intercom, "Navigator to pilot, fifteen minutes to IP."

"Roger Nav. Do you copy that Vince?"

"Bombardier to pilot, roger, I do."

When they reached the IP the formation would make a final turn toward the target, tightening up and preparing to drop their bombs when the leader dropped his. The different levels of the formation turned at different times. Lowell's element paused fifteen seconds after the first element made their turn.

Several minutes passed. They reached the IP and made the turn toward the target without mishap. The flak had indeed increased making the sky look like a Fourth of July fireworks display. With the Norden Bombsight, the bombardier could make slight adjustments in the flight path, but the pilots still had main control. The lead bombardier in the section would drop a smoke flare indicating he was releasing his bombs. This was the signal for all the bombardiers in the section to toggle their bombs. The time that elapsed between when they saw the smoke and when they toggled their bombs, carried the rest of the tightly formed planes to the prescribed drop position.

At the drop, Vince called over the intercom, "Bombs away!" which wasn't really necessary because the plane took a leap up with the lightening of the load and every one aboard knew they'd dropped the bombs.

Lowell announced over the intercom, "I've got it!" and took full control of the plane again to make the turn toward the rendezvous point and head for home.

The flak was still very heavy and suddenly Zo called to say that plane number 5386 was smoking a lot. Lowell told the crew to keep an eye on it and see if it dropped out of formation.

Lowell thought, *We've seen two planes in trouble. I wonder how many we didn't see.*

The course going home was close to the route taken on the way to the target. They never flew exactly the same route in an effort to throw off enemy fighters and the gunners on the ground. The flak was still quite heavy at this point. The Germans would shoot down as many planes as possible in an attempt to keep them from returning on another bomb run.

Lowell was still sweating under his flying suit but he also felt a sense of relief at having delivered his first blow against the enemy. Suddenly the trap door between the cockpit and the navigator's compartment opened and Myron's head appeared. He gave Lowell a big thumbs-up and Lowell knew what that meant: Jew had finally 'bombed the crap out of them Nazis'.

Flying over the sea again and away from the flak, the trip home became routine. Lowell asked Vern if he wanted to take a break and he said he did. Lowell made sure he had taken the portable oxygen bottle with him and then settled back for the trip home. He hoped Vern would not be too long because he needed some relief as well.

One of the problems for air crews was how to relieve themselves on missions. The plane was equipped with a relief tube that worked fine at lower altitudes; however, the tube froze at higher altitudes like those flown during the bombing missions and the crew could not use it. Therefore, the new crews learned that their steel helmets could serve the purpose. In a few minutes at fifty below zero it would freeze; then they could merely turn the helmets upside down and dump the frozen waste out of the aircraft.

In a short time, Vern was back and Lowell unstrapped his harness, connected the portable bottle, stiffly climbed from the seat and made his was to the back of the plane. He plugged his intercom into the system and asked the crew if they were okay. Wayne reported that he heard shrapnel hitting the wings and Lowell looked out but could not see any evidence.

He said over the intercom, "Well, I'll have to explain that to Sergeant Goldstein, won't I."

The guys all nodded their heads and Lowell knew they were probably smiling under their masks.

He returned to the cockpit, but allowed Vern to fly for awhile. As they flew on, the formation loosened a little and Lowell's thoughts drifted to how many planes they had lost besides the one they saw go down. Every plane carried ten crewmen and he thought about all of them. Remembering when they first arrived at Sulensborne and their assignment to a hut, he had wondered why there were so many empty bunks and assumed they were men who had rotated. He later learned they were mostly men lost on missions. Jerking himself back to the job at hand he signaled to Vern that he was taking control again and concentrated on staying in formation and keeping the ship tucked in.

When they reached the field, the formation flew over the landing runway and then turned to the left allowing for severely damaged aircraft or those with wounded to land first. Being one of the last, the *Grizzly's Roar* flew for nearly twenty miles from the field until they turned to head in for the landing. This was necessary to space the aircraft and prevent any mishaps. Lowell remembered that during the training flights and some of the lectures, the instructor made a point of doing everything to prevent an accident. It would have been too bad to have a crew survive a mission and then crash on their home field. After landing, Lowell taxied to their assigned parking space. This accomplished, he spoke to his men over the intercom.

"Well men that's one; only twenty-nine more to go."

Vern reached over, patted him on the shoulder and said, "Good job Low."

The hatch down in the nose opened, Jew stuck his head up and complemented him on a good mission. Lowell appreciated all the comments, but was not sure he deserved them. It was a routine mission. The gunners, Myron and Vince had to unhook their guns and ammunition and return them to the armament shack for cleaning. They looked around the plane to be sure they were not leaving any equipment. Crew members returned all flight equipment, such as the parachutes, to the equipment shack and then attended the interrogation.

As they entered the interrogation shack, they received a shot of whiskey if they wanted it, which most of the crew took though many men turned it down for various reasons. At interrogation the men told about everything they witnessed that might be of importance to intelligence. Of course those crew members who saw 2754 go down related that information and Zo reported the smoking plane. The interrogators also asked about fighters, how heavy the flak was, and how the formation flew.

After being asked if they could think of anything else, the interrogation officers finally said, "Good mission men, the trucks to the mess halls are waiting."

Riding on the truck to the mess hall Lowell was surprised at his hunger and looked forward to a hot meal.

As they lined up Myron said, "Boy am I hungry!"

"Yea me too," replied Vince.

Lowell agreed as they all received their food. He was surprised that the crew was not talking about the mission yet, but after they'd had their fill of food, they began to talk.

Vern said, "Low, do think that was the typical amount of flak?"

"Well, it was somewhat less than my practice mission with Lieutenant Buckner, but I suppose it depends on the target."

"Yea, one of the guys I was talking to in the Officers Club said that," replied Myron.

After eating, they went to quarters and Lowell said, "Boy, I'm going to have a very long shower; I feel dirty."

Vince said, "Yea, I wonder why."

Vern added, "Well I know why. Low and I sweat like butchers up there."

Lowell nodded with a smile on his face and Myron said, "Why would you sweat? All you had to do was steer the plane."

They all laughed and began to take off their uniforms and get ready to shower.

When they were through, Myron said, "I'm going to have a long nap."

Vince and Vern agreed and they flopped down on their bunks.
Lowell reached under his bunk for his writing kit and

Myron gave a moan and said, "Your not going to write a letter are you?"

"No, just a short note."

My Dearest Wife,

Well, today was the big day, Our first mission as an intact crew. The guys performed very well and I am so proud of them. We have a very good bunch of men. Jew got us right on target and Vince dropped the eggs right where they belonged.

How are things with you? I think about you all the time and wonder how you are making out. Are you busy at the yard? Jew said he heard from Betty and that you girls talk nearly every day. That is so nice to hear.

We did not fly for the last three days because of weather so we went into Sulensborne and took some more food for the needy families. Myron asked the pastor about a synagogue and he said the nearest one was in London. I hope we can get down there soon so he can meet with the Rabbi.

I have seen quite a change in him since we have been here; he is much more serious and thoughtful. I hope he doesn't change permanently, I liked him the way he was. Don't say anything about this to Betty; I don't want her to worry.

Lowell went on with more everyday stuff and then ended with:

Please keep the letters coming. You don't know how important they are to me.

To you I give my life and love forever.
Your husband,
Lowell

*****

The next morning Lowell woke up and looked at his watch. It was nearly 0700, far later than they usually were awakened. He remembered that he was supposed to report to the Link Trainer for a session. He got out of bed and noticed that the other men were still in bed. He didn't want to disturb them so he quietly dressed and went to the mess hall for breakfast. When he entered, he noticed that Lampson was already there.

Lowell got his food and joined him at the table. "You scheduled for the Link today?"

"Yea, I really hate that, but I guess it might help us to get home some day so it is okay."

"Yea, I agree."

After eating, Lowell reported to the hut for his Link training.

A sergeant said, "You Lieutenant Andersen?"

"Yes."

"Okay lieutenant, climb aboard."

Lowell climbed in. The sergeant observed him put on the headphones and seat himself within reach of all the instruments. He closed the hood and Lowell heard a voice over the headphones explaining in a bored voice what they were going to do. Lowell took the control stick and fixed his eyes on the instruments.

After about thirty minutes of concentration and sweating, (it was very hot in the "box" as the boys called the Link) the sergeant said, "Okay lieutenant, I think you've had enough."

The top of the trainer lifted letting in light and Lowell took a few minutes to adjust his eyes. The top was on hinges and lifted like the opening a large box or trunk. Lowell climbed out thankfully and realized his shirt was soaked with sweat. The sergeant said, "Lieutenant, you did real good; how long have been flying?"

"Oh, we just got here. I just completed the first mission with my crew."

"Well you did good."

"Thanks sergeant."

Lowell walked out of the building and started back to his hut. Someone called his name and he turned to see who it was. Larry Bishop was coming across the street.

"How was it Low?"

"Oh, you know; hot and dark just like coffee. You up for a session today?"

"Yea, I guess it's better than sitting around the hut all day."

"You're right. Say, how about a little basketball this afternoon?"

"That sounds swell! What time?"

"Oh I don't know. Why don't we see who's interested before we set a time."

"That's okay, well I had better get in there. See ya."

Several of the guys decided to join the game, Dave, Larry, Myron and of course Lowell. They met at the gym and divided into two-man teams: Lowell and Dave against Myron and Larry. Larry was an all league basketball player from Iowa and Dave played for his high school in Missouri.

The game continued for most of an hour and Lowell and Dave were up thirty-seven to thirty-three. There was a lot of bantering about who was the best, all in good fun. They had only an hour of gym use to determine a winner.

The game had gone on for nearly fifty-seven minutes when Myron said, "Okay, we have three minutes to go so let's make it work. What do you say Larry?"

Larry agreed as he passed the ball to Myron. Lowell was guarding him, moving with him down the court. Myron made a fake as if to go to his left, but Lowell knew he would never go left being a right-handed player so he still stayed with the right side. Myron started to dribble and Lowell stole the ball from him and started to dribble down the floor when Larry suddenly streaked by and took the ball back. Myron was breaking for the basket and Larry passed it to him. Myron had an easy lay-up and the score was thirty-seven to thirty-five.

On the inbound, Lowell threw the ball to Dave who started to dribble when Myron moved in on him and stole the ball. Larry broke for the basket and Myron passed him the ball. Larry didn't have an easy lay up because Dave was between him and the basket. That didn't prevent him from scoring. He stopped, set and shot a two handed set shot that ripped through the net, tying the game 37-37.

Lowell looked at his watch and called, "Time!"

"What? It can't be!" replied Myron.

Larry said, "Yea, it is; so I guess we tied."

Myron was still griping as they walked off the court, but Dave came up to him and said, "Face it fellow, we tied!"

They laughed and went to the shower room as another group entered the gym.

*****

That night the signal went up for a maximum effort the next day with call at 0400, which gave an indication that it would be a long mission. Lowell got that feeling in his stomach again and began to worry that he might do something to cause problems for his crew. He had talked it over with several of the more experienced pilots and they said they felt that way at first but learned that it usually didn't happen.

The lights came on and the duty sergeant called, "All right sirs up an at 'em. Chow in thirty minutes. Briefing in one hour."

The men threw back their blankets and swung their feet to the floor. Lowell looked around the hut and saw that every one was getting up. They dressed, did what little was needed in the latrine to look presentable and walked over to the mess hall. It was nearly full yet very quiet. They went through the line, found an empty table and sat down. Larry's navigator came over and asked if they had heard what the mission was and they shook their heads.

When they had finished they cleaned their trays and walked over to the briefing hut. Lowell and his crew again chose seats toward the rear and sat down. Larry and Dave's crew moved slightly forward based on their experience. The other crews in the hut had flown ten missions. That made them very experienced. Lowell knew that if you made fifteen to twenty missions, you were one of the most experienced crews on the field.

As they sat there waiting for the briefing officer, Lowell asked Myron, "Do you think it gets easier the more missions you fly?"

"I don't know, but I'm feeling really tense on this one. I thought the second one would be easier, but I guess it isn't."

"Yea, that's what I mean.

Suddenly they heard the ATTENTION command yelled from the back of the room and the men leaped out of their seats as the colonel came down the aisle and mounted the stage. The usual AT EASE MEN came next and the crews sat down.

The colonel began, "Today will be a maximum effort and a long mission. Okay major, open the shade."

As the major pulled the map cover back, there was an audible gasp from the gathered airmen. The ribbon went all the way to Berlin. Lowell looked at Vern who just stared and raised his eyebrows.

The colonel went on, "You see it men. We're going all the way today. All the way to the capital. To Berlin!"

There was the usual chatter from the audience and then the colonel said, "Now, I'll turn you over to Major Booker."

The major came up on stage, greeted the men and explained significant times to start engines, taxi, and other important points. He then dismissed the bombardiers and navigators for their briefings. Continuing with the pilots, he explained the route in further detail, what they might expect of the enemy, provided the map coordinates and had the sergeants pass out the individual information sheet. Lowell noticed his assignment to the lower formation and to one of the last take-off times again. He wondered how long it would be before his assignment would move him up.

The men next addressed the routine of gunners drawing their guns and ammunition and the bombardier arming the bombs, getting their parachutes and boarding the trucks. They arrived at the *Grizzly's Roar* and Sergeant Goldstein was waiting for them. They conducted the walk-around as the rest of the crew boarded the plane and began to prepare the positions for a very long flight.

The take-off was smooth and Lowell turned toward the Buncher Beacon and began to climb. After several flights over the beacon, they were at altitude and joined with the rest of their element. Lowell wondered how he would do when it was cloudy. He had heard the other pilots briefly mention it is quite scary. Reaching their formation altitude, they were all in formation headings for the North Atlantic and Berlin.

Soon they were over enemy territory and Lowell instructed the gunners to test guns and watch for enemy aircraft. They could see flak splashes up ahead where the ground gunners were shooting at the lead formation. Soon enough they could feel a slight shock as rounds began to go off nearer and nearer. Again, Lowell and Vern dripped with sweat from the strain of trying to keep in formation. This was a signal since they were getting close to the target and had to close up the formation even tighter. The anti-aircraft fun fire was also increasing. At their briefing, they had learned that their target, Berlin, was the most heavily defended city in Germany.

Vince called, "IP coming up."

Lowell responded, "You've got it!"

The bombardier had some control of the plane with the Norden Bombsight until he dropped the bombs. Lowell and Vern still had to keep the plane level and on course. The Norden could only control the rudder to skew the plane slightly.

A few minutes later Vince called, "Bombs away!"

Grizzly's Roar lunged upward as the heavy load left the aircraft.

Vince said, "Your airplane again."

The little trap door between the nose and the cockpit opened and Jew stuck his head up and raised his thumb. Lowell repeated the gesture and thought, *Yea Jew; we bombed the crap out of them.*

The formation began to turn on the homeward bound course and the crew of *Grizzly's Roar* breathed a little sigh of relief although they still had to fly through flak sent up by anti-aircraft planes around Berlin. Lowell could feel the sweat running down his back.

He reached up and wiped his goggles to clear them when Zo came on the intercom yelling, "Plane hit!"

Lowell answered, "Who? What number is it?"

"I can't tell. It must have had a direct hit. It just blew up."

"Try to identify the number and placement."

There was no response from Zo for some time and then he said, "I don't know, it was off to our left and below us."

Lowell answered, "Okay Zo, thanks; we'll find out when we get home."

They flew on through the flak for some time. Several bursts were close enough to shake the plane violently, which caused some concern for the crew. Being very new to combat missions, they did not realize that this was very normal. Lowell was gripping the control wheel so tight that his arms were beginning to cramp and he realized that he must relax or he would totally lose control.

*****

When they were out over the sea again and the flak was gone, Lowell reminded the gunners that they needed to be alert for enemy aircraft even though their little brothers were with them. Little brothers were the P-51 *Mustangs* that protected them all the way to their target and back. The earlier fighters, the P-38s and the P-47s did not have the range nor did the British fighters. Lowell gave silent thanks for the North American engineers who had designed the P-51 and the British who provided the Merlin Rolls Royce engine that gave the *Mustang* the range to accompany them all the way to the targets. The protection provided by the *Mustangs* greatly reduced the threat of enemy fighters. Now, if someone could design something to prevent the flak, that would make daylight bombing almost hazard free.

After the flak free flight over the North Atlantic and the Channel, they approached the field. Lowell received instructions to fly in a holding pattern and was given runway instruction. He knew that the ships with wounded aboard would be allowed to land first.

Finally, their turn came and they lined up on the assigned runway and Lowell brought it down with his usual skill. After taxiing to the parking area and shutting down, he reminded the gunners to unload the guns and unused ammunition and then de-plane.

Sergeant Goldstein came aboard and asked if everything went okay. Lowell responded in the positive and said, "Okay sergeant, it's you're airplane again."

The crew all climbed down from the *Grizzly's Roar* and waited for the truck to take them to debriefing. The gunners would have to go to the armament room and turn in their guns and then would meet at the debriefing hut.

Suddenly Gabe yelled, "Look at that!"
He pointed to the south where the returning planes were coming in for landings. They all followed his pointing finger and saw a B-17 coming in on the approach with smoke pouring out. From where they stood, the boys could see that part of the nose and tail of the plane were missing and there was a giant hole in the side. They all watched in horror as the pilot brought the damaged plane down in what was a very controlled landing.

After it landed and came to a stop across the field, they all stood for awhile as the ambulances and fire equipment rushed out to the ship. There were expressions of disbelief on all faces that had witnessed the heavily damaged plane make a miraculous landing.

Every man had the same thought in mind: *How could a plane that shot up bring the crew home?* Later they learned that the bombardier had died immediately plus the navigator and two of the gunners received wounds, but all others made it safely home.

Lowell entered the hut. This time he accepted the shot of whiskey and waited his turn at the table.

The officer called, "Next!"

Lowell walked over and sat down. The debriefing didn't take long.

As it ended Lowell asked, "Sir, how many planes went down?"

"I don't know lieutenant. Next!"

Lowell got up and waited for a few minutes until Jew was finished and they walked out together. They were very subdued as they proceeded back to their quarters. When they entered, Dave was lying on his bunk with his hands behind his head looking up at the ceiling. Glancing at

Larry's bunk, Lowell noticed it rolled up.

Dave looked over and simply said, "They didn't make it."

Lowell and Myron looked at each other for a minute and then Myron asked, "Was that their ship that blew up?"

"Yea, I think it was. We saw it but couldn't get a number."

Lowell responded with, "Same with us."

While they were cleaning up for chow, Myron said, "Ya know, it is a wonder when you think about that ship we saw land so shot up and then think about Larry's just blowing up. You got to think that if it doesn't explode the 17 will bring you home."

"Yea that was something wasn't it?"

After cleaning up and going to chow, no one in the hut seemed to be up to doing anything else. They were all very tired and turned in much before lights out.

Everyone except Lowell, who took out his writing kit.

My Dearest Wife,

Well we had our second mission today, Halloween. It was a long one if you know what I mean. We did okay and think Vince hit the target right on the nose. We felt a little flak but nothing very close.

Lowell wanted to talk about Larry but didn't want to worry Helen unduly.

We don't think we will fly tomorrow. Usually we don't have two missions in a row. How are things at home? I bet the twins had fun trick-or-treating. It seems funny to go into town and not see Halloween decorations all over the place. Of course, they don't have decorations of any kind. The country has really suffered in this war, particularly the children. I received your letters yesterday. Boy is it great to know I have something you have actually touched. Keep 'em coming.

The weather is beginning to turn a little bit towards winter so maybe we won't fly as often. Jew, Vern and probably Vince will go to town tomorrow although we might have to do some training exercise. I hope not.

Lowell went on for a few more lines and then signed off as usual.

To you I give my life and love forever.
Your husband,
Lowell

It was very difficult to enter the hut and see the empty bed that was Larry's, but after several days, there were replacements. One afternoon as the boys were lying around reading and writing letters, a corporal entered.

"Sirs, let me introduce you to Lieutenant Van Dyke, Anderson and Booker."

The men got off their bunks and walked over to shake hands with the new lieutenants and later learned their full names They were Kenneth Van Dyke from Wisconsin, Thomas Anderson from Ohio and Osgood Booker from Alabama. Van Dyke was a co-pilot in another crew, Anderson a pilot and Booker the navigator in Anderson's crew. They had just arrived in England a few weeks before and their story was very similar to Lowell's crew. They had taken their training in Texas and came over on a troop ship rather than by aircraft.

As Myron came up to Anderson, he said, "Oh my God, not another Swede!"

Thomas looked confused until Lowell said, "Don't pay any attention to him lieutenant; he can't tell the difference. I'm Lowell Andersen, a Norwegian. We grew up together and he has never gotten it right."

They had a good laugh at that and after introducing himself, Vern said, "Here, let me help you with that stuff."

The others also offered help and the new men picked out bunks. Osgood, "Os" asked, "Why are these bunks empty; did the guys finish their missions and go home?"

Myron looked at Vern and then said, "Well no, they are missing in action."

Os looked totally devastated and said, "Oh my God, I'm sorry."

No one responded until Vince said, "Well, chow will be in a few minutes, so why don't you guys throw your stuff on the bunks and we'll show you the joys of the 247th."

Ken, Tom and Os settled into the hut very nicely. As they went through their preliminary training, they had lots of question for the more experienced crews. Experienced, that is, with three or four missions. The usual questions included, "What's it like over the target? How long are the missions? Are there any enemy fighters?"

When asked the first question of Myron, he shrugged and said, "Oh, I don't know; I usually sleep on missions."

He did find almost an equal in terms of humor in Os, who was somewhat of a practical joker and kept the hut in turmoil most of the time. His favorite joke was to put things in a guy's boots. One day Lowell got up to go for chow and slipped his boots on only to feel something in the toe. He shook out a hard-boiled egg.

"Okay Os, you've gone too far this time!" Lowell exclaimed as he threw it at Os.

"I don't know what ya'alls talking about, but thanks for the egg; I won't have to go to chow now."

Myron spoke up and asked, "Say Os, what does ya'alls mean any way?"

"Why it means all of ya'alls. Didn't you study English in that high school way out west?"

Myron looked at Lowell and said, "I guess Miss Large Bottom forgot to teach us that plural form."

A slight laugh from the others in the hut and Os said, "Don't ya'alls know how to speak the King's English?"

The fall wore on with increasing weather changes. Lowell and Myron as well as several of the other crewmen didn't find the dark damp days too disturbing.

One day Jew said, "Ya know – this is a lot like Oregon isn't it?"

"Sure is but not as much rain."

*****

Around Thanksgiving, the weather closed in on them and the boys learned that there probably would not be a mission for several days. They also learned about the availability of passes. Lowell, Myron, Vern and Vince decided they would try to make it to London. Lowell said he had always wanted to see it and Myron agreed that old Miss Large Bottom had instilled in them the desire; he might as well go along. Vern and Vince looked confused until Lowell explained that Miss Large Bottom was their social economics and English teacher in high school and that she always talked about London with reverence. She was born in England but the family had immigrated to the United States when she what a little girl.

"Everybody in the school liked her, but she had the biggest butt you ever saw."

They laughed and Vince said, "Well, let's go see - What was her name? Miss Big Butt? Let's go see her favorite city!"

"No, Miss Large Bottom, we were very nice boys and wouldn't dream of using butt."

"Yea, I bet," responded Vern.

They checked on transportation and found there was an army bus that would take them to town where they could get a train to London. The next morning the boys rose early, dressed, ate chow, picked up their passes and waited for the bus to the train station. When they arrived at the station, there were many soldiers waiting and a few civilians. The train pulled into the station and they climbed aboard. As they boarded, they talked about how different the trains were here than in the US.

The passengers were mostly US service men, a few British soldiers and a few civilians. One was a very attractive young woman who was sitting with an older lady, most likely her mother. She sat demurely with her hands in her lap and her eyes down cast. Even as married men, Lowell and Myron had to admire her. Lowell noticed the worn look of her clothes, the lack of makeup and yet that did not detract from her beauty. When Lowell realized he was staring, he jerked his head around and looked at Jew who was smiling at him. Lowell was embarrassed but managed a slight smile.

"Well, it doesn't hurt to look does it?"

This caused Jew to laugh aloud causing several men to turn and look at them, which made Jew laugh even louder.

Vern said, "What's going on with you two?"

"Oh nothing, I just caught this old married man staring at that young girl."

Vince chimed in with, "Yea, I think every guy on the train is staring at her."

The train made several stops and finally began to enter the outskirts of the city. Every now and then there was a damaged building, evidence of the terrible bombing Germany subjected London to during the blitz.

As the train pulled up to the platform, Myron said, "Boy, did you see those blown up buildings?"

Lowell said, "Yea, I'll bet the buildings in Germany look the same."

"I hope so," replied Myron.

They walked from the station out to the street where several taxis were waiting. They were the typical London taxis with an open driver's compartment.

Vince said, "You know, I saw pictures in the National Geographic once about the London taxis but I never thought I would see one."

"Yea, well let's see what they will charge to take a trip into town."

They approached one and asked the driver how much and he replied in a very cockney accent the amount. Lowell asked if he knew of a good hotel that wasn't too expensive.

"Right-ou gentlemen, hop in."

It was a bit crowded for four big American men, but they managed. He drove them along some very deserted streets and arrived at a hotel named the Carlton.

"Many Yanks stay at the Carlton when they're in London. 'Er you are gentlemen."

The boys got out of the taxi and Lowell asked, "How much would you charge to show us around London tomorrow?"

He replied, "Right-ou gentlemen; let's see now, say eighteen pounds."

Lowell did a quick calculation, decided it was around fifty dollars and asked the others what they thought. The group agreed upon the rate as reasonable.

Lowell turned to the driver and said, "Okay, can you be here about nine tomorrow morning?"

"Right-ou," he responded as he pulled away and was gone.

Myron said, "Well, I wonder if we will ever see him again.

As they entered the Carlton, Lowell looked around and said, "It looks a little seedy don't you think?"

"I don't care; I could sleep on a park bench tonight. I'm really tired," replied Vern.

All agreed that though it was not the Ritz, it probably would do for a couple of nights.

As they approached the desk, a middle-aged man said, "I say there Yanks, what can I do for you?"

Lowell looked at the others and realized they were waiting for him to say something and he said, "Well yes, do you have a room that will accommodate us four?"

"Well let us see, yes, I have a room with two beds and two couches that will accommodate you all."

"How much?"

"Let's see, eight pounds six."

Lowell did a quick calculation again, realized that was close to twenty America dollars and responded that seemed a little high. The clerk scanned his book and said, "I say, I do have a room that will accommodate four for five pounds."

That was just under twenty America so he said, "Okay, we'll take it."

That night they walked around the neighborhood until the blackout came just at dark. They had not eaten, but there was a little café in the hotel and they decided they would have a light supper. Light it was. The meal consisted of boiled vegetables, a hard-boiled egg, what they called a mash, which turned out to be a potato like dish and tea. They became acutely aware of the food shortage in the city.

Returning to the room Vern said, "Boy, how do these people live on this?"

As they settled down, Lowell reached in his B-4 bag and took out his writing kit to the groans of the rest of the boys.

He said, "Oh, I'm just going to write a few lines."

Just as he wrote *My Dearest Wife*, the lights went out. They all laughed and Vince said, "Maybe you could borrow a match from Myron."

"Aw quiet you guys, go to sleep!"

The next morning the boys were up and around before 0800 and ready for breakfast. They dressed and went downstairs to eat. The lady seated them and handed them menus. They looked them over and found them written in English; however, they had no idea what they were reading. When she came back and asked for their order, they inquired about some of the items and all decided on a mush like cereal, a banger, and tea. The banger turned out to be one small very flat tasting pig sausage. Asking for a cup of coffee they learned none was available. When the group finished, they went out to the street to wait for the taxi.

Myron said, "Boy if I ever come up here again, I'm going to bring a big sack lunch."

They all laughed and Vince said, "Yea, I think about how the people back home gripe about the shortages and rationing."

"Yea, I guess the folks back home don't even know what it is like to be in a war."

Everyone nodded in agreement just as the cab pulled up and said, "Ou now, are you all ready to go?"

Myron, always the comedian said, "Right ou old chap, we are."

The driver laughed and said, "Hop in then. What would you like to see?"

"Oh everything I guess," replied Lowell.

Myron in an uncharacteristic mood said, "I would like to go to a synagogue, if that's possible?"

"Right ou old chap, you're Jewish then?"

"Yea."

The driver said he it would take time to get there but the route would pass several points of interest. He started the taxi and off they went for their tour of London. A barrier of sand bags surrounded many landmarks. The driver took them as close as he could get to the well guarded Parliament and Big Ben. As they traveled around the city, they saw more and more devastation, which again saddened Lowell. The cathedral nearby was an attraction as well.

Finely the driver said, "Here we are, Portland Street and the synagogue."

Myron and Lowell laughed at the street name, Portland.

"Do you think it would be okay to go in? asked Myron.

"Right ou, well I think so," said the driver.

Myron got out as Lowell asked, "Do you want me to come?"

He replied, "You can but you don't need to."

Lowell decided to wait in a shop across the street with the rest of the boys. They'd spied some pastries displayed in the window and invited the driver to accompany them. As they entered, the shop owner looked up with some shock and asked if he could help them. The driver explained the situation and the shop owner nodded in understanding, smiled at them and showed them to a table.

As they finished their tea and "biscuits," Myron came in with a very satisfied look on his face.

Vern asked, "Well, what happened?"

Myron laughed and said, "Oh not much, I met with a rabbi and we talked for a few minutes and said a couple of prayers. He asked me if we didn't have a rabbi on base and I told him I wasn't sure if we did or not. Do we?"

They all looked at each other and shrugged their shoulders. "Well I'll ask when we get back."

They continued the tour seeing St. Paul's, several galleries and the famous London Bridge. They made a lunch stop at a small restaurant where they found the fare no better than that at their hotel.

When they were back in the taxi, Vince said, "Boy I'm never going to complain about army chow again."

They all agreed that in comparison, the base food was quite good. The tour ended at their hotel and they arranged for the driver to pick them up in the morning and transport them to the train station for the return to Sulensborne.

That night as they lay in bed, Myron said, "You know that rabbi talked to me about the revenge thing; I think I'll try not to be so intent on bombing the crap out of those Nazis."

Lowell looked over at his friend and said, "Oh really, what happened to that eye for an eye stuff?"

Myron looked quite surprised and said, "Why dear friend, I think you got me on that one!"

A little laughter and they both settled down for the night, Vince and Vern were already snoring.

The next morning following another lack luster breakfast of mush, bangers, and bread with the taste and texture of sawdust, they checked out of the hotel and waited in the lobby for the taxi. It finally came and they climbed aboard.

The driver said, "Right ou, the station then?"

"Yes, that's right," replied Vern.

At the station, they had almost an hour's wait for the train that would take them north to Sulensborne so they decided to look around. It was the same story, very tired and shop worn people were waiting or walking around. The magazine shop had newspapers with stories about the war. Lowell noticed one about Japanese Kamikaze planes sinking the American aircraft carrier Intrepid.

He asked, "What are Kamikazes?"

Everyone looked at him and shook their heads.

The man behind the counter said, "They're suicide planes that crash into ships."

Vern asked, "How do the pilots get out?"

"They don't. That's why they're suicide planes."

The boys looked at each other in disbelief.

Vince said, "Why would anybody do that?"

They agreed they didn't know.

On the train ride back to base, there wasn't room for all four in the same car so Vince and Vern went forward to the next. As the train rumbled along, Lowell thought about the Kamikazes and wondered what their parents must think. Probably there was some religious meaning to it, but it sure wasn't what he wanted in life or death. He also was thinking about the devastation they had seen in the city. He wondered how much he had contributed to the devastation of the cities of Germany.

Finally, Jew poked him in the ribs and said in his best smarty voice, "A penny for your thoughts soldier."

Lowell laughed and said he was just thinking about those Kamikaze boys.

Myron, in a more serious vein said, "Yea, I thought a lot about that too. I guess they were just brought up to think differently than us."

Lowell agreed just as Vince came up the aisle and said, "Hey you two Oregon boys, there's a guy up in the next car from Oregon."

"Really, where?"

"I can't remember the town, why don't you come up and talk to him."

To which Myron, in his usual slice of sardonic humor said, "That's a good idea, if I stay here Low will have me crying thinking about those poor Kamikaze boys."

They got up and followed Vince to the next car, where he introduced them to a sergeant sitting across from Vern.

Vince said, "Sergeant I forgot your name but these are the two friends I was telling you about from Oregon."

The sergeant looked up, extended his hand and said, "I'm Bill Jacobson."

"Glad to meet you Bill. Where in Oregon are you from?"

"Well I've lived in several places. I was born in Nebraska and we moved to Dallas when I was just two. My dad worked in a mill there."

Myron said, "Well I'll be darned, we're from Drayville."

The sergeant looked at Lowell and said, "You were the catcher on the baseball team weren't you?"

"Yea, were you on the team in Dallas?"

"Yea, we played you guys when I was a senior."

"What year did you graduate?"

"Forty one."

"Yea, we're forty two."

Vince looked up at the ceiling of the train car and then said to Vern, "Vern, this Oregon must be a pretty small place." He looked over at the sergeant and said, "Everytime we run in to somebody from Oregon, these guys knew him back home."

The sergeant said, "Well, where they're from is only about fifteen miles from where I live."

He looked up at Lowell and said, "I remember you hit a home run with a man on and beat us four to three."

Myron spoke up and said, "Yea, and I was the one on. If it hadn't been for my great double, his home run would have only tied the game."

They laughed and Vern spoke up and said, "Don't mind these guys sergeant. They're always on each other."

Lowell asked, "Where are you stationed?"

"I'm at Sulensborne how about you guys?"

"Same."

"How did you guys end up at the same base?"

"Not only the same base I got stuck in the same crew with him," replied Myron.

"That's really strange. How did that happen?"

Myron warming to the situation said, "I don't know. I guess I screwed up and they wanted to punish me."

Vince chimed in saying, "See what we have to put up with sergeant? Although they really do like each other."

"Says who?" replied Myron.

They reminisced for awhile longer and finally Myron and Lowell left after finding out what squadron Bill was in and agreeing to try getting together some time later.

The train finally got to the Sulensborne station. Bill, Vince and Vern got off together and met Myron and Lowell. They walked out front of the station and spotted an army bus. Lowell went over and inquired if they could catch a ride back to the base and the driver said they could. He was there to pickup some new replacements but was sure he would have room.

When they got back to the base, Lowell said, "Let's go over to the officer's club and see if we have a mission tomorrow."

The boys responded with a positive comment and they walked down the street until they got to the club. They entered and found a few men there, some playing pool, some cards and some just sitting and reading or sleeping. Lowell spotted one of the new pilots from his section, walked over to him and asked if they had a mission tomorrow. He pointed to the board and Lowell read, *Maximum Effort.*

That meant that they would probably all be flying. The wake up call was set for 0430, which suggested a flight of some distance. He shared the information with Vern, Vince and Myron who groaned in unison.

That night, the inevitable writing kit came out and Lowell started.

My Darling Wife,

Well with this bad weather, we had a few days off so we went to London. Boy, those poor people sure have it rough compared to us Americans. We saw so much devastation and ruin that we wondered if they would ever be able to get back to normal.

Lowell went on to describe their tour, the driver and Myron's visit to the synagogue.

He came out after talking with the rabbi and believe it or not, he was in a very serious mood. We also met a man from Dallas. You won't believe this: he was a on a baseball team we played against in high school! He's a sergeant in another squadron but seemed like a nice guy.

He went on a few more pages and then sighed off with the usual.

To you I give my life and love forever.
Your Husband,
Lowell

Home

Helen walked up the steps to the Andersen house and rang the doorbell. She smiled as she heard the twins arguing who would get it, but David was faster and he tore open the door. The argument was not over as Diane kept yelling at him that it was her turn. When they saw who was at the door, all argument stopped and they greeted their sister-in-law with a warm hug and a welcome to come in.

Mrs. Andersen came out of the kitchen wiping her hands on her apron. "Why Helen, what brings you here at this time?"

"I was on my way to work and I wanted to come over and invite you to our house for my dad's birthday party Saturday night."

"Oh that is just lovely and of course we would like to come. What time?"

"Well Mom is fixing dinner and we usually eat around six. Oh and by the way, presents are not expected."

David, looking somewhat perplexed said, "You mean a birthday party without presents. That's dumb."

His mother scolded him but Helen just laughed.

Diane said, "Could I make him a card?"

"Why that would be very nice Diane. I think he would really like a card from you."

"Oh boy!" she responded as she ran up the stairs to her room planning the card on the way.

Mrs. Andersen and Helen both laughed.

"Helen dear, won't you come in to sit for a minute?"

"Oh, I really need to get to the lumber yard but maybe for just a minute," Helen replied.

They talked for several minutes and then Helen said, "We need to get any packages in the mail if we want them to get to the boys around Christmas. I don't know what to send; I suppose cookies. Lowell says food packages are always welcome."

"Yes, I have the same problem. Diane is embroidering a handkerchief in 4-H for him. She is really taking it seriously."

They both laughed lightly and then Helen got up to leave. Mrs. Andersen stood and they embraced for a few minutes. Mrs. Andersen walked her to the door and gave her another little hug, which went on far longer than either had expected. They had become very close in the past few months with the common concern they had for Lowell.

"Thanks for the invitation Helen dear; we'll see you on Saturday then."

Helen descended the stairs and walked up the street. She turned and waved. Mrs. Andersen watched her go thinking to herself, *What a wonderful girl. We are so lucky she is part of our family.* She closed the door and walked back in to the kitchen to resume her daily chores.

England, Seventh Mission

The wake up call at 0430 was always a shock, even though they knew it was coming. The boys got up, dressed and walked over to the mess hall where the smell of sausage and eggs greeted them. Lowell, Myron, Vince and Vern went through the line with their trays, received their food and chose a table. They sat down and sleepily began to eat their breakfast. When they were finished, they cleaned the trays and left for the briefing hut.

The briefings were all the same. Held in a large theater like building with a stage and a curtain covering the large map, the captain came on stage and called for their attention. As the colonel approached all the men jumped to their feet. The colonel gave them an at ease command and told them to take their seats. He said the usual words of welcome and motivation and then turned to Major Booker motioning for him to remove the curtain. This time the red ribbons went all the way to Regensburg, bringing a low murmur from the men.

The colonel said, "Yes, that's right were going to hit the Messerschmitt plant again. Good luck."

With that, he left the stage to the usual "ATTENTION" and the major bid them to sit. The briefing continued with the pilots remaining in the central auditorium, and the navigators and bombardiers departing for another part of the building for their briefing. Lowell received his slip of paper with their startup time, runway information and his position in the formation. Since the fifth mission, the *Grizzly's Roar* had moved up to the middle element in the formation.

After the briefing, they hopped a transport vehicle to the armor room for their guns, to the equipment room for heavy suits and parachutes, then re-boarded the trucks for the trip to the *Grizzly's Roar.* Upon arrival, Lowell started the pre-flight check and walk around. When finished, he boarded the plane and along with Vern and Bob did the cockpit check and pre-startup procedures. Because the *Grizzly's Roar* was no longer in the back of the formation, they had less time to wait before starting the engines.

Lowell watched the time very carefully and finally said, "Okay, let's turn 'em."

Bob leaned over and tapped the gauges as Lowell called start engines. Vern, watching out the right window to be sure the ground crew was clear, gave Lowell the okay and he started the right outboard. When all four engines were running, they reduced throttle to a slower RPM and waited for their turn to taxi.

Again at lift off, Lowell was surprised at how heavy the plane felt with the big bomb load and fuel they were carrying. They picked up the Buncher Beacon and began to fly the looping climb to altitude. Lowell was also surprised that on this mission, the seventh, he was beginning to feel relaxed and ready for whatever came.

As they formed up and headed towards the Channel and North Sea, Lowell told the gunners to test their guns and to be sure the oxygen was flowing. They responded appropriately and Lowell thought, *I sound like Coach Roberts giving his inevitable his pep talk at the beginning of a season. This crew is certainly coming together as a team.* A slight smile crossed his face, which he would not have wanted Vern to see, and Lowell was glad for his mask. Vern's voice on the intercom jerked him back to reality.

"Low, number 2174 on our right wing is weaving all over the place."

"Roger, pilot to right waist, can you see 2174?"

"Roger on that, I don't see any trouble though."

"Well keep an eye on him for awhile."

"Roger."

Lowell tensed up a bit. Glancing out the right window at 2174, he noticed that aircraft was not only weaving but going up and down as well. He couldn't remember who was flying 2174 and he didn't have time to look at the paper right now.

The formation kept climbing until they reached bomber stream altitude. Lowell reminded the gunners to keep an eye out for bandits and keep their guns charged. As they crossed the coast, the turbulence increased causing Vern and Lowell to concentrate more on their position and effort to keep the plane at proper altitude. Suddenly Dave called, "Right waist to pilot, 2174 just dropped back and down. Looks like he's in trouble and is turning back."

"Roger, Dave; thanks."

Lowell looked over at Vern and they both shook their heads. Lowell tried to remember who was flying it but couldn't. He just hoped they could get home okay.

As they closed up the formation with 2174 gone, Lowell was again reminded why the pilots didn't need heated suits as the sweat ran down his face and back. Both he and Vern were on the controls now trying to keep the plane steady. Flak was increasing the closer they got to the target. Lowell looked over and noticed that Vern had not put his helmet on and he tapped his head to remind him. Bob called to report that another plane was falling out of formation and smoking badly, but he didn't know which one it was.

Lowell said, "Roger, look for chutes."

After a short time, Bob reported that he could only see three chutes. Lowell thought about the other seven men in the crew and wondered if they made it out safely.

After what seemed like hours of fighting to stay in formation and being bounced around by the flak bursts, Myron came on, "Nav to pilot, IP in fifteen minutes."

"Roger nav."

Right on time Vince called out the target and assumed partial control of the airplane. Lowell and Vern watched the dial indicating what the Norden Bombsight was giving them for corrections.

With the correct distance from the target determined and the signal given, Vince called out, "Bombs away!"

The plane surged upward, which was very dangerous even though they had opened up the formation somewhat and no plane was directly above them at the moment. After dropping their loads, the bomber stream began the turn for the return trip. Flak was very heavy and the crew of the *Grizzly's Roar* could hear it hitting the plane.

Suddenly Gabe called out from tail, "They got number 2185!"

Lowell and Vern were so busy they couldn't look at the sheet so had no idea which crew had been hit, they only hoped it wasn't one of their close friends.

"Watch for chutes."

Finally, the always-welcome North Sea came into view. Although this meant no more flak, fighters were still a threat. They made it back to base without further incident and flew the holding pattern since they had no damage or wounded.

As they de-planed and boarded the truck to the debriefing hut, Lowell thought about the strain of the missions. Yet in spite of his weariness, he felt very hungry. After debriefing, he waited at the door of the hut for Jew and the other crewmen.

When they came out Lowell said, "Do you guys want to eat?"

"I sure do," replied Vince.

They walked in silence to the mess hall and entered.

Vern said, "Did we get an ID on those planes we saw go down?"

"Yea, the one who pulled out and turned around was Clark's. They didn't know anything about them and I guess the other two were Charlton's and Wall's," replied Lowell.

Myron answered, "Yea, I kind of knew Charlton a little; we had a beer at the club a couple of weeks ago."

The next morning they got to sleep in for awhile because there wasn't a mission. The new men - Osgood, Anderson and Van Dyke - had training missions to fly and they were up and gone when Lowell opened his eyes and looked around. He was surprised that he had slept while the three were getting ready. Flying a long mission was very taxing. He looked over at Myron who was still sleeping and noticed that Vince was sitting at the small desk writing.

"Writing to that girl Vince?"

He turned and said, "Oh, yea I couldn't stay awake long enough last night."

"Have you eaten?"

Myron rolled over and said, "Would you guys go eat and let us sleep!"

Lowell laughed and got out of bed reaching for his clothes.

Vince finished the letter to his girl and said, "Ready to go."

Vern came to life with, "Just a minute guys I'll go with you."

The days went by with the weather getting stormier. Several missions were scrubbed and on one, they were turned back just at the Channel because of bad weather over the target. They got credit for the mission, however, which pleased them.

Fall gave way to winter. They hadn't heard anything about Larry and his crew though they didn't hold out much hope. The weather changed and became very cold. Clouds covered most of Northern France and much of Germany as well. The missions were still long and the main targets were the railroad yards and switch tracks. The Allies were trying to cripple Germany's ability to move troops. They'd crossed the Rhine, liberated Paris and the holidays were coming.

As Christmas approached, they could feel the anticipation of victory in the commanding officer's somewhat relaxed attitude. They received more passes. With no mission to fly for a few days, the boys decided to go to the Officers Club and have a few beers. As they entered, Lowell saw a notice on the bulletin board and called it to Myron's attention. He walked over and read.

ATTENTION ALL MEN OF JEWISH FAITH.
THERE WILL BE A MEETING IN THE CHAPEL FOR ALL MEN OF JEWISH FAITH AT 0920 ON 12 DECEMBER 1944.
YOU ARE ALL URGED TO ATTEND.

Myron turned to Lowell and said, "I wonder what that's all about?"

"I don't know. Let's see, the twelfth is tomorrow isn't it?"

"Yea, I guess I'll go and see what's up."

On the morning of the twelfth, Myron rose early enough to have breakfast first and then go to the meeting. After they had eaten, Lowell asked if he wanted him to go along and Myron told him it wasn't necessary.

"Besides, don't you have a Link training session?"

"Oh yea, I forgot. I don't like that darn thing."

"Well buddy, we need you to know how to fly in the dark just in case we are late coming home."

So, Lowell went off to the Link and Myron went to the chapel. Around noon chow, Lowell had finished his training and as usual, although it was very cold he came out from under that hood with perspiration running down his back. He decided to go back to the hut and shower before eating and besides, maybe Jew would be there and he could find out about the meeting.

As Lowell came out of the latrine, Myron was just entering the hut. Vince was lying on his bunk reading and Vern and Os were each taking a nap.

Vince looked up and said, "Well, what was that all about?"

Lowell stopped in the door and listened to Myron's response.

"Well, it seems that they have gotten information that a lot of Jewish men are being taken out of POW camps and sent to work camps. The high command has authorized and recommended that we carry phony ID and if shot down, we destroy our tags."

Lowell responded with, "No kidding, what about our escape kits?"

"Well they said we would be issued new ones if we wanted them."

"Are you going to get a new one?"

"Yea, I guess I will."

They stood around looking at Myron until he said, "Hell, we're not going to get shot down and that's final. I'll never speak to you if that happens Low; so fly good and dodge the flak."

There was a little laughter and Myron said, "Well let's go eat. I'm hungry.

After chow, they returned to their hut and Lowell reached into his footlocker for his writing folder. Myron made the usual moan, but did the same. Lowell knew that he was writing to Betty as often as he wrote Helen.

My Dearest Wife,

Well no missions today; bad weather, so we are just lying around the hut and writing letters, reading and so forth. I had another session in the Link this morning. You remember; I've told you about the Link Trainer before.

Something odd happened today. They called all the boys of Jewish faith together and met with them. They advised them to carry false ID in case they are ever shot down because the Germans are not treating the Jews very well. I ask you not to say anything to Betty, but I think Myron will tell her. Also, don't worry about us getting shot down because the Germans are about licked and they don't put up much resistance.

How is everything with you? I'll bet everyone is getting ready for

Christmas. Mom wrote that the twins are fighting over the toy catalog again this year; nothing changes. I don't know if I will get any Christmas shopping done, but will make it up to you when I get home.

Lowell thought about the silk scarf he had purchased with the squadron's insignia on it and had sent it early in the week. He hoped she would like it.

We are hosting a group of kids from the town this year and most of the guys are looking forward to that. We continue to take stuff from the PX into the church for them. They have brought a lot of kids from London up here to get them out of the danger area and so there are a lot of kids without parents.

He went on with another page telling about what they had been doing and asking questions about home and then signed off in the usual manner.

To you I give my life and love forever.
Your husband,
Lowell

*****

On Sunday December 17, they got word that the Germans had broken through American lines in the Ardennes Forest area of France and Belgium. They wondered how that would affect them and their missions. There were some targets available, however, so the boys got in their tenth mission.

The colonel called a meeting of all the men in the squadron and reported the progress of Germany's offensive. It gave the men some concern when they learned that the Germans had overrun several American divisions in their attempt to get to the coast where the Allies had stored a large amount of supplies. One of the officers raised his hand and asked if they were going to try and help.

The colonel replied, "No, with the weather, high altitude bombing would be more dangerous to our own troops. We will look for targets of railroads and so on, that might be used to supply the offensive."

After a few more questions, the colonel assured the men that the war was in no danger of being lost, "It might take a few more months to finish the Germans, but we'll still beat them."

Once dismissed, Lowell, Myron and Vince walked out together and decided they would go to the officers club for a beer and some snacks.

*****

On the way back to their hut, they went by the mailroom and picked up their mail. Lowell had two letters, and two packages from his folks and Helen. One letter from Coach Roberts was addressed to both Lowell and Jew. Lowell smiled at that, remembering his thoughts on the mission.

He said, "Hey Jew, we got a letter from Coach Roberts addressed to both of us, but my name is first so I'm going to read it first."

"Oh go ahead I'm going to read mine from Betty."

When he got back to the hut, he tore open the one from Helen even before he showered.

My Dearest Husband,

I hope this finds you well and happy, or at least as happy as you can be. Everything is just swell here. We had a good year at the yard with a little building starting up again and lumber is a little easier to get. We still have trouble getting anything with steel in it, however.

I ran into Vern Dickerson's mom in the grocery store yesterday. She said they had finally gotten word that Vern is a prisoner somewhere in Germany. She seemed very happy about it. Imagine waiting eight months to hear something after they listed him as missing.

Lowell thought about that and was glad to hear Vern was okay.

He rose up and said, "Hey Jew, Helen said she saw Vern Dickerson's mom and they have gotten work he is in a prisoner of war camp in Germany."

"Really, well that's great. Betty was just telling me that she and Helen just went to the first Drayville basketball game. It was a loss to North Union thirty-eight to thirty-one."

"I guess without us they aren't very good this year or NU has really improved."

Lowell returned to Helen's letter.

I went over and had supper with your folks and I don't think you will recognize the twins when you get home. They have grown and are actually becoming people. HA HA! Your mom put together one of her outstanding dinners. She'd saved meat stamps for several weeks. It was really fun.

My dad's birthday party was really fun too. Diane made Dad a card and he just laughed and laughed about it. It was so cute he put it up on the mantel and it is still there. Diane was so proud but of course, David had some smart remarks about it.

Helen went on for a few minutes with local news and then some personal loving stuff that made Lowell tear up a little.

Oh, I ran into Coach Roberts this week and he asked for your address. Have you heard from him yet? He said he tries to write at least one letter to all the boys he has had in sports. That's really nice of him, don't you think? Well it is getting late and Dad is expecting me at the yard early, so I will close for now.

I will love you forever and ever.

Your loving wife,

Helen

He then opened the package from Helen. It consisted of another picture of her with the twins, some very stale and broken cookies, and a scarf. He smiled thinking that they had gotten each other the same present. The package from his mom, which was pretty much the same except a handkerchief from Diane with an embroidered inscription: *To Lowell, I love you a lot*

This brought tears to his eyes as he thought about his little sister. The note said that she had made it in 4-H. This made him smile. The package also contained a sketched picture of a B-17 that wasn't bad from David. There was a note as well saying he had drawn it from a picture he saw in the post office. His folks wrote a nice note that included comments from both his father and mother, and finally there were the much-appreciated cookies, stale and broken but so good.

He opened the letter from Coach Roberts last.

Dear Lowell and Myron,

I can't believe that only a couple of years ago you guys were playing sports in high school. This war has caused a lot of changes in everyone's life. I ran into Helen Speer, oops I mean Andersen; you have to forgive me I still think of her as that beautiful high school girl.

As Lowell read that line it caused tears to well up in his eyes with the memory of her as a high school girl.

Anyway she said you guys were serving together and in fact in the same airplane crew so I thought I would kill two birds with one stone by writing one letter.

Lowell looked up and laughed at the reference to "killing two birds." Myron came around and looked over Low's shoulder to see what was so funny.

Lowell turned and said, "Back off Jew; you can read it when I'm through."

"Okay, okay!"

Lowell read on.

Well, our football season was not very good, not like when I had you boys on the team. We lost to Willamette 24 to 14, but beat Mitchell 13 to 7. Anytime we can beat them, it is a good season. The only other victory this season was over Fir Grove 21 to 6.

Basketball season is just getting started...

Lowell looked up at the date of the letter: November 30.

We have had a fairly good pre-season so far beating Lincoln of Portland 39 to 27 and Dallas 41 to 28. We had the district jamboree again which was fun, but with the gas shortage, only four teams showed up.

He went on to tell a little more about what was going on at school and then closed with a proper salutation.

Lowell tossed the letter over to Myron and lay back on his bed. It wasn't five minutes until he was fast asleep.

Later that night they checked the board and found out they were to fly the next day.

Lowell said, "Boy am I glad I got that little nap."

Myron responded with, "Little nap, man you were sawing logs like crazy!"

They laughed as they walked towards the mess hall for evening chow.

*****

Their tenth and eleventh missions were to hit railways, switchyards, bridges and anything that would prevent the Germans from reinforcing or sustaining their attack in the Ardennes. Lowell sensed he was much more relaxed than earlier. He hoped that he wasn't becoming complacent, a sure way to become careless, leading to disaster. There was the flak to contend with and that ever present threat of fighters. Now there was the appearance of the new ME-262, the first jet powered aircraft to fly; and of course the close formation in rough air, which always made the pilots tense.

After their eleventh, they again had a few days off because of weather. During this down time, Lowell and the rest of the pilots in the hut had to endure training in the Link, as well as other training such as evasion techniques if shot down, which reminded Lowell of Myron's situation. Walking out of one of the survival meetings he asked Jew if he had followed through on the recommendation about ID.

"Nah, I'll get around to it soon."

"Damn it Jew; they wouldn't have told you to do it if it wasn't important!"

"Yea, yea, I know. I'll do it!"

His friend's response angered Lowell, a rare occurrence. He reached over and punched him on the shoulder saying, "Do it!"

Myron looked at him and they smiled at each other with "that" look, which said *I love you*.

As Christmas approached, signs of the holiday began to appear around base. Crewmen decorated the mess hall when time permitted and several reminders appeared in the huts as well. On the night of December 23, they went over to the Officer's Club and saw the notice that they had a mission the next day.

Letting out a groan, Vince said, "I thought everyone would get a little time off for Christmas."

"Yea, what if we run into Santa and his sleigh?"

Lowell said, "Well, if Lieutenant Rothstein will keep us on course, I imagine they have planned to fly us around Santa's course."

"You just keep it straight and level and I'll get you there."

After a little pool and a beer or two, without Lowell partaking, they returned to their hut and bedded down. Lowell reached into his footlocker, took out the writing kit and wrote a short note to Helen telling what they had been doing. He found it more difficult to write positive things to her without going into the missions, which he had decided never to do.

The next morning was December 24, Christmas Eve; however, it was mission day, their twelfth. They rose at the usual time for breakfast chow and briefing. Entering the briefing hut, Lowell realized he was getting used to the routine. They hadn't flown a mission since the nineteenth and he had begun to relax a little, but upon entering the hut, all the anxiety came back.

The colonel climbed the stairs to the stage and greeted them, "Morning men."

The men responded with the usual, "Morning sir."

He wished them a merry Christmas and got right to the point.

"Today we are going to contribute to what is being called *The Battle of the Bulge*."

He then turned to the major and motioned to have the curtain drawn back. The ribbon extended well in to Germany to a place called Babenhousen.

Pointing to the map the colonel said, "We are hitting an airfield in this city where much of the Luftwaffe aircraft are based. When the weather breaks, we don't want their fighters to combine with the ground forces and possibly extend this offensive."

He then turned the briefing over to the weather and ordnance personnel. With the bombardiers and navigators released to attend their briefings, the pilots stayed for the information they would need, including the sheets of paper listing their take-off positions and placement in the formation. Lowell showed the information to Vern and they smiled, both savoring the moment of moving up in the formation, which demonstrated a trust in their ability.

The routine for getting to the *Grizzly's Roar* was the same and after the walk around with Sergeant Goldstein was completed, they boarded the plane and went through the cockpit check: engines started, gauges checked. Then they waited for the signal to taxi.

They made the climb out over the Buncher Beacon without mishap and as they reached the formation altitude Lowell suddenly became aware of his relaxed state. He recalled a warning given during training: *When missions become routine and you think everything will go okay, trouble can crop up and cause you problems.* Shrugging his shoulders, he took a tighter grip on the wheel. He called the crew and told the gunners to charge guns and test. He then admonished them to be careful where they shot. Bob Wright was now standing between him and Vern monitoring the gauges. He tapped Lowell on the shoulder, gave him the okay sign and returned to his position to test his guns.

The mission went on as planned. They hit the IP right on time, made their drop right on time and turned for home. Due to the cloudy weather, the flak was not overly heavy although they got a couple of pretty good jolts. Lowell could hear it hitting the plane and he called for reports on any damage or injury. Hearing none, he continued flying toward home.

Returning to Sulensborne, they landed and went through the routine of debriefing, turning in chutes and guns, and going to the mess hall to eat.

As they walked out of debriefing, Lowell asked, "Did you guys see any planes go down?"

Vince said, "No, but number 1951 was smoking quite a bit from the left outboard."

Lowell said, "I hope they didn't go down. Wouldn't it be terrible to be shot down on Christmas Eve."

On the way to the mess hall, they went by the mailroom and asked about mail. Lowell got two letters from Helen and one from his folks. Vern came out with a shoebox size package under his arm.

"What have you got there, Vern?"

"Well, it's a package from my coach's wife, you know the folks I lived with in high school."

Lowell responded with a nod of his head and Myron said, "I hope it's something to eat."

"Well it probably is. Mrs. Palmer is a very good cook."

When they entered the mess hall, they noticed that the cooks had decorated it with pine bows, some paper things that looked like Christmas Bells and had carols playing from a phonograph.

It made them feel good although as Jew noted, "I sure miss home today."

Vince said, "Did you celebrate Christmas back home?"

Lowell laughed out loud and Myron said, "Yea, being the only Jewish family in town, we had to with all those Swedes around, but we usually went to Portland to synagogue for our celebration."

Lowell said, "Yes, he had it both ways. He got both Hanukkah, and Christmas presents!"

"You know guys; he has never been able to tell the difference between a good Norwegian and one of those Swedish guys."

"By the way Low, what is the difference?"

It was Myron's turn to laugh as Lowell answered, "Don't tell anyone Vince, but only the 'son' and the 'sen' on the end."

As they got in line to pickup their trays and food, Myron said, "Don't believe him; there is a lot of difference."

CHRISTMAS 1944

The next day was Christmas. Lowell woke, looked out the window to bare brown earth with the rain falling in buckets and said to no one in particular, "Well, it's just like Oregon, another Christmas without snow."

Vince rolled over and said, "Good, back home we got very tired of having to shovel the walks Christmas day so the relatives could get to the house for Christmas dinner."

The squadron planned a big Christmas celebration for the children of Sulensborne and most of the crews volunteered to help prepare. They got up earlier than normal on a non-flying day, dressed, and then went over to the mess hall to decorate for the festivities. After breakfast, they asked the mess sergeant what they could do. The mess sergeant and his crew had already done much of the decorating but they still had more to do before the party. Because he was used to ordering the young officers around, he had no qualms about giving them directions.

After some time, he brought out plates of Christmas cookies he had fixed and said, "Help yourselves to some cookies and coffee men."

They thanked him and walked over to the table where the cookies were.

Lowell said, "I'll be darned, those are just like the ones my mom sent except these aren't in pieces."

"Yea, I remember them well; boy this reminds me of home," replied Jew.

They stood around reminiscing about home until the sergeant said, "All right gentlemen, I didn't mean for you to take all day eating cookies. The kids will start arriving in a couple of hours, so let's get at it."

There were about two-dozen men there to help and they pitched in to hang more streamers and wrap the small gifts to place under the tree for the children. Lorenzo had chosen that job and as Lowell came over with another arm full of small gifts, he noticed tears in his eyes. He looked up, saw Lowell and wiped his eyes.

"Sorry lieutenant. I guess I got a little home sick."

Putting his hand on Lorenzo's shoulder Lowell said, "I understand where you're coming from Zo. I got a little emotional when I opened the packages from my family."

Zo nodded and returned to his task.

The Christmas tree had been up for some time but several of the men added ornaments. Myron was up on a ladder hanging a streamer when the mess sergeant came up to him.

"Lieutenant Rothstein thanks for coming. I apologize for not having any Hanukkah decorations."

"That's okay Sarge. I'm used to it and don't mind."

When they had finished decorating, they stood back and admired their work. The mess sergeant came out, patted several of the men on their backs and complemented them on a job well done.

Myron said, "Boy I wish it was Christmas every day if he would be that friendly."

There were "Merry Christmases" being wished all around and everyone was in a good mood, unlike a normal day when they were usually sullen and quiet. Suddenly the door opened to a loud "HO, HO, HO" and they turned around to see someone enter wearing a Santa costume, or at least as close to one as he could get. He had a large bag over his shoulder and he walked around the room asking the men what they wanted for Christmas. All the men laughed and several, Myron included, played along with him.

Through the beard, Lowell recognized Sergeant Goldstein when he came up to Jew and said, "And what would you like for Christmas young man, or do you celebrate Christmas?"

Jew playing along said, "Santa, I would like to spend one night with my wife, and yes I celebrate Christmas, don't you?"

All the men laughed knowing both Myron and the sergeant were of the Jewish faith, but also knowing they were both characters.

The frivolity went on for awhile and then Santa said, "I must move along for I have many stops to make yet."

He again wished them Merry Christmas and after a few more HO, HO, HOs, left the mess hall. The laughter subsided as the room quieted and the men went into their own thoughts. The mess sergeant came out and asked for quiet. He announced that the busses had just left to go pick up the children and they would be back in about an hour or so. The men were free to go back to their huts but should be back before the kids arrived.

Just then, the door to the mess hall opened again and the colonel accompanied by the major and Captain Eagleston entered.

The colonel shouted, "Merry Christmas men."

They responded with a Merry Christmas as well. There were only a few places in the army that the men did not have to jump to attention when a superior officer entered. One was a church and another was the mess hall. The colonel went around the room shaking hands with the men.

When he came up to Lowell he said, "You're Andersen aren't you?"

Lowell, somewhat shocked that the colonel would know him answered weakly, "Yes sir."

"Well, keep up the good work Andersen."

He shook hands with the rest of the men at the table and made the rounds through the room before leaving.

After their departure, Jew said mockingly, "You're Andersen aren't you?"

Lowell kicked him under the table as the others at the table laughed.

"Boy thanks a lot Low; he knows you. Now we'll probably get every dirty job in the squadron," replied Vern.

They all knew that in the army, anonymity was the best protection.

As they walked back to the hut, Os said to Vern, "Boy, this makes me home sick, how about ya'll?"

"Yea," replied Vern. "And I didn't have much of a home."

Os said, "Really, where did ya'll live?"

"I spent many years in a home for orphans."

"Oh, I'm sorry."

Vern reached out, gave him one of those friendly man-to-man punches on the shoulder and said, "That's okay Os."

Lowell thought of the Vern he knew when he first joined the crew and the story of his life as told that day in Spokane.

Back in the hut, they sat around telling stories about Christmas back home. Sitting on his bunk thinking about home and Christmases he had celebrated, Lowell remembered one in particular when he was about twelve. The twins were babies and he woke to their cries. He jumped out of bed and ran down stairs and there was his brand new bicycle under the tree. He didn't even get dressed but grabbed the bike and started towards the front door.

His father said, "Where are you going Lowell?"

"I'm going to go ride my bike!"

"Well it's raining cats and dogs outside so get dressed first and you might say Merry Christmas to me and your mom."

Lowell smiled with the thought and Jew said, "Thinking about home?"

"Yea, about the year I got my bike."

"Yea, I remember, you rode down to my house and had to bring it up on the porch so it wouldn't get wet, remember?"

"Yea, you got yours the same year."

"Yea and we rode all over town. You were late for breakfast and your mom was really mad at both of us."

"What ever happened to yours?"

"Oh I don't know, I suppose I just threw it away."

"I fixed mine up and gave it to David."

Lowell laid back on his bunk. The next thing he knew, Vince was shaking him awake and said it was time to go to the mess hall to get ready for the party. Lowell got up and noticed that Jew was already gone.

"Where's Jew?"

"Oh he went to mail a letter."

When they returned to the mess hall, a phonograph was playing Christmas music, all the cooks were wearing Santa hats and the mess sergeant was greeting everyone with much more warmth than he usually displayed.

Jew was already there and Lowell walked over and asked, "What's up?"

"Oh nothing, we're just waiting for the kids to arrive. Sarge said they should be here any minute."

The colonel came in again and several men who were sitting jumped up.

He said, "Now look men, this is Christmas and we are here to give the children of Sulensborne a little Christmas cheer, so forget that sir stuff and let's devote the whole day to the kids."

The men all nodded and smiled their approval of what he said. Lowell noticed Zo, Wayne and Niggs sitting at one of the tables. He walked over and greeted them with Merry Christmas and they returned the greeting.

Lowell said, "You men all ready for the kids?"

Wayne asked, "Lieutenant, are all these kids orphans?"

"No, as I understand a lot of them have been brought from the cities where the major bombing is being carried out."

"Why would they do that?" asked Zo.

"I guess this is safer from the buzz bombs than staying in London."

A corporal came running into the room shouting, "They're here!"

The boys went outside where several big army buses were just pulling up in front.

The sergeant yelled, "Okay men, let's help them."

Lowell and the boys moved out to the first bus as the driver opened the door. Several dozen very wide and very small eyes were peering out of the windows. The driver came out first.

Bob Wright stepped into the bus and said, "Here, let me help you out."

He picked up the first child, a small girl, and handed her to Myron who put her down on the ground. She looked very scared and unsure about what to do. She didn't want to let go of Jew, who looked at her and then looked up at Lowell who was waiting to help another child.

He said, "I guess I've found my date for the party."

As the bus emptied, the older children started to come out without assistance. Lowell noticed a similar scene being acted out at all the buses lined up on Mess Hall Street. Lowell looked up and saw a little boy about eight or nine, come down the steps.

He immediately thought of David and he reached out, took the boy's hand and said, "My name is Lowell, what's yours?"

He answered, "Andrew."

"Well come on Andrew; let's go inside out of this rain."

As he turned to go, he noticed Zo holding a little girl's hand and talking to a very attractive young woman whom he thought must be one of the staff from the orphanage. They went inside and Lowell got quite a thrill looking at all the children's eyes widen when they saw all the decorations, food and presents. He could hardly keep his composure he was so overwhelmed with emotion. The colonel was standing by the door greeting all the children. He seemed to be enjoying himself immensely. Lowell remembered someone saying he had two children about the ages of these at home.

Lowell looked around the room and spotted Jew and the little girl sitting at one of the tables.

"Come on Andrew, let's join this man; he is a friend of mine."

Andrew nodded his head and they walked over to Jew and the little girl.

He looked up and said, "Low, I want you to meet Helen."

Lowell was shocked for a minute but said, "Well hello Helen; this is Andrew."

Myron reached out his hand to shake Andrew's, but he wouldn't let go of Lowell's.

The day was full of food, games, presents and a lot of companionship. Every once in awhile Lowell would look around the room. He noticed that Zo, the little girl and the young woman were still a threesome.

He finally walked over to them and Zo stood up and said, "Lieutenant, I would like to present Abigail, he indicated the little girl, and this is Margaret Hammond."

"Glad to meet you Abigail and you too Margaret; this is Andrew Jones."

They visited for a little while and then it was time to distribute the gifts. Santa Claus, or St. Nicholas, came in with a flurry and with the help of several men with green beanies on their heads began to pass out the presents. The children were very excited and it seemed to bring the more shy ones out of their shells. Finally, the day was over and the men took the children out to the waiting buses for the ride back to town. Lowell said goodbye to Andrew and Jew to Helen who clung to him and he had to lift her to the steps. When he turned around, Lowell noticed tears in his eyes, but said nothing because he was sure he was showing some tears as well.

As they turned to go back into the building and clean up, Lowell noticed Zo was still talking to the young woman, Margaret. He nudged Jew in the side and pointed.

Jew said, "Well look at that, Zo met a girl."

"Now don't go kidding him about it okay."

"Sure, sure."

Later, while they cleaned up the mess hall, Zo came over to Lowell and said, "Lieutenant, what do you think of Margaret?"

"Well, she is a very nice looking girl."

"Yea, I got her address and on my next pass, I'm going to look her up. She said she lives with her mother and an aunt in town and works at the children's shelter. Her father is in the RAF; he's a gunner on a Lancaster."

"Well that's just swell Zo; good luck."

After the party and clean up, Lowell was surprised at how tired he was. As they were walking back to their hut, he said, "Boy, I'm almost as tired as when we fly a mission."

Vern agreed, as did Vince and Os. When they had settled into their bunks again, Lowell reached into his footlocker and got out the writing kit.

My Dearest Wife,

Well, Merry Christmas darling. We had the day off today and entertained groups of children from the village. We helped decorate the mess hall earlier and it looked very much like Christmas although it is hard to get Christmas decorations like those at home here.

I'll bet you guys had quite a Christmas morning. You said you were going to go to the folk's house after you had Christmas with your family. I'll bet the twins are waiting patiently for you to bring their presents. I sent them each a little gift and I hope they arrived before today.

Darling, I wear the scarf all the time; it is really warm and fits right in to my uniform. Most of the pilots have scarves, but mine is the best.

Lowell went on talking about what was going on with him and the crew and closed with the usual.

To you give my life and love.
Your Husband,
Lowell

Home

With dinner over, Mr. and Mrs. Andersen, Helen and her folks were sitting around the fireplace sipping a class of Christmas cheer. The twins were playing with their new toys on the floor and they were listening to Christmas music on the radio. The mood was very mellow and everyone was at peace; however, thinking about Lowell and what he was doing tainted Helen's mellowness. He had written right after Thanksgiving that they were going to host a group of children from the village.

Mr. Andersen interrupted the mood by commenting to no one in particular, "Well, I hope this is the last Christmas we spend with a war going on."

His wife said, "Oh Ethan, why do you have to bring up the war?"

"Well I was just thinking about the offensive the Germans have mounted."

Mr. Speer said, "Yes I have thought the same thing. From the news you would have thought that we just about had it won."

"Oh Dad, I don't want to talk about it," replied Helen.

David looked up and said, "Are we going to the movies?"

Helen said, "Yes we are, but it's a little early."

"Are you going to call Betty dear," her mother asked.

"Yes, we decided we would go about 6:45."

"What's playing?"

"It's a comedy with Laurel and Hardy. I don't remember the name."

The room fell silent until interrupted by the phone. Both David and Diane jumped up.

Diane said, "It's my turn to answer it!"

Their mother said, "David, let your sister answer it. It is her turn."

Diane ran out in to the hall where the phone was located and they could hear her talking. In a few minutes she came in and told Helen it was Betty. After a short conversation, Helen came in and asked her dad if she could have the car, it was really raining. He said yes and she told the twins to get their coats on, they were supposed to pick up Betty in ten minutes.

The movie was quite funny and they all enjoyed it. Betty suggested they go by Smiths for a coke or something. Helen said she had eaten about all she could for one day but the twins begged and they decided to go.

Walking down the street to the ice cream parlor, Betty said, "What do you think the boys are doing today?"

"Well you know they wrote that they were giving a party for the children, so I guess they did. Of course, it is very early in the morning in England."

England

The orderly came in at 0400 as always and awoke the men for their mission. It was a maximum effort day, which required everyone. Lowell rolled out and groaned.

Jew said, "I've changed my mind, I don't think I want to go today."

Vince threw something at him as they all got out of bed. They dressed, walked slowly to the mess hall for breakfast, though after the meal yesterday, they weren't very hungry. The briefing hut was nearly full when they got there and joined the rest of the crews. When the colonel came in, they all jumped to their feet at the sound of ATTENTION, as usual. He greeted them and said he hoped everyone got what he wanted from Santa for Christmas.

Someone in the back shouted, "I didn't sir; I'm still here!"

That brought about a round of laughter from the group and a smile from the colonel.

"Well, remember men, at least we got to sleep in warm dry beds last night. Those poor guys in the Bulge slept in cold wet foxholes, if they slept at all."

He went on with a little more pep talk and then turned it over to Major Booker who ascended the stairs and motioned for the removal of the curtain. When it came down, a groan went around the room. Berlin!

The briefing continued with the usual procedures of dismissing the navigators, bombardiers, and other crew members for their individual briefings. The major continued with bomb load, course and the warning to keep a tight formation when approaching the target. After their dismissal, Lowell and Vern waited outside for the rest of the officers. The enlisted men had departed for the plane. Vince and Myron had to draw their guns and all of them their chutes.

The procedures at the *Grizzly's Roar* were the same. Lowell and Sergeant Goldstein did the walk around while the rest of the crew boarded the plane.

When he was finished Lowell turned to the sergeant, extended his hand and said, "We'll bring her back in one piece."

Sergeant Goldstein saluted and said, "I know you will sir."

The preflight check, the warm-up and take-off and the climb to formation altitude went on without a hitch. They headed out over the North Sea, tested their guns and received the warning from Lowell to keep their eyes open. They flew along for some time until they were close to the target and Lowell ordered helmets on as they were approaching flak country.

Shortly thereafter Myron's voice came on with "Nav to pilot, IP in twenty minutes."

"Roger Nav; you got that bombs?"

"Roger," replied Vince.

Suddenly Niggs shouted out on the intercom, "Sir, I see one of them funny airplanes!"

"Pilot to ball, make your report properly."

"It's one of the jets and he is really coming."

"Niggs, where is he!"

"At our six, low."

Lowell looked over at Vern who was already writing it down on the pad next to him. When he finished he looked out the right window for a time.

Suddenly he exclaimed, "Jesus Christ, there he goes."

Dave and Bob both shouted at the same time, "I see it too!"

"Well make notes you guys, so you can report it."

There was a lot of talk over the intercom until Lowell said, "Okay guys, that's enough. Clear the air."

The flak started in earnest as the plane shook and they could hear pieces of metal hitting the plane. Suddenly Zo called out, "They've hit one, and I think it's 1064."

Vern looked down at his ship placement sheet and said, "That's Ken's ship."

"Pilot to crew. Watch for chutes."

"Left waist to pilot, I don't think there will be any, the whole ship blew up and I think it knocked down another one."

Lowell and Vern looked straight forward thinking about another empty bunk in their hut.

Following the usual routine, Vince took over partial control of the ship, making slight adjustments to line up the Norden Bombsight on the target.

Toggling the bombs, he pronounced, "Bombs away!"

Lowell took over total control of the ship and began the turn for home. This was always one of the most dangerous parts of the mission. There were several hundred planes making a turn at once and of course, the flak was constant.

On this mission, everything went as planned as they flew out over the North Sea again.

Bob came up to the cockpit and asked, "Wasn't Ken in your hut."

"Yes."

They approached the base, received the landing instructions and Lowell brought the *Grizzly's Roar* down without a hitch. As he went to their parking place, he and Vern went through the shut down procedures.

Lowell spoke over the intercom, "Well men, that was number thirteen. It's behind us."

They had been all talking before Christmas that the first mission after the holiday would be their thirteenth.

The Interrogation was routine except for the report of the ME 262 and Ken's plane. Afterwards, the boys met for a meal and then headed back to the hut.

Lowell said, "I really hate to go back to the hut and see that empty bunk."

"Yea, I know what you mean," replied Myron.

*****

The fourteenth mission was somewhat of a milk run. The target was a small effort near the area where the Germans had broken through; a railroad-switching yard in Western Germany near Cologne. After debriefing, they went by the mailroom. Lowell received two letters from Helen in the mail that day. He opened the first one, dated December 19, and read it.

My Dearest Husband,

How are you darling? Everything is fine here except of course the weather that is typical Oregon December - rainy and cold. I hope you get or got my present OK. It was hard to pick out something you might need and want.

Your mom mailed a package the same day I did. I guess there is something in it from the twins; Diane was so excited to know if you liked it, so be sure and write her and let her know.

Lowell had a moment for guilt because he had not yet written a letter to the family thanking them for the gifts. Helen went on:

We have been very slow at the yard this month, but we are getting more and more building material in now. We see this as a signal that this war is drawing to a close. Oh, I hope so darling, I want you back so badly.

This surprised Lowell a little, Helen hardly ever wrote about anything of a depressing nature.

Betty and I still have lunch together a couple of times a week and take the twins roller- skating and to the movies when there is a good one playing. Betty and I don't usually skate; we decided we only did that to meet boys and we don't need to now. (ha ha)

I visit your folks every week and your mom seems very up-beat.

I will love you forever and ever.

Your loving wife,

Helen

The second letter was much the same with more Merry Christmas information, which made him very home sick. After reading it, he reached in his locker for his writing kit to write to the twins and his folks.

Dear Diane,

Hi squirt; how is school? I bet you're really doing well; you are the smartest one of us Andersens, but don't tell David I said that.

Boy, I really like that handkerchief, every time I have a runny nose I take it out and blow and read the message you embroidered on it and think of you.

He went on to tell a little about the Christmas party they had for the kids and then signed off:

Your loving brother,
Lowell

He then wrote a little note to David telling him he had the picture of the B-17 pasted up in his locker. Then a short note to his folks and by that time, he was so tired he couldn't do another. Though he wanted to write to Helen, he decided he would do it the next day, as they probably wouldn't fly.

Their fifteenth mission was longer but uneventful and after landing, Lowell came on the intercom and said, "Well men, we're half-way there, just fifteen more to go."

The interrogation went as usual with nothing outstanding to report. They found out later that only four planes failed to return, but one had diverted to Sweden with engine trouble on the inbound flight. There had been quite a point made to the men that they only went to neutral Sweden as a last resort, when they truly felt that they could not complete the mission or make a safe return to base. Of course, Myron had a lot to say about going to Sweden and being able to talk Swedish.

That night after chow and a good hot shower, Lowell and Myron went to the Officers Club for a beer. None of the other men in the hut felt like going so the two went alone.

As they sat sipping their beer, Myron asked, "Low, do you think you and Helen will start a family as soon as you get home?"

"Well, we've talked about it in our letters, but I want to finish school first. How about you guys?"

"Betty wants to but I feel the same as you."

"You know, there has been a lot of talk about some kind of veteran's program that will pay for our college when we return; so I guess money may not be a problem."

"Yea, I read something about that in *Stars and Stripes*," replied Jew.

Lowell asked, "Do you think you will go to Emmons when you get out?"

"I don't know, maybe Oregon. I would like to look into business or law maybe."

"You mean you would go to the 'duck' school? The University of Oregon?"

"Well, that's better than Oregon State College, the 'beaver' school."

"Yea, I guess. I think I would like to maybe go back to Emmons for awhile and then maybe look into architecture."

They finished their beers and Jew said, "I'm going back to the hut; I'm really beat."

"Me too."

However, when they got back to the hut, Lowell took out his writing kit.

My Dearest Wife,

Well, we finished our fifteenth today, just fifteen more to go and we're done. I wonder if the war will last long enough for us to get in that many more. Jew and I were at the Officers Club tonight talking about when we get home. Did you know he was thinking about business or law at U of O? It was a surprise to me. I guess I surprised him a little when I said I would like to look in to architecture. I have told you that haven't I?

The weather is very poor this time of year so we are only flying every five or six days, which suits me just fine. I sure have a good crew; Bob Wright, our engineer, is one heck of a swell guy. He really knows B-17s. I'm glad I've got him.

Well, how are things going back home? I suppose the twins, especially David, has already broken some of his Christmas toys. He usually breaks at least one on Christmas morning. I sure miss those little devils.

Lowell went on to tell about several new men in the squadron and more about the weather. He asked Helen to send some more cookies as all the men loved them. Then he closed:

To you I give my life and love.
Your Husband,
Lowell.

*****

On the sixteenth mission, deep into Germany, the *Grizzly's Roar* took several hard hits from flak. There were no other sightings of the jet fighter, but the flak was bad enough. Zo received a slight cut on his left leg from a piece of shrapnel that came through the side, though it was not serious enough to warrant anything but a band-aid. All the crew kidded him about it but he just shrugged it off.

Wayne said, "Yea, if it had been a little higher maybe I would have had to take over that girl in Sulensborne."

The crew all laughed as Zo slugged him on the shoulder. Lowell smiled at the joke, but mostly smiled with pleasure to see how the crew had come together. The weather again closed in, but the good news was that the infantry had broken the German's offensive and were beginning to push them back slightly. The weather had given the Army Air Corps a few good days. They had resupplied the troops, raising hell with the German support system and much of their front line. One incident occurred when a flight of P-47 *Thunderbolts* caught a group of German tanks in the open and destroyed or disabled over fifty of them.

The door of the hut opened and the mail sergeant came in announcing mail call. All the men sat up as he walked down the aisle calling out names and sailing the envelopes to the men sitting on their bunks. Lowell got three letters, two from Helen and one thick one from his mom, which he assumed included two from the twins.

The first from Helen described a New Year's party thrown by several of the girls whose husbands or boyfriends were away at the war.

It was fun, almost like those slumber parties we had in high school. Oh, I guess you don't know what they were like. Anyway, we sat around, talked about old times, mostly high school and, shared the latest news about our men. There were also several occasions when we had a good cry.

Did you know that Robert Carson died in the Pacific? He was in the navy and something called a Kamikaze hit his ship. What ever is a Kamikaze?

Lowell rose up, looked at Jew and said, "Hey Jew, Helen just said Bob Carson was killed by one of those Kamikazes."

Jew skimmed down Betty's letter before he answered and then said, "Yes, here it is, Betty said the same thing."

"That's too bad, he was a nice guy."

"Yea, and sharp too."

Bob Carson was a year ahead of the boys and was editor of the school paper, worked on the year book staff, and was student body president their junior year. Lowell thought about Bob for a minute and remembered a time when they were in grade school. He was probably in the sixth grade and Bob the seventh and they had gotten into a fight on the way home. Bob was not much of a fighter, but being a year older, gave him all he wanted. He also remembered when he got home with a bloody nose and a torn shirt his mother forced the truth out of him and then walked him over to Bob's house to apologize to him and his mother. It was a hard lesson to learn, but he never fought again and he and Bob became sort of friends after that.

*****

After several days rest without a mission, the signal went up; they would fly the next day.

Looking at the board Myron said, "Well, I guess the war isn't over yet."

The call again came at 0430 with the announcement that morning chow would be in thirty minutes.

The men all moaned and Os said, "Boy I can hardly wait for that Spam and pancakes."

Jew responded, "I thought all you southern boys ate grits."

"Yea, before my friends and neighbors got me this job, but now I love all the food ya'll Yankees eat!"

All of them reluctantly got out of bed except Vern.

Lowell looked over at him and said, "Come on buddy, rise and shine."

Vern dragged himself out and sat on the edge for a minute. Lowell asked him if he was okay and he said he'd be fine. Breakfast as expected consisted of Spam, hotcakes and very strong black coffee, none of which Vern availed himself. Again, the men didn't drink a lot of coffee because of what happens at 30,000 feet to one's bladder.

The briefing pretty much followed the standard. Attention was called, the men jumped up as the colonel entered.

"At ease," he said. "Good morning men."

He requested the curtain's removal and the ribbon showed a mission to central Germany. The target was a railroad-switching yard. After the briefing, the men followed the usual routine of boarding the trucks, going to the Grizzly's Roar, doing the walk around, climbing aboard and waiting for the start up and take-off. Lowell noticed that Vern was not his usual talkative self and he asked if he was okay.

"Yea, I guess I'm just tired today."

"Yea, I guess we all are."

The take-off time came and the usual climb to formation altitude now routine to the crew. They formed up with the flight and headed out over the North Sea. Testing the guns, putting on oxygen masks and as they reached the enemy coast, donning the helmets felt routine. Of course, there was the flak to contend with. Several close bursts rocked the *Grizzly's Roar* as the crew heard pieces of shrapnel hitting the plane.

They completed their run and Vince reported that he thought they had hit the target. Lowell turned the plane and headed for the rendezvous point where the formation would again tighten up and set course for home. Lowell reminded the crew to keep their eyes open because if any fighters came up, it would be on the way out. He looked over at Vern and he was just sitting staring straight forward. He was too busy to ask, but wondered what was going on with him.

The flight home was customary, although because of several damaged ships some with wounded on board, the *Grizzly's Roar* had to fly the holding pattern before landing. After a routine interrogation, all of the crew except Vern went to the mess hall for a meal.

When he declined, Myron went over to Vern and said, "You okay buddy?"

"I'm fine, just really tired so I think I will go back to the hut and have a little rest."

Vince, Myron and Lowell watched Vern walk away and then Vince said, "Low, what do you think is wrong with Vern?"

"I don't know, but he sure is acting strange."

Jew said, "Well, let's go get something to eat."

After eating, the boys went back to their hut for a shower and a little rest. Vern was already in bed though not asleep. Lowell went over and asked if he was okay and he said, "Yea, I'm fine, just really tired, that's all."

The boys hung out for awhile and then went over to the Officer's Club for a beer before they turned in. Vern did get up and go with them but not for long.

Before they even finished their first beer he said, "You know guys, I think I will go back to the hut."

"Okay Vern; take it easy and we'll see you in awhile."

When they got back to the hut, Vern was fast asleep so no one tried to talk to him. Myron and Vince talked for a few more minutes and then turned in. Os, Larry and Tom were still out so the hut was quiet. Lowell reached into his footlocker, took out his writing kit and began.

My Dearest Wife,

Well, today we finished our seventeenth, over half the way finished. It was a very ordinary mission and we flew it just great. I hate to think this, but I feel I am getting used to them. The only concern was with Vern. He seems to be acting very strange. I don't think he feels very well. I hope he is not getting sick; he has become a very good co-pilot. All the guys like and depend on him.

We went into town early in the week and took food for the pastor. Gosh, I hope these people get along better after this war is over. They are sure nice. I think that after the war, it would be fun to come back here with you. I'd love to introduce you to some of the people we have met.

Zo is still seeing the girl he met at the Christmas party. I think it is getting very serious. She is a very nice girl and Zo seems to like her a lot. I haven't seen any of the kids we had at the party, but I guess they are okay.

Lowell went on to talk in generalities and then signed off with the usual.

To you I give my life and love.
Your Husband,
Lowell

The next morning, Vern said he thought he would skip breakfast that he wasn't feeling too well. Lowell told him he should probably check in to sick call, but Vern said he would be okay. He was just tired. When they returned from breakfast, where they had made plans to go in to town, Lowell checked on Vern and he was lying in his bunk shivering. He leaned down, put his hand on Vern's forehead and found it to be very warm.

"Okay buddy, you're going to sick call right now!"

"Yea, I guess you're right."

Vern slowly got out of bed, pulled on his clothes while still shivering and Lowell walked with him to the infirmary where he took his place in line after checking in with the medic at the desk. Most men hated sick call because some men who went there were slackers trying to get out of flying. Many of the medics looked on them in the same way.

When Lowell returned to the barracks, Jew and Vince were all ready to go to town. Jew said, "You'd better hurry, the bus leaves in fifteen minutes."

"Yes, I'll be ready."

Vince asked, "Is Vern alright?"

"Oh yea, but he sure has a flaming temperature."

The boys caught the bus and just sat silently for the twenty-minute ride into town. It wasn't much of a town; however the town's people always treated them with great respect and appreciation. It was located right in the middle of England's major farming area of East Anglia. The US built bases there because of the flat nature of the terrain. The Americans were not aware of what a hardship that presented to the British people because the troops had more than enough to eat at the base. Lowell always tried to sneak a little bread, or butter and sometimes sugar when he was going to town. He took this to the pastor with whom they had become quite friendly. Many of the boys did the same and in some of the mess halls, the mess sergeants would cast a blind eye to the practice.

After a few hours in town, the boys usually got bored with the warm beer and returned to base. At least they had some form of recreation on base. When the bus stopped at the Officers Club, Lowell said, "Let's go see how Vern is doing."

Entering the aid station and inquiring about Vern, the medic on duty told them of his transfer to the base hospital. They asked him what was wrong with Vern, but he couldn't tell them anything; they would have to ask the doctors. They hurried over to the hospital, asked to see Vernon Stewart and learned he was in the recovery ward. They asked what was wrong with him and received the same answer they had gotten at the aid station. After receiving directions, they proceeded down the hall until stopped at the door by an orderly who inquired as to the nature of their business.

When told what they wanted, the orderly looked at an admitting book and then said, "He has had an emergency appendectomy."

Lowell asked, "Can we see him?"

Referring to the admitting book, the orderly said, "You'll have to come back tomorrow after the doctor sees him again."

The next day Myron and Lowell went back to the base hospital again to try to see Vern.

The orderly looked at his chart and said, "Okay, but he is still pretty groggy."

Entering the ward, they asked the attendant which bed Lieutenant Stewart was in, and learned he was in number twelve. They proceeded down the aisle between the beds until they recognized Vern.

He looked up at them and said, "Do we have a mission today?"

Lowell answered, "I don't know, but you don't buddy. I don't think we could get a bed in the right seat."

Jew put in, "Course we could put one in the bomb bay and secure it to the first stick of bombs."

Vern laughed a little and then grabbed his side, "You bastard, don't make me laugh!"

Myron looked a little frightened and offered an apology.

"Damn, I hate to miss a mission; it'll put me behind and when you guys finish the thirty and go home, I'll still be here."

Lowell looked at Myron and made a facial gesture meaning, oh yea, we didn't think of that.

Lowell responded with, "Well maybe you can make them up in another crew."

At that time a nurse came by and said, "Okay lieutenants, it's time for another shot. You'll have to leave."

Lowell and Myron shook hands with Vern and walked up the aisle. They stopped at the bed of another pilot they knew who had taken some flak in the side on a previous mission. After a short visit, they walked out of the hospital.

"My God, I didn't ever think about that, where are we going to find a replacement for him?"

Lowell just shrugged and said, "Oh, they'll find someone. Damn, I sure don't look forward to flying with another co-pilot."

When they returned to their hut, Os said, "Oh Lowell, the orderly was in and ya'll's suppose to report to the orderly room."

"Oh thanks Os; did he say what it was all about?"

"No, he didn't."

Lowell walked out and turned towards the orderly room. He tried to guess what the call was about and as he reached the steps, he had decided it had to do with Vern being out of flying for awhile.

He entered and gave the corporal his name, "Lieutenant Andersen reporting as ordered."

The Corporal said, "Oh yes, lieutenant, have a seat. I'll tell the major you're here."

Lowell did as instructed. The orderly knocked and entered the major's office.

He heard the major say, "Okay, send him in."

The orderly came out and bid Lowell to enter. He did so with the proper military salute and report. The major told him to have a seat.

"Well lieutenant, I've been informed that Lieutenant Stewart is off flight status for awhile so you'll need a co-pilot."

"Yes sir, I do."

"Well I've assigned Lieutenant Marshall, Peter Marshall. He has just arrived as a replacement but seems to look okay."

"Can I meet him sir?"

"Yes, I've told the corporal to have him report. He should be here in a minute."

With that, the corporal knocked on the door again, stuck his head in and said, "Lieutenant Marshall, sir."

"Okay, send him in."

The door opened and a very young looking lieutenant entered and proceeded to report. He was about Lowell's height with blond curly hair. He had a little Errol Flynn mustache that many of the men in the squadron wore.

The major said, "Lieutenant, this is Lieutenant Andersen. You'll be flying right seat for him until his regular co-pilot gets out of the hospital."

Lowell stood and extended his hand to him and said, "Glad to meet you lieutenant."

"Okay men, if there isn't anything else, you are dismissed. I'm sure you will want to take a little while getting acquainted."

They left the major's office and out in the orderly room, Lowell said, "Lieutenant, why don't you come with me and I will introduce you to the rest of the crew."

"Okay sir."

"Hey, drop that sir stuff, we're both lieutenants."

Lieutenant Marshall looked somewhat embarrassed and said, "Sorry."

Lowell had called a crew meeting for 1000 hours to talk about Vern and what might happen. He didn't realize they would give him a replacement so soon. As they entered the hut for their meeting, the crew members were sitting around in various degrees of dress.
Myron looked over his shoulder when he heard the door open and yelled "ATTENTION!"

As Lowell led Lieutenant Marshall into the room, he said, "Knock it off Jew."

He and Pete walked up to the front of the room and he said, "Men, I would like you to meet Lieutenant Pete Marshall; he will be flying right seat until Vern recovers."

They all nodded hello but Lowell noticed the looks of skepticism on their faces. "Why don't you all introduce yourselves?"

They all looked at each other and Vince gave a little wave and said, "I'm Vince Bracketts, the bombardier."

Jew waved and said, "Myron Rothstein, navigator."

They all went around until the last man, Gabe who said, "Sergeant Miller, tail gunner."

Lieutenant Marshall responded with, "Glad to meet you all. I'll try to learn your names as soon as possible and I will do my best to fit in."

With that, the faces of the crew softened and Zo spoke up and said,

"Hell sir, none of us fit in this group of characters."

That brought laughter and a relaxing of tension. Lowell took the floor again.

"I don't know when our next mission is but I have scheduled a training run for tomorrow at 0900, weather permitting."

That brought a small moan from the crew, but nothing larger than that. Lowell dismissed them and asked Pete to walk out with him.

When they were out of earshot of the rest of the crew, Lowell said, "Pete, you are now a member of one of the best crews in the eighth. I know everyone thinks that, but we really believe it. And, I am glad to have you."

With that, he reached out and shook his hand again. Just then Myron came up and extended his hand as did Vince and Bob.

Pete looked a lot more at ease and Myron said, "Well, let's go over to the Officers Club and get better acquainted."

They found that Pete did not drink so he just had a coke, but sat down and talked with the boys. They found out he was from Indiana and had one year of college when he enlisted in the army. He, like Vern, wanted to be a fighter pilot, but there was more need in the multi-engine aircraft. He hoped someday to transfer to fighters. He said his dad died in an industrial accident when he was eight years old and his mom had worked hard to provide for him. He was an only child and had spent a great deal of his young life living with his grandparents.

As the afternoon wore on, the orderly room clerk came in and put up the MISSION TOMORROW sign to a chorus of boos and yells. He just smiled and gave back in kind.

Lowell said, "Well men, I guess we will have to postpone that practice mission and teach Pete here everything he needs to know on a real one."

They looked at Pete, wide eyed at the thought of flying his first real mission.

Myron patted him on the shoulder and said, "Don't worry Pete, except for take-offs, formation flying, bomb runs, and landings, Lowell here does everything else pretty good so you won't have much to do."

That caused everyone to laugh including Pete.

Vince said, "You've got to know, these two grew up together and Jew is always on Low's rear about something."

"Well, someone has to do it."

The boys got up laughing and Lowell said, "Well, we'll see you at briefing tomorrow."

Looking somewhat worried Pete asked, "What time should I get up to be ready on time?"

That brought a ripple of laughter and Vince said, "Oh don't worry about that lieutenant, someone will make sure you're up."

Home

Helen woke up before her mother called her and lay in bed thinking about Lowell and their future. She wondered how soon he would be home. *When will this terrible war be over so we can become a family?* With those thoughts, she wondered if Lowell would want to start a family as soon as he got home or would he want to wait. One of the girls she had known at Emmons told her that when her husband came home after completing all his missions, he was not the same. Helen hoped and prayed that Lowell would not have changed that much.

"Helen dear, are you up? Remember Dad needs you a little earlier today because it is payroll day!"

"Yes Mom, I'm up."

Helen dragged herself from the bed and walked over to the bathroom for her shower. She could never feel clean with a bath in the morning and preferred a shower, though a bath at night did help her sleep better. After showering she went downstairs and was at the table while she watched her mom busy herself in the kitchen. She thought about her life and her most prominent memory of her mother, in the kitchen.

"Mom, was Dad very different when he got home from World War One?"

Her Mom thought awhile and said, "Well dear, remember we weren't married yet, but I think he had matured a great deal if that's what you mean."

"One of the girls I knew at Emmons said her husband was quite different when he came home."

"Yes, I think we here at home have no idea what the boys are going through over there and we need to be patient with them when they get home."

"I think when Lowell comes home everything will be just fine."

"Remember dear, our life has been pretty much the same while theirs has been very different."

Helen thought about that for a minute. *I wonder what he will be like when he gets home. His letters always talk about how he looks forward to coming home and how happy we will be again. I sure hoped this war doesn't change him too much.*

EIGHTEENTH MISSION

Lowell finished a letter to Helen, and then turned in not knowing whether they would wake to a late breakfast or at 0430 for a mission. He lay in bed thinking about Helen, his folks and Drayville. He wondered how he would feel being back there after what he had gone through.

He looked over at Jew who was lying with his hands behind his head indicating he was not asleep yet.

"Jew, you asleep?"

"Na, just about though."

"What do you think it will be like to be home in Drayville again after this?"

There was a long pause and then he answered, "Oh, I don't know; I suppose we won't feel the same. Some of the guys I knew in Texas said people tend to treat you the same, but you don't feel the same at all."

"Yea, that's what I was thinking. I don't see how we could feel the same after what we have been doing for the past few months."

They both fell silent for a time and then Jew said, "Well, I guess we will have to just wait and see."

"Yea. Good night."

There was no response from Jew so Low turned over and in a few minutes he was asleep. At 0430, the duty sergeant came into the hut and turned on the lights.

"Okay sirs, rise and shine, breakfast in thirty minutes and briefing in one hour."

Os said, "I thought we weren't all flying today."

"Everyone is flying today sir. The weather cleared and there is a maximum effort on so better grab those socks sirs!"

Several of the men let out with a groan and somebody threw a shoe at the sergeant. They all lay there for awhile more considering the day ahead.

Lowell finally said, "Well, I guess that means we had better get up."

As the men rose from their bunks Vince said, "Ya know, when I get home if anyone wakes me at four thirty in the morning I think I will kill 'em."

They all dressed and left for the mess hall, encountering a typical English winter morning; wet, cold, and very hazy. Lowell wondered about their target and the role the weather would play. As they entered the mess hall their new co-pilot, Pete, joined them. Lowell nodded to him and asked him to sit with them during chow.

Jew said, "Well I guess someone woke you up okay."

Pete had a sheepish smile on his face and answered, "Yes, you were right."

They went through the line and received their pancakes, Spam and coffee. Finishing their meal, they departed the mess hall for the briefing hut. Entering the room, they found a row with four empty chairs and took them. Dave and his crew were sitting behind them and Os with his crew in the same row. As always, there was some talking amongst the men and a good share of laughter. Suddenly the call to ATTENION came. The men jumped to their feet as the colonel came into the building and up the center aisle to the stage.

Climbing the steps he gave them the usual greeting, "Good morning men."

After at ease was given, he gave them a little pep talk and motioned for the curtain to be removed. There was the typical low murmur of voices when they saw their target. Again, the tape stretched all the way to Berlin, the most heavily defended city in Germany.

Lowell thought, *Today I'm flying with an inexperienced co-pilot. Can I trust him enough to take the controls? I know he's experienced several practice flights, and from all reports he did quite well . . .*

The shuffle of the navigators and bombardiers leaving the hut for their briefing brought him back to reality. The weather officer was explaining that they should have good weather at 32,000 all the way to the target. Another officer discussed the expected resistance the men would encounter. Lowell heard him say that they could expect heavy antiaircraft fire, but very few fighters. It was some comfort to the crews, but not a great deal.

As usual after the briefing, the gunners, navigators and bombardiers went to the armory and drew their guns and ammunition. Lowell and the other pilots waited outside for them, and then they all boarded the trucks to the flight line. Pete asked a few questions about this process and Lowell answered as best he could.

When they got to the flight line, Sergeant Goldstein greeted them and Lowell introduced him to Pete.

Lowell said, "Everything ready Sarge?

"As ready as I can make it."

Walking over to Vince, Lowell asked, "Are all the bombs armed?"

Vince replied, "Just about."

Lowell and Sergeant Goldstein started their walk-around with Pete following along behind.

Lowell asked a few questions and then said, "Looks good Sarge."

Sergeant Goldstein nodded his head and said, "Your airplane now sir; take good care of it."

"You got it sergeant!"

They climbed aboard and Lowell picked up the headphones and mike. "Pilot to crew, every one aboard?"

There were several "rogers" and then Jew came on and said, "You know, I don't think I'll go today; let me off."

Lowell did not respond but realized Pete was looking over at him.

"Oh pay no attention to him lieutenant; he thinks he's a comedian."

Pete smiled and picked up the pre-flight instruction clipboard. Lowell looked over and was pleased that he remembered what to do. They started going down the checklist one item at a time. A recent experience depicted in a training film brought home the importance of the preflight check list. On a training flight, a new crew member forgot to release the control locks and they ran off the runway into a grove of trees killing the men in the nose of the plane. After the accident, there were several meetings on the subject of following the preflight check list procedures. The crews did not forget the lesson.

As Pete read off the items and Lowell answered "roger" the time finally came to start engines. The *Grizzly's Roar* was number twelve in the flight. Lowell consulted the sheet provided at the briefing to be sure he had the time of engines start and taxi correct.

After confirming, Lowell said, "Ready to start engines."

"Roger, starting engines. Clear on the right."

Pete opened his window and yelled, "Clear" to the ground crew.

Sergeant Goldstein was standing by with the fire extinguisher and Pete called out, "Clear."

Lowell pushed the start button and the usual high-pitched whine began.

"Contact!"

Pete leaned over and switched on the magneto for the right outboard.

"Magneto on!"

The engine fired once, letting out the expected big cloud of smoke as it sprang to life. They repeated the process until all four engines were running. Bob stood between Pete and Lowell carefully watching the gauges. He reported that all gauges were reporting a routine start. Lowell increased the throttles, the RPMs increased to a taxi level and then he backed them off. Again, Bob reported everything was normal as Lowell backed off the engines to idle speed.

When it was time to taxi to the main runway for take-off, Lowell increased the power and released the brakes. The take-off was without incident and they climbed over the Buncher Beacon until they reached the prescribed altitude and joined the formation. On this mission, the *Grizzly's Roar* was in the middle element.

As they flew out over the North Sea, Lowell gave the gunners permission to test guns. The chatter of twelve 50-caliber machine guns caused a vibration throughout the plane. The gunners reported that all guns were firing properly and Lowell acknowledged their reports.

After some time they began to see flak bursts. Lowell spoke to the crew over the intercom.

"Pilot to crew, black spots in the sky, let's all put on those helmets."

They only wore the steel helmets, or steel pots as most of the men referred to them, when they were in danger of getting flak inside the plane. The helmets provided some protection from the small pieces of metal thrown from the exploding shells.

They flew on until Jew announced the IP and Vince switched on the Norden Bombsight. As they approached the target, they followed the procedures for dropping their load.

Vince called out, "Bombs away!"

The aircraft surged upward with the lightening of the load. Lowell took full control of the plane and flew on for the prescribed time until the turn for home.

The flak was heavier than usual. A few minutes after making the turn, a huge explosion rocked the *Grizzly's Roar* and stunned Lowell for a few seconds. He felt something hitting his helmet and small items hitting him in the neck that felt like small bee stings. When he regained his senses, he looked over at Pete.

He saw a gapping hole in the side of the ship and Pete slumped over in his seat. The plane was beginning to fall off on the right wing and loose altitude. Lowell reacted immediately by applying left rudder and rotating the controls to the left.

He called on the intercom, "We've been hit! Is everyone okay?"

He heard the crew respond "rogers" and Lowell said, "Jew, get up here, Pete's been hit!"

The small door between the pilot's compartment and the nose flew open and Myron's head came up. He looked around the cockpit and when he saw Pete, he disconnected his oxygen and headphones and climbed up in the cockpit.

Picking up the portable oxygen bottle from behind the seat, he plugged into the intercom and asked, "What in the hell happened?"

Lowell responded with, "We took a near direct hit!"

Vince then stuck his head up through the hatch and Lowell ordered him to come up and help.

"Jew, get Pete out of the seat and see if you can stop the bleeding," said Lowell.

The impact blew Pete's helmet off and his oxygen mask was hanging from the hose. Myron first replaced the mask on Pete's face and then examined the wound. He was bleeding profusely from a large gash in his neck. Myron did as instructed and began applying pressure on the wound to stop the bleeding.

Lowell said, "Vince, get in the seat and give me a hand."

As Vince climbed in the right seat, Lowell said, "Get on that left rudder and apply pressure or we're going to go into a spin."

Bob dropped down from his station and asked if he could be of any help. Lowell told him to stay at his station and if they needed him, he would call.

Vince and Lowell fought the controls and finally got the ship leveled out. Lowell looked at the altimeter and realized they had fallen nearly ten thousand feet. He called the crew and reminded them to keep their eyes out for enemy fighters although at this stage of the war, they were not the major threat. They flew on and Lowell told Vince he wanted to try to regain some altitude.

Dave McDonald's panicked voice came on the intercom with "Lieutenant, the right inboard looks like it has been torn loose and is on fire!"

Lowell looked out and there was heavy black smoke and flames coming from the cowling. "Bob, get down here, we have fire!"

Bob Wright was a very calm person and he approached all emergencies the same way. He came down, plugged into the intercom and oxygen and just as calmly reached over and pushed the extinguisher button. The fire and smoke visibly lessened, but did not go out.

"Dave, what does that inboard look like now?"

After a short pause he answered, "Sir, it is still burning and it seems to be hanging down like it's been torn loose."

Lowell thought for a minute about what to do and how much he wished Vern were with him. The thought made him feel guilty with Pete's condition as it was. He said to himself, think idiot think! Suddenly he remembered another lecture in training. They learned that when engine fires were not too severe, some times you could dive a plane and extinguish them. Lowell asked Bob if he thought they could dive it out. Bob replied it was worth a try.

Speaking into the intercom Lowell said, "Pilot to crew, we have a small fire in the right inboard and I am going to dive to try and put it out, so hang on."

"Okay Bob, keep your eye on the airspeed and altimeter and call them out every few seconds."

With that Lowell instructed Vince to keep his foot on the left rudder and push the controls forward. The ship went into a shallow dive and Bob begin to call out the speed and altitude.

"180, twenty-five thousand, - 195, twenty thousand, - 203, twenty thousand."

"Dave, can you see, is it still burning?"

"I still see smoke, but no flame!"

"215, eighteen thousand, - 223, seventeen thousand."

"Okay, I'm going to level out. Vince, help me. Grab the controls and pull back."

Vince complied and the *Grizzly's Roar* leveled out. Lowell stole a quick look out the right side and did not see any flame, but it was still smoking. By the time they got it leveled, they were down to less than fifteen thousand feet.

Both Lowell and Vince were sweating profusely from the strain. Lowell looked at Myron and asked about Pete and he reported that he had gotten the bleeding stopped. Lowell called the crew again and warned the gunners to keep a sharp eye out. The enemy loved to find wounded planes flying low. They made easy marks to add to their kill numbers.

Lowell said, "Men I don't know if we can make it back to base or not, I am going to try to climb, but she's very sluggish. We may have to bail out."

Myron said, "Low, I don't know if Pete will make it if we bail out. I've got the bleeding stopped but if I take my hand off, it will probably start again."

Lowell thought for a minute and then called Bob.

"Bob can you see anything that might prevent us from keep this plane in the air?"

There was a pause and then Lowell said again, "Bob do you copy?"

"Roger, the fire seems to be out, but I don't know the condition of the outboard."

"Dave, can you see the right outboard, what does it look like?"

"The fire seems to be out, but I see fuel trailing back from the wing."

Lowell thought about that for a minute and then asked, "How does that outboard engine gauge look Bob?"

Bob answered, "It looks like the oil pressure is dropping and the temp is rising."

"What does that mean?"

"Well it means the oil lines must be damaged."

Lowell thought for a minute and then made a decision.

"Pilot to crew, there is a very good chance that we will not make it back to base." He let that sink in, then said, "Lieutenant Marshall is unconscious and bleeding, we have the bleeding stopped but if we put him in a chute, he will never make it to the ground. We can't abandon the ship so I will stay with it and see if we can find a place to set it down. You all have to decide what to do. You can jump or stay with us. Give it some thought and then report."

Only a few seconds passed before Niggs responded, "Stay with you," followed by affirmative responses from the rest of the crew.

Lowell looked back at Jew who nodded his consent. Vince said, "You'll need help putting it down so I'll stay too."

Lowell nodded and settled back a little. He thought for a few minutes and remembered one of the lectures in training, which focused on lightening the ship if engine power was a problem.

"Pilot to crew, we've got to lighten the ship, so let's dump anything we don't need: guns, ammunition, tools. Niggs, get out of the ball we'll drop that too. Wayne, do you think there is any chance we could contact the base."

"I don't think so sir and besides we might tell the Germans what's going on."

"Yea you're right. Okay Vince, let's see if we can gain some altitude back. Gently pull back on the controls but don't let up on that right rudder."

The *Grizzly's Roar* started to climb but after a few feet, began to shudder and shake.

Lowell said, "That's not going to work. Let up Vince."

Bob, scanning the instruments said, "The left engines are beginning to heat up too. Probably that dangling engine is putting a strain on them."

They continued to lose altitude until they were down to 10,000 feet.

Lowell called, "Pilot to crew, you can take off your masks now. Through them out with the bottles."

They flew on in silence for a few minutes. Lowell looked back at Jew and Pete. Myron was looking down at him and trying to make him more comfortable. Vince was staring straight ahead and Bob focused on the instrument panel.

"Pilot to crew, look for any clear place where we might set down, no trees, and fairly flat. I don't think we will be able to lower the gear so it will have to be a belly landing. It looks like we have snow and that might help, but it also might hide something, so look carefully. Wayne, Jew is busy and can't get a fix on our location, can you try? Niggs, get up here into top turret and Gabe you get in the nose, watch for a landing spot. Everybody keep your eyes open."

After several minutes, Gabe called out, "Sir, I think I see a spot."

"Where? Give us a location."

"It's off the left side and it looks to be several miles ahead."

Zo called out then, "Yea, I see it; it looks big enough."

Lowell was straining to see the clearing but couldn't get high enough above the nose to see it.

"Where? Where is it? I can't see it!"

"About eleven o'clock sir," replied Gabe.

Looking just to the left front Lowell said, "Yea, I see it! It might do."

They flew on for a few minutes until Lowell got a clear sighting of the spot. It was fairly clear of trees with just a few small ones and did not look like there were any large boulders. He requested Gabe to look through the binoculars for boulders under the snow.

Gabe asked, "Where are the binoculars?"

Myron answered, "Hanging just behind my seat."

"Oh, I see em."

Several more minutes passed and Gabe called again, "I don't see anything that looks like a large boulder."

"Are there any ditches or large humps that you can see?"

A few more minutes passed which seemed like hours to Lowell.

"Damn it Gabe, do you see anything?"

"No, nothing except those small trees."

Lowell thought for a few minutes and told himself to relax. Bob put his hand on his shoulder and squeezed, which helped relax him some. If Bob thought he could do it, then he guessed he could.

"Pilot to crew, we're going to put this thing down. It will probably be rough, so find a place and sit down. Use anything you can for padding and hang on."

Lowell again became silent as he looked out the front at the open space. He calculated what he needed to do to line up properly for a straight on landing. As they approached, he noticed that the area was not level, but was on the side of a gentle slop. He wanted to land up hill rather than take a chance of becoming a toboggan and sliding into the trees.

"Alright, Vince, we're going to turn slightly to the right and then turn fairly quick to the left to line up. We want to land uphill. You got that?"

"Yea."

"Okay, when I tell you, turn the controls slightly to the right and let up a wee bit on the left rudder. Okay are you ready?"

"Yea."

"Turn the controls!"

The *Grizzly's Roar* began to turn to the right until Lowell was satisfied that they would be far enough below the opening to make the left turn for a straight in landing.

"Okay, straighten the controls and get back on that left rudder," ordered Lowell.

He looked out the left window until determining the aircraft was in position for making the approach correction.

He said, "Okay Vince, what we're going to do now is turn the controls to the left keeping pressure on the rudder. Bob, I will need you to get on the throttle controls and reduce power slightly so we can make a large turn to line up."

They both answered in the affirmative and Bob reached down for the left engine throttles.

He called out on the intercom, "How's it look Gabe? Are we lined up?"

"Yes, it looks like it's just fine."

"Okay, Gabe I'm going to start the turn soon. Keep me informed of how we are lined up and when you think we are straight, sing out and then get the hell out of the nose!"

"Roger."

"Okay, start the turn now."

Vince and Lowell turned the controls to the left and Bob reduced power allowing the control surfaces to over ride the pull of the two left engines. The plane began to turn to the left. Lowell was pushing so hard on the left pedal that he felt a cramp developing in his leg. The turn continued until Lowell couldn't see the area out the left window.

"How does it look Gabe?"

"Looks good lieutenant."

Just then Zo, in the top turret, said, "It looks great sir."

"Okay, when we clear the trees, you guys get out of those turrets and brace yourselves."

"Bob, when Gabe calls out that we are clear, cut the engines and switch them off. Now, begin to reduce power. Vince, when Gabe yells and Bob cuts the engines, pull back as far as you can on the controls."

Lowell could hear the engines begin to slow down as Gabe kept calling out until he yelled, "We're clear!"

Gabe scrambled out of the nose and climbed over Pete and Myron to the radio compartment where he could sit with his back to the forward bulkhead. Bob cut the engine switches killing the power and, hopefully, fire danger. Lowell and Vince jerked back on the controls causing the nose to rise slightly putting the tail on the ground first. When it hit, the front of the aircraft slammed to the ground and the whole plane bounced several feet in to the air. It then hit the ground again with a terrible crash and settled down, beginning to slide along the snow-covered ground. The dangling engine caught causing the plane to slue to the right. After several more yards, the *Grizzly's Roar* came to a stop bringing the boys back to the earth safely for the last time. The crew sat there for awhile catching their breath.

What am I going to tell Sergeant Goldstein? Lowell thought.

Jerking back to reality, he spoke into the intercom, "Okay, gather up anything you might need, coats, food, gloves, don't forget your escape kits and get out. Make for those trees on the right and gather there!"

Jew looked up and with that impish smile said, "Happy birthday Low, and welcome to Germany."

Lowell had almost forgotten; this was his twenty-first birthday.

England

Vern lay in the bed listening to the planes coming back from the raid. He tried to count them but couldn't separate the number of aircraft from the constant roar of so many engines. He laid back and drifted off, though he was feeling so much better than when Low and the crew visited him right after the surgery.

He didn't know how long he had slept but he suddenly woke up to see Os, Larry and Tom standing over his bed. They were smiling down at him and when he opened his eyes.

Os said, "Well, ya'll look lots better today fella."

"Yea, I feel a lot better. Where's Low and Jew?"

The others looked at each other for a minute and then Larry said, "Vern, they didn't make it."

"What?" Vern tried to sit up but the pain in his side jerked him back to reality and he winced and fell back on the pillow.

"We were just turning away from the target when they were hit by flak."

"How many chutes?"

"Well," said Tom, "The ship didn't go down, they were able to maintain formation for awhile and then they began to lose altitude. We watched as long as we could and finally they were way below us and we lost sight of them."

"Did anyone else report in debriefing?"

"Yea, several crews saw them. The last report was that they looked like they were maintaining some control and possibly looking to set her down."

"That would be just like Low; never give up."

"Yea, he was good."

"What do you mean *WAS*? He still is good."

"Yea, you're right, you're right, you're right."

Vern lay back again and looked at the ceiling for a minute then said, "Thanks for coming by guys. Come back again."

They looked at each other and then turned to leave and Os said, "Vern, I'm sure they are okay. Lowell is a great pilot and if anyone can pull them through, he can."

Vern nodded and turned his head, and as the men left, he thought of those guys as the only family he had had for a long time and now they might be taken away from him. As tears welled up in his eyes he thought, *It just isn't fair. I should have been with them.*

On The Ground

Lowell, Vince, Bob and Myron managed to get Pete back through the bomb bay and out of the aircraft. While they were carrying him, Myron's hand slipped off the wound and he noticed that the blood had stopped squirting. He looked up and met Lowell's eyes for a minute and he shook his head in the negative. Myron thought the same; Pete was dead. Just outside the plane, the right wing had scraped most of the snow off the ground and they laid Pete down. Lowell removed his gloves and Pete's and tried to find a pulse but could not. Bob opened Pete's flight jacket and listened for a heartbeat for several minutes and then rose up and shook his head, Pete Marshall was dead.

Zo and Dave came back to the plane where the others were working over Pete.

Dave asked, "Is he okay?"

With his head bowed, Lowell said, "No, I think he is dead."

The others joined them, they all stood around Pete's body in silence for a minute.

Gabe, who was the most religious of any of the crew, said, "Sir, can I say a few words?"

Lowell hadn't thought of that. "Yes, sure. Please, go ahead Gabe."

The boys all removed their flight helmets and Gabe gave a short spiritual prayer asking the Lord to take Pete unto himself. At the Amen, Zo and Niggs crossed themselves as their good Catholic up bringing taught them. The words moved Lowell and he patted Gabe on the shoulder.

Myron nodded his head and said, "That was nice Gabe."

They stood there for a few more minutes and then as if something had suddenly occurred to him, Lowell jerked his head around and looked at Myron.

Myron gave him a questioning look and said, "What are you looking at."

"Did you do what the chaplin told you to do?"

Myron lowered his head and said no. "I didn't get around to it."

"Damn it Jew, why didn't you?"

Very defensively he said, "I just never got around to it."

Vince said, "You mean that thing about the ID?"

"Yea that's it."

They all looked around for minute and then Lowell turned to the rest of the crew and said, "A couple of weeks ago, the chaplain called all the Jewish men together and told them that the Germans are taking Jews out of the POW camps and sending them to slave labor camps. The chaplain told them to get themselves phony IDs without the Jewish name on them."

All the men looked at Myron and then Gabe said, "Sir, Lieutenant Marshall is dead. Why don't you take his tags?"

Myron looked at him shaking his head and Lowell said, "That's a very good idea. Do it."

"I don't want to take his tags, what will I do with mine."

"Throw them away."

After several minutes of silence Niggs said, "Lieutenant, there's nothing wrong with it. I'm sure it's better than being taken to one of those forced labor camps we've heard about."

"Okay, it's settled then," said Lowell.

Kneeling beside Pete's body, Lowell gently removed his tags and the second lieutenant bars. He also searched all his pockets to be sure there was nothing else that could identify him. He rose and handed the tags and bars to Myron and said, "Okay from now on you're Second Lieutenant Peter Marshall. Start learning your new serial number,"

"What are we going to do with his body?"

There was another thoughtful pause.

Vince said, "Why don't we just put him back in the plane, the Germans are bound to find it eventually and give him a proper burial."

So, they lifted Pete's body back into the plane, closed the door and Lowell said, "Okay, let's get out of here."

As they made for the woods, Lowell walked up beside Myron and said, "It'll be okay Jew."

"Yea maybe, but I still don't feel good about this. What will they tell his family?"

"Well in talking to him yesterday, he said he had only one family member, his mother."

Myron nodded and continued to walk through the snow. Lowell put his arm around his best friend.

"Hey buddy, I don't want to lose you."

When they were deeper into the woods, Lowell called them together.

"Okay guys, we've all been through training on how to avoid capture if shot down, but that's in a classroom and we are here. I would like to hear what you all have to say."

Before anyone could answer, the snow began falling.

Gabe said, "Dang, it's snowing again."

Zo said, "Well you know, it will help to cover our tracks"

Lowell had never thought about that and what Zo said pleased him.

"Okay guys, you know that we were trained to move only at night and sleep in the day time," he said. "We need to move west and south because we know that is where our forces are moving. Does everyone have their compasses?"

They all nodded in agreement and Lowell added, "Okay, the first thing we need to do is get as far away from the plane as possible, so let's get going."

"Myron, I mean 'Pete', what was our position when we were hit?"

"Well, we had just made the turn north, so I suppose we were only a few miles north of Berlin. We must have flown another fifty miles before we came down. That would put us close to Wettenberg."

"Okay, we don't want to go near any large towns, so I suggest we swing more westerly. Are there any other large towns around there Myr– I mean 'Pete'?"

'Pete' looked at him with some disquiet on his face and answered, "There are a lot of towns in Germany, but I don't think any very large ones."

"Okay guys, let's get going. We'll travel on a heading of say, what 'Pete', 270 degrees?"

"Yea, that should do it; I guess."

"What about moving in the day time, is that a problem?"

"Well, if we stay in the trees, I don't think they can see us. What do you guys think?"

After a moment Niggs said, "I think YOU need to make the decision; we trust you Low."

Lowell was overwhelmed with that comment and almost teared up with emotion.

"Fine, but I want input at anytime. I don't care if you have stripes on your sleeve or bars on your shoulders, I will consider every idea and we will follow the best. Remember, we no longer have a navigator named Lieutenant Rothstein, we have a co-pilot named Peter Marshall."

They all nodded and then Lowell said, "Okay, let's get on the move. Stay under the trees as much as possible and if anyone hears engines or talking don't yell out, make some kind of motion for everyone to get down and no smoking. They'll smell the smoke miles from here."

They walked for several hours and then Lowell said, "Let's take a break and have something to eat. Remember guys, we don't know how long we will be so don't wolf down your rations, they may have to sustain us for a long time."

They sat under trees where the snow was less and ate. Wayne asked, "Sir how far do you think we are from the American lines?"

Lowell looked at him and then said, "'Pete', can you answer that?"

'Pete' didn't respond until Vince elbowed him and said, "I think Low is talking to you."

"Oh, well by my calculations, but remember I'm just the co-pilot, I think we are several hundred miles yet."

Wayne turned again to Lowell, "Do you think we can make it out?"

Lowell sighed, looked up at the sky where snow was still falling and said with some frustration, "I don't know WE, I just don't know." He got up and walked a distance away.

The whole crew looked at him. They had never heard such desperation from their pilot.

'Pete' spoke up with, "Guys, you know I have known Low since we were in grade school and he has always known what to do. In high school he was the captain of both the football and basketball teams. He was the all-state catcher on the state all-star team and if anyone can lead us out of here Lowell Andersen can."

There was a moment's pause and then he added, "Even if he is a Swede."

That brought a round of laughter for the first time from the crew since they had taken off on this mission. They were well aware of the running banter about Lowell's nationality. Lowell turned around and looked, smiled with the realization that Jew must have said something funny and rejoined the group.

Lowell said, "Okay guys, let's get going, I think we can cover some ground even if it is daylight, I doubt that any airplanes will be up looking for us as long as we stay in the woods. We should be fine."

They made their way through the woods for several hours until it began to get dark. Lowell called a halt for a short break and a bit of food. By the time they had finished, it was almost totally dark.

"Okay men, listen up," Lowell said. "I want one man in the lead a few yards ahead of the others to give warning of any hazards in our path or any signs of civilization. Who'll be first"?

Dave spoke up, "I will, I'm used to being lost in the woods."

That brought a few more snickers from the men as he got up and walked into the dark.

"Good, be sure you keep an eye on the compass. If you need more light, we will form a shelter and strike a match or something," said Lowell. "Okay men, let's form a single file and stay in sight of the man in front of you. If you lose sight of the man in front of you, call out, in a hushed voice of course."

With that he got up, signaled Dave to take the lead and said he would be tail end Charlie. Jew thought that was just like him, taking the responsibility for all the crew.

They stumbled through the woods for several hours. Lowell had no idea what time it was as he had lost all track of how long they had been walking. His biggest concern was that one of the men might stumble and get injured or worse yet, get off the trail and lead part of the crew astray. The snow had let up a bit, but there was no moon to guide them. He thought by the way he felt that it was time for a break so he whispered to Gabe, who was walking just ahead of him to pass the word up to stop for a few minutes.

As he entered the circle of men he counted to be sure everyone was there. No one talked or smoked as per Lowell's instructions. He remembered his days of hunting when you could smell cigarette smoke for a surprising distance.

"We've been walking for nearly nine hours and I figure we're at least twenty to twenty-five miles from the plane, what do you guys think?" Lowell asked.

'Pete' said, "Yea, I don't think you're far off Low. We must be walking about three miles an hour."

After a few minutes, Lowell whispered, "Okay, who wants to lead?"

Vince got up and said, "I'll lead for awhile."

"Good. Okay. Let's move out and don't forget to keep an eye on the man in front of you and if you lose sight, tell the person behind you before you speed up."

Again they trudged through the snow-covered forest for some time. Lowell wondered if they were in one of those famous German forests that they had studied about in school. He thought about home and Helen, *I wonder what she's doing and how she will take the news I've been shot down. How long will it take the army to notify her and my folks*?

A whispered message passed back from Gabe jerked him out of his thoughts back to reality. He asked Gabe to repeat and he said, "Lieutenant Bracketts wants you up front."

Lowell made his way to the head of the column where 'Pete', Vince and Bob were kneeling down behind a pile of old tree limbs. He said, "What's up guys?"

"We've come to a clearing and it is 0500, said Vince. "Dawn should be breaking soon and I spotted what looks like a deserted shack at the edge of the woods."

"Let's have a look."

Lowell crawled out from behind the limb pile and walked bent over to the next row of trees along the edge of the clearing. He could not make out the building until Vince came up beside him and pointed.

Lowell thought for a minute and said, "That might be a good place to hole up for the day, can you see how big this clearing is?"

"No, but it is far enough across that we can't see any trees on the other side."

'Pete' came up and said, "What gives?"

"Vince spotted a building out there in the clearing and it looks abandoned. We thought it might be a good place to spend the day."

"Where is it?"

Vince pointed in the direction and 'Pete' said, "Oh yea, I see it. What do you suppose it is?"

"Well from the stories we used to read about this part of the world, it could be a herder's shack, or hay storage."

"That sounds good, why don't we go have a look?"

"Okay, Jew you stay here in sight and Vince and I will crawl up and have a look."

'Pete' caught on that Low had violated his own rule about his name but said nothing. Vince and Lowell walked in the tree line until they were even with the shack and then bent over to a near crawl and approached the building. When they got to it they sat down with their backs against the outside wall and listened for awhile. Hearing nothing, they made their way around to the door opening and peaked in.

Because of the lack of light, they could not tell much more. They entered cautiously and felt around until they had explored the entire space. It seemed to be a bare room with a dirt floor. There was a little straw on the floor, but the smell was almost overpowering. However, it was much warmer than outside.

Lowell asked, "What do think?"

"I think it beats the heck out of sleeping in the woods."

"Yea, me too. I wish I could see more and tell what is around here."

They walked back to the men and explained the situation.

Vince said, "It doesn't smell good, but it is dry and considerably warmer."

The men gave it some thought and then Zo said, "Heck, I'm used to the smell of cow manure; it will probably make me homesick. I vote we move in."

That brought a slight laugh from the rest of the crew as well as agreement with Zo's suggestion. So, the crew moved in and settled down. Lowell set up an hourly guard change and he took the first shift. The smell was bad but it didn't take the men long to ignore it and fall asleep.

As the day wore on, the shifts changed and everyone was getting some sleep.

Suddenly someone was shaking Lowell and whispering, "Lieutenant, I hear motors and voices."

Lowell took a minute to realize it was Gabe shaking him. "What's up Gabe?"

"I said I hear voices and motors."

Lowell jumped up and crawled over to the door. When he looked out, a huge wave of fear spread over him. Outside he could see two army trucks and solders dismounting not fifty yards from the shack. There was a road not noticed last night that ran directly through the clearing.

He jumped back and said, "Men, we're in trouble. We didn't notice a road just fifty yards or so from the shack. There are solders coming directly towards us with their weapons at the ready, I think we've had it."

"Can we make a run for it?"

"I wouldn't advise that, they are less than thirty yards away and I'm sure they could pick us off. I don't think we have any choice but to surrender. Be sure you have no incriminating information on you. Let's take out our 45s, hold them in a non-threatening way and don't give them any reason to start shooting. Sorry men, I guess I didn't do the right thing."

They all started talking at the same time scolding him for the statement. Soon they heard a voice speaking in very broken English.

"American, come on out with hands up!"

"We're coming out!"

"For you der var iss ofer."

CAPTURE

The Germans searched them and took their weapons. As they loaded onto the truck, Lowell noticed only older or very young men guarding them. They looked quite nervous and he hoped that none of the men would do anything foolish. The German guards climbed into the truck after what appeared an argument as to who was going to ride in the back with the prisoners and who got to ride in the warm cab. The older man won and climbed into the cab and the two young men got up in the back with the crew.

The truck started and Lowell said in a low voice, "Let's just keep still guys and don't do anything stupid. These kids look nervous enough to shoot first and asked questions later."

One of the boys yelled in German. Lowell interpreted the words to mean shut up, and he acted accordingly.

The Germans took the crew to a small town several miles from the area of their capture. As they moved down what looked like the main street, people stood on the sidewalks and just looked at them. The Americans had been told that many of the common citizens were quite hostile towards airmen for the bombing campaign, but these people showed no reaction at all. Perhaps it was because their town had not been bombed.

The truck pulled up in front of a stone building with one door and no visible windows. Lowell wondered if it was a jail. Speaking in broken English, the Germans told them to dismount and, as the solders kept their rifles at the ready, marched them inside. The inside looked as bleak as the outside; it was cold in both appearance and temperature.

Led through a door and down a short hall, the Germans ushered them into a small room with no windows. There were no furnishings; no place to sit except the cold floor.

'Pete' said, "Boy, I don't care much for their hotels in this town."

There was very little response to his humor as the men began to sit down. The room was so small that they had to interlace their legs just to sit.

Lowell said, "Is everyone okay?"

There were several yeas and okays.

"Well, I don't think this is anything permanent," Lowell added.

"How long do ya think we'll be here sir?" Dave asked.

"I have no idea, but we have to be ready for questioning somewhere along the way. You all remember our briefings about this sort of thing."

Lowell heard several affirmative responses and said, "Let's see if we can get a little rest and remember, don't do anything that might provoke them."

Gabe asked, "Like what sir?"

Before he could answer, Vince spoke up and said, "Well, you know, quick moves, moves that they might see as threatening."

Bob spoke then saying, "And don't reach inside your coats. They might think you are reaching for a gun or something."

After some minutes of silence Lowell asked, "Pete, how you doing?"

"I'm okay."

"Have you done your home work?"

"Yes, O7385263."

"Good."

During that first night of captivity the crew was very uncomfortable. They were hungry, scared, cold and trying to sleep on a rough cement floor. Lowell lay on the hard floor thinking about what he must do to keep the crew safe. He felt so overwhelmed by the situation that he wanted to just curl up and cry.

How will Helen and my folks react when notified about my status?

What will they tell Betty and Jew's parents? How long will we spend in prison before the war ends?

The thoughts tumbled through his mind, yet in spite of them, he fell asleep for about two hours.

Suddenly the door of the cell flew open striking Gabe on the shoulder. A guard entered with a large pot of something that smelled like heaven to the starving men. It was their first exposure to what would become one of the staples in camp, watery potato soup. He placed it on the floor along with some tin bowls. Though it was far from what any of them would call a meal, the boys dug in and finished the entire pot.

'Pete' said, "Boy, I don't know when I've eaten anything that was as awful, but tasted so good."

Several of the crew agreed.

Lowell asked, "Did any of you sleep?"

Several said they had and Zo added, "Yea I did, but for me who grew up sleeping on the floor of a bunk house half the time, this wasn't that bad."

As the other members of the crew good-naturedly chided Zo for his remark the door flew open and an officer entered. He motioned for the men to get up. They rose to their feet and the officer motioned them to follow him out of the room. Entering the hall, Lowell noticed two armed guards standing there who fell in behind the crew.

The officer led them through an outside door to a waiting truck parked along the curb. He told them to get in the back and the two guards climbed in after them. Unlike the open truck that first picked them up, this truck gave some protection from the cold with a canvas cover. The engine started, the truck pulled away from the curb proceeding down the street and out of town. They traveled for what seemed like hours before hearing other traffic noise.

Dave said, "I think we're coming into a city."

Several of the men stood up trying to look out through the canvas. The guards yelled so they sat down. Then they heard train noises.

Lowell said, "Sounds like a train station."

They all agreed as the truck suddenly stopped. The guards jumped down to the ground while motioning the crew to climb down and line up before herding them across several sets of tracks toward a railroad boxcar that sat on a siding. They opened the boxcar door, indicating that the crew should climb aboard. Once on board, Lowell found there was just enough light to see others in the car.

One of the men standing by the door said, "Welcome aboard the prison express men."

Lowell said, "You guys prisoners too?"

"Do you know where they're taking us?" asked Dave.

"Nah, they never tell us a thing," said the airman. "I don't think these guards know anyway. There isn't much room but find a place and have a seat."

Leaning forward he extended his hand to Lowell, "I'm Lieutenant Jack Copeland."

Just then they heard a huge bang and the car lurched backwards signaling they were being coupled to an engine. Lowell tried to look out the slot at the top of the car but he couldn't see much.

Lieutenant Copeland said, "We've been in this car for three days now and most of the time we're sitting on a siding somewhere."

"Have they fed you anything?" Lowell asked.

"Yea, thin potato soup and some very course bread."

"Yea, us too."

Several of the others close by stepped forward and introduced themselves.

Lowell asked, "Were you flying 17s?"

"Nah we're all mixed, I flew 51s; I don't know what these guys were flying."

"24s," replied one of the men from the dark. "I'm Jim Carson and this is Bob Prichard my co-pilot."

Prichard leaned over and shook hands just as three other men came up and introduced themselves. They were members of Lieutenant Carson's crew.

As his eyes adjusted to the dark, Lowell realized that the car was nearly full of men. His crew introduced themselves, but found it difficult to shake hands in the dark.

Vince asked, "I didn't think we had many twenty-fours left."

"Yea, we're out of Italy."

"Oh, you're from the fifteenth."

Dave asked, "When were you shot down?"

"Over a week ago, they've been running us all over Germany."

The train rumbled out of the town and into the open country. By this time it was almost dark, which explained why they spent so much time on sidings, the Germans did not move trains in daylight, there were too many Allied aircraft just looking for trains to destroy.

Lowell thought, *What a travesty it would be to be killed by one of our own planes.*

They traveled all night until they reached another town. As they pulled into the station, they were again shunted off to a siding. The men were given some more of that thin potato soup and bread. Asking if they could get out and stretch, they learned they'd only be there for a short while. Suddenly they heard sirens going off in the city. They tried to see out of the slot at the top, but couldn't.

Knowing that railroad yards were prime target for the Allied bombs caused panic among the men This came closer to home when they heard explosions coming nearer and nearer. Several of the men started banging on the door of the car and demanded to be let out. Lowell had never been so scared in his life. The explosions got louder and shook the car.

Finally a guard unlocked the boxcar door and slid it back. The men jumped down and ran away from the railroad station. Lowell noticed that the Germans were scared too.

Lieutenant Gibson yelled, "Come on guys, let's get the hell out of here!"

They all followed him across the tracks and to an open field beside the station. They found a slight depression in the ground and jumped in and lay down with their faces buried in the ground.

The raid went on for nearly fifteen minutes and then ended as suddenly as it began. The men began to look up and one or two of them rose to their knees. Lowell got up and looked around asking if everyone was okay.

'Pete' said, "Good lord is that what a raid is like on the ground?"

The guards rounded up the men and took them back to the railcar. As they entered it, a truck pulled up and several more airmen received instructions to climb into the car.

Lowell said, "How many more are they going to load in this car?"

"Oh, I don't think the Germans are too concerned about our comfort," said Lieutenant Copeland.

They spent most of the day at the station and as it began to get dark again, the engine hooked up and they were off. It got colder as the night wore on and the men were getting hungrier. It had been several hours since their last meal, if you could call thin soup and course bread a meal.

Zo said, "My God I'm hungry!"

Lowell responded, "I think we all are Zo. Don't think about it."

His response brought a smile to his face, it was what his mom used to tell him just before a meal was set on the table. He thought about the many times he turned up his nose at some of her offerings. He'd never do that again.

'Pete' sitting next to him leaned over and asked, "Low, have you thought about what the army will tell Betty and my folks?"

"Yes, I have and I suppose they'll just report that we're missing."

They both leaned back against the wall of the car and fell into their own thoughts.

Home

Helen was working at the desk in the office when the door opened and a man came in. She recognized him as one of the builders in the neighboring town.

"Hello Mr. Cooper. May I help you?"

"Yes, I don't suppose you have any two by sixes do you?"

"I think we do. How long and how many do you need?"

"I need eight footers, say about six."

"I'll go out and ask my dad. It will be just a minute."

Out in the yard, Helen asked, "Dad do we have any eight-foot two by sixes?"

"We only have a few," Mr. Speer responded.

"Okay Dad, thanks."

Returning to the office Helen noticed the man looking at the picture of Lowell she kept on her desk.

Hearing her come in he looked up, embarrassed, and asked, "Your boyfriend?"

"No, my husband. He's in England flying B-17s."

Mr. Cooper's face looked sad as he said, "Nice looking boy. I lost mine at Normandy."

This information hit Helen hard. She'd never met anyone who had actually lost a family member. After she completed the order for the lumber and Mr. Cooper left the office, Helen got up from the desk, went into the restroom and broke down. She could not seem to stop crying. She sobbed her heart out. She knew Lowell was okay, but talking to the customer seemed to bring out that nagging ever-present fear that was always there since Lowell entered the service.

After awhile she heard a knock on the door and her father asking, "Helen dear, are you okay?"

"Yes Dad, I'll be right out."

She wiped her eyes, washed her face and opened the door. Her father was standing there and took her in his arms.

"Go ahead dear, let it out," which brought out more sobs and she buried her face in his shoulders.

A short time later he said, "Why don't you go home; we're not very busy today."

"Oh that's okay Dad, having your shoulder has helped a lot. I don't know what came over me. Mr. Cooper was looking at Lowell's picture and told me he had lost a boy in the war. It just hit me, that's all."

"Well, I'm sure Lowell is just fine. It's almost noon, why don't you call Betty and go to lunch?"

Helen looked up at her dad and the panic was replaced with the very warm and loving feeling she had for her father.

"Okay Dad, I'll just finish this invoice and give her a call."

Germany

The train rumbled through the night. The guards had taken the airmen's watches so they could not determine the time of day. Lowell thought it must be morning. He moved his legs, trying to stretch a bit.

Niggs said, "You awake Lieutenant?"

"Yea, I guess."

"How long will it take for them to let our folks know we're shot down?"

"I don't know Nigel; I suppose several weeks. They will probably wait until they have enough information."

"Will they tell them we're just missing or that we're dead?"

"Oh I don't think they'll tell them we're dead. They usually don't do that until they have proof."

"Yea, I suppose."

"You have a large family at home Niggs?"

"You know us Catholics; we all have big families."

Lowell smiled at that and replied, "You have a girlfriend?"

"No, not really. There is this girl from school who lives down the street that I kind of like. We've been writing to each other. I think when I get home, I'm going to go see her and ask her to go out with me."

"That's a good idea Niggs."

They both fell silent listening to the rumble of the train. Lowell could hear someone in the car sobbing.

He thought, *Some of these men are probably just out of high school and not more than eighteen or nineteen. I feel old even though I've only been out of school for three years and I just "celebrated" my twenty-first birthday.*

The train slowed down as they entered another town.

Where are we? What's coming next? Lowell wondered.

When the train stopped, he heard voices yelling and truck motors revving up. The rest of the men began to stir, waking up and asking the same questions Lowell thought.

Finally a couple of guards pushed the boxcar door open and motioned for the men to get out. Confused, they complied. Lowell saw trucks lined up next to the train station. The guards motioned the airmen to climb aboard, providing them with a clue that maybe they had reached their destination. After getting into the back of the trucks, they departed. As they left the station, Lowell noticed a sign on the side of a building. It was probably the name of the town, but he had never heard of it.

The back of the trucks where the men sat had no canvass covering and wind was very chilling. They rode in the open trucks for some time huddling together for warmth, which helped a little.

Someone asked, "Do you think we're going to the prison camp?"

There wasn't any reply but Lowell figured it wasn't their final destination. He was correct. Arriving at a camp known as a Dulag Luft, the airmen off-loaded from the trucks and entered one of two large buildings connected by a covered passageway. Here, the guards ordered their prisoners to strip out of their flight clothing. The airmen were photographed, finger printed for prison ID and issued large coveralls.

After that ordeal, the guards led them through the passage way and placed them in individual cells. Lowell looked around as he was instructed to enter and caught 'Pete's' eye for moment. He had never seen such fear on his friend's face in all the years they had known each other.

The good news was that the individual cells were warm, very warm. At twelve-feet-long, five-feet-wide and twelve-feet-high, each cell provided a cot, a table, a chair and what looked like a button to summon the guards. There was a rusty metal pot on a little stand that Lowell realized served as a bathroom. He had never felt so depressed in his life.

He thought, *How long will I be here? What will happen to me and my men?*

Walking over and sitting on the edge of the cot, he discovered that the mattress was filled with something less than down, probably wood chips. After some time the door of his cell opened and a guard motioned for him to come.

Exiting his cell, Lowell followed the guard down the hall to a small room, entered and received instructions to sit. There was a desk and two chairs arranged one on either side. He sat on one of the chairs and waited. Some time later, the door opened and an officer entered with a note pad and pencil. He sat down and introduced himself as Lieutenant Munsenburg. The lieutenant sat down across from Lowell and began asking the questions Lowell had learned during his training about what happens in the case of capture.

"Where are you from lieutenant?"

Lowell answered in the prescribed fashion, "Second Lieutenant Lowell Andersen, O-76594392"

"Oh come on lieutenant, you can do better than that. I know your serial number and rank. What were you flying?"

"Second Lieutenant Lowell Andersen, O-76594392"

"What was your target when you were shot down?"

"Second Lieutenant Lowell Andersen, O-76594392"

This cat and mouse game went on for nearly thirty minutes and finally the lieutenant rose and said, "Well, that's all for today. Do you have any questions?"

Thinking for a minute Lowell said, "Sir, will I get my things back?"

"What things?"

"My clothes, watch and dog tags, personal items?"

"Oh yes, they will be returned to you in awhile."

With that the lieutenant turned and left the room. The guard stepped forward and motioned Lowell to leave the room. When he entered the hall, he caught sight of Vince being taken down the hall, probably for his interrogation.

Later as Lowell lay on his cot he thought, *Lieutenant Munsenburg speaks perfect English with a slight British accent. I wonder where he learned it.*

The door of his cell was opened again and a guard brought in food. It consisted of the small bowl of potato soup, some bread and a cup of coffee. The smell reminded Lowell of how hungry he was. The guard set the food on the table and left. Lowell eagerly went over and began to eat. The soup was very watery and the bread very hard and course. The coffee was ersatz made from something Lowell could only imagine. All that considered, the food tasted wonderful as it had been nearly eight hours since his last meal.

After several more interrogation sessions, Lowell found himself feeling a slight kinship with his interrogator. This was dangerous. He could not establish any trust with the German. He was the enemy. However, following one fairly short session Lowell asked him where he learned English.

Lieutenant Munsenburg looked at Lowell for a minute and said, "I attended university in England."

"Oh, what did you study?"

"Anthropology. Did you attend university?"

"Kind of, I went to a little local college in my home town."

Suddenly Lowell froze with the realization that he had given away some personnel information. The lieutenant looked at him, got up, turned and left the room. As the guard came in to get him, Lowell realized that the lieutenant did not pursue his mistake, which made him feel a little friendlier towards his enemy.

As Lowell entered his cell, he discovered his clothes and some of his personnel items stacked neatly on the table. Sorting through them he found his pictures of Helen and his family much to his relief, though the Germans kept his wallet. He immediately changed into his uniform and laid the coveralls on the table. Just as he finished changing the door opened and the guard brought in his meal. He picked up the coveralls, nodded to Lowell and left, locking the door behind him.

After a week of this routine, a guard entered his cell one day instructing Lowell to gather up his personal belongings and come with him. Lowell didn't have many personal items so it only took a minute to follow the guard's instruction. Once outside, he saw 'Pete', Vince and several of the other officers standing in a very loose formation and joined them.

"What's going on?"

Vince said, "I guess we're being transferred."

"Where is the rest of the crew?" Lowell asked.

'Pete' answered, "I guess they've separated us from the enlisted men. We may not see them again."

Lowell thought about that and felt terrible. He looked around, saw Lieutenant Munsenburg and raised his hand motioning him over.

The lieutenant approached and Lowell asked, "Sir, where are they taking the enlisted men?"

The lieutenant looked around as if to see if any of the other officers were watching and said, "They are going to a different camp."

Lowell looked at 'Pete' and Vince, who shrugged their shoulders. Lowell felt he no longer could watch out for his men and became very depressed. His crew were 'his' people and he felt very protective toward them.

The guards loaded the men into trucks for the trip to their permanent home. It was cold even though the trucks were covered. The road was rough and the bouncing made sleep impossible. Lowell, 'Pete' and Vince talked about their lives before the war, their ladies, and parents. Finally one of the officers looked out of the back of the truck and announced that the sun was coming up. All the men stirred slightly and several moved to the back to look out.

After what seemed like forever, the truck made a turn, slowed down, and the men in the back announced that they could see a camp. It was a large cleared area in the middle of a small forest. Buildings were lined up five to a row with many rows. A barbed wire fence divided the rows. Surrounding the entire camp was a much higher and stronger wire fence with guard towers every few feet and loops of barbed wire on top.

As the trucks pulled up to the main gate, the airmen heard other prisoners shouting questions.

"How's the war going?"

"Where you guys from?"

"Any news from the front?"

No one in the trucks responded. They were shocked by hearing the men yelling.

Prison Camp

Over two weeks since their capture, they finally learned that this was their permanent prison camp, Stalag Luft II, located in eastern Germany 100 Kilometers or approximately sixty miles south of Berlin. Off-loaded from the trucks, the guards marched the airmen through the gate into the camp's outer area. There were two sets of wire fencing. One fence surrounded several structures serving as administrative buildings. An inner fence surrounded the prisoners' quarters.

The new arrivals were very nervous as they stood in the road outside the commandant's office. They didn't know what would happen next. After a few minutes a German Luftwaffe colonel came out on the porch and greeted them in very good English; however, they were so worried that in later discussions none of them could remember what he had said.

The German's assigned the airmen to barracks. Lowell and 'Pete' found themselves in the same barracks but Vince was separated from them. The camp itself was divided into five, separate compounds. Officers occupied two of the compounds and enlisted men the other three. Learning that enlisted men were located in Compound D and officers in Compound B, Lowell hoped to find the rest of the crew at some point.

Entering their assigned barracks, Lowell was very glad to have 'Pete' with him. The building was not unlike barracks in the United States during the early part of training; the bunks were made of wood with no sign of springs and again the wood chip filled mattress was the only sign of comfort. A wave of depression swept over him. He saw cabinets against the wall for personal items, including the issue of rudimentary toilet articles consisting of razors, toothbrushes, soap, towels and a comb received from the Germans. As far as privacy was concerned, there was very little in a prisoner-of-war barracks. The windows had large crudely constructed shutters, closed at night to prevent light from providing Allied planes with direction.

A captain came out of one of the rooms introducing himself as Jack Folsom, the barracks commander. A fighter pilot, he didn't look much over eighteen years of age. He told them to find an empty bunk and move in.

"How many of you are there?"

Lowell responded, "Only three officers survived the landing, but all the enlisted men are here too."

Captain Folsom asked, "Have you received your toilet articles?"

"Yes, we have," said Lowell. "Our other officer hurt his shoulder during the landing. Are there any medical facilities in the camp?"

The captain laughed and said, "Sorry, yes we have a flight surgeon who was taking a joy ride when he was shot down. He's quite good, but he doesn't have much to work with. Didn't the Germans look at him when you were picked up?"

"Yes, just barely, they said he could have it fixed when we got to camp."

"That's what they say about everything; I'm sure Doc Kinnion can do something for him."

Lowell started to salute and then thought better of it and asked, "Sir, do we salute here?"

Folsom laughed and said, "Nah, unless you really want to. Get settled and when you're through, come on in for a little talk."

It didn't take Lowell and 'Pete' long to settle. After placing their small German-issued personal kits into a cabinet, they walked down the row of bunks to the captain's room. He stuck his head out of this door and asked them to come in. As they entered the room, the captain bid them to sit on his bunk. He explained about the routine of the barracks and the camp in general. He told them that they did their own cooking in the barracks when they got Red Cross packages with canned food, because they had a man who had been a professional chef in civilian life. They'd turned one of the small rooms at the end of the barracks into a kitchen.

"The commandant is an okay guy for a Kraut as long as the men behave themselves."

"What about mail sir?"

"The Red Cross man only comes about once a month or so. That's the only time we receive or send mail out."

After a little more explanation of the daily routine of camp, Captain

Folsom asked if there were any questions. Lowell looked at 'Pete' and both shrugged.

Then 'Pete' said, "Sir, would it be possible to see the camp commander, I mean the US commander?"

Folsom raised his hand and motioned them to follow him. He took them into the shower room and turned on several of the showers before continuing.

"We never know when one of the ferrets are under the barracks listening. Anytime we want to talk about anything we don't want them to hear, we come in here or go out for a walk around the fence. What did you need?"

The boys were very confused by this action but 'Pete' said, "Well, I would rather not say now, but will try to explain later."

"Well, I suppose you can, but he is usually very busy and I don't know how long it will be before you could see him."

"That's alright sir, I can wait."

Several days passed with the boys trying to learn the camp routine and trying to get used to the meager meals of what they called sawdust bread, a little sausage and the ever-present watery vegetable soup.

When they asked about the food the man across the aisle said, "Well, we aren't getting many parcels these days."

Lowell looked at 'Pete' with a perplexed expression on his face and saw that he also didn't understand. "What are parcels?"

"We receive parcels from International Red Cross every so often."

'Pete' asked, "What's in 'em?"

"Canned food, cigarettes, candy, shaving equipment, letter writing kits – –."

"Do you write letters home?"

"Yea, but we never know if they're sent or not."

Lowell asked, "Do you get mail?"

"Yea, but it takes several months. The last time I got a letter from home was just before Thanksgiving."

"How long have you been here?"

"Well, I was captured in July of forty-four but I've only been here in this camp since the first of January."

They heard a whistle blow which brought a moan from all the men.

Captain Folsom stepped out and said, "Okay boys, time for PT."

Lowell and 'Pete' looked at the man across the aisle and he said, "Our US commander thinks if we go out every day and exercise we have a better chance to survive."

They rose and Lowell extended his hand and said, "I'm Lowell Andersen and this is M– Pete Marshall."

"I'm Jim Slatery, sorry to meet ya."

It took Lowell a moment to understand, but he caught on.

After a few days, the boys began to learn the camp routine. The "appells" or roll calls, meant standing out in the weather for as much as an hour while they were counted. They also began learning the language and terminology of the camp. "Cooler" referred to a cell used for punishment. They called the guards "Goons," and "Ferrets" meant guards who were constantly on the alert for escape plots. They referred to themselves as "kreigies," which was a word taken from the German word for prison.

A couple of weeks passed. One day as they entered the barracks after their mandatory physical exercise, Captain Folsom opened his door and called for Lowell and 'Pete'. A full colonel, whom they recognized as the Allied Camp commandant was sitting at the desk. They immediately jumped to attention and saluted.

The colonel said, "Oh forget that! I'm Colonel Chandler," and beckoned them to follow him. He led them to the shower room and repeated the procedures used by Captain Folsom earlier.

"I understand you men wanted to see me."

"Sir, there's something we feel you should know," answered 'Pete'.

The colonel looked down at some notes he had and said, "Lieutenant Marshall isn't it?"

"Well, that's what we wanted to talk to you about. You see sir, I'm Jewish; my name is Rothstein. A couple of weeks ago, the chaplain in our unit called all us Jewish guys together and told us the Germans were taking Jewish men out of POW camps and sending them to slave labor camps and that we should consider taking false ID in case we were ever captured."

The colonel looked at Captain Folsom who nodded his head and he said, "Yes, we have had several of them removed from this camp in the past few months. Go on lieutenant."

"When we were hit Lieutenant Marshall was wounded severely and after we landed, we discovered he was dead. Well, I didn't obtain my new

ID before the mission. After we landed, Lieutenant Andersen here asked me if I had done what the chaplain suggested and I told him no. Well, he explained my situation to the crew and one guy suggested that I take Lieutenant Marshall's tags and throw mine away."

Lowell picked up the story at this point. "You see sir, we all thought about what the chaplain back at Sulensborne had told Myron, and we wanted him to do it. He wouldn't hear of it until he was sure Lieutenant Marshall was dead so we worked on him for awhile and could not revive him so Lieutenant Rothstein finally took his tags and ID."

Speaking to Myron, the colonel asked, "What did you do with your tags?"

"Well, we were free for a couple days and I threw them in a little stream we found."

The colonel got up and said, "I don't know how this will be reported to his family or to your family for that matter, but I think the fewer people who know about this the better. So, Lieutenant Rothstein will be Lieutenant Marshall while he's here."

Myron and Lowell thanked the colonel as he left and looked at Captain Folsom.

Shrugging, the captain said, "I think the colonel will make it okay."

As the boys left the shower room, Myron looked at Lowell and asked, "Do you think the colonel was upset about what I did?"

"I don't think so, why?"

"Well because I have been giving it a lot of thought and I have some serious doubts."

"What do you mean?"

"Well, what is the government going to tell Betty and my folks? And what about Marshall's folks? What will they tell them?"

"I guess we didn't think of everything when we encouraged you to do it, but it's too late now so let's make the best of it, okay?"

They returned to the barracks and Lowell went to his bunk and lay down; he began to think about Helen and his folks.

I wonder if they know yet. How will Helen take it? What will they go through knowing that I'm missing and maybe dead?

He knew that the army would list him as missing until they had proof of his death or capture. Then they would notify his folks and Helen about the nature of his status. He wanted to write home but would it be sent?

Home

For the past several weeks, Helen had been beside herself with concern. It had been over three weeks since she'd received a letter from Lowell. Betty was in a similar state as were the boys' parents. She decided to try not to worry about it too much though it was very hard. They were probably very busy; however, she had always received at least one letter every week.

Another week went by. The phone rang at work. It was Betty, who was very excited and wanted to meet. Betty told Helen that her mother had come to the shop with a telegram from the army. The telegram announced that Myron was listed as missing in action. Helen immediately went into her father's office with the news and asked if she could call home. Her father reminded her that her mother was playing bridge at the club that morning and told her to go to the telegraph office instead.

As she left the office, she encountered a man from the telegraph office entering the yard. He had an envelope in his hand. Helen felt her knees become weak and her breath came in short spurts.

He walked over to her and said, "Mrs. Andersen?"

Helen responded, "Yes?"

Handing her an envelope, he said, "This arrived for you."

Tearing it open, Helen read the telegram.

THE SECRETARY OF WAR DESIRES ME TO EXPRESS HIS DEEP REGRET THAT YOUR HUSBAND, SECOND LIEUTENANT LOWELL ANDERSEN HAS BEEN MISSING IN ACTION IN GERMANY SINCE FEBRUARY 23, 1945. IF FURTHER DETAILS OR OTHER INFORMATION ARE RECEIVED YOU WILL BE PROMPTLY NOTIFIED.

Signed by the adjutant general, the first sentence sent a wave of panic throughout her entire body; however, in its entirety the message lowered her anxiety one notch.

Helen thought, *At least it isn't the dreaded death message.*

Returning to her father's office, she showed him the telegram.

"Dad I need to go over to the Andersen's house and tell Lowell's mom."

"Perhaps you should take the telegram to the station first and tell his dad. He might want to go with you to tell his mom."

Her father was right.

After reading the message, Mr. Andersen said, "Hop in the car Helen. We'll go tell Mary together."

After informing Mrs. Andersen and having a little cry on her shoulder, they all sat down and the phone rang. It was Mrs. Rothstein. She and Lowell's mother talked for a few minutes.

Upon hanging up she said, "Betty got the same telegram. She and Gertrude are coming down. I suggested that she call Aaron and invite him to come as well."

"Good idea, how about Betty's parents?"

"Oh I didn't think about them," Mrs. Andersen confessed.

That afternoon saw the gathering of the Rothsteins, Miles and Speer families at the Andersen home. They discussed the meaning of *missing in action* and pondered whether it meant the boys were being held captive. They also wondered if the army *really* knew about their boys' status or if they would soon receive a worse message. It wasn't a happy gathering by any means, but it wasn't exactly sad either. After several weeks of not hearing anything from Lowell or Myron, at least the telegrams brought some news. The consensus was to wait and see.

By late afternoon, Mrs. Andersen suggested, "Why don't we all have dinner together?"

Mrs. Rothstein said, "I just finished peeling some potatoes and could bring some canned vegetables."

Mrs. Miles added, "I have some pork chops in the refrigerator if that would be okay."

She looked at Mrs. Rothstein who smiled and gave her a little hug. As if by magic, within a short time a buffet meal was laid out on the Andersen's dining room table consisting of small hamburger patties, pork chops, a bowl of mashed potatoes, a bowl of mixed canned fruit and a large platter of canned vegetables. There was the remainder of two pies, and a layer cake one of the ladies had left over. Of course, there was also a loaf of Mrs. Andersen's famous home baked bread and a basket of rolls.

At the announcement that dinner was ready, the twins jumped up and ran to the table.

"Please let the guests go first you two!" said Mr. Andersen.

David said, "But there's so many of them."

The adults laughed and Mrs. Miles told them to go ahead and fill their plates. The twins did not wholly understand what was going on. They only knew that some news had arrived about their big brother that was not really good news but not really bad either.

After they had eaten and began to talk about going home, Betty said to Helen, "Helen, let's go for a walk."

Looking at Betty with a very puzzled expression on her face, Helen said, "Okay."

The girls excused themselves and as they put on their coats and left, their mothers watched with concern.

Walking a short distance, Betty said, "Helen, I am really worried; just after Christmas I got a letter from Myron and he said the Jewish boys had been told to carry false ID because the Germans were taking them out of prison camps and putting them in slave labor camps."

Helen said, "Yes I know, Lowell mentioned it in a letter too, but he didn't know if Myron would tell you so he thought it best I not say anything to you. I'm very sorry."

"Oh, that's okay Helen. I was going to tell you anyway but I just couldn't face the fact that they might be shot down."

They walked awhile longer until it started to rain and they turned to walk back to the Andersen house.

Betty asked, "Do you think we should tell our folks?"

"Well, that's a difficult decision. I really don't think it is my place to tell anyone, but it's up to you."

"Yea, but with what the Rothsteins have gone through in this terrible war, I don't think they could face the fact that Myron might end up like their other family members. I don't think I will tell them."

"That's probably wise Betty," she reached out and put her arm around her friend's shoulder.

POW Camp

Lowell and 'Pete' kept very close to each other for the first few weeks until they got acquainted with some of the other prisoners in the barracks. There was one lieutenant from Tacoma, Washington with whom they became quite friendly. He'd played basketball at Western Washington State College and Lowell kind of remembered him from the Emmons and Western game. His name was Myron Garretson and as Lowell remembered, he played as a shooting forward on the team. They had several conversations about who had the best team although Lowell knew that Western had beaten them fifty-two to forty. Because of the name, Lowell had to be careful not to divulge anything about Jew. Sometimes when one of the hut mates called Myron, 'Pete' would look up until he realized they were talking to Garretson.

Lowell still didn't know for sure that his crew was in the enlisted men's compound. He had made several inquiries with the senior officers, but no satisfying response. One of the guys in the barracks suggested that he needed to earn their trust because, on occasion, the Germans planted English-speaking spies amongst them in an effort to gain information.

Daily routine was quite boring with appells each morning that consisted of a head count and a report accounting for all of the men, which usually took over an hour. The Germans were very methodical in their prisoner-of-war record keeping; however, during this activity the prisoners stood out in the cold. After appell, they ate a breakfast of sawdust bread, some very weak ersatz coffee and once in awhile some sausage, which was a very welcome addition even though they had no idea what it was made from. Lunch, or noon chow as the men called it, usually consisted of the thin potato soup with the ever-present sawdust bread and some vegetables once in awhile.

Lowell often thought of the German family who lived a block away from his home in Drayville. They'd invite them to dinner occasionally, and served marvelous meals and he wished these Germans would do the same.

In the boy's barracks with the chef they ate a little better when the Red Cross parcels came and there was also a little contraband food available. Several guards willingly exchanged American cigarettes for smuggled food. Quite often a group ate better than the rest of the camp through these means.

Not all was gloom and doom, however, as the boys discovered one day on their walk around the fence line. A strange event took place. From between the huts two guys appeared. They wore what looked like worker outfits and carried with them saws, hammers, a wheelbarrow and some kind of clipboard.

As they approached the main gate, a prisoner nearby whispered, "Don't look at them!"

Lowell could hardly keep a straight face as he realized they were prisoners in a daring escape. They went to the gate pointing at the board and talking as if they had some problem. One looked up and yelled in German to open the gate. The guards did and they walked through to freedom, albeit, short-lived. The Germans brought them back under guard three days later and they spent two weeks in solitary confinement.

*****

After several weeks in camp, the colonel sent for Lowell, who responded quickly.

"Lieutenant, let's go for a walk."

Important discussions took place on walks around the compound or in the shower room where the noise of the showers would drowned out their voices from prying ears.

As they started their walk, the colonel asked, "Lieutenant, do you know a Vernon Dickerson?"

Lowell was somewhat shocked and answered, "Why yes, I went to high school with a Vernon Dickerson."

"Well it seems that there is a Vernon Dickerson in the enlisted compound who thinks he knows you."

"Really?"

Continuing, the colonel said, "I've received a message from the enlisted men's compound and that this Vernon Dickerson has asked about you."

"Sir, how in the world would Vernon know I was here?"

"Oh there are ways. Isn't part of your crew in Compound D?"

"I don't know sir; I haven't been able to find out."

"Well, somebody over there knows you; this Dickerson found out somehow. Would you like to see him?"

"Why yes I would! Can it be arranged?"

"Yes it can. Be in my hut after lights out on Thursday and we will see, and remember, don't talk about this in your hut!"

"Sir, Lieutenant Marshall also went to high school with him, can I bring him along."

The colonel looked at him for a few minutes before asking, "Isn't that the fellow that – –?"

Lowell anticipated the colonel's meaning and said, "Yes sir, it is."

"Well, we'll have to get to this Dickerson and warn him somehow."

"What if I bring Lieutenant Marshall with me and he waits out of sight until I have a chance to talk to Vernon."

"That sounds okay. Do it."

Lowell felt somewhat perplexed about the whole situation as he left the colonel. Vernon was listed as missing in action before the boys left the States. Helen wrote that his mother said she'd received a message from the army that he was a prisoner of war, but the chances of them being in the same camp was way beyond reason. Even though as teens they didn't get along, he was excited about the opportunity to see him.

Then he thought, *What about Jew?*

When he got back to his hut, 'Pete' was lying on his bunk.

"'Pete', let's go for a little walk."

They went out side and joined the parade of men walking around the compound.

Lowell said, "Okay buddy, hold on to your hat. Vernon Dickerson is in Compound D and he has found out I'm here and wants to see me. Can you believe that?"

"Well I'll be damned."

"Now, the problem is you. What are we going to tell Vernon?"

"Well I would like to see him. Maybe we can meet outside and warn him."

"The colonel told me to be in his hut after lights out, so I don't think we can be outside."

"Yea, okay."

"Anyway, the colonel and I thought you could come to his hut and you could wait out of sight until I could explain it to Vern."

"Okay, that sounds like it'll work."

As Thursday approached, Lowell found that he was more and more anxious to see Vernon. He talked to Jew on their parades a lot and they reminisced about high school days.

There was a system of guides that moved men around the compound after dark. Lowell and 'Pete' were ready as the lights went out and the candles came on. The men had learned that to have any activity after 2000 hours they had to provide their own lighting and a thriving business in illegal candles sprang up. It was well known that the Germans knew about this; however, unless the prisoners set the barracks on fire, they didn't care.

Soon through a hidden entrance, an officer appeared and asked for Lowell.

"Here!"

The officer looked them over and provided a briefing about what to do and the route to take. They followed the guide out through the hidden entrance, waited under the building until the searchlight passed and sprung out running bent over to the next building. The procedure was repeated until they came to the colonel's building where they again entered through a hidden door. They came up into one of the small rooms reserved for high-ranking officers. The colonel greeted them with a finger to his lips and motioned for 'Pete' to stay put and bid Lowell to follow him.

They entered the shower room and Lowell noticed that all the showers were already running. The colonel told Lowell to keep his voice at a low level. Lowell looked across the dimly lighted room and saw a man standing.

He approached Lowell and said, "Low?"

"Vernon?"

Vernon stopped in front of Lowell and just stared at him. He reached out and shook his hand.

"God it's so good to see a familiar face."

"Yes, yes it is!"

As Lowell stepped up to Vernon he noticed how thin he was. He remembered Vernon as a fairly husky kid who weighed around 165 pounds in high school. He put his arms around him in a bear hug and they both laughed.

Vernon said, "Boy, I would never have guessed you would ever do that to me."

"It's okay, buddy. I have another surprise for you. Jew is with me."

"What?"

"I said Jew is with me, but we need to talk before he comes in."

Lowell explained the situation that Myron was in and Vern shook his head in understanding.

"Yea, they came in just last month and took two Jewish guys out of our hut."

Lowell motioned towards the door and Myron entered.

"God, I didn't think I would ever be glad to see you J– –."

Stopping mid-word, he looked at Lowell and Myron.

"'Pete'!"

Lowell asked Vernon, "How did you know I was here?"

"Oh a new guy, Bob Wright, moved into our barracks along with several other guys who said they were in your crew. We got to talking about where we were from and Bob said his pilot was from Drayville and I asked his name and boy was I surprised to find out it was you."

They stood and talked for nearly twenty minutes, Vernon told the story of being shot down and bailing out and Lowell and Myron told about their experiences.

Myron asked, "Did he say anything about me?"

"Ya know, that's a funny thing, he started to say something and then stopped and when I asked him what he was going to say, he just said, 'oh nothing' and that was it."

"Yea Bob is a great guy," replied Myron.

Vernon was a bit surprised to learn that Lowell and Helen were married, but congratulated him nevertheless. The colonel came in at that point.

"Well, we need to break this up. We've got to get Sergeant Dickerson back to his side."

Lowell asked, "Sir, will it be possible to meet with Vernon again?"

"No, I don't think so, but you could arrange for meetings during your parades around the wire."

They thought that would be fine and agreed on a time in two days.

"Vern, would you ask Bob to bring any of the crew with him?"

"Sure, the more the better. The Goons get suspicious if only a few guys are parading."

The next morning the prisoners woke to a fresh blanket of snow.

One of the guys looked out the window and said, "Boy that almost looks good."

The others just moaned. Lowell got up and looked out the window and commented on how deep it looked.

A lieutenant from Ohio asked, "Have you ever seen snow before?"

Lowell replied, "Yes, but we only get a few inches and it's usually gone by the end of the day."

They all laughed and then Lowell remembered they'd arranged meet Vernon on the walk around and wondered if the snow would affect their plans. Captain Folsom came out of his room and looked at Lowell and motioned him to the shower room.

They turned on several showers and then the captain said, "I don't think this is a very good day to meet your friend."

"Yea, I guess not. Will someone let him know?"

"Most of the men will stay in on a day like this so I don't think that will be a problem."

*****

The days became endless and food became an obsession with all the men. As the war dragged on the food supply became shorter and shorter in Germany and the German army barely had enough to feed the troops. Red Cross packages became increasingly important to the prisoners. At times the prisoners gave some of the friendlier guards food for their families. There was one guard in particular that all the men seemed to like a lot. His name was Werner Schoker. He spoke flawless English and one day Lowell asked him where he learned to speak so well. He looked at Lowell and asked if he had ever heard of a little town in New York called Hamondburg. Lowell said he hadn't and asked why.

"Well lieutenant, I was born there and lived there for most of my life."

"How did you get in the German army?"

"When that bastard Hitler called all loyal Germans to return to the Fatherland, my father did. Things were not going too well in the States with the depression and all, so my folks decided to come back."

"How old were you?"

"I was fifteen, just starting high school and was playing on the football team and of course we didn't have football as we knew it in Germany. I could never catch on to that soccer."

"How did you end up guarding us?"

"Well, I was on the Russian front and got badly wounded so when I got out of the hospital, they sent me here."

An officer came around the corner of the huts and Werner said, "I better go."

Lowell wondered what would happen to him and if there was any way to put in a good word for him. He thought he would ask the colonel about it. He knew from civics classes that any American citizen who served in an army of a country fighting against the US would have their citizenship revoked.

As time passed, the boys learned of some fun activities in camp, like the band that played instruments provided by the YMCA and held periodic concerts. A theater group also performed plays and hoops attached to the walls of some of the barracks provided basketball opportunities; however, the only balls available were actually soccer balls. When it snowed, outdoor activities were limited. Unfortunately, as the boys learned, the greatest problem for POWs was boredom.

Lowell and 'Pete' set up a schedule with the enlisted crew and Vernon Dickerson to meet on their walk around. The first meeting of the entire crew brought great relief to Lowell. They scheduled a regular meeting across the wire every third day; they knew an everyday event would bring unwanted attention. As they walked around the fence on their respective sides, Lowell always asked about their welfare and how they were feeling.

They always answered in the same way, "Okay sir."

That was about all they could accomplish before they got to the corner of the compound. On the next circuit, they could continue their talk.

One particular day when Vernon was with them, Lowell asked, "Vern, do you remember that game we played against Grant from Portland?"

"Vern responded immediately, "I sure do, I scored the winning basket. Do you remember?"

"Yea, I remember but do you remember who passed you the ball?"

"Ah, I don't think I do."

Lowell was taken aback with his response until he stole a glance across the wire and saw that Vernon was smiling.

"You dog, you do remember!"

At that point, Zo came in to the conversation with, "You guys must have been good friends in high school."

'Pete' laughed and said, "That's the most incorrect statement you could have made Zo!"

"Yea Zo," put in Vernon. "He stole my girl friend and worst of all, he married her."

Remembering how beautiful Helen was when he met her in Spokane, Wayne said, "Well, I think I would have tried to steal her too Vern."

As they turned the corner of the compound, everyone on both sides of the fence was laughing. Then, noticing the guard in the corner tower looking down at them, they went their separate ways.

As they walked along the outer fence, Lowell thought of what Wayne said about his beautiful Helen and one of the strongest waves of depression since he had been in captivity swept over him.

Home

It had been over a month since Helen and Betty received word that the boys were missing in action. One day, the phone rang on Helen's desk at the lumber yard.

Picking up the phone she heard her mother say, "Helen dear, a letter has arrived from the War Department."

A very cold feeling pass over her and she said, "Open it Mom and read it to me."

"I'd rather not dear. Why don't you come on home?"

"Okay mom. I'll be home in a few minutes."

When she told her Dad, he got up from his desk.

"Come on honey, we'll go home together."

As they entered the house, Mrs. Speer was sitting on the davenport and the telegram was lying on the coffee table. Helen looked at it with much concern but walked over, picked it up and opened it.

THE SECRETARY OF WAR DESIRES TO INFORM YOU THAT YOUR HUSBAND, 2nd LIEUTENANT LOWELL ANDERSEN IS BEING HELD AS A PRISONER OF WAR IN GERMANY. ANY FURTHER DETAILS OR INFORMATION WILL BE FORWARDED TO YOU IMMEDIATELY.

As before, it was signed by the adjutant general. Helen took a deep breath and said, "He's alive!"

Mrs. Speer immediately went to her daughter and took her in her arms and they both began to cry with happiness. Then her thoughts turned to Betty.

"I must call Betty."

Her father cautioned her to be careful because maybe she didn't get the same message. Helen thought about it and the happiness she felt suddenly turned to dread. How would she ever approach Betty?

The next few weeks were a terrible time for Helen after receiving the news. Betty had not mentioned anything about a notice and Helen realized she did not receive a message. She spent a lot of time with Betty, but felt there was now a distance between the two very good friends.

Letters Home

One day as March approached, word went around the camp that the Swiss Red Cross was coming to bring new mail and parcels, and could also take letters out of the camps, after careful censoring by the Germans, of course. With the Red Cross due to arrive within a week the men busily wrote to their families. Lowell had several letters already written to Helen and some to his parents, with hope he could mail them.

'Pete' came to Lowell and said, "Let's go for a walk."

It was one of those cold brisk late winter days in Germany, but no new snow had fallen for a few days.

Once outside, 'Pete' said, "What'll I do? I want to write to Betty in the worst way, but if the Germans get a hint, they will know."

Lowell thought for a minute and then said, "Let's go talk to the colonel."

When they went through the necessary chain of command, the colonel joined them in the yard. They explained the situation to him. After walking nearly a full circuit of the yard, the colonel paused.

"Why don't you write as Lieutenant – it's Marshall isn't it?"

'Pete' nodded.

The colonel went on, "Use your wife's maiden name maybe, but send it to her, and talk about something only you and she know about. You know, plans for the future and so on."

They walked on for awhile and then 'Pete' said, "Yes, that'll work. There are several things only we know about."

They thanked the colonel and turned toward their hut.

Lowell asked, "What are you going to write about?"

"Well, there were some things that happened when we were dating that I haven't even told you about."

They both went to work feverishly writing. Lowell talked about what they were doing and then had an idea of how he could help Jew with his problem. He wrote:

I don't know if you know this, but Myron is not with us, but there is a guy named Pete Marshall who I feel like I've known all my life. It has to do with that letter I wrote you from England. He even wants to come home with me when this is over.

Lowell leaned over and showed 'Pete' what he had written. He read it, thought a minute and said, "Yea, that's fine."

'Pete' leaned over and handed Lowell his letter, which began with *Dear Betty Miles.* Lowell looked up at him and continued to read.

My name is Pete Marshall; I am a friend of Lowell Andersen and your husband. Myron is not with us here but I think he told you about that in a letter from England. He was such a serious fellow but because I was such a good friend, he told me several things about you two like the time at the river when he almost got your clothes off under the blanket. Boy - that must have been something!

"You did that? Why didn't you tell me?"

"I don't tell you everything."

'Pete' continued the chitchat in his letter and signed off after a few more lines.

Well, we were told to keep this short so goodbye and I think I will come to Drayville with Lowell when we get out and meet you.

All the best,

Pete Marshall

They reread their letters several times and decided they would be okay. 'Pete' took his into Captain Folsom, the barracks chief and after reading it, the captain thought it was okay. The Red Cross soon arrived and took the boys' first letters home to their wives since their capture.

Home

The phone rang at the lumber yard. Helen answered, and heard her mother say, "Hello dear. I thought you'd like to know that the Red Cross delivered a letter for you today. I think it might be from Lowell."

In her excitement, Helen didn't even tell her father where she was going. She jumped up and ran out of the office and started for home. When reaching the house, she burst through the front door and her mother, who had seen her coming up the sidewalk, handed her the strange looking envelope. Ripping the envelope open, and with tears of joy streaming down her checks, she read the first words from her husband in several months.

At that very moment, Betty walked up the front walk to her parent's house, and reached in the mailbox fixed to the wall beside the front door. There were three envelopes and as she sorted through them, she nearly fainted as she came to one that looked very different. It was addressed to Betty Miles, but the address was correct. The envelope was some what worn looking and a little soiled, the handwriting looked very familiar. She went in the house, took off her coat and sat down to open the strange envelope. As she tore it open, she discovered a strange looking form. Hearing her daughter arrive, Betty's mother came into the room.

"Was there any mail Betty?"

"Yes, there is a very strange letter. It looks like Myron's handwriting on the envelope, but it's addressed to Betty Miles."

Her surprise increased as she started to read the letter. When she finished it, she felt faint.

Her mother, showing concern, asked, "What is it dear?"

"I don't really know Mom. It doesn't make sense."

Her mother reached out, took the letter from her daughter's hand, and read it. When she got to the part about the incident at the river and stopped reading.

She said, “Oh my,” and handed the letter back to Betty.

Both women sat down and looked at each other.

Betty said, “I don’t have any idea who this Pete Marshall is, but he’s talking about things that only Myron would know.”

Just then, the phone rang and her mother went to answer it, listened, and then said, “Dear it’s Helen.”

Betty got up, took the phone and said, “Hello.”

Helen said, “Betty I got a letter from Lowell and he said something very strange. Did you get any strange mail today?”

“I sure did. I got a letter from a Pete Marshall and it is very odd also. You want to come over and talk about it?”

“Okay, I’ll be right there.”

When Helen came in she noticed that Betty was holding one of those funny envelopes in her hand and she felt like a terrible weight had been lifted from her shoulders.

She asked, “Did you get a letter from Myron?”

Handing the letter from ‘Pete’ to Helen, Betty said, “No. I received this. Read it.”

Helen gave Betty the letter from Lowell, and the two women read each other’s letters. After a few minutes they looked at each other.

“I don’t understand this. What are they trying to tell us and where are they?” said Betty.

Looking her friend in the eyes she said, “Dear, I have a confession to make to you. Several weeks ago I got another telegram from the War Department informing me that Lowell was a prisoner of war. I wanted to tell you but Dad encouraged me to wait and see if you got one too. And when you didn’t mention one, I felt so guilty that I knew my husband was alive and you didn’t know.”

“Oh Helen, that explains a lot, I have been worried for the past few weeks that I had done something to offend you. You were acting so aloof. I don’t know how I would have reacted knowing Low was safe and not knowing a thing about Myron.”

The girls fell into each other’s arms for a long hug.

Betty said, “So, what do these weird letters mean?”

“I don’t know. Read that line about Pete coming to Drayville again. I think ‘Pete’ is Myron!”

“Yes, and read this part where Pete talks about what we did at the river. Myron would never tell anyone that."

"You did that?"

Betty smiled and said, "Well yes, but that's all we did. And what about this line about how serious Myron was. That's not the Myron I know."

Pointing to a paragraph in the letter Helen said, "This is what convinced me. Here, where Low is talking about Myron."

She took Lowell's letter from Betty and read it out loud, "*There is a guy named Pete Marshall with us who I feel like I have known all my life. He even wants to come home with me when this is over.*"

"Betty, you do remember when the boys wrote about what the army wanted the Jewish boys to do?" asked Helen.

"Yes, carry a false identification," said Betty. "That must be it! The letter from 'Pete Marshall' is really from Myron – I'm sure about it. He's alive and going by his false name."

"Yes, that must be it!" Helen exclaimed. "Oh honey, I am so happy for you."

The girls rose and hugged each other again.

Betty said, "Helen, I want to thank you for sparing my feelings about that notice and I don't want you to ever feel guilty for it."

They resumed their embrace and Betty's mom came over and hugged them both.

POW Camp

Lowell lay in his bunk trying to sleep, but hunger, loneliness and worry kept him awake. The days were going on toward spring, but in spite of the better weather, the kreigies did not feel any improvement in their lives. The food got worse, the Germans appeared to be more and more tense and with the melting of snow, the circuits were becoming walks through mud. Still, everyone was sure that the war was near completion.

The American camp leaders worked very hard to keep up the prisoners' moral and warned them to not incite the guards. An incident in the enlisted men's compound brought home their warnings. The previous week the men heard several shots, but no one knew anything about what caused the gun fire. Lowell watched for Werner and spotted him standing by a barracks wall.

He walked over, turned his back to him, which was a position they had worked out to communicate, and asked, "What happened over in the enlisted men's compound?"

Werner looked around and answered, "Oh there was a problem. A guard got edgy and shot a man."

"Is he dead?"

"I don't know. They took him to the hospital."

"Thanks Werner.

Lowell asked, "Is there a way I can put in a good word for you?"

Werner responded with a slight smile on his face, "The colonel has already assured me he will do so."

Lowell replied, "Okay Werner. Take it easy."

In the next few days, word spread around the camp that the solider had survived and that the colonel had met with the leadership from the enlisted compound and warned them to keep the men under control. They did not want anyone killed this close to the end.

Red Cross parcels arrived less and less frequently and the food provided by the Germans became nearly unpalatable. Lowell and 'Pete' were in better shape than many of the men in the barracks. As fairly 'new' arrivals, they had more body fat.

The only good news was the increased moderate weather and disappearance of the snow. The guards grew tenser. Lowell learned why from Werner. Apparently the Russians were on the outskirts of Berlin.

Conditions grew worse. The Germans seemed preoccupied about the direction the war was taking. They took less and less interest in what the prisoners were doing. Garbage was collecting in piles all around the compound. No transport arrived to pick it up. Colonel Chandler finally persuaded the commandant to let them haul it outside the fence by convincing him that no one would try an escape this late in the war. Lowell and 'Pete' volunteered just to spend some time outside the wire. Besides, they were probably some of the best-conditioned men in the camp due to their short imprisonment. It was messy work, but it meant a few minutes of freedom each day.

A rare humorous incident happened one day as they came in from their daily PT. The boys walked in and flopped on their beds.

Captain Folsom entered his room and yelled, "What the hell are you doing here!"

They all jumped at that and suddenly the door of the captain's room flew open and one of the ferrets came running out looking very embarrassed. The captain followed him out shouting at him.

Returning with a big smile on his face he told the others, "He was sound asleep on my bunk!"

Those few moments of humor did not offset the terrible boredom and hunger experienced by all. As the weather got better they spent more time outside. The guards got so lax that 'Pete', Lowell, and Vince could stand at the fence and talk to the rest of the crew. 'Pete' and Lowell spent more time talking about old times with Vernon. They reminisced about sports, girls, town gossip and anything else that took their minds off the present situation.

One day during one of their talks, Lowell said to Vernon, "Do you remember that time when we were juniors and you were with Helen in Smith's and J – I mean my friend and I came in and you were holding her hand?"

"Yea, I kind of remember that."

"Well, I remember it well. I thought you two were going steady or something."

Vernon lowered his head and laughed, "Well, to tell you the truth, Helen was telling me she didn't want to go out with me any more and I was holding her hand trying to convince her to go steady, but when she saw you and your friend, she pulled her hand away and got up and left."

Lowell thought awhile and then did remember that she agreed to go steady very soon after that.

He said, "Gosh Vernon I'm sorry, but not too sorry."

"Oh that's alright Low. Every one in school knew she had a big crush on you, even me."

Just then a guard came into view in one of the towers. He motioned them to move on.

'Pete' said, "See, I told you that you didn't have anything to worry about."

With spring came the opportunity to play baseball. Discovering some good old American baseball equipment, the boys went behind the barracks and played some catch. There wasn't room for a full diamond, but they were able to scratch out an infield. They spent more and more time outside, yet because of the lack of nutritious food, they didn't have the energy to play very long. Once in awhile someone hit the ball over the fence and they'd yell at the guards to retrieve it for them. The enlisted men didn't have the same privileges, but the officers were able to slip some balls and a bat through the fence.

Werner came and watched them play. He told Lowell that he wished he could join them, but he would get in deep trouble if he played with the prisoners. Another guard, an older man who had lived in the US for several years, watched them play also. He discussed life in America with the boys on occasion. He told Bill Wilkins, one of the guys who played, that he loved baseball and played when living in the States. The guys heard rumors that they could bribe him with cigarettes for food, or anything else, and that he was very sympathetic to the Americans.

After one particularly exciting game, he came up to Lowell and said, "I see Babe Ruth and Lou Gehrig play one time in New York."

Lowell was stunned that a German guard was so much into baseball and asked, "Really, when?"

"I live in New Jersey as a boy. A neighbor take us boys to a baseball game in the city. It was New York Yankees and Boston Red Socks. New York beat five to three." Grinning, he added, "The Babe hit a two run homer to win!"

"You saw Babe Ruth and Lou Gehrig play?"

"Yes, I did."

"So you lived in America?"

"Yes, until I was fifteen and then my folks move back to Germany."

Lowell inquired about the old man and found out his name was Crouse and that he would help the prisoners on occasion. He asked Werner about him one time and Werner said that he was one of the old people that the German army was now drafting. Lowell didn't mention that everyone he talked to said Crouse would get them things on occasion as Werner himself did. He was still wary of anyone who wore that uniform.

Lying in his bunk, Lowell realized his thoughts centered on food and not Helen. This shocked him, but then he smiled to himself about his instincts. Survival was utmost in everyone's mind.

Captain Folsom came out of his room and said, "Okay guys, time for a little PT."

His announcement was met with a bunch of moans and groans, but the men got off their bunks and straggled outside. The captain led them in some jumping jacks and a few pushups.

"Okay guys, now for a little run around."

He led them around the compound twice which seemed to be a severe struggle for some, but 'Pete' and Lowell made it in good shape. After PT the boys wandered over to the fence where some of the enlisted men stood watching them run.

Lowell said, "Don't you guys have anything better to do than watch us?"

A sergeant said, "We just love to watch you officers run."

There were a few laughs at that and then 'Pete' said, "Can you get Dickerson for us."

As they were talking, they always kept a watchful eye on the towers though at this stage of the war, the guards were much more lax and really didn't pay much attention to them talking across the wire.

Vern, Dave McDonald, and Zo came around the corner and approached the wire.

Lowell said, "Hi guys. How are things?"

"Well should we say just great?"

'Pete' asked, "Did you guys get to send letters?"

Bob answered, "Yes, we did but we couldn't say very much."

"That's good. At least our families know we're okay."

They all agreed. At that time, a ferret they didn't like because he was still very zealous about his job, came around the corner and yelled to get away from the fence. They all thought that he must be a member of the Nazi Party.

The men knew that the war was not going well for the Germans, not only from the looks of the troops who passed by the camp, but from the informational sheet, or "camp newspaper" that made the rounds nearly every night. It was a neatly typed sheet and was smuggled from barracks to barracks and the prisoners learned to look forward to it. It was well known that the information came from the British Broadcasting Company; however, they were never sure how it got to camp. The assumption was that there was a radio somewhere, although the bigger question was how it was typed. Lowell asked Captain Folsom one time and he just smiled. One theory held by some of the men was that a friendly German was responsible.

Home

Helen was concentrating on a lumber order when the door of the office burst open and the twins rushed in. Diane jumped around the desk and gave Helen a big hug while David began to play with the pencil sharpener attached to the side.

Diane said, "Helen, Mom wants you to come to dinner tonight and bring your folks."

"Well, that sounds swell Diane."

David spoke up then and said, "And then will you take us skating?"

"Oh David, you weren't suppose to say that until she agreed."

Helen laughed and gave her another hug and said, "I'll be glad to take you skating, but remember we have to help your mom clean up first."

"Well, you can do it fast can't you?"

"Yea, David is afraid that Joyce Smith might leave early," said Diane.

"I am not. I don't care anything about Joyce Smith."

"Oh yea, how come you write her name on your notebook all the time?"

Helen said, "Now kids, let's don't have a fight right here. You run along now and tell your mom I accept and that it will only be me, Mom and Dad are driving over to Willamette to their card club tonight."

"Okay, see you at six," said Diane as the two youngsters rushed out of the office.

Helen sat there a few minutes and smiled at the thought of those two being related now. She sure hoped that when she and Lowell had children, they would have a little of the twin's energy.

That night after dinner as Helen helped clean up, Mary asked, "Dear, what do you think it will be like having Lowell home again? I don't mean just home, but what do you think he will be like?"

"I've given it a lot of thought Mary and I don't really know. I've heard that we need to give the boys time to adjust back to civilian life though and I suppose in Lowell's case, being in prison and all, it might take a little longer."

"Well, I know you can handle it dear. You better get going now. David and Diane have had their skates out since this afternoon!"

Helen dried her hands, gave her mother-in-law a hug and thanked her for the meal. In the living room Ethan was sitting by the radio smoking his pipe and listening to the news.

He looked up and said, "The Russians have Berlin surrounded. Won't be long now."

"I hope not. Ethan, where do you think the boys are?"

He got serious and said, "Honey, I don't know, but I'm sure they will be liberated soon. You hear of prison camps being liberated all the time."

"Yes, I guess so. Well, whoever wants to go skating better come with me!"

David and Diane jumped up and grabbed their skates.

Ethan said, "Here kids," and handed them each a fifty-cent piece. "Don't spend this all at once."

"Gosh thanks Dad," said David and Diane went over and gave her father a hug.

POW Camp

Spring brought much warmer weather; however, it rained most every day. The guys in the barracks kidded Lowell about being from Oregon and probably he didn't mind the rain at all. 'Pete' got caught up in it and responded in a defensive way. Lowell gave him a glare, which caused him to remember his situation and cover his comment.

"Yea, I have an uncle who lives in Oregon and he says that it's a myth that it rains all the time."

Lowell responded, "Yea, it sure is, but it does rain a lot. We have some snow too, but it usually comes in the night and early morning. It's gone by afternoon. That's the kind of snow we like!"

A guy from Minnesota said, "Well, we have snow in November and it's usually gone by April!"

Everyone laughed as Lowell responded, "Yea, I was born in Nebraska and even though I left when I was very young, my folks talk about all the snow they had."

Although life in the camp was very severe, life went on. The theater group prepared to present a play and everyone looked forward to seeing it. It was one of those feel good shows about a family in the US who lived an idyllic life in a Mid-Western town. There was, of course, a father, mother, two children, a girl and a boy, and the nosy neighbor. Men, for lack of small children and girls, played all the roles. A prisoner, who lived in the next barracks, was very small in stature and played the little girl and another smallish fellow played the brother. A man who lived in the same barracks as Lowell and 'Pete' assumed the role of mother. The play was well done and all the men enjoyed it. Even the guards came to watch, and even though many of them did not understand the language, they seemed to like it.

In the yard the next day, Lowell, 'Pete' and Vince were doing a walk around when Werner approached them laughing.

He said, "That was a great play last night. You know, when I was in high school we did that as a student body play and I played the little brother."

Lowell was amused at the thought that a German had performed in an American play, but then he remembered Werner was not really a German. He had been born in the United States and spent most of his life there.

Food became the prisoner's sole obsession. What the Germans provided wasn't enough to sustain life for any length of time. Lowell had never started smoking and 'Pete' had quit, so the boys had several packs of American cigarettes stashed, which served as better barter than money and could buy more. The cigarettes bought an occasional loaf of bread and some meat, usually sausage. Werner was their main source, but once in awhile even he couldn't get anything.

Lowell laid in his bunk trying not to think about food. The only way he had any success was to concentrate on Helen and home. He thought about the time when they competed in the Emmons speech tournament together and he gave her a ride back to school.

He still felt like a fool every time he remembered what she said: "All the girls think you are the nicest boy in school."

He smiled as 'Pete' looked over at him and said, "What are you laughing about?"

Lowell told him and 'Pete' said, "Are you still thinking about the dumb answer you gave her?"

"That's what makes me feel stupid. I didn't say anything."

By this time, many of the men in the barracks knew that there was a special relationship between 'Pete' and Lowell. They told several of the men that were now their friends and they felt they could trust about their little secret. Jim Slatery figured it out one day by himself when he accompanied 'Pete' and Lowell on a walk around.

"Ya know it seems like you two know a lot about each other. More than comes from just being crew mates."

It took them by surprise and then 'Pete' said, "Yea, we do." Pausing, he added, "We grew up together."

"What's wrong with that? Why are you keeping it a secret?"

Lowell and 'Pete' looked at each other for a few minutes and Myron said, "My real name is Myron Rothstein."

Jim looked somewhat shocked and then said, "Oh that explains it. You're Jewish."

"Yes."

They walked a little further and Jim said, "I don't know a thing."

Lowell said, "Keep it that way, okay?"

"Keep what?" replied Jim.

"Exactly."

As they continued their walk, 'Pete' thought, *It sure feels good to tell someone the truth. It's getting harder to keep up the charade with the war approaching an end. I can't wait to be myself again.*

As they continued the circuit, each one in his own thoughts, Lowell said, "Jim, you were in college when you enlisted weren't you?"

"Yea, I had just finished my freshman year at Northwestern."

"What were you majoring in?"

"Mostly girls and baseball. I was sure that I would get an offer from a pro team what with all the regular guys in the service. But, my draft board started breathing down my neck so I enlisted."

"Yea, my dad wanted me to at least start college, so I did. 'Pete' went right in after high school."

"How come 'Pete'?"

"Well, I was a year older when I graduated because I missed a year in grade school with scarlet fever."

It felt good for the boys to be able to talk about their youth and not be guarded about what they called who and so on. Jim had become a trusted friend and someone with whom they could let their hair down, so to speak.

'Pete' asked, "So you played baseball did you?"

"Yes, I played in high school but only lettered one year. I went to a very large school and it was hard to make the team."

'Pete' said, "Well, our esteemed friend here was an all state catcher in high school."

"Did you play in college?" asked Lowell.

"Yea, I made the team, but Northwestern was pretty big so there was a lot of competition. I only got into a couple of games."

"What did you play?"

"Oh, mostly outfield, but a little first base as well."

'Pete' said, "We went to a pretty small high school so we played all three sports."

Lowell added. "Yea, some of the guys played four."

"How did they do that?"

"Well, a couple of them were pretty fast so the track coach had them running when we didn't have a game."

"Wow, I can't imagine that. How big was your high school?"

"What Jew? Maybe around 350 our senior year."

Jim looked a little confused and then said to Lowell, "What did you call him?"

Lowell looked embarrassed and then said, "Oh, we had nick names that we called each other."

"Yea, we did too but to call a Jewish boy that in our school would have gotten you into a fight."

'Pete' looked at Lowell and said, "See Low, I should have been slugging you much harder."

"Oh shut up, 'PETE'!"

They all laughed and continued their walk around until they came to the barracks and entered.

As March came, some of the men busied themselves preparing gardens for spring planting. The boys wondered why. It was common knowledge that the war could not go on for much longer. Talking to Captain Folsom, Lowell asked what he thought.

"It gives them something to do," he replied.

Lowell understood. Boredom competed with hunger for the most disconcerting aspect of being a prisoner-of-war. He had slowed down writing to Helen. Though he knew he might never mail his letters, he wrote to her nearly every day.

One day as they were sitting on the steps of the barracks taking in the spring sun, Werner walked by and made a motion indicating that he wanted to talk to them. 'Pete', Vince and Lowell got up and followed him around behind the barracks out of sight of the towers.

When he thought it was safe, he turned to the boys and said, "Colonel Rickered told us today that the SS may be taking over the camp."

"What does that mean?"

"Well, it could mean a lot worse treatment."

Is he going to tell Colonel Chandler?"

"I don't know, but I wanted you guys to know. If that happens, you guys will have to be doubly careful about what you say and do."

When they went back to the barracks, Lowell knocked on Captain Folsom's door and asked if he could talk to him.

The captain said, "Yes, come on in."

By this stage of the game, they were a lot less concerned about being overheard and many times didn't even bother to go to the shower room.

The captain said, "What is it Andersen?"

"Well sir, our friend on the other side of the wire just told us that the commandant told them that the camp might be taken over by the SS."

The captain looked at Lowell for a minute and said, "Oh that must be what the colonel wants to see us about. He's called a meeting for this afternoon."

As the word spread around the camp, the men became very tense. Everyone was worried that if the SS did take over, they might do terrible things. There were stories about prisoners being executed by the SS for little or no reason. 'Pete' did not display any more concern because he felt his cover was pretty solid. He did talk to Captain Folsom and was assured that his situation was not common knowledge and that there was probably nothing to worry about.

MOVE & LIBERATION

April came and with it much nicer weather. They hadn't had snow for several weeks; however, food was scarcer than ever. The Red Cross parcels were now nonexistent. They all knew that the war was not going well for the Germans. Day after day, the men watched defeated looking German troops passing by on the road outside of camp.

Then President Roosevelt died. Word spread around the camp like wild fire, and someone named Truman was America's new president. Most of the men in the camp had known only one president. He had led them out of the Great Depression and through most of the war. Dying this close to victory – it seemed a terrible shame that he would not see the end. It was a sad day for the prisoners. The Germans did not seem to react the way the boys thought they would. Werner came by and offered his condolences.

He said, "Ya know, he was my president too."

Several days later, whistles, shouts and bangs awakened the camp as the guards came into the huts. It was much earlier than usual and everyone wondered what was going on. They were instructed to get up and fall out for appell. When they came out to the assembly area, Lowell looked around and saw that the camp seemed to be the same.

"I wonder what in the world is going on?"

'Pete' said, "I don't know."

As they assembled, the camp commandant climbed to the small stage, speaking to them in his usual excellent English.

"I am here to tell you that you will be moved."

This information caused a stir among the men. The colonel stepped from the ranks and approached the commandant. The boys in Lowell's formation could not make out what they were talking about, but the colonel listened for some time and then called all the barracks chiefs together.

When the barracks chiefs finished listening to the colonel, they came back to their groups. Several of the men were yelling at Captain Folsom about what was going on. Captain Folsom held up his hand and motioned them to gather around.

"Men, we are being moved. I don't know why nor does the colonel, so just go in, gather up your stuff and wait to be called."

Many questions were thrown at the captain.

"Where are we going?"

"How long will it take?"

"Are they going to turn us loose?"

The captain answered them all in the same way, "I don't know. Just do as you're told!"

As they gathered up their few possessions, Lowell looked at 'Pete' and asked, "Well what do you think?"

"I have no idea. I guess we better do what they tell us."

After several hours, the call to fall out again came and the men assembled in the yard. They talked, looked around, and waited.

'Pete' said, "I don't get it. Why would they move us this late?"

"I don't know. You just can't figure the German mind sometimes."

Just then a German junior officer and several enlisted men came around the barracks with several large sacks that they threw on the ground. The officer walked over to the colonel and said something to him. The colonel looked very disgusted and turned to the men again and called for the barracks chiefs to form up around him.

After a short talk, the barracks chiefs began to pick through the sacks that the men realized were full of mail. The chiefs began to call out names and when Lowell's was called, he went off to the captain who handed him a bundle consisting of several letters. Lowell realized they were the letters he'd written to Helen and his folks for several weeks. The Germans never mailed them.

After more time the guards came down from their towers and the men received instructions to get into a march-order. Just then Werner Schoker came by.

Lowell said, "Werner, what's going on?"

Werner looked around, walked over to them and said, "The Russians have broken through our lines. They've crossed the Oder River and will probably be here in a few days."

"Well why don't you just let them liberate us?"

"Oh, you don't want to get in the hands of the Russians."

'Pete' said, "Oh I don't know. Things couldn't be worse."

Lowell and 'Pete' picked up their equipment and started to form up. Lowell noticed the enlisted men were also out in the assembly area and forming up. Finally they got the order to march and as they left the camp, some of the men cheered and yelled as they passed through the gate, but Lowell didn't feel as deeply as those who had spent over a year in Stalag Luft II. He wanted to stay and be liberated by the Russians rather than walk into the unknown as they seemed to be doing.

They marched the rest of the day and well into the night. There was no food except what they carried and only a few breaks. As they lumbered along, Lowell wondered if this was somehow a humanitarian effort on the part of the Germans. As Werner said, they didn't want to be turned over to the Russians. Lowell didn't understand that, after all they were allies, but maybe the Germans knew something they didn't. Finally at around 2000 hours they were allowed to fall out for the night. A large grass covered field along side the road looked to the men like heaven on earth. They fell to the ground. They didn't even think about food. The ranking officers came around to check on the men as best they could. Mainly they were warning them not to wander off. Any German soldiers they might run in to would probably shoot and the civilians weren't very friendly either.

Around 0500 hours the guards roused them, though few of the men had slept much, and told them to fall in on the road. Several of the men yelled for food, but none was forthcoming. Lowell reached into his sack where he had his meager supply of food.

He said, "Hey 'Pete', you going to eat something?"

"Well, I don't have much, but I guess I should have something."

They stumbled down the road chewing on some very dry bread with a little cheese. At times the guards told them to get off the road when a convoy of Germans passed. They noticed that many of the vehicles were horse drawn and very weary and emaciated horses were pulling some of the trucks.

'Pete' said, "Boy, it looks like a dying effort from a dying army."

"Yea," replied Vince who had joined them the night before as they fell. "I remember pictures of the defeat of Napoleon when he retreated from Russia. It looked a lot like this."

"The troops don't look any better fed then we are," replied Lowell.

As they continued along the muddy road, a commotion caught their attention up ahead. The guards yelled to get off the road again. The boys looked up and down but could see no convoy.

Suddenly some one shouted, "Look, planes!"

Lowell looked up in direction he was pointing and saw several small specks on the horizon. As they drew closer, he realized they were P-51s. Many of the men jumped up and waved until the planes opened fire. It was only a short burst until the pilots realized their mistake and ceased firing and pulled up from their strafing run.

Men were yelling, "Why would they fire on us?"

A captain nearby said, "Well, they don't know who we are. To them we look like a large group of men moving along a road."

The P-51s climbed, made a turn and came down very low wagging their wings in recognition of the prisoners. Several of the guards started to raise their rifles to fire, but the prisoners close to them grabbed the barrels and deflected the shots. The boys learned later that several of the prisoners were hit, but luckily no one was killed.

Though the guards gave the men rest breaks, by late in the day, men began to fall out along side the road. A few trucks accommodated some, but most were picked up by friends and dragged along. Other prisoners, not in much better shape, carried their buddies on makeshift stretchers.

Again around 2100 hours the guards told them to fall out into a field. This time a field kitchen provided the prisoners with the usual fare of thin soup and very hard bread. The prisoners didn't complain. They were hungry.

Lowell, Vince, and 'Pete' found a small clearing, sat down with their food and ate.

Vince asked, "How much longer will we have to keep this up?"

"I don't know, but if it's much longer, many men won't make it," replied 'Pete'.

Lowell said, "Ya know, I wonder if they aren't doing us a favor by moving us."

"What are you talking about?"

"Well, you remember what Werner said about the Russians. Maybe they are moving us to where we can be liberated by the Americans," replied Lowell.

There was a moment of silence while they all thought about Lowell's comment.

Vince said, "Yea, I bet that's it. The camp commandant seemed like the kind of fellow who might do that."

'Pete' said, "Oh come on Vince, the commandant is just following orders like all good Germans do."

They all sat there thinking and chewing on their hard bread.

Finally Lowell said, "I don't care. I'm going to try and get some rest."

They all nodded and then laid back on their packs. In a short time all three were asleep.

The next morning they awakened as usual around 0500. They had slept fairly well until around 0330 when it started to rain. They didn't have much protection and were all wet and cold. The German guards told them to fall in so they moved to the road and started walking again.

After several hours, Lowell looked over at one of the German guards walking along with them. It was Crouse, the guard who loved baseball and was helpful to the prisoners. He was in his late fifties, about his father's age. He was stumbling along and nearly fell several times. His rifle had slid off his shoulder and was being dragged on the ground and seemed to be more than he could stand. Lowell moved over to him and reached out and removed the rifle.

The guard looked up at him and said, "Donka."

Lowell just smiled and slung the rifle over his shoulder and carried it for the man.

Bread

The third night, they arrived in a small town with several ruined buildings. One large building looked like some kind of warehouse. It had a near-intact roof and they were told to fall out and move in. Some of the prisoners began to wander around the town and look for food.

A sergeant came by with several loaves of bread and 'Pete' yelled, "Where did you get that bread?"

The sergeant yelled back, "Look for yourself!"

'Pete' looked at Vince and Lowell and said, "Want to take a look?"

"Yea, that would be okay."

They went out into the street and began to wander around. Captain Folsom, lying near the door said "Where you going men?"

"To look for food," they replied.

"Well, be careful. Remember this is still an enemy city."

"Okay."

They walked down the street and 'Pete' asked several guys whom they met, "Have you guys seen any goons lately?"

"No, I think they're probably shacked up in some of these houses."

They turned a corner and there on the street was a bakery with the lights on.

"Well." Lowell said, "Shall we go in and see what is going on?"

Vince said, "I don't want to steal from him even as hungry as I am."

"Who said anything about stealing, I'm sure Lowell still has those Red Cross cigarettes don't you Low?"

"Yes, I do."

They went to the back of the building and tapped on the window and the baker looked up. His eyes widen and he reached under the counter and took out a gun that looked like a shotgun. The boys dropped down and started to crawl away when the back door opened and the baker came out. They stopped.

Vince raised his hands saying in his high school German, "Don't shoot! We want to buy some bread from you. We were not going to steal it."

Vince only understood about one word in ten.

"I think he wants a pack a loaf. How many do you have?"

"I've got four I think."

"Well, lay them on the counter and let's see what he does."

Lowell put the cigarettes on the counter. The shopkeeper put down the gun, reached over to the shelf and handed four loaves to them. Just then Captain Folsom came up to the door and the shopkeeper grabbed his gun again. Vince convinced him the captain came with them.

Captain Folsom said, "What's going on guys?"

Lowell and 'Pete' explained that they were trading cigarettes for bread and the captain said, "Well, I don't feel that we need to buy anything from this guy."

"Yea, but with that double barrel pointed at us, we didn't think we had much choice."

Captain Folsom then reached into his coat and took out two packs of cigarettes and offered them to the shopkeeper. He looked at them and reached back on the shelves and handed the captain two loves of bread.

Folsom took the bread and said, "Let's get out of here."

Turning to leave, 'Pete', Lowell, and Vince followed him out of the shop down the street.

That night was a little better with the fresh bread. The boys and Captain Folsom shared their bread with the men around them. Accompanying the usual watery soup and a little cheese contributed by others, it seemed like a banquet. Anything in their stomachs helped – and the fact that they weren't sleeping in a field helped most of the men get a fairly good night's sleep.

The next morning the routine was slightly different. The Germans allowed the men to sleep in and it wasn't until almost 1000 hours that they told them to fall in.

Vince asked, "Do you think they let us sleep a little longer out of sympathy?"

'Pete' said, "Boy Vince, you sure don't understand the Germans very well."

Lowell said, "Oh take it easy 'Pete', he didn't mean anything."

The order to march was given and the trek down the muddy road began again. About mid-day they came to a fairly major river where the Germans told them to fall out. With only a temporary bridge, they had to wait their turn to cross. The men walked down to the shore and sat or slept until they were told to fall in again. The guards led the prisoners across the temporary bridge between convoys. The men tried to figure out which river they were crossing, and finally someone suggested it must be the Elbe. One airman who knew German geography well said if it was the Elbe, then they had traveled over fifty miles since leaving camp.

Lowell did a little figuring and remembered a time in Boy Scouts when they'd hiked twenty miles, which took them only about five hours. This was their third day since leaving camp.

He said, "Hey 'Pete', you remember when we did our hiking merit badge in scouts?"

"Yea."

"Didn't we do that in about a half a day?"

"Oh, I don't know. Maybe a little longer I guess."

"Well we sure aren't making very good time if we've only covered fifty miles in a little over two days."

"Why you want another merit badge?"

Lowell reached over and slugged him on the shoulder.

'Pete' looked up at him and smiled saying, "That really felt good buddy."

They gave each other that look meant to express how much they meant to one another.

Vince walked up to them and asked, "What were you talking about?"

"Oh Low was just reminding me of the hike we took in Boy Scouts."

"Oh."

Another day passed and at the end the guards again told the men to fall out. Later, they consumed the usual meal of soup and coarse bread. Lowell, 'Pete', Vince and Jim Slatery grouped together. They sat talking for awhile. Captain Folsom came by and joined them.

Lowell asked, "Do you know what happened to the enlisted men?"

"I think they are traveling the same direction, but on a different road."

"Captain, you got any idea how much longer this is going on?"

"I wish I knew, but I don't."

Vince said, "Well, I would settle for where we're going."

"Yea, and why they are moving us," added 'Pete'.

"Oh that's easy. I don't think the commandant wanted us to be turned over to the Russians."

Lowell looked at 'Pete' and smiled, meaning *I told you so.*

After what passed for evening chow, they began to look for places to sleep. 'Pete', Lowell, Vince and Jim found a fairly dry place under some thick brush and crawled in.

A little later 'Pete' said, "Ya know, I don't think I want to be Pete Marshall anymore."

Lowell rose up and looked at him and asked, "Why?"

"Well, I don't think the Germans care anymore who they have and I'm tired of having to remember who I am. Oh I don't mean I'll go tell them, but between us, I am now Myron again."

Vince and Jim agreed and after a few minutes, Lowell said, "Okay buddy, but let's don't spread it around just in case."

The next morning the men got a good surprise, the sun was shining and it seemed much warmer. It even made the morning fare taste a little better. As they lined up for the soup and bread, the colonel came by talking to the men as he passed. When he got to the boy's little group he asked about how they were doing.

Vince responded, "How much longer is this going on sir?"

"Well, I talked to some of the German officers and they said we were being sent to a small camp just a few hours away, so I guess it will end today."

"Sir, do you know about the enlisted men?"

"Oh yes, they were taken to a different camp on the other side of the river. They are already settled in I'm sure."

That made Lowell feel a little better, knowing his crew might be okay. They gathered on the road again in groups resembling in no way a formation and started to walk. With the warmth of the sun and knowing it was supposed to end today, the march was not bad at all. After a few hours, they laboriously climbed a small hill up to a flat plain with a view.

Myron said, "Look! That looks like an airfield."

Captain Folsom, who was walking along side said, "Yea, the Germans like to put POW camps near strategic sites in the hopes that we won't bomb them. It didn't work though because we used to come down and shoot 'em up anyway. We always liked to see the prisoners out waving at us. I didn't realize what that really meant to them until I became one."

"From the looks of all the wrecked planes, you did a pretty good job."

"Well, we tried."

The camp was a few hundred yards off in the distance and from what they could see it was not a very large camp by POW-camp-standards. Lowell saw towers, barbed wire, rows and rows of huts, and could tell a small stream ran beside the camp, which stood at the edge of the woods. Lowell thought, *In better times this was probably a nice place to camp.*

Getting nearer to the camp, the boys saw men standing along the wire fence. There was no shouting of questions this time. Apparently everyone knew the status of the war. The men looked like every prisoner in every camp in Germany. There was a mixture of clothing. Most men had long hair and most were unshaven and thin. Lowell wondered how they looked to those inside.

Guards opened the gates and the new arrivals entered. The men inside greeted them with nods; some waved and a couple asked where they were from. Once in formation, a German officer came out of the administration building, climbed up to the platform and began to speak in understandable English.

"Welcome to Stalag Luft VI. It is useless to try an escape. If we all wait patiently, the war will be over in a short time."

He got down from the platform and left the compound. Colonel Chandler mounted the platform and spoke to the men about divisions and assignments to barracks.

He said, "Remember men, this is already a very crowded camp and we are the newcomers, so be aware that this has been home to most of these men for a long time."

Lowell, Myron and Vince were assigned to the same barracks. When they entered, they were greeted by a major and told to find a place to throw their stuff and settle down.

"I don't think we will be here much longer. From what we hear, General Patton's not far off," said the major with a knowing look.

Just as in the other camp, the prisoner's had a way of getting the news. There was even a periodic one-page newspaper.

The boys looked around a little and one of the prisoners said, "Here guys, there's an empty bunk down at the end."

Lowell thanked him and they talked for awhile and decided they could all share it.

The old "Jew" humor raised its head again when he said, "Okay, but if you guys ever tell anyone back home that I slept with you I'll kill you."

That brought smiles to their faces, but only for a little while.

As they laid their stuff down, they heard someone in the next bunk say, "Where ya from?"

Vince answered, "I'm from Colorado; these guys are from Oregon."

"Yea, there's a guy down at the other end from Oregon. I don't know where."

Lowell made a mental note to try to find him; it was always good to meet someone from home.

Lowell asked the man next to him, "Were you here when they bombed the airfield?"

"Yea, several times. They came in low and did a job every time."

"Our barracks chief was a fighter jock and he said he had done that several times and the prisoners came out and waved."

The man smiled slightly and nodded his head.

The first night at the new camp was quite different. No slamming of the shutters, no lights out, and no ferrets snooping around under the barracks. The boys wondered about that, but the older men said they hadn't done that for some time. They guessed the commandant wasn't all that concerned. This camp, being hastily built, had no shower rooms or rest rooms as there were in Stalag II. The privies consisted of four-holers lined up at the end of the rows of barracks and the showers were outside in canvas covered tents. The water came from large tanks spaced every so often throughout the camp. The water was slightly warmed by wood burning stoves.

After a couple of nights, Lowell, Myron and Vince worked out a system of sleeping. They had two bunks, an upper and a lower, for the three of them. One night two would share the lower bunk and one would have the single. Every night it would be rotated so that each man would have a bunk to himself every third night. With the additional prisoners, the camp was very crowded. The food was even scarcer and the new arrivals sensed some resentment from the older inmates, though most accepted them for what they were, prisoners just like themselves. Lowell, Vince and Myron became quite friendly with the next-door neighbor. His name was Ken Marzak and he was from New Jersey. He had been a navigator on a B-24 out of Italy and was shot down in August 1944. He had gone through navigator's school at the same base where Myron had taught though they didn't know each other.

Lowell found the boy from Oregon. He was from Medford and his name was Ralph Fredrickson. He said he'd been to Drayville once with his father who was a logger. He had come up to the county to look into buying some timber, but didn't.

"Yea, we've got a lot of trees in the county," put in Myron.

Lowell added, "My wife's family owns a lumber yard in town."

"I will probably go back into logging when I get home. With the depression over, I'll bet there'll be a lot of building going on."

Lowell hadn't thought of that, but suspected he was right.

Not all the Germans had given up on the war. There was one guard who was just as zealous now as many Germans were at the beginning. His name was Martin something and all the prisoners had been warned not to mess with him. The older inmates told stories about him beating prisoners with his night-stick for not stepping out of the way when he came down the walk. It was very evident that the rest of the guards didn't like him much either. When Lowell heard about Martin, he warned Myron to be very careful and watch his true identity.

Myron thought for a minute and nodded his head and said, "Yea, I'll be careful."

One of the things that Martin had a habit of doing was sneaking into the compound at night and listening outside the huts for conversations that might intimidate a prisoner. He listened for things such as guards who were accepting bribes or prisoners who might be dealing in contraband. Even at this late stage of the war, Martin had not given up and was still practicing his clandestine spying. One night one of the men in Lowell's hut took a chance and opened one of the shutters to let in a little fresh air.

He immediately closed it again and turned and whispered, "Martin is standing at the window in hut twenty-seven listening."

Someone said, "Let's get the bastard!"

Someone else said, "We had better ask the major."

One of the guys knocked on the major's door and when he opened it, the major was asked to come out; there was something they wanted to talk to him about. All the men were gathered around in a circle and several held their fingers up to their lips indicating that they should whisper. After explaining what the situation was, the major asked what they had in mind. No one answered because no one had thought that far ahead.

After a few minutes of silence, someone said, "Let's sneak up behind him with a blanket and wrap him up and throw him down the hole of one of those crappers."

After a minute of silence, the major said, with a big smile on his face, "I don't know a thing about it. I'm going to bed."

Once the plan was finalized, the kidnap crew was chosen. There were three men who somehow had kept themselves in reasonably good condition and were quite large. They got some blankets and rope and decided on the route around the barracks and which crapper they would drop him in. Most of the men could hardly keep from laughing out loud with anticipation. Lowell, Myron, and Vince were caught up in the caper as well, but they hadn't been dealing with Martin for as long as most of the men and had not built up the hate. Lowell shuddered at the thought of what it would be like down in that hole with all that sewage. The smell alone was enough to kill a man. A final admonishment was given to the kidnappers not to tie him up too tight. To kill him, even at this stage of the war, was something the Germans could not ignore, even a guard that the Germans didn't like.

The kidnappers slid silently out the door. Part of the German's more relaxed attitude meant they no longer used the floodlights to scan the compound at night. The chosen men sneaked silently around the end of the barracks, peeked around the corner and saw Martin still listening at the window. The larger of the two kidnappers, a man named Frank Osborne who had been an all-star football player at Michigan State, crept up behind him and suddenly he turned. Frank grabbed him covering his mouth with his hand and pinning his arms to his side. Martin did not have his rifle with him. That probably would have prevented the prisoners from carrying out their plan.

There was a slight struggle before the next man wrapped a towel around his head to cover his mouth preventing him from yelling. The third kidnapper then threw the blanket over him and tied the rope. Martin's struggling made enough of a noise the men in number twenty-seven opened the shutters to see what was causing it. Realizing what was going on, those who could see began to laugh though they didn't know what the total plan was. Frank and his crew picked up the struggling Martin and began to carry him toward the outhouses.

Most of the men could not see the final results of the plan, but later the kidnappers told the story. When they got Martin into the crapper, he was still struggling and they had some problem getting him down the hole. They had decided to put him in feet first to prevent him from drowning but he kept spreading his legs. Finally one of the men wrapped his arms around Martin's legs and they were able to complete their mission. They reported that the effluent only came up to his waist. The men were laughing so hard they could hardly talk.

They went to sleep that night with smiles on their faces. To get a little bit back at those Germans who were still treating them like lesser men was something that made them feel good. Lowell kind of felt sorry for Martin, but he had not experienced the cruelty that the guard had perpetrated on the older prisoners. They didn't have any sympathy toward him at all. The next morning at appell, Martin was not present and the prisoners never found out why.

The days continued to get better and the food continued to get scarcer as spring continued to progress. Lowell, Myron and Vince stayed very close to each other. They sensed, as all the other prisoners did, that the end was near.

One day out on the front steps of the barracks, Vince asked, "What do you think they told Pete's family about him?"

Myron rose up and looked at him and then replied, "I don't know, but I am going to find out when we get home."

Lowell looked at them both with some concern and said, "I imagine they reported him missing in action. You remember how long it was before we heard Vern was a prisoner."

They settled down with their thoughts, mostly about food and attaining their freedom. Captain Folsom came out of the barracks, stood for awhile and looked out over the landscape.

Vince turned to him and asked, "Captain, do you think the Germans will just let us go or will they try something?"

"I don't know Vince. The colonels feel they will probably just disappear one day."

Lowell said, "I've heard rumors about shooting prisoners rather than letting them go."

"Oh, I don't think that will happen," said the captain. "The commandant of this camp is a Luftwaffe officer and they are usually pretty good guys."

They all fell silent again with their own thoughts.

Lowell thought of Helen, of course, and had a moment of fright when he couldn't bring up her face in his mind. He had noticed over the past few weeks that the longer he was imprisoned and the hungrier he got, the more difficult it was to remember things from home and that alarmed him.

Liberation

One morning in early May, things changed. Shouting and yelling awakened the prisoners. Lowell jumped down and ran outside but couldn't see what all the ruckus was about.

Vince followed him out and shouted, "Look the guards are gone!"

Lowell looked up at the towers and saw they were empty. There was no one walking the perimeter of the fence and the administration building seemed to be vacant. The colonel came by and everyone was shouting at him. He shook his head indicating he didn't know what was going on either. Finally the senior officers got the men settled down and in some order.

The two colonels climbed to the platform and shouted, "Gentlemen, the Germans have abandoned the camp, so I guess that means the war is over. We have just heard that the Germans have quit fighting, but we don't know if it's official or not!"

Most of the men in camp knew there was some means of communication either by clandestine radio or from friendly guards. The prisoners always seemed to know what was going on.

The announcement was greeted with a mixture of reactions. There was much cheering, some men broke down, others just shook their heads, but all were in a state of high emotion. The colonel then asked all the barracks chiefs to gather at the north fence.

The men stirred around as the officers met. Finally, the meeting broke up and the barracks chiefs led their men to various corners of the compound where they could talk.

Captain Folsom and the major serving as barracks chief called for silence.

"Men, the colonels don't know what is going to happen next, but they are sure we will be liberated soon," said the major.

That brought a huge cheer from the gathering. The major raised his hand for silence and continued.

"They're going to try to contact our troops. We have men breaking into the motor pool right now to see if there are any vehicles left. So, you guys must be patient and don't do anything stupid this late in the game. Remember the civilians don't like us much and they may still be hostile."

The men shouted many questions to the major, but he just shook his head indicating he didn't have the answers. After the meeting broke up, the men milled around the compound for a time and suddenly they heard a motor running. They all looked toward the sound and saw a motorcycle with a side-car come from the motor pool. A lieutenant was riding it and Colonel Chandler was in the sidecar. A cheer went up from the nearly 2,000 men behind the wire. Shouts of encouragement caused the colonel to raise his hand in a victory sign. The motorcycle headed across the abandoned airfield and turned westerly, disappearing into the woods.

The prisoners were so excited that they didn't even think about hunger until word spread that they had broken into the supply warehouse and found some food. The men who had been designated as cooks were going to prepare it and it would be ready in a short while. For every four rows of barracks there was a mess hall off sorts. That meant that each hall had been built to serve about 400 men. With the over crowding they now were expected to serve nearly 600, which meant it took considerable time to serve a meal. However, with the meager rations found in the storage warehouse, it didn't take long to serve the thin soup, hard bread and moldy cheese.

With their stomachs a little fuller, the men were more relaxed. They lay around, some on their bunks in the huts and some outside. The colonel felt that the main gate should still be closed to prevent anyone from leaving camp and possibly getting in trouble outside. They still thought of the commandant's warning about SS troops.

Word spread about the camp that in one of the buildings, broken into by the prisoners, they found bags of letters written by the prisoners and never sent. Lowell looked at Myron and they both shrugged.

Myron said, "I guess that happened in all the camps."

Lowell, Myron and Vince along with several of the other men from their barracks sat on the steps, one of their favorite places of late.

Lowell said, "I wonder how the enlisted men are doing?"

Vince responded with, "I suppose their guards have left as well."

"I hope so."

"Do you think the crew is still in touch with Vern?"

"I guess they could be."

This pointless conversation went on for several more minutes and then Vince said, "I think I will go in and see if I can catch forty winks."

To which Myron replied, "You can do that anywhere, anytime."

As he rose Vince feinted a kick in Myron's direction and entered the hut.

Myron, Lowell and several of the other men sat outside for some time.

Finally Myron said, "I think I'll join Vince for awhile."

With a little more food in their stomachs and the relaxed state of the camp, sleep became the most important thing on their minds.

Lowell thought, *I could be holding Helen in my arms in just a few weeks.*

He said, to no one in particular, "How long do you think it will take to get us home?"

There was no immediate answer, but finally some one said, "Oh I don't know, I suppose several weeks. They'll probably ship us home on the slowest transport they can find."

That brought a slight chuckle from the gathered group. Their thoughts about getting home were interrupted by the sound of an engine. The men all jumped up and ran to the fence closest to where they heard the sound. As it grew louder, more and more men gathered. Suddenly, the motorcycle with the colonel in the sidecar came up the slight rise that separated the camp from the airport. Following the cycle was a jeep with several men in it and two trucks. A tremendous cheer went up from the men and they began to push forward pinning the front row of men against the wire fence. Lowell, being in the front, was barely able to squeeze out around the gathering just as Myron and Vince came out of the hut.

Myron asked, "What's going on?"

"The colonel and some help are back!" shouted someone in the crowd.

Myron spotted Lowell worming his way out of the press of men.

"What are they talking about?"

Myron could not see over the large group of men gathered at the fence.

"The colonel just came over the hill followed by a jeep and two trucks. That's all I know."

The excitement spread throughout the camp as the main gate was opened to let the colonel and his entourage enter. The men were all shouting questions and the officers in the jeep stood up and held up their hands for silence, which took some time.

The colonel shouted as loud as he could, but his words were drowned by the men yelling, "WHAT'S HE SAYING? WHAT'S HE SAYING?"

When the rear flap of the two trucks opened and soldiers began to dismount, they looked at the prisoners and the prisoners looked at them. The prisoners had not seen anyone so healthy looking and well fed in a long time. Several of the prisoners came up and shook hands and several even leaned down and kissed the rescuers on the back of their hands. The recently arrived troops were overwhelmed with all the gestures the prisoners were making towards them, not understanding the gratitude.

Finally the colonel and some of the ranking officers got the men quiet enough so the captain could explain that they were part of an advanced element of the Seventh Armored Division and that they had been sent to the camp to assist the prisoners in anyway possible. They had brought medical supplies, several nurses and one doctor. The colonel talked to the medical people who immediately headed for the infirmary. Though the nurses wore those very baggy army coveralls, the prisoners stared at them. They had not seen any women for a long time and if a vote had been taken, they would have been voted the most beautiful women in the world.

After a few more minutes of consultation, the colonels mounted the jeep again and called for silence. They instructed the barracks chiefs to meet in the corner of the compound. The captain was talking to the soldiers he had brought. When finished, they dispersed to various points along the fence and four soldiers were stationed at the main gate.

Myron said, "It looks like we are now the prisoners of the Seventh Armored."

That brought a slight laugh to the men who heard and a lieutenant said, "I think that's so everyone doesn't try to take off. Though the war is over there is still the threat of the SS and those angry civilians."

They all nodded their heads in agreement. Finally, the barracks chiefs were instructed by the colonels and signaled for the men to gather in various spots around the compound. Captain Folsom and the major called for quiet and began to explain the situation.

"Okay men, here is the poop. The main units of the Seventh Armored are about a day away and until they get here, we are to stay inside the compound and wait. There are trucks carrying food a couple of hours behind this lead group and when they get here, we will eat."

This brought a loud cheer from the men. Captain Folsom held up his hand for silence and said,

"Now guys, you haven't had much solid food for awhile so you need to be careful. It will be a shock to your systems and if you overdo it, you could become violently sick."

Someone in the back yelled, "Yea, starving to death can make you violently sick too."

All the men laughed including Captain Folsom and the major.

Someone also called out, "Sir, is the war over for sure?"

The major answered, "Yes!"

That brought another cheer from the men.

Captain Folsom again raised his hand and said, "Okay men, remember what we said and let's don't do any thing foolish this close to the end. Remember, the German civilians don't like us very much."

When the meeting broke up, Vince, Myron and Lowell started walking back toward their barracks. Myron said, "Boy, I can hardly wait for that food to arrive."

"Yea, but remember what the major said, take it easy."

On towards evening, the men were beginning to wonder if the food trucks would ever arrive. Suddenly motors were heard once more. Though they knew the war was officially over, everyone held their collective breaths. Their anxiety ended when the canvas top of an American truck came over the small knoll separating the camp from the airport. A huge cheer went up from the men when they realized that it must be the food trucks.

The first trucks to be unloaded were two that carried portable field kitchens, followed by the supply trucks. It took nearly two hours to get the kitchens set up and running, meanwhile all the prisoners were told to go to their huts and wait until they were called. Finally the men were notified that chow was ready.

As they lined up with eating utensils, they noticed that the chow was field rations consisting of canned meat, some over done vegetables, very dry crackers and coffee. There were also cigarettes for those men who still smoked. As their turn came, Lowell noticed that the men serving the food provided each prisoner with only a small portion. Some complained and begged for more, but an officer was at each line told them to be careful and move along. Later there were quite a few men who became sick from the first rich food they'd eaten in many months. Lowell kept warning Myron and Vince to eat slowly and not take big gulps as some of the men were doing.

Myron said, "My God, Low, you sound just like my mother."

"Yea, well if she were here, I am sure she would tell you the same thing."

"Okay Momma, I'll be careful!"

That night the boys went to bed with out the gnawing ache in their stomachs from hunger. The next morning when they responded to roll call, the person who mounted the stand was not German. Colonel Chandler addressed the men.

"Did everyone get enough to eat last night?"

There were several "Nos" but by in large the more common responses were cheers. The colonel went on to explain the next steps in their liberation. Several camps had been set up as disbursement points after D-Day for liberated prisoners, mostly near ports. All liberated prisoners were being taken to those for examination and some rehabilitation. The camps were all named after American cigarettes and this group would probably be going to Camp Lucky Strike, which brought another round of cheers. He continued by explaining that Camp Lucky Strike was located near the city of La Havre in Northern France.

The colonel listened to several questions from the men. How long will they stay there? How soon will they be moved? Will they be shipped home right away? He told the men he didn't know the answers to their questions yet, but as soon as he did he would let them know.

As the roll call broke up, Lowell, Myron and Vince started to walk back to their huts. They were joined by Ralph who said, "Boy when I get home to Oregon the first thing I'm going to do is go to Lithia Park in

Ashland and drink a whole gallon of that water."

"What water?"

"There's a spring in Lithia Park that has Lithia water that's supposed to be good for you but it is the worst tasting stuff you've ever tasted."

Vince asked, "Then why are you going to drink it?"

"Well, that used to be one of the things us guys did to tease people who didn't know about it and it is one of those things I think of when I think of Medford and I really believe I miss it."

Myron and Lowell looked at each other and shook their heads.

That night the boys went to bed with dreams of home on their minds.

Lowell thought for awhile and then said, "Jew, do you really think you will go to Emmons when you get home?"

"Well, maybe a year, but I have been thinking about what to do with my life. First, I'm going to get reacquainted with my wife. That'll probably take about twenty minutes. After that, I'll decide what to do. I have been thinking about maybe going to law school."

"You can't get that at Emmons can you?"

Myron thought a few minutes and then said, "Nah, I guess not, but I could get my undergraduate stuff there and then maybe transfer to the U of O."

"Yes, you did mention going to the 'duck school' before."

They both fell asleep with a near full stomach for once in a long time.

The boys awoke the next morning after sleeping better than they had before they'd been captured. Lowell wondered why they hadn't been roused, and then he remembered all that had happened in the last two days. As he got out of bed, walked to the door of the hut and looked out at a beautiful morning, he reflected upon being a prisoner-of-war, not seeing his wife and family for many months, and not knowing what was in store for the future.

Vince came out and asked, "Are the trucks here yet?"

"No, not yet."

"Didn't the colonel say they would be here in a day or so?"

"Yea, but don't forget, that was only yesterday."

"You're right."

Myron came out and said, "Is chow ready?"

"I don't know. We haven't heard."

A sergeant came around the barracks and asked, "Sirs are all the men in there up?"

"No, not all, why?"

"Well wake 'em and tell 'em that chow is ready."

The boys went back in the barracks and announced that chow was ready. The men still sleeping stirred and started to get up. Just then they heard an engine, which gave them a moment of concern. They were still a little concerned about the SS even though they had surrendered. It turned out to be another jeep with an officer in the right seat. The men were disappointed that it wasn't the group of trucks to take them to the new camp.

After the morning chow, there was another roll call and when the men had all gathered, the colonels mounted the platform and requested quiet. A major climbed up beside the colonels and began to speak.

There were several shouts of, "We can't hear you."

The major turned to the colonels in desperation and Colonel Chandler began to shout.

"Men, the major has brought us some great news. Because we have an airstrip so close, they're going to fly us out. There will be several transports arriving in a few days to begin the evacuation."

This news brought a huge cheer that drowned out any more words by the colonel. When the men settled down the colonel went on to say that the wounded would be evacuated first, followed by the men who had been here the longest. Lowell, Myron and Vince looked at each other and knowingly nodded that they would probably be there awhile longer since they were relatively new prisoners. The roll call broke up and the men went back to their huts.

The next few days were agony for the prisoners while waiting for the planes. The boys spent most of their time sitting outside if the weather permitted and talking about what they would do when they got home.

Myron asked Lowell, "Low, do you think you will play sports at Emmons?"

After a thoughtful moment he said, "Oh I don't know. I don't think sports competition will mean much to me after this."

Ken asked, "Did you play before you went to the service?"

"Yea, one year, I played basketball and baseball."

Jew spoke up saying, "I think you were an all-league catcher weren't you?"

"Yes, but remember most of the guys were in the service so it was like a freshman league then."

Those days waiting to be evacuated were the most painful days Lowell had ever experienced. Every man continued to scan the sky for the promised evacuation planes. The colonel had further information about the situation. He said that the order to use aircraft came from General Eisenhower who directed the Transport Command to make available as many planes as possible to liberate the men held in POW camps.

All the barracks chiefs had been summoned to a meeting with the colonels and an officer from the air corps who would be responsible for the evacuation. All the men were anxiously awaiting word of when they would be evacuated.

When the meeting broke up, each barracks chief summoned the men in their huts and explained the situation. It seemed that the runways of the field next to the prison were full of bomb craters and strewn debris. The colonels requested volunteers to ready the field for landing. It would require several days' work, but the planes could not land until the runways were safe. The volunteers would meet by the main gate at 1000 hours ready to go to work. Nearly every man in the camp showed up at 1000 hours. The colonels were overwhelmed and had to have the barracks chiefs weed out men who were not physically able to do manual work. Several of the men at the gathering were on crutches and several had arms in slings.

When they saw the crowd, Jew said, "What happened to that old army saying, 'never volunteer'?"

The job of readying the airstrip took the better part of a week. The craters caused the most trouble. They required filling and leveling. The men located a few wheelbarrows and carried the rest of the fill material in buckets. Several men who had built roads and runways in civilian life stepped forward to supervise and an air corps engineer arrived to examine the work. He finally gave his approval for the planes to land.

While the work on the airstrip went on, the colonels along with the barracks chiefs were busy putting together evacuation lists. They had the sick or wounded men on the first flights followed by the men who had been in prison longest and finally the able bodied men with less time behind the wire. Once the field was ready, the whole camp was on edge waiting to hear the motors of those transports coming to take them out of this place of confinement.

Lowell, Myron, Vince and Ken were sitting on the steps of the hut talking about nothing in particular when Ken said, "Listen!"

The boys became silent and heard the faint drone of aircraft engines. Before long every man in camp was rushing out of the huts and looking skyward.

Someone yelled, "There they are!"

The boys looked around to see who had yelled and which direction he was pointing. They all followed his finger and recognized several C-47 transports coming over the horizon. The planes circled the field that had been hastily cleared by the prisoners and made safe for landing. The army had set up a temporary tower in the back of a truck to give the pilots landing instructions. The planes began to land to the cheers of the men and one after another taxied to the parking area.

It would take about two days for all the men to be evacuated from the camp. After helping at the landing strip, Lowell, Myron and Vince volunteered to help load the men who needed assistance. This kept them busy for a few hours, but when that job was finished, the colonel thanked them and told them they could return to their huts.

Lowell thought Myron was acting kind of strange and he asked his friend, "Jew, is something wrong?"

"I was just wondering if I should still be using Pete's name."

"Oh yea, I kind of forgot about that. Why don't we ask the colonel now?"

"Oh, I don't want to bother him."

"I don't think he will care. Colonel, do you have a minute?"

"Yes, what is it?"

"Sir, you remember that I spent most of my time as Pete Marshall and I wondered what I should do when we get to Lucky Strike?"

"Oh yes, you're Rothstein aren't you?"

"Yes sir."

The colonel thought for a minute and then said, "Well when we get to the camp, I'll check on it and let you know. Because that was an official policy, I don't see a problem. We'll just have to be sure the families are notified."

"Thank you sir."

As the colonel turned and the boys started to walk back to their hut, Myron said, "Damn, this is the part I have been dreading every since I took his name. What will his mother think?"

"I don't know Jew, but now she probably doesn't know and that will be some relief."

"I'm going to find out where she lives and stop and see her on the way home."

"Yea, well I'll go with you."

"Would you?"

"Sure buddy, someone has to make sure you don't screw up."

Myron reached out and punched his friend on the arm. Lowell just smiled thinking that was the first time he had done that since they were shot down. The old Jew had returned.

When their turn came, Myron and Lowell were loaded on one plane while Vince was on a second. There were nearly forty men to a plane so seating was on the bare floor. Lowell was one of the first to load and was seated at the front of the plane. After take-off, he stood up and looked in the cockpit. The co-pilot turned, saw him watching, reached over and handed him a set of headphones so he could listen in. When he had them on, the co-pilot asked what he had flown.

Lowell answered, "The 17-G."

The co-pilot said, "Yea, that's what I thought I was going to fly, but this guy needed someone to make sure he always landed wheels down so they hooked me up with him."

Lowell noticed the pilot smiling and nodding.

He said into the mike, "Yea my co-pilot wanted to fly fighters, but he turned out to be one very good multi-engine pilot."

The pilot spoke up saying "Well, I can't say that much about my co-pilot."

They all laughed and then Lowell asked, "How long a trip is it to camp?"

"Oh, about two hours."

Lowell nodded and removed the headphones and handed them back to the co-pilot. He returned to his seat and Myron, who was seated several men from him, called out with a question but Lowell couldn't make out what he said because of the engine noise.

Many of the men had put their heads down between their knees and were asleep. Lowell thought he would try it, but had no luck; he was too excited. The drone of the engines was mesmerizing, however, and after some time he too assumed the position and caught a nap.

The change in tempo of the engines woke Lowell. He knew from the sound that they were letting down for a landing.

One of the men seated by a window said, "Looks like we're going to land."

There were several comments and some talking as the noise of the engines decreased. They all visited a little before landing. The jar and squeal of the tires as they hit the runway announced that they were on the ground. They taxied for awhile and then came to a halt. The crew chief, gently stepping over the men's legs, made his way to the rear of the plane and opened the door kicking out the stairs to the ground.

"Okay men, you can deplane now."

The men rose, anxious to see their new camp and freedom. As Lowell's turn came to climb out of the aircraft, he saw Jew waiting for him below. There was no camp in sight which gave them a moment of concern.

Then they saw an officer in a jeep. He stood up and said, "Okay men, climb aboard the trucks. We've got a few minutes ride to the camp."

CAMP LUCKY STRIKE & HOME

The trucks rumbled along the rough roadbed for a few minutes and then slowed to turn into the camp. When they stopped the driver walked around back to lift the canvas flap and the men got their first look at Camp Lucky Strike. It was a tent city, capable of handling many thousands of troops. Following D-Day, it was used as an assembly and embarkation point for incoming troops and now it served as a debarkation point for not only liberated prisoners, but also other troops who had finished their tours of duty.

Lowell spotted Jew looking at the camp.

He walked over and said, "Well, welcome to Camp Lucky Strike airman."

Just then Vince found them and said, "It sure looks better than Luft II."

"At least the men look better."

An officer came up and said, "Okay men, follow me."

He led them into the camp and around a row of tents.

"Men, this is the shower room where we get rid of those unwelcome little guests you have brought with you."

The boys looked at each other and laughed. They were all infested with several kinds of unwelcome little guests. They stripped the old uniforms off, piling them into one pile and placing their personal items in another.

"Okay, now go in the showers. You can take as long as you want."

The sight of all the men walking around outside naked was a bit humorous. Entering the showers, they felt the very welcome heat of the water. There were several groans of pleasure and some laughing about the water being too hot. After the shower, they were sprinkled with DDT to kill the little unwelcome friends and told not to wipe it off. They looked like a bunch of flour-covered statues. The officers directed them to the supply room where they drew new clothes. They were told not to complain about the size because that was all they were going to get.

They received an issue of several sets of underclothes, fatigues, mostly too big, several pairs of socks and shoes. Myron got a lucky draw because his shoes were the exact size while Lowell and Vince drew shoes several sizes too big. They also received mess kits, shaving and toilet kits and writing materials.

Lowell asked, "Will we be able to write home?"

"Of course."

They were led back to collect their personal items. They noticed that their old clothes were gone.

Jew asked, "What do you think they will do with our old clothes."

Lowell looked at him and said, "Do you really care?"

This brought a shrug from him.

Next they were assigned to tents. Lowell, Myron, Vince and Ken found themselves assigned to the same tent. When they saw the army cots with real mattresses, clean sheets and those wonderful GI blankets, all thoughts and concerns left them. They quickly made up their bunks and crawled in for the best sleep they'd had in several months. The next morning they were not awakened by any harsh shouts or bangs. The men woke up of their own accord, rose, dressed and received directions to their mess hall, which they entered to the smell of bacon, ham, eggs and coffee. Of course Lowell made a fuss at Jew about not offending the cooks and he should take some ham, which he did with a nod and a threat to Lowell about not ever telling his mother.

After chow, the men were told they would be debriefed, which brought several groans of near pain. It was not like those the flyers went through after a mission. They were lined up in front of a clerk at a typewriter and asked their name, rank, serial number, when captured, where held and home town.

As they left the lines, Myron said, "I wonder if the colonel has taken care of my little problem?"

"I don't know, but I would guess it could take awhile."

Following their debriefing, they gathered in a compound to listen to an officer address them from a stage over a PA system.

"Welcome to Camp Lucky Strike men. During your stay here, you will take your first step towards rehabilitation back into your normal lives. First on the agenda is putting a little meat back on you guys; we don't want you to go home and scare your families to death now do we?"

Several shouts and cheers greeted this comment.

Continuing, he said, "Those canteen cups you were issued are part of that. You will find around the camp at nearly every tent, a kettle of eggnog. We want you to dip in and have a drink every time you see one. Are there any questions?"

A shout came from the back asking how long they would be at the camp.

The officer said, "I was coming to that. We're not sure, but we will try to get you home as soon as possible, maybe a couple of weeks or so."

This brought moans from the group. The officer held up his hand and started to say something when several jeeps and a staff car pulled in to the compound.

The officer said, "Okay men, look sharp; we have a very distinguished visitor today."

The staff car came to a stop and the right front door opened. An officer got out and opened the back door. The men were all looking as a head emerged. Next came his star-topped shoulders. When the visitor looked up a gasp arose from the entire contingent of ex-prisoners as they all recognized General Dwight D. Eisenhower with that very familiar smile. He raised his hand to a loud cheer. As the general was escorted to the stage, every man in the group was clapping his hands in a round of applause. The general greeted the officers on the stage and then walked up to the microphone.

"Good morning men and welcome to freedom."

This brought an even louder cheer from the men.

The general talked for several minutes and thanked everyone finishing with, "What can we do for you?"

From the middle of the formation a voice yelled, "Send us home!"

The general laughed and raised his hands again, turned and said something to the commanding officer and then did something that surprised all the men, including the camp commander. He dismounted the stage and began to walk among the men, shaking hands and talking to several. As he approached near Lowell and Myron, Lowell just stood there staring. Myron pushed past him and reached out for the general's hand.

Lowell heard the general ask where he was from and when Myron answered, he said, "Oh yes, a very beautiful state, I love to go fishing there."

Myron responded with, "Well come on out some time sir and I'll show you some good fishing."

As the general passed by, Myron stepped back beside Lowell who looked at him and said, "That was a dumb thing to say."

"Well not any dumber than just standing there staring."

Several men pushed up to Myron and began to fire questions at him as to what he and the general talked about. Myron, picking up his usual flare for the ridiculous responded, "Well he asked if I thought he'd conducted the war okay and I just said it was okay."

That brought several BS remarks and several shoves and a lot of laughter.

The excitement of the general's visit kept the boys going for several hours. When they returned to their tents, one of the guys told Myron there was a sergeant here looking for him with a message.

"You're supposed to report to the orderly room when you get back."

"Okay, thanks. Low, will you go with me?"

"Sure, if you want me to."

When they entered the orderly room, which was in one of the few wood frame buildings in camp, Myron told the desk sergeant who he was and the sergeant told him to report to a Major Arnt at camp personnel.

After a few requests for directions, the boys found the HQ building and walked in. There were several desks arranged in typical army style with partial walls screening off the offices. When Myron told the desk sergeant that he was to see a Major Arnt, the sergeant got up, knocked and entered one of the doors announcing Myron, then signaled for him to come in.

The sergeant made an effort to stop Lowell from entering until Myron said, "He's with me," and the major motioned for them both to enter.

"Well I take it you're Lieutenant Rothstein," looking at Myron.

"Yes sir and this is my friend Lowell Andersen."

The major rose and extended his hand to the boys.

"Well lieutenant, I understand there is a little identity problem here."

"Yes sir, you see just before we started the last mission, we were told we should carry false ID because the Germans were taking Jewish boys out of prison and sending them to work camps."

Myron went on to explain the whole situation.

Finishing his story he said, "So I took Lieutenant Marshall's dog tags and destroyed mine."

The major asked, "What about the rest of his identification, bill fold and so forth."

"Well sir, we never carried anything except our tags."

"Oh I see. Well what we need to do is get you properly identified and Lieutenant Marshall's family notified. So, if you tell the sergeant outside that you need an ID form and give him the information on Lieutenant Marshall, I believe we can straighten this whole thing out."

The boys rose and Myron said, "I'm sorry for the mess sir."

"That's alright Rothstein I fully understand. When my folks came to America their names were Arntstein. I'm Jewish as well."

Lowell spoke up saying, "Oh sir, one more thing. We would like to get in contact with our crewmen, is there any way we can?"

"Why yes, go to the camp HQ. It's just down the street from here. Ask for them by name."

"Thank you sir."

The boys saluted and walked out of the office. Myron got the proper forms and filled them out, hopefully to again be Myron Rothstein. They gave the clerk the information on Pete Marshall including giving him Pete's tags, which Myron still had. The sergeant told him to come back in a couple of days and they would have new tags for him.

As they walked down the mud street, they spotted a large tent with guards in front and many men coming and going. They walked up to one of the guards and asked if that was the camp HQ. He told them it was and they entered. It was quite spacious with many desks and the clicking of typewriters.

They stood there for a few minutes before a sergeant asked, "May I help you gentlemen?"

They told the sergeant what they wanted and he directed them to another desk. They walked up to what looked like a very busy corporal and waited.

He looked up and said, "May I help you sirs?

They explained they wanted to contact their crew members. He asked the names and wrote them down on a small piece of paper and reached over for a very thick folder.

After scanning it, he said, "Well I see a sergeant Ellingston, Wayne; McDonald, David; Miller, Clark; Martinez, Lorenzo; they're all in block E-134, tent eighteen and let's see, there's a Risen, Nigel; and Wright, Robert, they're in tent twenty-one in the same block.

"Thank you corporal; oh, is there a Dickerson, Vern any where?"

The corporal turned a few pages and said, "Yea here he is; same block, tent twenty-three."

They thanked him again and left.

As they walked back to their area to get Vince, Myron looked at Lowell and said, "Maybe we should have asked how to find block E-134."

"Yea, I guess we should have."

After getting together with Vince, they found a large sign board with a map of the camp. It looked like block E-134 was about a mile away.

Walking down the temporary street of the tent city, they discovered that at Camp Lucky Strike, the segregation of enlisted men and officers was not as strict as it had been in the other camps. There were officers and enlisted men sitting around talking and smoking. Vince walked up to one group and asked the directions to block E-134.

A sergeant spoke up and said, "We're in F-142, it should be just down the street."

They thanked him and continued to walk. At each intersection they discovered there were signposts indicating block and number. Just as they turned the corner toward E-134, a voice called out, "Lieutenant Andersen!"

All three turned to see Zo running up to them.

"How are you sirs? We wondered if you guys were here."

"Yea, we wondered about you too. Are the rest of the crew with you Zo?"

"Sure, come on I'll show you." As he led the officers toward their tent, he asked, "When did you get here?"

"Probably the same day you did. What day was it Jew?"

"Thursday, I think."

Zo said, "Oh, I see we're back to Jew. Did you get that all straightened out?"

Myron answered, "Well, I hope so."

After the reunion with the crew, Lowell asked, "Have you seen our high school friend, Vernon Dickerson?"

"Yea, he's just up the street. I'll go get him."

"Thanks Zo, that'll be swell."

In a few minutes Zo entered the tent with Vernon. They exchanged greetings and updates and as Vernon and Jew stood there talking, Lowell was reminded how much he disliked him in high school and how little that meant now. That night during their reunion, the boys made plans to get together again the next day. When they got back to their tent, the boys put the newly issued writing kits to good use. Of course with V-Mail, they had to write sparingly, but both Myron and Lowell wrote daily to their wives.

My Dearest Wife,

Darling, it feels so good to write this to you and know that you will get it. We are in a rehabilitation camp in Northern France called Camp Lucky Strike. We don't know how long we will be here, but everyone says that it could be as long as several weeks. We arrived the day before yesterday, had our first hot showers, new uniforms, clean beds and best of all some good old Army C Rations. Remember some of my letters during training talked about how I hated C rations? Well, I will never again say that.

Now it's time to clear up a mystery. I hope Betty got the letter from Jew when we were in camp and was able to figure it out. Jew is fine and sharing a tent with me. I won't go into detail, but in the POW camp he had to assume a different identity so he took the name of our co-pilot, Pete Marshall. Pete was filling in after Vern had an appendicitis operation. Pete was wounded when we were hit and died before we got down on the ground, so Myron was Pete Marshall all the time we were in camp. I'll write more later.

To you I give my life and love forever.
Your husband,
Lowell

Home

The phone rang in the lumber yard office and Helen put down the invoices she was working on and answered it in the usual way, "Speer Lum – –."

She stopped mid-word hearing her mother's voice, "Helen, George from the Western Union was just here with a telegram from the War Department and I sent him to the yard. He should be there in a short while."

"Oh Mother thanks so much. I'm sure it's the one we've been waiting for."

Just then the door to the office opened and George came in with a big smile on his face. George was the elderly gentleman who was the chief operator at the office. Helen hung up on her mother and greeted the messenger. He reached over the desk and handed the telegram to Helen who tore it open with trembling hands and read it.

THE SECRETARY OF THE ARMY WISHES TO INFORM YOU THAT YOUR HUSBAND, 2ND LIEUTENANT LOWELL ANDERSEN HAS BEEN LIBERATED FROM A GERMAN POW CAMP AND IS NOW IN A REHABILITATION CAMP IN FRANCE. LIEUTENANT ANDERSEN WILL BE HOME AS SOON AS HE IS PROCESSED.

Someone signed it for the Secretary of the Army. Helen started to reach for her purse to tip George, but he held up his hand.

"No need Helen, that look on your face is all the tip I need."

Helen thanked him and started out to the yard to tell her Dad when the phone rang. She picked it up to hear a very loud Betty shouting something Helen could not even understand.

She said, "Betty, calm down. Did you get a telegram from the army?"

"Oh yes, I knew it all the time. Myron couldn't be dead. I was sure he was alive!"

Just then Mr. Speer came into the office with a big smile on his face, "What is all the excitement about."

Helen ran into her father's arms and handed him the telegram.

Of course being who they were, the good news called for a get together and a meal. Mrs. Andersen and Mrs. Miles organized it along with Myron and Helen's folks. Uncle Norwood joined them and opened the celebration with a very long prayer.

That night, Helen stayed up late writing one of the longest letters she had every written to Lowell. Of course with the V-Mail restrictions, she couldn't send it all and had to reduce it to the required page. She had no idea where to send it, but would keep it until she got an address for him.

Camp Lucky Strike

As they sat in the sun of Northern France, and reveled in their freedom, Jew said, "Low, what do you think about visiting Pete's mother on the way home?"

After thinking for a few minutes, he answered, "Well, the most important thing on my mind is home and Helen, but I think it is a very good idea."

They both fell silent again into their private thoughts, mostly about their wives, homes and the future.

As the days got warmer and warmer, the boys had a chance to see some of the area around the camp. They got together with the crew and visited the Normandy beaches that were still littered with the debris from the D-Day invasions, spent time in a nearby town and even had a quick trip to Paris.

Unlike London, Paris did not show near the effects of bombing. There were a few damaged buildings, but all in all, the city of lights was very much intact. The people, however, looked very haggard and worn. Food was not very plentiful though the boys managed to have what they considered a Paris type dinner.

Standing in front of the Eiffel Tower, Zo said, "Man, I never thought I would ever see this thing. I remember in school we read about it and I didn't pay much attention."

"Yea," replied Wayne, "I always thought it would be something like the towers we had at home to store grain in."

Lowell looked at him and said, "Well this wouldn't hold much grain. There are a lot of holes."

They all laughed and moved on. The boys did get a sample of what the Parisian girls were like. A school group, probably high school age, came by as they were looking at the Arch de Triumph and the single guys became more interested in them than the Arch. There were so many American GIs on the streets that the girls paid little or no attention.

Upon their return to camp, they were told that mail had arrived. The boys hurried over to the post office tent and both had letters from their wives that they took back to their tents and tore open. Lowell settled in to read the words written by Helen.

My Darling Husband

I can't tell you the relief that swept over me when I got the telegram telling me you were safe and in an American camp. Of course Betty was in the same state as I. We did figure it out about Myron from what he had said in the one letter we received from the prison camp, though we were never sure until today.

Do you have any idea when you will be home? Mr. Vance was in the yard yesterday and said that usually they ship the former prisoners home first. Will that be the case with you guys?

The letter went on with a few short updates from home. With the V-Mail restrictions it could only be one page long and Helen's letter closed too quickly.

Waiting for your return and to hold you again.
All my love forever,
Helen

One day they heard it was possible to hitch a ride to England on one of the transports bringing supplies over for the troops on the Continent.

"Why don't we go talk to the CO and see if we can get back to

Sulensborne."

"Yea, maybe our stuff is still there and we can get it back," replied Myron.

After making several inquires, they learned that there was a shuttle flight going back and forth nearly every day. After further inquiry, they were told to go the airfield to see if there were any available seats. At the field they were told that getting over to England was not a problem, but to be careful because on the return, the planes were very crowded with supplies and there might not be room.

As they left the field, Lowell said, "I'll go talk to the boys and let them know what we are trying to do, but can't give them any guarantees."

When Lowell told the rest of the crew that they could get to Sulensborne but the return trip might be somewhat doubtful, they all agreed that getting home was more import and to forget trying to get back to their old base. Lowell was very relieved because he felt the same way.

The days again wore on and on and the boys were wondering if they would ever get home. One day, an assembly was called to announce that they would be processing men for shipment home. It could take up to two more weeks, but the trip across the Atlantic was only a few days now, instead of the two or more weeks it took to come over.

Leaving the assembly, Jew said, "I suppose they will send the guys who have been in prison the longest home first."

"Yea," responded Vince. "We didn't spend near as much time as some of the guys. Remember that captain in Luft II that was shot down in 1943?"

Lowell nodded his head and said, "Yea, I don't know how anyone locked up that long could survive."

Homeward Bound

The day finally came when the boy's names appeared on the roster for shipment home. They would leave in three days by way of Le Havre where their ship would be waiting. The trip would take about five days.

As they were in the showers the day of their departure, Lowell looked around and realized how much weight the men had gained in the weeks at Lucky Strike. Good food and all that eggnog had done its duty. Though still quite thin, they were not the skeletons they were when they arrived. At the briefing the day before, they learned they would not receive special accommodations as was usual for officers, but would mix with the enlisted men. This suited the boys just fine.

They walked to the trucks and took a last look at Camp Lucky Strike.

Lowell said, "Boy, I can't believe how good this camp looked when we arrived and how glad I am to be leaving."

Vince said, "Yes, it meant a lot to us, but compared to going home it doesn't hold a candle,"

They all agreed and climbed aboard the truck.

The relatively short trip to Le Havre seemed to take forever. They bounced along on recently repaired roads until they thought their teeth would be jarred from their heads. The convoy did stop once to allow the men to disembark and relieve themselves. As they were standing along side the road, several trucks came along in the opposite direction and stopped just past their convoy. They were trucks transporting Germans back home. The American's began to yell obscenities at them though Lowell noticed it was done with smiles on the faces of the yellers. A whistle blew and the officers in charge began to order them back into the trucks. As they were waiting their turn to load, the convoy commander walked by, stopping beside Lowell and Myron and said, "Man I have never heard of such a stupid thing."

Myron asked, "What's that sir?"

"Giving those Krauts a pee call right across from us."

The men around him all laughed and one of the men said, "Yea, funny some one didn't cross the road and use them for relief."

They all laughed and continued to load into the trucks. Arriving in Le Havre, the men got out of the truck on the dock along side a tied up ship. A navy officer, with the ever-present clipboard, stood at the gang plank. He stepped up on the gangway and called for their attention, informing them that this was the USS Winslow, a troop ship. and that it would be quite crowded so officers and men would be mixed on board. Most of the men didn't care; they just wanted to get aboard and get going.

As they heard their names called, the boys were pleased that the three of them received an assignment to the same compartment.

They had not seen the rest of the crew and as they climbed the gangway, Vince said, "I wonder where the men are?"

"I don't know, but notice there are several gangways to the ship, they must be at one of the others," Lowell responded.

They were directed down into the ship and were stunned by the odor emitting from the hold.

Myron said, "My God, what the devil is that smell?"

"I don't know, but I think I'm not going to like it very much!" replied Vince.

Their assigned compartment was on the second deck. As they ascended the odor became more pronounced and they began to cover their noses.

Lowell said, "Oh come on guys, it doesn't smell half as bad as Luft II did."

"Yea, I guess you're right Low," said Myron.

Their compartment was a long barracks type room with three aisles running lengthwise and double rows of bunks stacked five high on each side of the aisle. The boys found an empty stack of bunks that were not taken and Myron threw his bag on the bottom bunk. He asked, "Oh sorry guys, should we flip?"

Vince said, "Nah, unless you want to Low?"

"No, let him have it. He would probably fall out of one of the uppers and I would have to explain to Betty how he met his demise on the way home."

As he fell into the lower bunk, Myron said, "Aw shut up you damn Swede."

Lowell realized they had not kidded each other for a long time so with a smile he said, "I told you, I'm Norwegian!"

"Same difference."

Again, that look was exchanged between the two friends that expressed feelings that young men would not express verbally. The speaker suddenly came on with an announcement.

"NOW HEAR THIS! NOW HEAR THIS!
CHOW CALL! CHOW CALL!"

Before sailing, they received directions to the mess hall. The men in the compartment were to go aft, which they discovered meant toward the rear of the ship to mess number twenty-seven.

Myron rolled off his bunk and said, "Let's go eat, I'm anxious to see if this navy chow is as good as it is supposed to be."

A man in the next row asked, "You haven't eaten navy chow before?"

Walking out of the compartment, Lowell answered, "No, we haven't."

"Didn't you come over on a ship?"

Lowell spoke up and said, "No we're all from the same crew and we ferried a 17 over when we came."

"You lucky devils, we spent twenty days aboard a ship with everyone sick as a dog. After the first day at sea no one ate at all except the few who didn't get sick."

"Oh so that explains the odor down here."

The man shook his head and stuck out his hand saying I'm Hiram Chapman. I was with the 432nd. What about you guys?"

"We were in the 315th out of Sulensborne."

As they walked down the passage way they exchanged a few more facts until they reached the mess hall. The food did smell good and again the boys noticed that there was a mix of officers and enlisted men. Lowell wondered if it would be possible to get together with the crew. Entering the hall, Lowell heard his name called and turned to see Niggs Risen waving from one of the back tables. The boys walked over and noticed that the rest of the crew seated there as well.

Lowell said, "Good to see you guys. What compartment are you in?"

Bob answered, "We're not all in the same, but have gotten together. We haven't found Wayne yet."

"Yea, we haven't seen any of you since we left Lucky Strike," responded Vince.

Zo spoke up saying "Boy, am I glad to be out of there."

"You said it. I couldn't stand lying in my bunk hearing the rats running around under the floor," replied Bob.

They all agreed. Myron said, "Well after we eat, let's meet up on deck and we'll look for Wayne."

Lowell asked, "Have you guys seen our high school friend, Vernon Dickerson?"

"Nah, maybe we can check the ship's muster list later," Gabe answered.

"Yea, maybe we can."

They all agreed as the officers left them to get in line for their food. Vince said, "Boy it's good to see those guys again."

"Yea," Myron said, "I don't think I will ever feel as close to anyone as I do to our crew."

"I wonder if Vern made it through. I tried to find out at Lucky Strike, but didn't have much luck," said Lowell.

"Well maybe when we get home we can try to get in touch with him," said Vince.

After chow, the crew met on deck. While discussing the best way to go about finding Wayne and Vernon, the speaker came on again.

"NOW HEAR THIS! NOW HEAR THIS!
THIS IS THE CAPTAIN SPEAKING,
PREPARE TO EMBARK!
ALL PASSENGERS REPORT TO THE COMPARTMENTS!
ALL CREWMEN TO YOUR EMBARKING STATION!"

Lowell said, "Well, I guess we will have to postpone the search for awhile."

They all moved to their respective ladders leading down to the bowels of the ship and to assigned areas. As they entered, there was an atmosphere of excitement. Lowell felt the same, leaving for home at last.

He had hardly conjured up the thought when Myron said, "Well, leaving for home at last."

Lowell smiled. Just then, they heard the ship horn blow and felt the engines engage and heard the swish of the propellers as they dug into the water. With the assistance of the tugboats, the ship began to move and a huge cheer resounded all around the compartment.

When the ship left the Le Havre channel and entered the North Sea, it took a huge dip and then rose as quickly. This motion kept up for some time and all the men began to think about the dreaded seasickness. After nearly and hour of the pitching and rolling, a soldier down the row and across from Lowell couldn't take it any longer and jumped out of his bunk and headed for the latrine. Several more men followed and the sound of them vomiting could be heard, prompting several more men to do the same. Lowell lay in his bunk feeling more and more queasy. He did not want to follow the other men, but felt he could not take it much longer. Then suddenly a man just across the aisle from him was sick in his bunk followed by several more and then Lowell followed suit.

He felt a little better, but needed air. The smell in the compartment was overwhelming. He threw his legs over the side and jumped to the floor.

"I've got to get out of here," he said as he went through the door and in to the passageway leading to the ladder and deck.

Jew followed him and when they came on deck, the fresh air immediately made Lowell feel better. Jew asked, "You okay?"

"My God I don't know Jew. I've never felt like that before, even on the carnival rides at the State Fair."

"Probably those other guys' being sick was the cause."

"I hope so. I don't want to feel like this all the way home."

That night was not a good one aboard the USS Winslow. The pitching of the ship caused many repeats plus many more became seasick. Luckily Lowell wasn't one; however, Vince was. Finally at about 2400, Lowell got down from his bunk and told Myron he was going up on deck. Myron said he felt like sleeping and wouldn't join him. When Lowell reached the deck, Vince was standing talking to a soldier.

Lowell approached them and asked, "Feeling better Vince?"

"Oh a little better when I got rid of that chow we had."

"Me too,"

"Oh by the way, this is Sergeant Amundson. He thinks there is a Vernon Dickerson in his compartment."

"Really, which one is it?"

The sergeant replied, "416."

"On the fourth deck?"

"Yea, but if he is the guy I think, he is pretty sick."

" Several of us are. Say, tell him that Lowell Andersen would like to meet him on deck tomorrow, okay."

"I'll tell him, but I don't know if he will be able to."

The second day out of Le Havre was much calmer. The ship continued to roll a little, but was much smoother. Lowell felt well enough to go with Myron, who never really got sick at all, to noon chow. After chow they went on deck for a little air. The weather was quite good and actually warm.

Standing at the railing watching England in the distance slide by, a voice said, "Low."

Lowell turned around and saw Vernon approaching them.

Myron said, "My God Vern, you look awful."

"Yea, I've been sick all night. You guys look good though."

Lowell responded, "Well, I lost all my noon chow, but feel much better. The crazy Jew boy here wasn't even sick at all."

Jew responded with, "Well, it must be heredity."

"Oh sure, all you Jews are used to the seas having been raised in the desert."

They all laughed and turned to look overboard again.

Vernon said, "Do you think things are going to be different when we get home?"

After a pause, Myron said, "I think we will be different, but probably not our families. They will just want us to be the same, which we aren't."

After another thoughtful silence, Lowell said, "Yea, that's the thing, we have changed but our families haven't."

After another pause, Vernon said, "Guys, I want to tell you something. I know you didn't really like me very much in high school and I guess I did act like a horses behind sometimes, but I hope we can be friends when we get home."

Both Lowell and Myron looked at him and then Lowell stuck out his hand and said, "Vernon, I was afraid of you. You were the rich kid in school and I was just a mechanic's kid."

"Are you kidding, you were the envy of every guy in school, with your looks and your athletic ability. What do you mean you were afraid of me?"

"I don't know. I guess it was when you were dating Helen."

"I told you in camp about that. Hey, we're on our way home. Let's be nice to each other."

Myron stepped in saying, "Well, I'm glad that's over with. I don't want to start having to counsel this guy all the time."

They all laughed and shrugged their shoulders. Just then the ship hit another trough and dipped down low.

Vernon said, "Oh my God; there it goes again," and headed for the rail.

On the Atlantic Ocean, the surprise was that the seas were much calmer than the North Sea. Some of the sailors told the boys, that is sometimes the case. Lowell and Vince had not been sick since that first day though many of the men aboard remained so.

The days passed with some warm enough they could be on deck with their shirts off and some when it was cold enough for a coat. It did rain several days and that made them feel like they were back in Oregon. The big pastime was to play card games. Many men gambled away all their back pay and tried to borrow more money to get back into the game.

The crew continued to meet on deck and on occasion, visit each other's compartments. As for gambling, Niggs seemed to be the only one partaking. However, he was not a loser. On one occasion he asked Lowell if he would keep some money for him and not, for any reason, give it back until they got off the ship in the States.

"Yea, okay Niggs. I'll keep it for you, how much?"

"Well, I've been pretty lucky and it's a little over two thousand."

"Yea, you seem to have an instinct to tell when guys are holding a good hand or when they're bluffing."

Niggs began to pull bills out of all his pockets and hand them to Lowell.

"Sir, this little nest egg will give me the start to ask that girl at home to get serious with me, maybe even marry me."

Lowell said, "Niggs, I don't think she is very concerned about money, just ask her. I'll go find an envelope and place this in the ship's safe."

"I don't know sir, I don't know how the navy will feel about gambling."

"Okay, I'll just find a good hiding place and put it there."

The days continued to pass until they had been out about one week when a bulletin went around the ship informing the men that instead of Boston as the port, they would arrive in New York . They planned to arrive in about three days. This was exciting news for the boys who lived in the city, especially Niggs. On the second day, the ships newspaper announced that they would enter New York Harbor around 1000 hours the following day. All the men were excited and planned to be on deck when that famous lady, the Statue of Liberty came into view. Lowell, Myron and the rest of the crew were not exceptions. At about 0830 Myron got out of his bunk and woke Lowell and Vince.

"What's up for God's sake?" Vince said.

"Well you don't want to miss the lady do you?"

"No," said Lowell.

"Yea, well we have to wait in line for chow so come on. Get up!" Myron exclaimed.

A man in the next bunk said, "I don't care what you do, but please do it outside."

They dressed and walked down the passageway to the mess hall. There wasn't much of a line so it didn't take long for them to get their food and eat. As they came out on deck, there were many men already there. Lowell asked which side she would be on and no one knew. Finally a sailor came by and told them the statue would be on the port side. The men began to hurry to the other side of the ship.

It didn't take long before the rails were full. As the harbor mouth passed by, there was much anticipation and a lot of laughter and talking. Suddenly the statue came in to view and a hush settled over the deck of the ship.

As the ship passed by, Myron turned to Lowell and extended his hand saying, "Thanks buddy."

Lowell looked at him with a questioning glance and said, "What do ya' mean?"

"You remember the Mitchell game when I blocked that big line backer so you could score and beat me for top scorer?"

"Yea."

"Well I said some day you'd pay me back and I think you have more than paid me back. I couldn't have made it through all this without you Low. We're even, which ain't bad for a Norwegian."

"Well, you finally got it right!"

The two boys stood there clasping hands and that look passed between them once more.

EPILOGUE

True to their discussion that day in the Officer's Club at Sulensborne, Lowell did return to Drayville and Emmons College where he majored in Science and Education. Unlike their plans, they did not wait until after college to start a family. Helen became pregnant in the fall of his first year back and in August of 1946 she gave birth to a girl they named Darlene.

Lowell graduated from Emmons with a Bachelor's degree in 1950 and received an offer to teach at Drayville High School. He accepted. This was only for awhile until he could look for something else. He assisted Coach Roberts in football, basketball and baseball, later taking over the basketball program as head coach.

Helen was pregnant with their second child by this time and Lowell, not finding anything else he liked better, spent his entire career in the Drayville School District working his way from the classroom to Vice Principal then to Principal and finished his career as Superintendent, retiring in 1984. He and Helen had two more children; a girl they named Chris and a boy named Curt. All three children were successful in life and provided Helen and Lowell with six wonderful grandchildren.

David and Diane grew up, attended college and had very successful lives. David became a doctor and Diane went on to teach Social Science at a small Mid-Western college. They finally learned to get along with each other. Ethan Andersen maintained the garage and as the automotive business grew after the war, was able to acquire a Ford dealership to add to the business. George Patterson, the mechanic who had worked for him for many years was made service manager. George's son Bob, after returning from the war, also started college, but after two years got married and needed a permanent job. Ethan hired him in sales where he was very successful. Ethan Andersen died in 1978 and Lowell, with the twins blessing, made Bob general manager under whose leadership the dealership branched out with two satellite agencies when the foreign car market invaded the US.

Myron returned to Drayville and attended Emmons for one year before transferring to the University of Oregon and graduating with a degree in business. He went on to attend the University of Oregon Law School and after passing the Oregon State Bar joined a firm in Portland practicing Business Law. He was elevated to full partner in 1968.

Myron and Betty like Lowell and Helen did not wait for graduation before starting their family. Both Betty and Helen became pregnant within weeks of each other and had their babies nine days apart. The Rothsteins out did the Andersens as they had five children who also went on to good lives and provided Myron and Betty with eleven grandchildren.

Low and Jew's relationship never changed throughout their lives. They remained fast friends and still embarrassed their wives with their bantering; mostly Jew's. Following up on the decision made during the journey on board the ship home, they got in touch with Vern Dickerson and became good friends. Their families all spent a great deal of time together.

The boys met regularly with the crew of *Grizzlies Roar* at group reunions. The first was held in San Francisco in 1955, ten years after the end of World War II. Soon after returning home at the end of the war, Lowell and Myron also made contact with Vern Stewart who had finished the war as pilot of another B-17. Vern stayed in the US Air Force retiring as a brigadier general in 1974 after commanding units in the Korean and Viet Nam wars. Lorenzo "Zo" Martinez returned to England and married Margaret. He brought her back to the US where they settled in Pierre and raised three children. Zo followed his father's footsteps and ended up as general manager of the ranch. The only crew member not accounted for was Wayne Ellingston with whom they were unable to make contact.

Charlie Smith finished the war without a scratch, returned home, graduated from college and medical school, married Linda Jensen and settled in Santa Maria, California where he practiced. Lowell and Helen kept in touch with them and would meet yearly half way between Santa Maria and Drayville. Once in awhile Myron and Betty would join them.

Osgood Booker and Tom Anderson were not as lucky, their plane took a direct hit on one of the last missions flown; all members of the crew were killed.

Werner Schoker, was able to get back to the states and after three years, regained his citizenship.

Myron and Lowell visited Pete Marshall's mother in Ohio on their way home. They spent two days with her. Myron never got over what he saw as his debt to Pete, which allowed him to survive in prison camp. He kept in touch with Pete's mother to the end of her life and every month, deposited money in her bank account. Toward the end when she developed several medical problems, all her expenses were paid.